Before the Dawn

Candace Camp

Cover Design: Anastasia Hopcus

Cover Photograph: Tasos Lekkas, via Pixabay

Other Titles by Candace Camp

Foreword

I'm so excited to be sharing the first Candace Camp Classic with my mom's readers. Candace Camp Classics will cover different time periods and places, but they were written with the same heart, lovable characters, and exciting storylines that endear Candace's Regency Romances to her fans. I've loved rediscovering my mom's older books and I am so excited that we are re-releasing them for new readers to discover, too. Before the Dawn is my absolute favorite with its wartime intrigue, lovely portrayal of friends who are more like family, and romance that grabs you by the heart and won't let go. I hope you will all love it too!

Anastasia Hopcus

Prologue

East Sussex, England, June, 1942

The road was hushed and deserted, squeezed between high green hedges. This late in the evening there usually wasn't even a cyclist or a walker on it, and cars were always scarce. But now an old, battered automobile nosed its way along the lane, trailing the thick smoke that spoke of rationed gas mixed with kerosene to make it last longer. The car passed through a moist green tunnel formed by trees arching thickly overhead, and slowed down even more to turn onto the dirt track beyond.

There were three women in the front seat of the car, all dressed in civilian clothes. It was a rarity nowadays to find as many as three people together, even women, without at least one being in uniform. The driver was dark and tall, a little too thin, with an air of crisp efficiency, the sort one could never imagine being late or forgetting something or losing her way. The woman seated next to the driver was also tall, and her slenderness was of the type often described as "willowy." Her hair was a light-catching red-gold, thick and curling; in the early summer warmth, she wore it pulled back, the ends forced under into a roll, its heaviness caught in a silk net. Her eyes were gray, clear, and candid, and her skin was a fresh, translucent white, her cheeks vivid with color. No one, seeing her, would have mistaken her for anything but an Englishwoman.

But just as everything about Jessica Townsend, from her hair to her clothes to her strawberries-and-cream complexion, cried out "England," there was something about the woman on the other side of her, against the passenger door, that said she was from Occupied France. The brunette was dressed, like the other two women, in a plain cotton summer dress; and though hers was of a poorer cloth and cut than Jessica's, it wasn't the lack of quality that made the difference. It was something more subtle.

The three women in the car knew wherein lay the difference. It was in the handbag the brunette carried that had been stolen from a refugee Frenchwoman and unaccountably not returned—even though the contents of the bag were found and turned in to the police. It was in the scuffed leather shoes she wore—they had been taken by another refugee in London to a repair shop and subsequently lost there. It was in the dress made from French-loomed cloth, sewn by refugees and fastened with buttons taken from other garments which were too torn and soiled to be used. And it was in a manner, a turn of speech, a Gallic inclination of the head—the result of a certain innate ability to mimic and weeks of training by a Frenchwoman. For the woman, while not English, was certainly not French, either, despite the ID card in her handbag that identified her as "Yvonne Pitot," ladies' maid. Her real name was Alyssa Lambert, and she was an American.

The narrow path twisted through trees and out again, ending in front of a small thatched-roofed cottage. The car stopped, and the three women climbed out. Alyssa looked around her. At nine o'clock, the place was still bathed in the mellow glow of the English summer twilight. The air was heavy with the sweet scent of dog roses and honeysuckle. It was a scene of serenity and timeless beauty, at odds with the tangle of nerves in Alyssa's stomach. It seemed as remote and unreal to her as a perfect movie set. She glanced at Jessica, standing beside her, and managed a small smile.

"Please wait," said the driver, whom they knew only as "Athena." She walked alone into the small house. Jessica and Alyssa waited in patient silence, knowing that the other woman had to check that anyone else involved in the operation was out of sight before they passed through the house. It was the rule to let each participant know as little as possible about the other workers or the scheme in general. A major bending of the rules had let Jessica accompany Alyssa tonight, a rare concession which had come down from Pliny himself. Jessica was sure her request had been granted only because Pliny knew her so well and respected her ability to keep her mouth shut. But there had also been a strange, unidentifiable emotion in his eyes when he had granted Jessica's request, something she had seen there more than once where Alyssa was concerned. Sorrow or regret, perhaps guilt, or simply a natural denial that someone with Alyssa's beauty and talent should be exposed to probable death. God knows, the thought of Alyssa in German-occupied Paris chilled Jessica to the bone. She dreaded the months of sitting at Evington Court, waiting for Alyssa's messages.

But now she returned Alyssa's smile as best she could, knowing she mustn't add her own worry to Alyssa's burden. Athena emerged from the cottage, stooping slightly as she passed through the low doorway, and motioned for them to come. Alyssa and Jessica walked across the small yard and into the house, following Athena through a narrow, dark hallway to a back room.

It was a small room of uneven height with plain white walls, its single window sealed with blackout curtains. An iron cot, a small table, and two wooden straight-back chairs were the only furnishings in the room.

"Not exactly the Ritz," Alyssa commented with a wry smile, strolling over to one of the chairs. She was tuned up and ready to go, but she knew that now all she could do was wait. Athena had warned her that there were often delays at this last, nerve-racking moment. There was no guarantee that the plane would arrive on time to pick her up—or even arrive at all. There were always other demands, other drains on pilots and planes, many with higher priorities than theirs. There was the possibility that something would go wrong with the plane at the last minute or that the weather might change, making it impossible to fly or to land. Athena had told her of delays of hours or even days. There had been one agent who had actually boarded the plane, then had to get off and return to the house to wait for another day. It was one of the things that was hardest for the agents, given as they were to independence and action.

Jessica sat down across the table from Alyssa, and for a few minutes the friends simply looked at each other, full of chaotic thoughts and feelings that they couldn't express—or deemed it wiser not to. Jessica studied Alyssa. She had done her best to hide the beautiful, sophisticated woman Jessica knew. The rather shapeless cheap dress somewhat obscured Alyssa's excellent figure. In a few months, when the weather grew colder, she would be able to disguise her form even further with bulky winter clothing. The clumsy, thick-heeled shoes distracted from the lovely line of her legs and ankles. Her once-manicured hands had become roughened over the past few months to suit her supposed occupation and station in life, and the polished nails were now bare and trimmed to the quick. She wore no jewelry and no makeup. Her luxuriant black hair had been dyed to a muddy brown and twisted back into a tight knot. But even stripped of makeup and deprived of the full glory of her hair, Alyssa was unmistakably lovely. There was nothing anyone could do to hide the perfection of her facial bones or the expressiveness of her large, deep blue eyes. This rare beauty would be a danger to her in the coming months; she was too noticeable. Too unusual. It would be hard for her to fade into the population, no matter how French she made her mannerisms, walk, and stance.

Alyssa knew tricks to change her appearance; it was part of her trade. But adding a disfiguring scar or wart or birthmark would make her stand out even more. Spectacles would hide her eyes, but plain glass spectacles would be a dangerously suspicious thing to wear if she should happen to be stopped and searched by a German soldier. The wrong color makeup and lipstick could make her skin unattractively sallow; eye makeup could be used to make her eyes appear smaller. But makeup in German-occupied France was a scarce thing now, a black market item out of the reach of a common servant such as she was supposed to be; again, if she were stopped, it would draw suspicion upon her. And the pencil lines of stage makeup to add age were too thick and obvious at close range.

Jessica felt a chill. Alyssa was too pretty by far. How long would it be before some German soldier noticed her? Wanted to have her? What would Alyssa do then?

Jessica swallowed and looked away, afraid Alyssa would see her thoughts in her eyes. She searched for an innocuous topic of conversation. What could one possibly talk about at a time like this? In a matter of hours her best friend would fly to France under cover of darkness to become a radio-telegraphist for a Parisian resistance group. The odds were high that this would be the last time Jessica would ever see Alyssa. It seemed impossible that they could be in this situation. Yet it seemed equally impossible that they could ever have been school-girls together, reading naughty French novels under the bedsheets with the light of an electric torch, giggling, daydreaming about their future. Alyssa had wanted to be a famous actress and fall in love with a handsome, powerful, exciting man. Jessica had just wanted to marry Alan.

Funny, they had both gotten their wishes—and, like the wishes in the fairy tale, they had turned on them and brought them pain.

Jessica sighed unconsciously. Alyssa didn't ask why she sighed. She could see Jessica's face and knew well enough what she was thinking. Jessica was far more scared for Alyssa than Alyssa was herself. Death didn't frighten her. Physical pain, perhaps—but she had the precious L-pill if that got too bad. But oblivion, blackness—she wouldn't mind that. She had been dead inside for almost two years now. Ever since Philippe...

She turned her mind away from that, as she always did. She summoned up a smile for Jessica, searching for something to say. "Well," she said at last, and her trained voice didn't reveal even a quiver, "it's a long way from Madame Brisbois's, isn't it?"

Jessica smiled genuinely at the thought of the strict Swiss finishing school at which they had met and become friends almost twelve years before. "Lord, yes. Mademoiselle Musson would be horrified to learn you are doing something so unladylike."

They continued to talk of things in the distant past: their friends at the school, the first few years of Alyssa's struggling career, Jessica's marriage. But they spoke of nothing recent, nothing important, nothing painful.

The time passed. The golden glow outside melted into darkness. The door opened, and Athena stepped into the room. Her face was pale, her eyes unreadable in the dim light of the room. "It's time."

Alyssa rose jerkily. Her hands were icy. She turned to look at Jessica; this might be their last meeting. The first three women telegraphists who had been sent in were all dead now or trapped in a German camp, worse than dead. Alyssa saw the knowledge in Jessica's eyes, too. Clear gray pools of honesty. Jessica had never been able to mislead anyone, even their once-dreaded headmistress. Alyssa opened her arms, and they hugged each other, a quick, hard movement. Then Alyssa spun away and strode from the room. Athena followed her, closing the door behind them. Jessica sat down again, clenching her hands together in her lap, and now the suppressed tears crept from her eyes and rolled down her cheeks.

Alyssa paused to let Athena come up beside her, and they walked together through the house and out into the field behind it. The Lysander waited for her, a black hulk against the dark sky. A pilot in RAF blue lounged beside the plane, arms crossed, waiting for her. Alyssa turned to the other woman. She'd worked with Athena for several weeks and in some ways was closer to her than to any other person alive, save Jessica. Yet she didn't know the woman's true name. She didn't know what to say or do at this last moment with her.

The other woman reached out and took Alyssa's hand, giving it a squeeze.

"Cleopatra," she said, looking at Alyssa. It wasn't hard to understand why Pliny had given her such an exotic code name. She was as beautiful as an enchantress, as poised as a queen. It seemed such a waste.

Alyssa returned the squeeze and broke the contact. She turned away. The pilot waited for her in silence. Funny. Two years ago when she flew into England, it had been her first time in an airplane. Now here she was, flying into France under cover of darkness, trained to parachute out if necessary, this low, slow, hedgehopping flight the least of the dangers awaiting her. Two years...before the fall of Paris, before Philippe. Before life had seized her in its cold, tight grip. It seemed a century ago. If only she didn't remember it so well.

She started forward toward the plane.

Chapter 1

The ungainly looking British Imperial Airways Clipper touched down on the water, its pontoons smoothly making contact, and eased into place at the docks. Moments later the passengers disembarked onto the long wooden pier. Among them was one woman, and as she walked away from the plane, heads turned to look after her.

She was a beautiful woman, out of the ordinary. She was taller than average, shapely, with long, lovely legs emerging from beneath the hem of her classic beige Chanel suit. Poised, graceful, her breeding showed in every line of her body, despite the rumpling inevitable from the twenty-one-hour-long flight from New York to Lisbon to Southampton. Her hair was coal black, glossy and thick, and it fell to her shoulders in a smooth cascade. A dainty hat sat atop her head, its net demi-veil shadowing her huge, vivid blue eyes, adding a touch of mystery without hiding any of their beauty. Thick black eyelashes outlined her eyes, tinting them with a sensual, smoky look.

The face below the hat was delicately triangular, with prominent cheekbones, and her skin was smooth and creamy white, tinged with color along her cheeks. Her features were regular and even, except for the upper lip, which was a trifle too short, often slipping up to reveal straight white teeth. This one slight irregularity added a hint of sexuality and vulnerability to her beauty, saving it from the coldness of perfection. Her mouth called to be kissed, and there were few men who could resist its lure.

Her name was Alyssa Lambert, and had she been in New York City, someone might have recognized her as one of the most beautiful and talented ingénues of the Broadway stage. Britishers saw only that she was a woman of beauty, taste, and elegance. And they were as correct as those who knew she was an actress. Her father was Grant Lambert, a distinguished American diplomat and son of an old New England family whose wealth was so well established that the Depression had made scarcely a dent in it.

It had been a long flight, and Alyssa hadn't slept much on the plane, but she was too eager to see Jessica again to waste the day in Southampton, sleeping off her travel exhaustion. Instead, she boarded an express train to London and by midafternoon she arrived in Victoria Station. There she hailed one of the ubiquitous black London taxis and told the driver to take her to the Ritz Hotel, where she always stayed when she was in London.

As she rode through the streets, Alyssa gazed eagerly around her at the city. She had loved London for years, ever since she had first visited it with her father when she was a child. Later, when she became friends with Jessica, she had come there often with her. The city was comfortable, dignified, without the bustle of New York, but rich in color and history.

It was as beautiful as ever, dearly familiar, with its gracious stone buildings and sturdy plane trees, its tidy little squares of greenery and surprising bursts of expansive parks and riotously colored gardens. But it was disturbingly different, too. War had put its mark upon it. All around were the signs of a city preparing for an air siege such as the Luftwaffe had launched on Warsaw last September. Crisscrossed tapes marked storefront windows, and sandbags had been piled against walls to absorb the shock of bomb blasts. Long trenches had been dug in parks and the small green squares. Strangest of all were the huge white barrage balloons, meant to discourage the dive-bombing Stukas. They floated like bizarre, lightweight elephants above the buildings.

The taxi stopped in front of the Ritz Hotel, and Alyssa looked up at the impressive white stone building with its massive carved heads. A doorman in a white-trimmed top hat and frock coat stood waiting on the steps. Another similarly dressed employee was sweeping the spotless sidewalk. Alyssa smiled. Well, at least the Ritz never changed.

Alyssa paid the taxi driver as the doorman hurried to close the door of the taxi for her and escort her into the lobby. Inside the hotel all was elegance and quiet, its cool marble floors, Aubusson rugs, and glass-dripping chandeliers so serene and removed from the world that Alyssa felt rested simply to be there.

Once in her room, Alyssa was tempted to lie down for an hour or two, but she resisted. After all, she hadn't flown all this way in the middle of a war just to take a nap at the Ritz. Instead, she washed her face and changed from her crumpled suit into a fresh linen dress before setting out for Jessica's house.

Jessica's home lay on a quiet crescent in Belgravia. Though they had kept up their friendship for years through regular correspondence and an occasional visit, Alyssa had never visited this house before, and as she exited the taxi, she looked up at it with interest.

A tall, narrow town house of a style known as Pont Street Dutch, unique to the Chelsea-Belgravia area, it was part of a row of connected houses, all four stories tall and no more than two rooms wide. Built of a dull reddish stone, each had an ornate, sharply peaked roof, jutting bow windows above the ground floor, and a black wrought-iron balcony on the second floor—or the first story, as the English called it. How like Jessica to live here, Alyssa thought, in a home quite English and subdued, yet with a flair, a romanticism, a spark of mischief and originality.

It had been those qualities that attracted Alyssa to Jessica when they first met. Alyssa was sixteen and a little frightened when she entered Madame Brisbois's boarding school and was placed in a room with Jessica Bainbridge. Jessica, with her serious gray eyes and blond hair pulled discreetly back and tied, appeared to be the model student. She made good grades; she studied; she was unfailingly polite to those around her, yet properly reserved. Alyssa thought, with a sinking heart, that she was a rather pretty prig and a bore—until a few nights after Alyssa moved in with her, when she awoke to find Jessica climbing out their second story window to attend a dance in the village below the school. Alyssa joined her, and they had been fast friends ever since.

Certainly Jessica was reserved and proper, but she also had a sharp, surprising sense of humor, and she could sparkle with merriment. She was quiet and easygoing, but given the right reason, she could flash into fire.

Alyssa knocked on the front door, hoping Jessica was home. Alyssa hadn't cabled her, wanting to keep her visit a surprise. A maid answered the door and showed Alyssa into an elegant, yet unostentatious drawing room to wait. A few moments later, there was the tap of high heels on the marble of the hallway, and Jessica appeared in the doorway, her face settled into lines of polite inquiry. Alyssa turned and smiled. "Hello, Jessica."

The other woman stared incredulously. Then a great grin of joy burst across her face. "Alyssa!" Jessica opened her arms wide, and Alyssa stepped into them. They hugged each other fiercely, then stepped back at arm's length to look at each other, grinning.

"Good Lord, I never expected to see you! When Doris said there was an American woman at the door, I couldn't imagine…" Jessica laughed with sheer pleasure and squeezed Alyssa's hands. Her wide gray eyes sparkled. Though no match for Alyssa's striking loveliness, Jessica was very pretty, with large, clear eyes, bright red-gold hair, and a marvelous, uniquely English complexion—translucent, dewy, and glowing with a natural high color that no rouge could ever duplicate. "Here, sit down, and I'll ring for tea. You must tell me all about this change-about. In your last letter you said you weren't coming for Claire's wedding…"

"I know. But the play I was in closed last week. No surprise; it was terrible. Not just the script. The two leads fought like cat and dog the whole time. I've gotten so tired of the theater. I'm tired of playing ingénues! After all, I'm twenty-eight years old now. How long can a woman go on playing pretty and sappy?"

Jessica giggled. "I've seen some women do it their whole lives."

"Well, not me. Anyway, there I was: the play over, feeling sick to death of my career and wishing I could see you and go to Claire's wedding. And Dad's in Paris right now; I could hop over there after the wedding. It's been almost a year since I've seen him. So I thought, why not? Of course, I couldn't take the *Queen Mary* with the U-boats prowling the Atlantic. But I knew I could catch the Clipper, and I've always had a secret urge to fly in an airplane."

"How was it?"

"Fantastic! Hanging up there above the clouds—it was so wild and beautiful."

Jessica smiled. "That's how Alan feels. But the couple of times he took me up in his plane, I just felt mostly ill." She grimaced. "But, tell me, weren't you afraid to come here, with the war and all?"

"What war?" Alyssa retorted quickly, and Jessica smiled wryly. "It's been seven months since England and German declared war on each other, and nothing's happened. At home everyone thinks England will sign a peace treaty with Germany soon."

Jessica sighed. "Yes. Everyone here is calling it the 'phony war.' But I've talked to people who don't think the peace will last."

"You think it will come to actual fighting?"

"How can it not? Hitler's a madman. He doesn't want appeasement. He wants the world under his thumb. We'll be polite; he'll keep pushing; and finally, when our back's to the wall, England will turn and fight." She fell silent as the maid slipped into the room with a tray, and Jessica began the ritual of tea.

Alyssa decided to change the subject to something more pleasant than the war clouds looming over them. "You look gorgeous. Marriage must agree with you."

Jessica smiled. "Almost seven years now, and we're still very happy." She had married Alan Townsend when she was twenty. Alyssa had been surprised that she had waited so long. Jessica and Alan had been neighbors since childhood, and as far as Alyssa could tell, Jessica had loved him from the day she was born. Jessica had joined Alyssa in flirting with the local boys from the village and the ones at a neighboring boys' school, but she never thought of them as anything more than a temporary diversion. Her heart was already given to Alan.

Alyssa had never been able to imagine being quite so steady-minded about anyone. Nor, when she met him during Jessica's "coming out" after they graduated, had Alan Townsend seemed to her to be a man to inspire such devotion. Two years older than Jessica, he was tall and lanky with thin, light-brown hair and a long, serious face. He spoke sparingly and smiled even less often. But over the years, as Alyssa got to know him, she discovered his charm. And it was obvious to everyone who knew them that he was mad about Jessica. They were "suited to each other," as Jessica's autocratic grandmother said, and while Alyssa couldn't imagine marrying a man who exhibited no more fire and passion than Alan did, marriage to him seemed to make Jessica happy.

"I just hope that Claire will be as happy," Jessica continued.

Claire Stanton had lived down the hall from Jessica and Alyssa at boarding school, and, being a fellow English girl, she and Jessica had formed a friendship before Alyssa arrived. The three of them had been friends until they graduated, Jessica forming the cornerstone of the relationship. Claire was considered the brains of their group, while Alyssa was the beauty, and Jessica the lady. Claire had gone on to study at a university and later had joined the Foreign Service, working in the British embassy in Spain, then in Poland.

"Tell me about Claire's fiancé," Alyssa urged, leaning closer and resting her arms on her knees. "She hardly said anything about him in her letter, except that he's Polish."

Jessica grinned. "You'll like Ky. He's terribly romantic. He even has a little dueling scar right here under his left eye."

"Ky?"

"Casimir Andrzej Dubrowski, more easily known as Ky," Jessica explained. "He's tall, blond, and very handsome, with that sort of stern, fiercely blue-eyed look. You know, the kind you expect to come riding in on a snorting steed, saber in hand, and pick a girl up and throw her over the saddlebow."

Alyssa chuckled. "Is *that* how Claire met him?"

Jessica joined in her laughter. "I don't know. I wouldn't put it past him. But Claire's positively close-mouthed about how they met. I'm beginning to suspect it involved something no one's supposed to know about."

Alyssa's eyes widened. "What do you mean?"

Jessica shrugged. "I'm not sure, exactly. Did you ever meet Claire's uncle? Ian Hedley?"

Alyssa shook her head. "I don't think so. I met her mother once; that's all."

"Well, I've met Ian several times, and he's very… interesting. I'm sure you'll meet him while you're here, and you'll understand what I mean. He seems quite ordinary, yet there's something rather compelling about him as well. Anyway, he's an importer—antiques and things—and he has a lot of contacts all over the world. I think for the past few years he's seen what was coming more clearly than most of us. He has been quietly collecting information… and friends… and favors."

Alyssa's voice dropped. "Are you trying to tell me that Claire is involved in spying? Are you serious?"

"Sound a little farfetched?" Jessica asked, smiling. "I thought so too until I started talking to Ian. He's very patriotic. Very knowledgeable. He's been rather a voice in the wilderness the past few years, warning us about Hitler's intentions. He told me a year ago that Germany wouldn't stop with Austria or Czechoslovakia; they'd want Poland. And he was right. No one would listen, but that didn't stop him. He's been working steadily on his own."

"Spying? And Claire's been working for him? I find all this a little hard to absorb."

"Yes, I think Claire was doing something for him in Poland. I think that's how she met Ky."

"I never thought of Claire as an adventuress."

"Me, either. But, then, lots of things I've never thought of have happened."

"Well, what is this Ky Dubrowski doing here in London?" Alyssa thought of the newsreels she had seen of the debacle in Poland, of Polish cavalry charging German tanks in a final, desperate struggle.

"He escaped. When Claire returned to London with the rest of our embassy staff after war was declared, she was worried sick about Ky. She was certain she'd never see him alive again. He was a pilot in the Polish Air Force, which the Luftwaffe destroyed. But somehow Ky managed to escape; he showed up here about six weeks ago to join the RAF, like other Polish flyers who escaped. And he and Claire are getting married."

"It sounds like something out of a book."

Jessica nodded. "Doesn't it? Everything's strange nowadays. People are marrying all over the place, as if they're trying to seize their happiness before the war comes. Or as if they'll somehow stave off the conflict. But Claire's deliriously happy. Wait'll you see her; her face glows. She looks like a different person from the woman who came back to London last September."

"I'm eager to see her."

"Don't worry. I'll call her and tell her you're here. We'll have lunch at the Savoy tomorrow. She can get away from work long enough for that."

"Where is she working?"

"In her uncle's business."

"The one into shady dealings?"

Jessica sent her a mock frown. "Not shady dealings, just... hush-hush."

"Ah. I see. I hope I'm going to get to meet this uncle while I'm here."

"I'm sure you will. No doubt he'll be at the party I'm giving for Claire and Ky this weekend. It will be enormous. Grandmother is graciously allowing me to hold it at her home because it's too big for mine. By the way, she wants to see you."

"Her Ladyship?"

Jessica smiled at Alyssa's nickname for her grandmother. "Yes. She thinks quite a bit of you, you know."

"Me? I would think she considers me terribly plebeian."

"Well, she does, but she accepts it because, after all, *all* Americans are plebeian. And she admits that for an American you come from a good family."

Alyssa laughed. "*My* grandmother would be thrilled to hear that."

"She says you have beauty and style—as women used to in her day, of course."

"Before they started cutting their hair and shortening their skirts," Alyssa supplemented.

"Precisely. Grandmother maintains that you could hide a multitude of bad features with long hair, long skirts, and a corset."

"I suspect she's right."

The two women smiled at each other. Then suddenly Jessica reached across the couch and clasped her friend's hand. "Oh, Alyssa, it's so marvelous to have you back."

*****

The Savoy Hotel was an elegant old place in the business district of London, its driveway famous for being the only road in England where traffic drove on the right, not the left. Its bar and restaurant were favorite meeting spots for the press, especially the American press, and it was particularly crowded these days, with the rush of correspondents to England and the Continent to cover the war.

Alyssa met Jessica there at noon the next day, radiant and refreshed after a good night's sleep. Snatches of conversation floated by as they followed the waiter to their table, the flat accents of Americans mingling with the crisper tones of the native Britishers: "… Sitzkrieg! How are you going to write about nothing?"

"…bloody nuisance. The PM says…"

"Churchill's spouting off about *Graf Spee*…"

"…but since the Finns surrendered to Stalin…"

"Get a load of those legs, would you?"

The maître d' seated them, and Jessica looked across at her friend quizzically. "Why is it that whenever I'm with you, I feel as if everyone's staring at us?"

Alyssa chuckled. "It's not just me, you know. There's a dark-haired man over there who's got his eyes set quite firmly on you."

"You're joking." Jessica swiveled her head to look. At a table against the wall were two men, one dark and rather broodingly handsome, the other supremely nondescript. The one with the black hair and brown eyes was studying her. Jessica turned back to Alyssa, her color flaming a little higher. "Well, what do you know? That gives the old ego a boost."

"I don't know why you should be so surprised. You're very attractive."

Jessica shrugged. "I get my fair share of looks. But I never expect to when I'm with you."

Alyssa rolled her eyes. "You want to know something? I intimidate most men."

"What?"

"Yes. It's the truth. I scare them off. All except the obnoxious ones, of course."

Jessica chuckled. "Now, Alyssa, I know that can't be true." She glanced toward the entrance. "Look, there's Claire." She raised her hand and waggled it, and Alyssa turned in her chair to get a look at their friend. Claire waved back and hurried toward them, arriving breathlessly at the table.

"Hullo. Sorry to be late, but Uncle had some last-minute things I had to do." She bent down to give Alyssa a half hug. "I'm so thrilled you came! I couldn't believe it when Jessica rang me up yesterday and said you'd made it after all."

"I wouldn't have missed it for the world," Alyssa assured her, trying not to stare at her friend. How much Claire had changed! Claire had never been unattractive, but she had been quiet and shy, lacking in confidence, a bookworm who had difficulty talking to people. When Alyssa first met her, she had worn her hair in an old-fashioned, unattractive style, was awkward with makeup, and seemed at a loss when it came to clothes. Jessica and Alyssa had managed to improve her clothes sense and hair style during the years they were at school together. But the last time Alyssa saw her, Claire still had that reticent air, a way of pulling back from a crowd until you'd hardly notice her.

But now she was turning heads. She wore a trim jacketed dress in a soft rose that brightened her complexion, and her hair was swept back from her face and fastened with barrettes in a becoming style. But the change was more than that. Her face glowed. Her eyes were bright and alive. She moved with poise and assurance. It was an inner change that showed all over her.

Claire sat down, and they ordered lunch. As they chatted, most of Claire's conversation centered on her fiancé. Alyssa began to burn with curiosity; she couldn't wait to meet this man who had made such a difference in Claire.

"You'll get to meet him at Jessica's party," Claire assured Alyssa. "He'll be off duty then. You'll love him; you can't help it."

Is this the same girl, Alyssa thought, who struggled to keep any boy she dated from meeting me, certain that he would immediately lose interest in her?

Claire had to leave as soon as they finished eating, sighing that tons of work were waiting for her at the office. Alyssa and

Jessica lingered over second cups of coffee and tea, then spent a leisurely afternoon wandering along Oxford Street, looking in store windows. They ended up in Fortnum & Mason, where Jessica bought caviar, chocolates, and a few other expensive groceries.

"I thought you had food rationing," Alyssa commented, watching her select her goods.

Jessica shrugged. "I haven't seen much sign of it. Except for fruit—that's scarce. The U-boats have been playing hell with the shipping."

Food wasn't the only area in which London seemed little touched by the war. As the days passed, Alyssa discovered that nearly everything went on as before. The cinemas were open, and restaurants and nightclubs were jammed. Stage productions had moved their curtain times up to 6:00 or 6:30 because of the blackout, but other than that continued with their business as usual. There were several successful plays and revues, including a scandalous nude review at the Windmill Theatre, in which the women stood onstage still as statues, their bare breasts and G-strings permitted by decency laws only as long as they did not move.

Jessica and Alyssa went to parties, to restaurants, and to tea at the Ritz. They bought tickets to the Palladium and to London's most successful revue, *New Faces*, where they listened to the latest hit song, "A Nightingale Sang in Berkeley Square" and laughed at jokes about the inactivity of British soldiers on duty in France. In the packed nightclubs, restaurants, and theaters, it was difficult to remember that the country was officially at war with Germany and had been since September of the year before.

Even though Alyssa knew there had been no real military activity since the declaration of war, she had expected to find a country somberly facing battle. She was amazed to find instead an air of frenetic gaiety, with everyone chasing madly, almost desperately, after pleasure in every form. She heard that the prostitutes along Piccadilly were doing thriving business even in the darkness of the blackout.

They only real reminder of the war was the blackout, and this was regarded as much as a nuisance as anything else. Almost the only deaths caused by the war had been pedestrians hit by vehicles at night, for the headlights of cars at night were covered over and only narrow slits or sidelights were permitted to shine, making it almost impossible for the driver to see—or for anyone to see the driver coming. When Jessica and Alyssa strolled home at night from dancing or the theater, looking for a taxi, they wore luminous armbands, called glowworms, or white umbrella covers, to catch what little light there was.

To Alyssa, who had spent most of her life in large cities, it was amazing how thoroughly dark the night was. The bright neon lights of Piccadilly Circus were turned off; no streetlamps glowed; no crack of light escaped around the edges of the heavy blackout curtains. Only the occasional dim glow of a car passing by lit the streets at all. It was eerie and dangerous. More than once Alyssa found herself stepping in a puddle or stumbling over a curb. Yet the inconveniences did little to keep the people from their frantic search for nightly fun.

It saddened Alyssa to find Londoners so unconcerned about Germany and with no eagerness to fight Hitler. She herself had been horrified by the news photos of the German Army and Air Force assaulting the country of Poland. And that had been only the latest, most bloody instance of Hitler's gobbling up every defenseless country around him. Earlier the world had watched Germany consume Czechoslovakia and Austria. Alyssa had been raised by a father with high ideals of fairness and justice, and such beliefs were ingrained in her. It revolted her to see the huge monsters of fascism plunder at will.

Her natural repugnance was strengthened by Hemingway's reports from the Spanish Civil War and those of another American foreign correspondent, S. E. Marek. His articles told of the economic, then personal sanctions against the Jews of Germany. He had written a particularly vivid and horrifying account of the "Night of the Broken Glass," in which the shops and homes of the Jewish section of Berlin had been looted and plundered and thousands of Jews hurt, even killed, in the process.

Marek had been quietly and firmly told to leave the country and had since been reporting from Paris. From there he had written of the French people's careless, unconcerned approach to the war. Alyssa hadn't been surprised. She had spent some time in France when she was at Madame Brisbois's, and though she liked the French people and their style and zest, she knew that they looked at life in an easygoing way. With their immense army and the enormous strength of the Maginot Line of defense fortifications, they considered an attack upon France something that wasn't worth worrying about.

Alyssa had assumed that the attitude in England would be different. She had lived in England for a while as a girl when her father worked at the embassy there. Later she visited Jessica frequently, often going home with her for holidays during school. Jessica's warm family gave her more of a home life that her own career-oriented father and troubled mother, and she came to regard England as her second home. She liked the English people, finding them fair-minded and incredibly tough beneath their cool, polite, rather effete veneer. When Germany invaded Poland last fall and England subsequently declared war, moving at last to stop Hitler's voracious appetite, Alyssa had been pleased. Now, at last, she thought, Hitler had bitten off more than he could chew. He'd find England tough to digest.

Yet here were the English still scrambling to find a way to make peace and engaged more in partying than in preparing for war. It left Alyssa feeling deflated, and she was glad now that she was to stay in London only another week before meeting her father in Paris.

Chapter 2

Jessica took a final glance around the long ballroom. The decorations were in place, the servants and caterers ready, the small orchestra setting up at one end of the room, and her grandmother was seated regally in a comfortable chair at the opposite end. Her grandmother gave her a low, stately nod, signifying her approval of the arrangements, and Jessica smiled. Grandmother's approval was not easily obtained.

Jessica went next to the large kitchen. Had she not held many parties in her life, she would have been frightened by the chaos she saw there. People rushed about madly, carrying bottles and food, setting up trays, bring boxes up from the pantry, preparing food. The caterer and his head assistant rapped out orders. The butler was sulking. The cook was shouting at one of the maids, who was crying. A footman was arguing heatedly with one of the caterer's employees. But Jessica had witnessed similar scenes often enough before to realize that this was a controlled chaos and that there wasn't a serious problem brewing.

She left the kitchen and circled around to the entryway, her high-heeled slippers tapping sharply against the black-and-white Carrara marble floor. She was feeling quite pleased with the evening. Everything seemed in order. She had on a Madeleine Vionnet evening gown which she had been saving for a suitable occasion, a soft off-white silk chiffon confection with a straight-cut sequined jacket of navy blue and off-white stripes. She knew she looked smashing in it; Alan had told her so. Alyssa was in London. Claire was deeply in love and getting married. And Alan was home, off duty for a week. It was going to be a perfect night.

Just as she stepped into the entry, she heard the clack of Alan's shoes coming down the stairs, and she looked up, smiling.

Alan smiled back at her. "Hullo, love. All set?"

"Yes, I think so." Since the party was at her grandmother's house and she had had a multitude of last-minute items to check, she and Alan had brought their evening clothes with them to dress here. Alan had just finished getting ready; his cheek was smooth from shaving, and he smelled deliciously of masculine soap and cologne. Jessica stepped up the bottom two steps to meet him, reaching up to plant a kiss on his cheek. "It's so nice to have you home."

Alan kissed Jessica affectionately on the forehead, careful not to disturb her makeup or her carefully coiffed hair. "It's nice to be home. Rochford Field leaves a great deal to be desired in terms of creature comforts."

"Is that what you miss?" Jessica asked in mock indignation, tilting her head back to frown up at him.

He chuckled. "My bunkmate isn't nearly as pleasant either."

Alan Townsend was a tall man, not quite handsome, but nice looking in a cool way. He had a long, thin face with a sharp nose and high cheekbones, a legacy from his aristocratic Norman ancestors. His eyes were gray, his hair dark blond and baby-fine, already beginning to thin a little on top. He managed to smoke a pipe without affectation; he was kind, if rather unemotional; and he fit easily into the mold of English gentleman. That, after all, was what he had been reared to be. He had been taught to live well but without ostentation, to be courteous to women and considerate of those who had been so unfortunate as not to be born a baron's son and reared in the Kentish countryside. Alan was not overly brainy nor did he perceive any need to be; he left those things to his two older brothers, who pursued affairs of state and the family business interests. But he had a healthy sense of humor and a surprising streak of daring. Easygoing and pleasant, he had only two passions in life: one was flying airplanes, and the other was his wife, Jessica.

His family's country estate bordered the lands of Jessica's father, Horton Bainbridge, and Alan and Jessica had played together as children. Alan had enjoyed Jessica's hero worship of him. She had followed wherever he led with unquestioning obedience. Her family was warmhearted, humorous, and full of life, quite different from his own rather cool and distant parents. His brothers had left home for school when he was only five, and his parents spent much of the year in London, leaving him alone at Avedon Hall with his nanny and the servants. He grew up lonely, and it was a joy for him to be at Jessica's house with her family. It was an even greater joy to bask in Jessica's admiration and love.

Their friendship had continued through the years, surviving separation when each was sent off to boarding school and even a period when Alan displayed a boyish disdain for girls. Alan found he could confide all sorts of things to Jessica that he wouldn't think of telling his parents or friends, and she was always fun to be with. But even as they matured, it never entered his head that she might be someone in whom he would have a romantic interest. Then Jessica had gone to school in Switzerland, and he hadn't seen her for almost two years, for he had chosen to spend his school holidays in the more exciting London. When Jessica graduated, she moved to London to live with her grandmother during the period of her "coming out." Alan met her at a party and almost didn't recognize her. And he fell hopelessly in love with her.

But Alan was not one to display his emotions easily; and after their long years of friendship, he was afraid that Jessica regarded him only as a brother. So he didn't rush into courtship or woo her with passionate declarations of love. Rather, he managed always to be around wherever she was, dancing with her at parties, inviting her to join him and his friends on outings. Because they were so often together, they came to be regarded as a couple, yet almost six months passed before he kissed her. That happened only because one day as they were strolling through her grandmother's garden alone, Jessica came to a sudden halt and inquired in an exasperated voice, "Alan, do you ever plan to kiss me?"

"What?" Alan stopped and turned back to look at her, his jaw dropping slightly. He could think of nothing to say.

"Bunny Fairley tells me she's certain you're mad about me, but I can't tell." Jessica's frustration had mounted over the months. She had loved Alan ever since she could remember. At first she had thought of him as the brother she had always wanted; but when she was about fifteen, she realized that she was in love with him as a woman loved a man, and the she wanted nothing more in the world than to marry him. She had been working on it ever since, flirting, dancing, even kissing other men as practice for the day when she would use these skills on Alan. She thought she had caught his interest at her coming-out party; certainly he was always around. Yet he still seemed to be only a friend, never saying a romantic word or trying to kiss her.

"Well?" she continued impatiently when he said nothing. "Is Bunny right?"

"Yes," he responded gravely. "I am quite mad about you."

Jessica made an inelegant noise and glared at him, her hands clenched on her hips. "Then why don't you do anything about it?"

Suddenly he smiled. "I suppose I shall." He took a step forward and leaned down to kiss her.

A year and a half later, they were married.

In the seven years of their marriage, Alan never once regretted it. They rarely quarreled and were still the best of friends. Alan never considered being unfaithful nor, indeed, had the slightest interest in any other woman. Though he was not the type to wear his heart on his sleeve, Jessica didn't doubted that he loved her. Nor had she ever doubted that she loved him. The most distressing part of the "phony war" this past half year had been that it separated them so much of the time.

Alan joined the RAF as soon as England declared war on Germany. He had an uncle who had flown for England in the Great War over twenty years before, and Alan grew up loving airplanes. His uncle taught him to fly when he was only fifteen years old, and he had never lost his love for soaring through the air. It had been only natural for him to join the Royal Air Force when he left school and was casting about for something to do. Military service, after all, was an acceptable occupation for a younger son in the Townsend line.

He had found he didn't much care for the military life, especially after he and Jessica were married, and he left the RAG several years earlier. But when war was declared, he re-signed immediately. Jessica hadn't expected him to do anything else. One had a duty to one's country, after all. Moreover, Jessica was convinced that Hitler must be stopped, even at the price of war. Still, it was hard to have Alan away from home most of the time, coming back only on weekend passes.

Now the two of them walked down the last two steps hand in hand, and took up their posts to greet their guests. Claire and Ky, the couple to be honored, came to the door. Guests began to trickle in and soon became a steady stream.

Alyssa arrived as the rush was beginning to slow down, and Jessica greeted her delightedly, then passed her along to Claire, who introduced her fiancé. "Alyssa, I want you to meet Casimir Dubrowski. Ky, this is Alyssa Lambert."

"Ah, yes, Claire has talked of you often." He took Alyssa's hand and bent over it in the Continental way while Alyssa took stock of him. He was very handsome; there was no denying that. Blond, blue-eyed, tall, with a tiny scar near his left eye that gave him a certain rakish dash, he spoke English well, with a soft accent. He was a bit stern, perhaps, but probably that suited Claire quite well. It was obvious that he had eyes only for her.

Alyssa smiled. She approved. "It's very nice to meet you." They chatted for a moment, and Alyssa moved into the ballroom to allow those arriving behind her to talk to the guests of honor. She paused for a moment on the threshold of the large room. She knew that there were those, like Claire, who dreaded entering a room full of people, particularly if she knew few of them, but to Alyssa such a situation presented a challenge. And she loved nothing more than a challenge.

Almost immediately a young man was by her side, asking her to dance. He was impossibly young, of course, but he looked like fun, and Alyssa agreed. After that, she didn't have a chance to sit down or even catch her breath until finally, after one dance, a middle-aged man approached her, smiling.

"Yes?"

"Allow me to introduce myself. Rolly Burchard, at your service."

"How do you do, Mr. Burchard."

"I won't be impertinent enough to ask you to dance; I never was much of a dancer, even in my younger days. But I've been sent as an emissary."

"Oh?"

"Yes." The older man nodded his head toward the far end of the room, where Jessica's grandmother sat. "By Lady Julia Stafford."

Alyssa smiled. She liked Jessica's grandmother. "Ah, I see. Then I can understand why you didn't refuse the duty."

He made an expression of horror, which Alyssa suspected was only half mocking. "My word, no. She's my aunt, you know."

He extended his arm, and Alyssa allowed him to escort her down the long, gleaming wood floor to the chair where Lady Stafford held court. The older woman held out a hand adorned with multiple rings. "Hullo, child. How enchanting you look. Here. Sit down next to me and tell me all about yourself."

"How are you? I'm so happy to see you."

"Humph! Then why haven't you come over to see me earlier? No, no need to answer that. I've been watching you bewitch every man in the place."

Alyssa chuckled. "Now, Lady Stafford…"

Julia held up a hand. "No. Don't try to squirm out of it. Or to apologize. Heavens, that's what a pretty young girl should be doing, not talking to some old dowager like me. It's precisely what I would have been doing at your age."

Alyssa could well believe that the old woman had bewitched men when she was young. Even now she was lovely, her snow-white hair twisted up into a tight coronet of braids, her blue eyes bright with interest, and her remarkably slim figure encased in a rich purple satin dress. It wasn't difficult to imagine her as a young woman, her thick brown hair in a flattering pompadour style and her body corseted into a perfect hourglass figure. Jessica said the family gossip was that her grandmother had had two lovers over the years, and Alyssa didn't doubt it. Lady Stafford had lived in a more permissive time than the present, during the reign of Edward VII. It wasn't at all unusual in those days for a couple to make an advantageous marriage, then go their separate ways, taking lovers for whom they felt real love and passion. More common for a man, of course, but not so unlikely for a wife either.

Julia studied Alyssa's dress. "Hmmm, that's a change, isn't it? A wide skirt, I mean, after all these years of clinging gowns. Who's the designer?"

"Molyneaux."

"Really? Interesting. I rather like it. About time to try something new, I should think. Now, tell me, have you met any fascinating men recently?"

"You mean since I've been in London?"

"London, New York. It doesn't matter. I just want to hear about your love life, it keeps an old woman from getting bored. All my granddaughters are deadly dull. Look at Jessica: in love with the same boy since she was a child. Never even looked at another man. What a waste."

"Don't you like Alan?" Alyssa asked, surprised.

"Oh, he's a good sort. Not one to set a girl's heart beating faster, though. No doubt he's a marvelous husband, but, personally, I find a *grand passion* much more intriguing."

"I'm afraid I don't have anything intriguing to report, either. No grand passions. The most interesting thing that's happened to me lately is that I flew over on an airplane."

"Frightful machines," Lady Stafford pronounced. "Well, if you have no fascinating love affairs to confide, tell me what you've been doing in the theater."

Alyssa settled down to an anecdote-filled description of the plays she had been in and the actors and actresses she had dealt with, making the older woman roar with her account of the petty squabbling and upstaging of the two warring leads in her latest production. A slight man with sharp features and bright, intelligent eyes hovered for a moment on the edge of their conversation until Julia noticed him. She squinted, being too vain to wear her glasses.

"I say, Ian Hedley. How are you? I should have known you'd be here. Claire's uncle, aren't you?"

"Yes. How are you, Lady Stafford?"

"Passably well, I suppose. And you? I hear you've thrown your lot in with Churchill and those hotheads."

A faint smile touched his lips. "I wouldn't say they're hotheads, precisely. Just realists."

"Of course, I've never agreed with Churchill's politics. But I can't like Chamberlain's backing down as he had. Looks bad. England never backed down in her history, even against the mightiest navy in the world. We whipped the Armada then and sent them scurrying back to Spain, and it seems a disgrace to give in to some strutting little paperhanger now."

"I agree."

"Alyssa, do you know Ian?"

"No, I'm afraid I haven't had the pleasure."

"This is Ian Hedley. Ian, Alyssa Lambert, a friend of Claire's and Jessica's. Good girl, even if she is American."

Ian's eyes lighted with amusement. "I've met a few of that breed who aren't all bad." He bowed slightly to Alyssa. "I'm pleased to meet you. Jessica and Claire are quite fond of you. In fact, I specifically came over to see you."

Alyssa's eyes widened slightly. "Really?" She couldn't imagine why Ian Hedley would seek her out. She had wanted to meet him; she'd been very intrigues with the idea of Claire's family harboring a spymaster. But why in the world would *he* have any interest in *her*?

"Of course," Julia said with a martyred sign. "All right then, you rude creature. Take her away, but you must promise to bring her back to me."

Ian led Alyssa away with a gentle but insistent hand at her elbow. "Would you like some punch?"

"That sounds lovely."

He got her a glass, then quietly steered her away from the crowd and through the entryway into the softly lit, deserted drawing room. Alyssa sipped from her glass and watched him, waiting. He sat down across from her and gazed back at her for a moment. "Well, my dear, Claire wasn't exaggerating about your appearance. You are a very beautiful woman."

"Thank you."

"Claire has told me of your other admirable qualities: intelligence, loyalty, a sense of justice." Ian took in Alyssa's raised eyebrows. "Don't look so surprised. Claire's quite smart about people. Jessica confirms her opinion. I trust those two young women. Very levelheaded."

"Yes, they are. But I don't understand—"

"Then let me get to the point. I forget how impatient you Americans are. Jessica said you agree with her that Hitler must be stopped. That war is inevitable and that we must do everything to prepare ourselves for it."

Alyssa tilted her head to one side, considering. "Yes. I've been amazed, I guess, at how lightly everyone is treating the idea of a war. I wish my own country were more aware of the danger, but, of course, there we're so separated from the conflict. But here…"

"Yes. It's right in our backyard," he finished for her. "Quite right. We ought to be paying more attention. Should have been for a long time. Unfortunately, I'm afraid it won't be long before we can't ignore it any longer. In the meantime, there are some of us who are doing what we can."

Alyssa's brows knitted. What if the world was he driving at?

"I understand that you're flying to France after the wedding."

"Yes, I am."

"Good. I want to ask you to do me a favor."

Alyssa's eyes widened. "You mean you want me to spy for you?"

Ian smiled. "My dear, please. You sound as if I'm asking you to be Mata Hari."

"That's what came to mind."

"Goodness, no," he assured her calmly. "You needn't steal documents or pour poison in some traitorous fifth columnist's drink. All I want is for you to keep your eyes and ears open while you're in Paris. Listen. Talk to people, all sorts of people, whoever you happen to meet, and remember what they say. Their mood, what they think about Germany, England, the war. What they're having trouble buying. Your father is a diplomat, a wealthy man. You are meeting him in Paris, are you not? Probably you shall attend parties, dinner, and such where there will be other men like him—wealthy, important, informed."

Alyssa frowned. "I'm sorry, but I think you have the wrong person. Father never says anything about his job to me; he's extremely cautious. And even if he did, I couldn't repeat what he entrusted to me. As for the other people I might meet—well, I wouldn't know what to do. What to ask. Whom to talk to. I haven't the first idea what's important. How could I discriminate between what's vital to you and what's trivial gossip?"

"Miss Lambert, you misunderstand me. I would never ask you to divulge anything your father told you in confidence. Nor would I expect him to tell you anything that couldn't be public knowledge. But, you see, since I am not in France or the United States, I can't be sure what is public knowledge there. That's why I need someone to tell me. You needn't be an expert; there's no need to know what we're looking for. I simply want your observant eye on the situation. Listen to what people tell you—and believe me, a woman as beautiful as you will find lots of men eager to talk to you. Then fly back here instead of going straight home, and tell me whatever you've heard. We'll sift through it to find what we need."

Alyssa gazed at him for a moment. "You make it sound very easy."

"It is. And it's safe; I wouldn't urge you to do anything that might endanger yourself. I don't want you stalking Nazis."

"I still don't understand how it will help you. How could I learn anything that your people couldn't?"

"I told you. You will go to parties where most people can't go, talk to men most people wouldn't meet. What you learn may merely corroborate what we've learned through another channel, or it may provide us with a piece that will fit into a part of a puzzle. A little tidbit might arouse our curiosity in an area we haven't explored before or show us a new direction. As for 'my people,' as you call them, I have very few paid employees. They're nearly all volunteers, as Claire is. You see, we aren't an official government organization. All we have is a few friends who are farsighted enough to know that the information we can glean now may be immensely important to us in the future. But at the moment our government is exploring avenues for making peace with Hitler, not ways to defeat him. Our group doesn't fit in with the present government; we are not recognized—we hope they don't even know we exist. So we have no money except what is donated and no help except what is freely given us."

"I see." And she did. She saw a bunch of amateurs gallantly struggling to stave off disaster for their country, facing facts their own government refused to accept. There would be war; she was becoming more and more convinced of that. When it came, England would need every bit of help it could get; not only arms and men, but vital information as well. "I'll do whatever I can," Alyssa promised softly, "if you really think I'd be useful."

"Good. I was certain you'd feel that way. Don't doubt your usefulness. I have several friends in the entertainment business, and they've done the same sort of jobs for me."

Alyssa stared. "Really?"

"Yes. You, of all people, ought to know that actors and directors aren't just a bunch of featherheads."

"Of course. But—well, I never imagined…"

"They travel a lot and everyone wants to meet them: kings, generals, businessmen, Germans, Swedes. You name it. It's amazing what people will brag about to a movie star. Well, then, it's arranged. You'll do it?"

"Yes."

Ian shook her hand. "Good-bye, then. I wish you a safe journey. When you return, just come by to visit Claire. I'll meet you there."

"But, wait! Is that it? Aren't you going to tell me anything? What to do? What to look for?"

"I already have. Listen and try to remember all you hear. Don't press for information; nothing will make people go silent more quickly."

"It sounds very vague."

"I'm afraid it is. You see, we're all working in the dark." He gave her a thin smile. "Good-bye, Miss Lambert. I'll look forward to hearing from you."

When he left the room, Alyssa simply sat for a moment staring after him. She could hardly believe that she'd agreed to gather information for a secret, nongovernmental organization. Alyssa Lambert, girl spy. A smile quirked her mouth. How absurd. She couldn't imagine herself coming up with anything they could use. Still…at least she would be doing something to fight the Nazis while the rest of the world was sitting on its hands. And—she couldn't deny it—she felt a little sizzle of excitement.

Chapter 3

Claire and Ky were married at St. Luke's Church in Chelsea, and the next day Alyssa flew to Paris. She was eager to see her father again—and eager to see Paris.

Alyssa loved Paris. It had a special quality no other city had, an indefinable charm that was part beauty, part sophistication, yet more than either. Its jumble of streets ran into each other at odd angles, forming islands of triangular buildings. Some of the streets were incredibly narrow and twisted, quaint and old, yet others were broad boulevards centered by wide strips of grass and trees, giving a feeling of spaciousness. Whereas London had spots of greenery in its squares and parks, Paris had trees in rows along the sidewalks and down the center of the boulevards. In spring the streets were alive and sweet with blooms. The buildings were beige or cream-colored stone with steeply pitched dark gray slate roofs, some decorated with black wrought-iron balconies. They were so graceful that their very similarity was pleasing to the eye.

It was uniform yet unique. Lovely. Charming. And somehow more. Alyssa had long ago given up trying to define the appeal of Paris and simply accepted the fact that she loved it. Whenever she came there, she felt suddenly invigorated, exhilarated, as if the air had an extra buoyancy.

She took a taxi to the George V, driving through the Left Bank and across the Prince Alexander III Bridge, lined with turn-of-the-century wrought-iron streetlamps, then onto the Champs-Élysées. It was a broad, beautiful avenue, its wide sidewalks lined with the brightly colored umbrellas and tables of outdoor cafes. Alyssa smiled. Before long, she would be sitting at one of those tables watching the parade of people go by.

It began to rain just as Alyssa emerged from the cab at the hotel, and the doorman scurried out to shelter her beneath his umbrella. Three tall stone arches led into the hotel, each set with a gold and black wrought-iron gateway. Just as Alyssa was about to step through the center doorway, an unusual couple walked out.

The man was rather short, only a couple of inches taller than Alyssa herself, with a wide chest and a heavy-armed, powerful build. A fat cigar was clamped between his lips. He looked more like a longshoreman that the head of a major Hollywood studio, which was what he was. The woman, however, looked exactly like what she was: the reigning queen of film comedy. Her chin-length waved hair was platinum blond, her eyes velvety brown and huge, and her small figure was full-breasted and enticing. The wide mouth curved invitingly, and there was a hint of mischief in her eyes. Thrown around her shoulders, sleeves dangling carelessly, was a white fox fur coat. She might have stepped straight off a movie screen.

Alyssa stared at the man and woman, and they gazed back at her with equal amazement. It was the man who broke the frozen tableau. He popped the cigar from his mouth. "Well, I'll be damned!"

"Lora! King!"

"Alyssa!" The blond woman grinned with genuine pleasure and came forward to hug her. Each kissed the air, Hollywood fashion, so as not to stamp the other's cheek with her lipstick.

"Whatever are you two doing here?"

Lora chuckled. "Don't be so amazed. We do get out of Los Angeles every now and then."

The man, Kingsley Gerard, stepped forward to claim his embrace from Alyssa. "How are you, Beautiful?" he asked her.

"Fine. And you?"

"Couldn't be better—unless you tell me you've decided to come back to Hollywood."

Alyssa laughed. "No, I'm a stage person, I'm afraid. I like to be able to see my audience and hear their applause."

Three years ago Kingsley had seen her in a play in New York and had enticed her to Los Angeles with a one-year contract with his studio, Royal. Her first role had been that of the beautiful society villainess in a comedy with Lora Michaels, Royal Studios' reigning star.

Alyssa had enjoyed working with Lora. Lora Michaels was a genuinely kind person, and all her years in the movie industry hadn't managed to spoil that. She had taken Alyssa under her wing, always friendly, helpful, and utterly devoid of airs, snobbery, or even jealousy. With her blond, sexy good looks and inviting figure, she usually played a wisecracking woman of the world, but beneath the sophisticated veneer lurked a certain innocent sweetness. One well-known actor had once described Lora as "a combination of Jean Harlow and Shirley Temple." It was this mixture that stole the audience's heart.

But as much as Alyssa liked Lora, she disliked Hollywood. The fawning fans, the publicity seeking, the cold lack of response in acting in front of a camera, all went against her grain. Most of all, she hated the contract system. The studios literally owned their contract players, and even the stars had little power against them. Just a few years earlier Lora herself had gone up against Royal Studios and even she, the studio's biggest money-maker, had lost. It was rumored that if it weren't for the fact that Kingsley Gerard himself had fallen in love with her, Lora's career might have been finished after her fight with the studio.

Alyssa gave Kingsley a grin. "Besides, you know I'm not photogenic." Lora had that magical combination of bone, skin, and personality that showed up vibrantly on film. Kingsley liked to say that "the camera loves her." It didn't love Alyssa. Somehow film paled the beauty that was so vivid in person.

Gerard snorted. "Photogenic, hell! So what if you're only half as pretty on film as you are in real life?" He made a sweeping gesture with his cigar. "That's still three times prettier than most women. You could have a big career at Royal."

"I didn't like the movies," Alyssa said, uttering what was to Gerard the greatest heresy in the world. "I'd rather go through the play from the beginning to the end, not jump around all over the place."

"You'd get used to it," King declared and stuck the cigar back in his mouth. He had a reputation for sensing star quality, especially in women; Lora had been his biggest find. When he had "found" Alyssa, he had been certain that he had another star on his hands. It annoyed him that Alyssa had gotten away.

Alyssa crossed her arms across her chest and smiled. She was one of the few people whom Kingsley Gerard did not intimidate. She couldn't deny the raw power he exuded, but when at six years of age one had sat on the knee of a famous and much-feared oil millionaire, wealth and power lost much of their power to intimidate.

Alyssa's father was an influential man in diplomatic circles. Had he not fallen in love with a woman who had no interest in the obligations of his career, he could have become ambassador to a major country. As it was, he had become a more-or-less secret adviser on foreign affairs to the President and a roaming troubleshooter for the Secretary of State. He moved among the powerful all over the world, and Alyssa, often called upon as a teenage girl to stand in for her mother on social occasions, had moved among them as well. Grant Lambert's daughter stood in awe of no one, including a Hollywood mogul.

"Come on, King," she said with a smile. "Admit it—if I had stayed at Royal, I'd have been a real thorn in your side."

King frowned at her, then relaxed into a grin. "True. You're even more cussed independent than Lora."

His wife rolled her eyes and talked past him to Alyssa, "Alyssa, what are you doing here? Don't you know there's a war on?"

Alyssa half smiled. "I'm beginning to wonder if Europe knows there's a war on. I went to the wedding of an old school friend of mine in London yesterday. My father's here in Paris, so I thought I'd pop over and see him before I went home." She paused and allowed a little grin. "And I might buy a few clothes while I'm here."

Lora shot back a conspiratorial smile. "I just may find the time for that myself. I'm ready to take on Chanel and Jean Patou."

"Not to mention Schaiparelli."

"Oh, yes. I'm going to stock up on 'Shocking.' How I love that perfume!"

"What about you two?" Alyssa asked. "Why are you here?"

"Business, what else?" Lora shook her head in mock disgust.

"I'm in talks with Claude Freret," King explained.

"The director?"

"Yes. I'm hoping to get him to come to L.A."

"I can't imagine Claude leaving France. When I met him, he seemed a very ardent Frenchman."

"Oh, he is. I wrote him over a year ago, offering him all kinds of money, but Claude refused. He said he wouldn't think of leaving France. But he's Jewish, and with France now at war with Germany, I would think he'd be more interested in my proposition." King grinned. "Besides, I'm always harder to resist in person."

Alyssa chuckled. "I know."

"We're having dinner with Freret tonight. Why don't you come with us?" Lora asked.

"Oh, no, I wouldn't want to interrupt a business meeting."

"That's no problem." King made a dismissive gesture. "I figure having Lora along will help sell Claude on the idea. You'd just make it twice as good. What director could turn down the chance to work with women like you?"

Alyssa smiled and shook her head. "No, really, I can't. I cabled my father that I was coming today and made a date with him for dinner tonight. I'd love to another day."

"Sure. And, listen, why don't we go shopping together?" Lora suggested. "I need your advice. Your taste is better than mine."

"I know that's not true," Alyssa responded. "But I'd love to shop with you. Tomorrow?"

"Yeah. That'd be great. The sooner, the better. See you tomorrow morning." As Lora and King walked away, she tossed back over her shoulder, "If you change your mind about dinner tonight, just call. We'd love for you to come along."

"I'll remember that. Good-bye."

As soon as Alyssa checked into her room, she rang the operator and asked for the American embassy, then sat down to wait, knowing from previous experience with the French telephone system that it could be quite a while before her call went through.

However, when the call at last came through, it was not her father on the other end of the line, but his secretary. "I'm sorry, Miss Lambert. He's not here. A meeting came up out of town, and he called yesterday to say he wouldn't be able to return to Paris for another two days. He asked me to apologize when you called. He said he would get in touch with you as soon as he returns."

"Oh. Thank you." Alyssa set the ornate receiver back on its pedestal.

She wasn't surprised that her father's business had come before her; it came before everything. When she was a child, she had blamed her mother for her parents' split-up, but as she grew up she began wonder if it wasn't as much or more her father's devotion to his "duty" that ruined their marriage; perhaps it even caused her mother's problems. With the world in the political mess it was, she knew her father would be terribly busy; why else would Roosevelt's chief troubleshooter in the State Department be here? Still, it disappointed her, as it always had.

With a sigh, Alyssa stood up and walked over to the window to look out. Now what was she to do the rest of the day?

She could choose a dress for dinner this evening and hang it out to be pressed. Lie down and rest from the trip. When she got up she could take a long, soothing bath, touch up her nails, put on new makeup. It was easy to waste an afternoon that way. But what about this evening? It stretched out long and lonely in front of her.

She picked up the phone again. "I'd like to leave a message for Kingsley Gerard, please. Tell him: 'I accept. Alyssa.'"
*****

When Philippe Michaude entered Maxim's, he was greeted with a smile. The maître d' immediately escorted him past the others who waited and through the cloth-covered tables to one with an excellent view of the room. A man was already seated there, and he stood at Michaude's approach.

"Ah, Philippe. Good to see you."

"Jean-Louis."

Philippe sat down with his back against the wall, looking over the spread of tables, and accepted the glass of wine which the other man poured for him. "Delicious."

"Trying to befuddle your sense," Jean-Louis said with a faint smile, "so you'll leap to put your money into my film."

Philippe raised an eyebrow. He had a cool, rather inexpressive face, made even more so by the light green color of his eyes. His features were sharp and straight, the skin stretched tightly over prominent cheekbones. His eyebrows were coal black, narrow slashes above his eyes, and his thick hair was equally black. He was considered handsome by most women; there was an elemental appeal to the apple-green eyes, fringed as they were by thick black lashes, and to the careless way his hair fell across his forehead. Tall and lean, well-dressed, with an air of sophistication that was close to cynicism, he was bright and talked easily and well; when he wanted to, he could be charming. Given the right situation, he could be equally cold and hard.

"Are you saying that I'd enter into your venture only if I were befuddled?" he asked now, his low voice teasing and lazy.

Jean-Louis threw up horrified hands. "Philippe, please! A joke, only a joke. It is an excellent investment."

Philippe shrugged. "The last film was. I made a nice profit."

Jean-Louis smiled, remembering. "Didn't we all? Ah, I wish they were all so easy."

"Put an actress like Louise Mignot in them, and they will be, I imagine."

Jean-Louis gave an extravagant sigh of admiration. "She is beautiful, no?"

"Beguiling." Philippe touched his face at the corner of his mouth. "It is the beauty mark here that does it. Irresistible." Suddenly he grinned. "Until you try to talk to her, at least."

The other man snorted with laughter. As an investor in Jean-Louis' last film, Philippe had attended a party at the studio, where Louise had sought him out. Jean-Louis had been surprised later to see Philippe leave the party alone, and he had learned a few days later that Mademoiselle Mignot was livid because the wealthy backer had turned down the hinted offer of her favors. Philippe's refusal was evidence of Michaude's intelligence; Louise as a vacant-headed, selfish harpy. But intelligence was one quality men usually didn't demonstrate around Louise.

"You like the cinema? The business?" Jean-Louis asked casually.

Philippe smiled faintly. "I enjoyed it, yes. A nice diversion. It was amusing to be on the fringes of it. Cinema is a world to itself. Too emotional for one to spend one's whole life in it. But I wouldn't mind continuing to invest."

"Good. I suspect you'll find it as irresistible as Mademoiselle Mignot's beauty mark."

"Ah, but I resisted that," Philippe reminded him, his eyes amused. Philippe Michaude had struggled his way to the top in the razor-sharp world of business, rising from a poor boy on the streets of Lyons doing odd jobs for a few centimes to the owner of one of the largest businesses in France. Compared to that world, the cinematic industry seemed a fantasy, a confection—intriguing, but too shifting and uncertain, too dependent on the vagaries of human nature to make it one's life. Still, he couldn't deny its pull; it held the thrill of gambling. And the boy from the streets still liked a little spice of adventure in his life.

A solicitous waiter took their order, and the two men settled back in their chairs. Philippe lit a cigarette and let his eyes drift over the room.

"Have you looked at the script I sent you?" Jean-Louis asked.

"Yes. He is a good writer. The script isn't the problem. You know that."

"Unfortunately, yes. A script can be fixed. I can't do anything about a war."

"Everything is uncertain. It's not a good time to invest in an entertainment that will take several months to develop."

"No more than four."

"Who knows what France will be doing in four months?"

"Even in a war, people will still want to go to the cinema."

"Perhaps."

"I don't know anything about wars—or business, really. But I know cinema." Jean-Louis sighed. "My studio is beginning to thrive—this crazy war comes at the worst time possible."

"Yes, it's too bad the generals didn't take your career into account," Philippe said drily. He glanced toward the doorway and froze. His cigarette burned unheeded between his fingers. All around the room heads turned to look at the group of four people who had just entered.

One of the men was small, with a bald head and a bobbing way of walking; he looked faintly familiar to Philippe. The other man was larger, though not tall, and an aura of power clung to him. He was obviously American, as was one of the women, a petite attractive blonde—an American cinema star everyone recognized. But Philippe hardly noticed her. It was the assured dark-haired woman beside her who caught his attention.

She was taller than the blonde, and her figure in the long, black sequined Chanel evening gown was slim, with full, soft breasts. The black satin dress caressed her white skin, shimmering with the same dark life as her hair, which hung down to her shoulders, curling under slightly at the ends. Philippe couldn't see the color of her eyes from where he sat, only that they were large and expressively beautiful. Her face glowed with color; it was perfectly, delicately formed. Her mouth was soft and vulnerable. She smiled at something the powerfully built man said, revealing small, even, white teeth. Philippe felt as if he'd been hit in the solar plexus.

"Who is that woman?" he asked softly. His cigarette burned his fingers, and he glanced at it as if surprised to find it there. He stubbed it out.

Jean-Louis glanced at Philippe in surprise. "Lora Michaels. The American—"

"No, not her. The other one. The beauty."

Jean-Louis cast an intrigued glance at Philippe and turned back to the party crossing the room. "I'm not sure. She looks familiar."

"She's American, too?" Lora Michaels obviously was, despite the French clothes. But the other woman moved with an elegance and poise that spoke little of nationality.

"I think so. The little man is Claude Freret, the director."

"Yes. I thought I had seen him before. Who is the other man?"

"Kingsley Gerard. He owns Royal Studios."

"Ah. Even I have heard of Royal Studios. Do you think she is his mistress?"

Jean-Louis looked amused. "Gerard is married to Lora Michaels, and I don't think she's so complaisant a wife as to take his mistress with them to Maxim's."

"She couldn't be with Freret."

Jean-Louis chuckled. "Of course not. She's the wrong sex for him. She was probably brought along to be a companion for him. For show, you know."

"I've seen her somewhere before." Philippe tracked her every move, noting the exquisite grace of her gestures. He wondered if she was, perhaps, a dancer. But, no, she didn't have the cold distance of a ballerina.

"At the cinema, I suspect. I'm almost positive she's been in an American film. But I can't remember…" Jean Louise rubbed his chin. "A Lora Michaels film; that was it. *Weekend Wife.*"

"Yes, of course. I saw it. She was the other woman, the femme fatale."

"Yes." Suddenly Jean-Louis' brow cleared. "Lambert. Alyssa Lambert. I knew I'd remember it eventually."

"She is more beautiful than in that movie." He remembered even then she had been quite enchanting. Her voice was beautiful, rich and low, soft in a way that drew one in.

"Yes. Some women are that way. Not photogenic."

A small smile touched Philippe's lips. "She certainly took my mind off Lora Michaels. I remember thinking I would rather have the siren, claws and all."

Jean-Louis watched Philippe. He hadn't taken his eyes off Alyssa. "I know Claude Freret," Jean-Louis said.

Philippe looked at Jean-Louis and smiled faintly, his green eyes narrowed and glittering. "Good. I have a sudden desire to meet him."

*****

Alyssa enjoyed the meal. The food was delicious, Lora was fun to be with, and it was amusing to watch Kingsley Gerard lock horns with someone as stubborn as himself. Claude Freret was a small man and seemed mild; Alyssa's first impression was that King would roll right over him. But when it came to taking Gerard's offer, Freret had no difficulty crossing one of the most powerful men in Hollywood.

"No. No. No," he said, shaking his head with each word for emphasis, and no matter how many times King came back to the subject or expressed it differently, Claude's answer was the same. He couldn't possibly leave France.

Alyssa watched King's anger and frustration building despite his supreme effort to keep it under control and maintain a pleasant face. Out of the corner of her eye she could see Lora glancing around the room, an air of unconcern on her face, but Lora's lips kept twitching, and she sucked her lower lip between her teeth. Alyssa knew that Lora was avoiding looking at her for fear she would burst out laughing. It *was* funny to see this little man obstruct the mighty Kingsley Gerard.

But she wondered how Lora could be so amused when she would be the one who would have the job of calming King down tonight after they returned to the hotel—but, then, maybe calming King down had its rewards. Alyssa wondered, not for the first time, if Lora loved Gerard. The consensus was that Gerard was so crazy in love with Lora that she'd have been insane not to marry him. No one would have passed up that kind of power and prestige. But, watching them together, Alyssa thought perhaps Lora loved King just as much as he loved her. The two of them reminded her of the French fairy tale "Beauty and the Beast." And hadn't Beauty wound up as ensnared by the Beast as he was by her?

All through the meal Alyssa had the feeling that someone was watching her, which wasn't uncommon. In New York she was often recognized; and even if no one realized who she was, her looks had attracted attention from the time she was a teenager. She had grown accustomed to staring, but not when it was as steady and persistent as this. She tried to ignore it, refusing to look around the restaurant for the person who watched her. But now and then she sneaked a peek, trying her best to appear casual.

Just as she finished her meal, Alyssa glanced up and her eyes met those of a man sitting on the opposite side of the room. She knew instantly that it was he who had been staring. He still gazed at her unabashedly, not even glancing away now that she had discovered him. He didn't leer, nor did he nod or smile at her. He simply smoked a cigarette and watched her, but there was something in his tightly drawn features, in his very carriage, that made Alyssa know that he wanted her.

She glanced quickly away, turning her attention back to Lora. Frenchmen were much more matter-of-fact about such things than Americans, much bolder. It embarrassed her a little, and she felt her pulse speed up. It annoyed her that she was letting this stranger make her uncomfortable.

Lora asked Alyssa a question, and she answered, her mind not really on the conversation. Almost involuntarily she glanced back at the man's table. He was no longer there. She looked around and saw him winding his way through the tables, walking toward her slowly but purposefully, a few steps behind a heavyset man. A little spurt of panic darted through her chest. What was she to do? But that was a silly thing to think. She knew what to do; she couldn't count the number of men who had tried to pick her up over the years. She had become adept at coolly polite rejection. The fact that this man was bolder than most meant only that she would have to give him an icier set-down.

She watched him walk toward them. He was tall and trim, and he moved with a smooth grace that European men felt no need to hide as American men did. There was power in him, Alyssa thought, just as there was power in Gerard, except that in this man it was covered by a layer of sophistication that made it no less dangerous.

He looked at Alyssa as he walked, only at the last minute pulling his gaze away from her as he swerved toward Claude Freret at the end of the table, still following the heavyset man.

The other man stopped beside Freret. "Claude! What an unexpected pleasure!"

Claude jumped up, all smiles. Alyssa suspected Claude would have greeted the devil himself with smiles if it offered him an opportunity to ward off King's pressure for a moment. "Jean-Louis! My good friend. How nice to see you."

They exchanged a few pleasantries, then Jean-Louis half turned to include the dark-haired man behind him. "May I introduce my friend, Philippe Michaude? He was involved in my Louise Mignot film last year. Philippe, this is Claude Freret, the famous director."

"Yes, of course, I've heard a great deal about you, Monsieur Freret." Michaude's voice was deep and appealing.

Lora leaned over and whispered a little tiger growl to Alyssa. "That one's a lady-killer. Frenchmen are so sexy."

This one was, at any rate. His gaze left Freret and flickered down the table to Alyssa. His eyes were light and lined by smoky lashes. They turned down a little at the corner, giving them a sleepy look. "Look at those bedroom eyes," Lora added in a whisper, shielding her mouth with her hand.

Freret hastened to introduce the two Frenchmen to the rest of the group, glad to have found reinforcements. "Please, allow me to present Monsieur Jean-Louis Deligne and Monsieur Philippe Michaude. Monsieur Deligne, he, uh makes the cinema, as you do, King. Jean-Louis, Monsieur Michaude, this is Madame Lora Michaels—I should say, Madame Gerard, the so famous American movie star. And her friend Mademoiselle Lambert. And, of course, this is Monsieur Kingsley Gerard, the owner of Royal studios."

"How do you do?" Philippe lifted Lora's hand to his mouth in a Continental greeting. "Mrs. Gerard. I enjoy your movies very much." Next he took Alyssa's fingers in his and slowly raised them to his lips. His hand was long and thin and firm around her fingers; his mouth brushed her skin with soft warmth. He gazed straight into her eyes as he kissed her hand. She saw that his eyes were pale green, the color of new leaves in spring, a cool color, but penetrating and intense. "Miss Lambert, I am pleased to meet you." He spoke in English, his voice seductively accented.

Alyssa's stomach turned cold, then hot. "Monsieur Michaude." She managed to keep her voice level.

Freret smiled encouragingly at Philippe and Jean-Louis. "Please, would you join us? We were about to have a liqueur after dinner."

"Yes, please do," King added grudgingly. Alyssa was sure he didn't care for the idea of any fellow countrymen bolstering Freret's stubbornness.

"Thank you. That is most kind." Michaude smiled at King, but his eyes went to Alyssa. He motioned for a waiter and asked him to bring extra chairs; and when the waiter returned with them, Michaude adroitly squeezed his in between Alyssa's and Freret's.

Alyssa could smell the faint fragrance of his cologne. Looking at him in profile like this, she could see that his lashes were extraordinarily long. She suspected that he usually had women falling at his feet. Well, this was one woman who would not.

"You must help me," Freret told the new arrivals. "Monsieur Gerard is trying to persuade me to leave Paris."

"Leave Paris!" Jean-Louis Deligne looked as shocked as if King had suggested that Claude fly to the moon. "Whatever for?"

"His life," King suggested dryly.

"His life?" Michaude's cool eyes moved to King with mild interest. "Has it been threatened?"

"A few times. By Adolf Hitler." King shook his massive head, exasperated. "Haven't you heard about the things he's done to the Jews? Claude's Jewish."

"Half Jewish. And I've never been particularly religious."

"That doesn't matter to Hitler. Have you seen S. E. Marek's reports? They're making Jews wear armbands with a yellow star on them, segregating them, taking away their money and privileges. Not only shopkeepers, but also people of status and prestige."

"Yes, but that is in Germany," Claude protested, waving his hands for emphasis. "I am a Frenchman!"

"So was Alfred Dreyfus," Alyssa put in, surprising everyone. So far she had kept her silence throughout King and Freret's argument. "You remember, the one Émile Zola wrote about?"

Philippe glanced at her sharply. Alyssa wasn't sure what the look meant—was he intrigued? Or just astonished that an American actress had read Émile Zola?

"Who?" King asked. "I don't know this Zola character, but I have looked at a map. It's not as far from Paris to the German border as it as from L. A. to Frisco."

"But, Alyssa, the Dreyfus case was long ago. Frenchmen would never do what the Germans are doing to Jews," Claude assured her.

"What if the Germans were in France?" King asked pointedly. "What if you lose this war? You know, the bookies aren't giving you guys good odds."

"Lose the war!" Jean-Louis jumped in now, horrified at King's suggestion. "But France has the greatest army in the world."

"The biggest," Philippe Michaude amended quietly.

"Exactly." King gave the Frenchman an approving nod. "Biggest isn't the same as the best."

"But the Maginot Line!"

"Jesus H. Christ!" King snapped. "Maybe it would have helped you a lot in 1914, but it's 1940 now. How in the hell do you think those forts will stop airplanes? They'll fly right over them. Haven't you seen what the Luftwaffe did to Poland?"

"That was Poland. France is different."

"Yeah, at least Poland had an air force for the Germans to smash. Anyway, the Maginot Line, even if it could protect you, doesn't run all the way along your border and it doesn't run between you and Belgium."

"Please," Lora put in in her husky voice. "Let's not have a war of our own right here. Okay, fellas?"

King grimaced and leaned back in his chair, shutting his mouth.

"You know, Claude," Lora went on sweetly, "King isn't asking you to leave France forever. He just wants you to sign a contract for a couple of years. Wouldn't you like to come to the U. S.? See California?"

"That is true, Monsieur Freret," Philippe Michaude agreed, and the director stared at Philippe as if he had stabbed him in the back. "You could go for a year or two. That way you'd be safe if anything did happen. And if not, you can come back—richer, and having worked with beautiful ladies like these. It doesn't sound too bad to me."

"But my life is here."

"It will still be here in two years, surely."

Claude blinked and was silent. Finally he said grudgingly, "Well... perhaps I will think about it."

"Great." King reached over and gave Freret a friendly pat on the shoulder. He knew when to let negotiations slide. "In the meantime, what do you say we all go out somewhere? I want to see this nightlife Paris is so famous for."

"But, of course," Philippe agreed with alacrity. "What about Shéhérazade? Or Suzy Solidor's?"

The others agreed, and Philippe stood up, reaching out politely to pull back Alyssa's chair. And somehow Alyssa found herself walking out of the dining room with her hand tucked inside Philippe's arm.

Chapter 4

Philippe stood back politely to let Alyssa pass out of the dining room before him. The back of Alyssa's dress was cut fashionably low, and the silk fabric was gathered into a rose nestled seductively at the base of her spine, drawing the eye to the sweet curve of her derrière. Philippe thought of running his hand down the smooth, creamy flesh to crush the saucy flower and caress the swell of her hips. As she walked, Alyssa's hair brushed the skin of her shoulders, and Philippe wanted to wind his hands through it and lift the hair from her shoulders, to touch his lips to that skin. He ached to have her. He had to remind himself to move slowly. A woman such as this was meant to be wooed. She required a slow seduction—flowers, sweet words, little gifts.

Philippe had moved so quickly to escort Alyssa from the room that he managed to separate the two of them from the rest of the group by several feet. Alyssa raised her face to look at him, and he was struck by the full power of her vibrant blue eyes. He wondered how long he would have to wait to kiss her.

"You surprised me, Monsieur Michaude."

"Please—Philippe."

"Philippe." Alyssa's melodic voice accented his name perfectly.

Philippe smiled. There was no need to correct her pronunciation.

"And your name is Alyssa?"

"Yes."

"May I call you that?"

Alyssa wouldn't have hesitated with another man. She was used to the casual manner of the theater. But addressing her by her first name so soon after meeting her was very informal in the French code of manners. He would probably interpret it in a way she didn't mean. So she replied coolly, "I see no reason for you to. After all, we have just met."

"But Alyssa is such a beautiful name." His tongue savored the word. "It is a shame not to use it."

Alyssa thought she could listen to the liquid beauty of his accent all night. Why was it that English on the French tongue made one think of satin sheets tangled around naked limbs? She steeled herself against the appeal. The practiced ease with which he had separated them from the others annoyed her. It was obvious that he was a man accustomed to seducing women—and just as accustomed to success.

It was equally obvious that he intended Alyssa to be the next victim of his charms. She couldn't deny that he was attractive—those sharp, handsome features; the finely cut lips; the thick black hair that her fingers longed to touch. But Alyssa had spent far too many years fending off men who thought actresses would fall into bed with any man if he played the seduction game right. She wasn't about to be one more in a string of women for any man, no matter how charming his smile or how much his accent melted her bones.

Philippe abandoned the subject of her name. "Tell me, why did I surprise you? By urging Claude Freret to go to the United States?"

"Yes."

"Pah!" He made a very French gesture, dismissing Monsieur Freret. "He'd be an idiot not to. Even Zola sought sanctuary in England when it appeared he was to be found guilty of libel. I was very impressed earlier by your knowledge on the Dreyfus affair, incidentally."

"Impressed because I am a woman or an American?" Alyssa teased.

"Ah, now you are trying to lay a trap for me." His eyes twinkled. "Shall I just say that beauty and intelligence are a rare combination in anyone?"

"A very neat way of slipping that trap," Alyssa responded. All right, she was flirting, but he was difficult not to flirt with.

"Hollywood holds much promise for Monsieur Freret." Philippe turned back to the earlier topic. "More money. Safety. A chance to direct you in a film. Most Frenchmen aren't such fools as to turn that down."

She smiled. "Thank you. But he wouldn't be directing me. I'm a stage actress."

"But I have seen you at the cinema, have I not? Jean-Louis and I discussed it. You were in a film with Miss Michaels."

"Yes. And I had the lead in another. But I'm not made for movies. I come across better onstage."

"You are even more beautiful in person, that's true." They stopped at the cloakroom. "But on film you are still beautiful enough for any man. Think of the millions whom you are depriving. I, for one, would very much like to watch you again at the cinema. I am not often in New York."

Alyssa backed off a step. The man was too attractive by half. She summoned up a cool smile. "I suspect you'll manage to console yourself."

She turned aside to give her ticket to the cloakroom attendant and waited, running the large black silk scarf she carried through her hand, not even glancing back at Philippe. But she found it hard to maintain her air of disinterest when the attendant returned with her cloak and Philippe wrapped it around her shoulders. His fingertips merely brushed her skin, but she felt it all through her body. Quickly she tied the strings at the neck before he could do so, then pulled on the gloves that covered her bare arms to above the elbow. She was relieved when King and Lora and the others joined them at the cloakroom.

It was utterly dark when they stepped outside. Alyssa sighed, thinking of the lights that had lit up the city before war imposed a nightly blackout—the quaint gaslights lining the Prince Alexander III Bridge, the floodlights on fountains and monuments, the soft glow of the streetlamps. "So sad. Paris darkened."

Philippe's brow furrowed. "Yes. The City of Light without her lights. Like a beautiful woman without her jewels."

"Filthy Boches!" Freret spat, his voice virulent with dislike, surprising them all. "They understand nothing but war."

A dimly lit taxi crept by and stopped for them. It as a squeeze to get them all inside. Alyssa was relieved—and a little disappointed—that Philippe politely took the jump seat at a distance from her.

But once they arrived at Shéhérazade he managed to seat the two of them at the opposite end of the table from the others and turned toward her, one arm resting on the back of her chair, creating an island of intimacy amid the crowd. Jean-Louis and Freret were deep in conversation on the favorite topic of each, French cinema. And Gerard, now that he had wrung at least a promise to think about signing a contract from the French director, seemed happy to ignore everyone but his wife.

There was a floor show featuring leggy, scantily clad women, but Philippe didn't glance at it. His eyes were only on Alyssa. It was very flattering, but she couldn't help but wonder if it was also too practiced. How many other women had he lavished this same attention on? Was he interested in her or in another conquest?

She had been around too many wealthy and powerful men not to recognize the power in Philippe Michaud. He was accustomed to getting what he wanted; it was there to see in the sharp assessing gaze when he glanced around the room, the ease with which he took command, the deference in others. Such men thrived on competition, seemingly always in a race to acquire, and women were often as much a commodity as a Bugatti or a mansion in the Hamptons.

Philippe offered her a cigarette from a flat leather case, and Alyssa shook her head. Her voice wasn't strong, her weakest point as a stage actress, and cigarettes ruined it. They sipped their drinks, and Philippe studied her face, his eyes lingering over her short, vulnerable upper lip. It was so hard to go slowly, to charm and reassure her, when all he wanted to do was kiss her until he couldn't think anymore, to slide his hands down the smooth fall of her hair and push it aside to expose the nape of her neck—smell it, caress it, taste it.

Philippe turned away, lighting a cigarette with fingers that trembled slightly. "So," he said, blowing the smoke away from her. "You are a stage actress. What parts do you play?"

Alyssa was startled. She had expected flowery phrases and romantic sighs, declarations of her beauty and of how she stirred him. She hadn't expected him actually to talk to her as a person. "Ingénues, mostly. Light comedy."

"And is that what you like to do?"

Alyssa shrugged, even more surprised that he had gone straight to the heart of her problem. "I love acting. I love the stage. So I enjoy any role, but…I am getting bored. The roles are the same. Sometimes I feel stifled!"

"What would you like to do?"

"Anything but a 'sweet young thing.' I want a part I can sink my teeth into. I auditioned for a role in a drama last year—a character part, not big. A lady of the night."

One of his eyebrows rose in amazement. "A prostitute? You wanted this role?"

Alyssa grinned. If Michaude weren't such a wolf, it would be fun to be with him. "It was a terrific part. A bad woman is a lot more fun to play than a goody-goody. You can get so much more out of it."

"She was a woman of great beauty? The mistress of powerful men?"

"No, just a common, garden variety streetwalker. One who drank too much."

He shook his head. "I don't think I understand theater people."

"Most people don't."

"Did you get this much-desired part?"

"No. The director said I did a good job, but I'm an ingénue. It's easy to get typecast. A director sees you in one play and you're good, so he decides to cast you in the same sort of part because he knows you can play it. You take it because you want to act. Then—you become known as that kind of role. They'll accept me as a little more sophisticated or funnier or more scatterbrained. But they don't want to see me in something really different."

"You were not a 'sweet young thing' in the film I saw."

"That's true. It was rather fun getting to be a wicked woman." Alyssa's eyes sparkled with mischief. "But I'm a stage actress, not a movie star. I don't like Hollywood or the studios; I don't like the way they shoot, with the story line all jumbled up. I even got tired of sunny weather."

"Did you work for Monsieur Gerard?" Philippe was fairly certain she must have, but he was at a loss for a better question to ask her. Watching Alyssa's eyes dance was distracting, and it was harder to think when his senses were filled with the smoke of Alyssa's voice or the smell of her skin mixed with a subtle yet tantalizing perfume he couldn't quite place.

"Yes. Royal Studios."

"He wants you back?"

"So he says, but I don't think he's serious. King simply hates the thought of someone leaving him instead of the other way around."

"I watched him tonight. He displayed a rather proprietary interest in you."

"King?" Alyssa's voice rose in amazement.

"Yes. Holding out your chair, touching your arm. I have to confess to a certain jealousy."

Alyssa laughed. "You must be kidding. Everyone knows he's crazy about Lora. He hardly looks at other women. Well, perhaps he looks, but he doesn't do anything about it. He used to have something of a reputation, but since he married Lora his only reputation is that of a faithful husband."

Philippe found it difficult to believe that a man could wish to be so faithful to the pretty blond woman when a devastating beauty like Alyssa was around. "If you say so."

"Believe me, it's true. He was just being nice. He felt he had to play escort to me, too, you see." She paused and smiled. "Though I have to admit that King would like the idea of having a woman on each arm. Besides, I think he has some lurking notion that he needs to be a good American male and protect me in a foreign country."

"He doesn't need to do that," Philippe replied in a low voice. Slowly he ran his thumb across her bare shoulder and up her neck beneath the soft veil of her hair, watching its progress across her pale skin. His mouth softened. "I can protect you better here. It is my country, after all."

His thumb was faintly rough against her skin, searing with heat. An answering warmth sprang up deep in Alyssa's abdomen. She wanted to shiver. She wanted to lean back her head and stretch like a cat, offering her throat to his touch. She swallowed and replied a little breathlessly, "Maybe I don't need protection from anyone."

Philippe smiled lazily, bringing his thumb back down her neck and along the hard ring of her collarbone, stopping at the soft hollow of her throat. His hand spread out over her neck and shoulders. "Oh, yes, I think you do. There are many predators around."

"Indeed. I think there's one beside me right now."

His teeth flashed in the dim light of the club. "But I won't hurt you."

Alyssa managed to get out a chuckle. It was difficult. With his hand on her, it was difficult even to breathe. "That's what the wolf said to Little Red Riding Hood."

He leaned closer, until his head was almost touching hers. "I promise, I never bite—well, hardly ever."

Her pulse was beating much too rapidly, and there was an iron band around her chest, tightening. This man was all too dangerous to her peace of mind. She couldn't remember when a man had stirred her senses so deeply, so quickly.

Philippe moved back, and his hand slid off her shoulder and onto the top of her chair. Alyssa was surprised at how much disappointment she felt. The floor show had ended. The lights on the dance floor had dimmed, and the band played. Couples moved slowly around the floor, dotted with sparkles cast by the revolving, faceted silver ball overhead.

Michaude turned to Alyssa. "Will you dance with me?"

"Yes." She ought to refuse just to show she was immune to him, but she didn't want to.

Philippe took her hand, and they walked to the dance floor. He liked the soft warmth of her skin against his palm, the slick hardness of her nails curled up against the back of his hand. He imagined those nails trailing down his bare back.

All evening he'd wanted to hold her in his arms, and now she stepped into them. It was intensely pleasurable to feel her hand on his shoulder, her arm against his, to curl his arm around her waist and touch the bare skin of her back. But it wasn't enough. Not nearly enough. His hand moved teasingly over her lower back, exploring the ridge of her spinal column and the soft flesh to either side of it. His hand pressed against Alyssa's back, moving her closer, so that their bodies brushed against each other as they moved. It was far too close to be polite, but not nearly as close as he wanted.

He leaned his cheek against her hair, drinking in the subtle, enticing scent of her perfume and luxuriating in the silken feel of her hair. Her breasts were soft against his chest. He knew she must feel his desire. He was fast running out of sophistication, it was the teenager bursting up from the streets who was running in his blood now.

Alyssa pushed lightly against his shoulder. "Monsieur Michaude," she protested. "I can hardly breathe."

He nuzzled her ear. "Then we have the same problem. You take my breath away as well." Reluctantly Philippe relaxed his hold, but he murmured, "Let me take you home."

"But—" She glanced around. "What about the others?"

"They've gone. Jean-Louis and Monsieur Freret left after the floor show. And Gerard and his wife just walked out."

"I should have left with them."

He grinned suggestively. "From the way they looked, I don't think they would have welcomed a third party. Gerard looked over here; he knows I will take you home."

"I don't need to be handed off to you to be taken care of." Alyssa stiffened. "I'm perfectly capable of getting home by myself."

"I'm sure you are. But I want to take care of you." He pulled her closer and dropped his head to hers, rubbing his cheek against her hair. It enticed him, luxuriant and sweet smelling.

Alyssa could feel his breath on her ear and it sent a shiver through her. "I think you'd better take me home."

It was only after she said the words that she realized she'd just agreed to exactly what he wanted. She was losing control of the situation. Alyssa wasn't prepared for the helpless yearning he aroused in her, this weakness that made her want to yield to his expert caresses. Her own body had never before betrayed her this way.

The taxi let them out in front of the flat gray canopy of the George V, and Philippe thrust several bills at the driver, hardly noticing the overlarge tip he paid him. They crossed the lobby and waited in front of the ornate elevators. This late at night only one was running. The elevator doors opened, and the operator pulled aside the folding metal gate. Alyssa gave him the floor number, and the young man rotated the handle, taking them up to the third floor.

At her door, Philippe smoothly took the key from her hand and opened the door, flipping on her light as he held the door open for her to enter. He started to follow, but Alyssa turned, putting her hands against his chest to stop him. "Hold it right there, buster."

"Buster?" He raised his eyebrow expressively.

She couldn't help but laugh, which didn't help her efforts to keep him at arm's length, but she said, "I don't recall inviting you in."

"You didn't. I am presuming on your hospitality." Philippe reached out to untie her cloak and eased it off her shoulders. Stepping closer, he put his hands on his shoulders, sliding them down her bare arms. Bending, he kissed the soft skin of her shoulders. His lips were soft and velvety; the kiss shot through Alyssa like electricity.

"I have been thinking about this all night." Philippe nuzzled her neck, his hands sliding up and down her arms.

"Philippe, we're standing in the doorway." She ought to push him back, but she did not. "Anyone can see us."

"I know." She could feel his smile against her skin. "That's why you should invite me in."

He nibbled at the hard cord of her neck. His hands left her arms to steal around her waist, pulling her into him. His body was so hot it seared her through their clothes. Alyssa wanted suddenly, intensely, to feel his hands upon her bare skin. The sheer force of her desire frightened her. "Philippe…"

"Alyssa." His voice was thick, and he returned unthinkingly, instinctively, to French. "How beautiful you are. Your skin, your eyes, your hair. Let's not play the game. Not tonight." His lips trailed up the side of her neck, moving under the veil of her hair. "Just let me love you."

"The game?" Alyssa pushed back against his encircling arms, and, surprised, he released her. She crossed her arms defensively over her chest. "I understand that seducing women is a game to you. But I have no desire to play."

"I don't understand." Philippe frowned. "I want you. You want me. Your body tells me that."

"Maybe I do. But that doesn't mean I'll hop into bed with you."

"My God, Alyssa, you're an actress." His voice rasped with irritation. "You can't expect me to believe—"

"An actress!" Alyssa's temper flamed, wiping out her treacherous desire to continue kissing him. "Of course. You're one of those archaic men who thinks the word actress is synonymous with whore. Well, I'm sorry you wasted your evening. But look on the bright side—at least you won't be out any money." She whirled away.

"Don't be a fool." Philippe followed her. "I never thought you were a whore, despite your peculiar desire to play one onstage. But the world of the theater is not known for its rigid moral code. It's not as if you were raised in a convent. You must know about men. You must have had lovers."

"And what if I have? That doesn't mean I sleep with any man who asks me."

His face hardened. "And that is what I am? Just any man?"

"I just met you!"

"And clearly you felt none of what I felt when we met," he said tightly. "I'm sorry. My mistake."

Alyssa flushed. She wasn't about to admit how very much she had felt. "You're twisting my words. I may be an actress, but I'm not easy. I'm not the prize in a game. And I have no interest in being another notch on your bedpost."

"That's what you think I've been doing? Chasing a trophy?"

"What else?"

"I wanted you. That's all. When you walked into Maxim's, I couldn't think of anything except how lovely you were and how much I desired you. I wasn't looking for another conquest.

Mon dieu, I couldn't even think straight. Yes, I pursued you. Yes, I tried to entice you into feeling the same desire I did. But I wasn't playing any game, and the only prize I was after was having you in my arms." He started away, then swung back. "You might want to consider, mademoiselle, exactly who it was that was playing games tonight."

With that, he was gone, leaving Alyssa staring after him speechlessly.

Chapter 5

Alyssa awoke the next morning with a pounding headache. She opened the curtains, revealing a perfect example of a lovely Parisian spring day, but the view didn't lift her spirits. Her father wasn't here and might not be for days. She had agreed to go shopping with Lora, but she didn't feel in the mood. No doubt Lora's bubbling spirits would irritate her and all the dresses would look terrible.

She wished the night before hadn't ended on such a sour note. Philippe had been witty and charming and very attractive—if only he hadn't been so arrogantly sure she would wind up in his bed. And then there was his parting shot that she had been playing games…when he was the one who had pushed his way into their party and spent the whole evening calculatedly seducing her.

Alyssa scowled, irritated all over again. Well, it hadn't been her fault the evening had turned out so badly, and she was not going to not let it bother her anymore. Pushing aside all thoughts of Philippe Michaude, she ordered room service. A breakfast as only the French could make it—thick black coffee and a roll hard as a brick on the outside and soft and utterly delicious on the inside—and a long, soaking bath lightened her mood.

There was a knock on the door as she dressed, and she answered it to find a bellboy, holding a long narrow box tied with a ribbon. Inside were nestled a dozen long-stemmed yellow roses, dewy with moisture and as vibrant as a burst of sunshine in the dark green wax paper.

Alyssa let out a breathy sigh at their beauty and lifted them from the box to sniff their aroma. A small white card tumbled to the floor. It read, "My deepest apologies" in a bold, black scribble, and it was unsigned. Even Philippe's apology smacked of arrogance. She ought to send them back. Instead, she picked up a vase to put them in and set it on the desk. The flowers seemed to fill the room and give it life.

There was another knock on the door, and Alyssa answered it. This time it was Lora. "You ready?" She stepped inside as Alyssa got her purse and jacket. "Oh, what gorgeous flowers!" She went to them and bent to smell them. "Mmm. Heavenly. I love roses."

"So I've heard." It was common knowledge that King sent a single red rose to Lora on the set every day.

Lora smiled, her eyes glowing. "Yeah. King's sweet that way. Who are these from? Mr. Michaude?"

"Yes."

"He seemed very smitten by you."

"He was very smitten by his glands."

Lora chuckled and sat down on the bed, tossing her purse down beside her. "You ought to be used to that by now."

"I am. It was just he was so—so damned expert at it. As if he'd done it a million times, and it was a game. You know: 'she will make this move, and then I will do this.'"

"He didn't look to me like he was playing. He looked *real* serious. Even King mentioned it."

Alyssa shrugged. "Well, it didn't come to anything."

"These flowers look like something."

"No. We had an argument when he brought me home, and he was—offensive. Anyway, he left in a huff. These are just an apology."

"Offensive, huh?" Lora's soft brown eyes gleamed with interest. "Exactly how offensive was he?"

"He expected me to go to bed with him, of course. And when I said no—"

"Your first mistake."

"Oh, come on. You aren't as tough as you like to pretend. I know it's ninety percent your image."

"You're probably right—but I am a terrible romantic." Lora smiled. "And I thought Philippe Michaude was *very* romantic."

"He was very pushy," Alyssa corrected. "The man clearly isn't used to being told 'no.'"

Lora's eyes widened. "Did he get rough with you?"

"No. Nothing like that. He acted as if it was a given I'd sleep with him. And when I wouldn't, he accused me of playing games. As if I was just making him chase me."

"Which isn't a bad idea. He'll appreciate you more."

"Well, I'm not interested in that."

"Why not? What do you have against him?"

"Lora! I don't sleep with men I hardly know."

"So get to know him. You don't have to go to bed with the guy. He's obviously willing to be strung along or he wouldn't have sent the flowers this morning."

"If we hadn't argued, perhaps I would have gone out with him again. But when I told him that I wasn't interested in being his latest conquest, he pointed out that I was an actress."

"Oh. That."

"Yeah. That. I hate that men assume we're easy game just because we act."

Lora grinned. "Well, you have to admit that people in the acting profession are a lot less straitlaced than the general public."

"I know. And my way of life is probably freer than it would have been if I'd remained a Boston debutante. But it doesn't make me a casual pickup. It doesn't mean I have to be a man's entertainment for the night."

"That's all he wanted?"

"What else?"

"I don't know." Lora shrugged. "But he looked to me like he was interested in a lot more than one night. Are you maybe..." She squinted, choosing her words carefully,

"...letting some bad experiences in the past color your judgement?"

"Well, it was something of a shock, going from being a 'nice' girl with a father no one wanted to cross to being considered easy prey," Alyssa admitted. "I've learned to handle them. Philippe's like all the others."

"How can you be sure?" Lora asked. "It's not like you really know him."

"Why are you on his side?" Alyssa asked.

"Oh, hon, I'm not. You know I'm your friend. It was just...I don't know, he reminded me a little of King."

"King?" Alyssa stared at her, thunderstruck.

Lora laughed. "Yeah, I know, Michaude's a Mr. Suave French Accent, let-me-kiss your-hand kind of guy, and King's, well, King. But I'm talking about the inside. I got the feeling he's pretty single-minded about what he wants; he doesn't fool around or try to impress people—he locks in on something and goes after it. Kinda like a torpedo."

"You might be right about that. I suspect he won't give up. He wants to win. But it's still just a game to him, and this is his next move." Alyssa gestured toward the array of flowers.

"A man's always going to try. You know that." Lora gave her the impish grin that won over movie-goers all over the country. "And sometimes games are fun."

Alyssa sighed. "Yeah, but this is a game I'm afraid I might lose."

*****

Alyssa and Lora toured the designer houses of the Faubourg Saint-Honoré, indulging not only in dresses, but in hats, luxurious scarves, shoes, handbags, and lingerie. They stopped late in the afternoon for a reviving cup of coffee beneath one of the brightly striped umbrellas along the Champs-Élysées and watched the people go by as they discussed their day's purchases.

"You know what the problem is, don't you?" Alyssa asked gravely.

"Yeah. King's going to lock me in my room when he hears how much I've spent."

"No. The problem is, how are we going to take all this stuff back on the airplane?"

"Oh, my God! You're right." Lora grinned. "The only solution is to stick to the lighter stuff. Tomorrow we'll go to the jewelry stores in the Place Vendôme."

They laughed and talked and finally turned wearily back to the hotel. Alyssa went to the front desk for her key and messages, and the clerk handed her a slip of paper and informed her that someone had called for her several times but had not left a message. Alyssa opened the slip of paper. Grant Lambert had left her a telephone number to call.

A grin spread across her face, and Alyssa took the stairs to her room instead of waiting for the elevator, eager to phone her father. She placed the call, and a few minutes later her father's modulated voice came across the wire. "Grant Lambert."

"Dad! It's me."

"Alyssa? I can hardly hear you. Bad connection. I'm back in Paris for a bit. I'm afraid I have a party tonight that I simply must attend. Could you come along? Not much fun for you, I'm sure, but I'd love to see you."

"No, that's fine. I'll be happy to go." She bit back her disappointment. She had to take the squeezed-in bits of time with her father whenever she could get them. At least she'd be with him, even if there would be other people around. Besides, she had promised Ian Hedley that she would listen to what people were saying, and what better opportunity could there be for that than a diplomatic party?

They said their good-byes, and Alyssa hurried to bathe and dress. She was ready and waiting in the lobby when Grant Lambert arrived. She wore the same Molyneaux gown that she had worn to Jessica's party and a discreet circle of pearls that

Grant had given her on her sixteenth birthday. When her father saw her, he broke into a broad grin and strode across the lobby to hug her.

"Ah, Lissy," he said, reverting to her childhood nickname. "You're more beautiful than ever." He stepped back. "You've surpassed even your mother in looks. How do you do it?"

She shrugged, dismissing the subject, and slid her arm through his. "It's wonderful to see you. It's been ages. Where are we going tonight?"

"Just a party given by a government official. But there's supposed to be another official there that I've tried to get hold of for days. His secretary's been putting me off, but tonight he won't be able to hide behind that officious young man."

They settled themselves in her father's waiting limousine and chatted all the way to the party. Alyssa made the most of her time alone with her father. She had learned to long ago.

The party itself was as dull as her father had predicted, but Alyssa listened to every conversation she could and tried to remember what was said. Fortunately, she had an excellent memory, the result of years of memorizing lines for plays, and she stored it all away, planning to jot everything down for Ian as soon as she returned to the hotel room—though she didn't hear anything that she thought Ian could find even remotely interesting.

She watched her father as he made his way through the crush of people, greeting everyone, smiling, expertly slipping away from those he didn't wish to talk to and just as expertly buttonholing those he wanted to see. He was a handsome middle-aged man: full white hair, bright blue eyes, un-aging strength in the bones of his face. Imposing. And yet a loving father, nonetheless. Though he had not spent as much time with Alyssa as other fathers did, she knew that he had given her many gifts—strength and independence, confidence in dealing with people and life, a sure sense of right and wrong, and the courage to act on her beliefs. He had done his best to instill his own virtues in her, yet he had managed not to criticize her mother's weakness to her. Alyssa loved him dearly, and she had come to respect him more and more every year. She had often thought that she could never marry a man who had Grant Lambert's devotion to his work, yet there were times when she wondered how she could love a man who was any less dedicated or any less principled. Perhaps that was the very reason she had never fallen deeply in love.

They returned to the hotel before midnight, her father beaming with pleasure at the fact that he had cornered his elusive official and wrung a promise from him to meet the following morning. "Dinner tomorrow evening?" Grant asked as he left her at her bedroom door. "I'm afraid I'll have to work straight through lunch, but I should be free by seven tomorrow night."

"Sounds nice. I'll be ready."

He frowned. "I apologize for having so little time right now."

"I promise, I'm quite capable of amusing myself."

"Yes, I suppose it's a bit late for me to worry about neglecting you," Grant admitted with a wry smile. "Love you, Lissy."

"I love you, too."

*****

Another spray of flowers greeted her the next morning, this time a delicate blending of spring blooms. There was no accompanying card. Alyssa called down to have another vase sent up and wondered how long Philippe would continue to pursue her. She had to admit that her resolve was weakening in the face of his persistence.

Had she been too hasty in judging him? Lora was right to say she didn't know anything about him really. She had labelled Philippe a playboy because he was handsome, wealthy, smooth and, well, French, which was admittedly biased and not really proof of anything. Nor did the fact that his kisses made her knees melt mean that he was a rogue. And she couldn't deny the unfairness of assuming he was a seducer because he was good-looking; that was, after all, exactly the sort of reasoning men used to think Alyssa was promiscuous.

Perhaps it wouldn't do any harm to see him again, provided he accepted that she didn't want to be rushed or chased or lured into his bed. She wanted only...only what? A picture of him came immediately into her mind. Tall, his dark hair tumbling casually down, his eyes watching her with smoky interest. She remembered the way his hand had moved up to impatiently to push back his hair. She remembered his hand on her shoulder, his thumb slowly caressing her neck.

Alyssa shivered. She'd better think about it carefully before she agreed to see him again. Otherwise she was going to find herself in trouble.

She went out again with Lora, but not to the Place Vendôme to buy jewelry as Lora had laughingly threatened the day before. Instead, dressed in casual dresses and low-heeled pumps, wide straw hats framing their faces, they took a taxi to the Left Bank and lunched at the Café de Flore. Sitting at one of the small tables clustered under the sidewalk canopy, they ate escargot in a buttery herb sauce and washed it down with a dry white wine while they watched the parade of unusual characters who flocked to the Latin Quarter.

Later they strolled through the incredibly narrow, twisting medieval streets, peeking into jumbled shops and dim cafes, and joined the youthful crowd along the "Boul'Mich." They wandered into the Montparnasse, even more heavily populated by artists, looking at paintings sold on the sidewalk, often hung on the black iron spikes of fences. Late in the afternoon, footsore and weary from their walk, they found a taxi and returned to their hotel, where Alyssa had to rush to get ready before her father called for her.

Grant took her to the Hotel Meurice for supper, but he was quiet and abstracted throughout the meal. Alyssa presumed that his meeting with the government official this morning had not gone as he had hoped. New lines creased his forehead, and for once he looked his age.

"Has it been bad?" she asked quietly. "Your mission here?"

Grant looked surprised, then sighed. "Not good, I'm afraid. I can't talk about it, of course. But I—things don't look hopeful. I've been in Germany and here, and the contrast isn't heartening. I'm afraid France is going to find herself on the road to hell soon. Hitler's a madman. But clever, too. And Germany's strong. United. I don't suppose France will ever be in that state."

Alyssa smiled faintly. "Probably not."

"I'm afraid I have bad news for you."

"What?"

"I'm leaving Paris tomorrow morning."

"Another mysterious meeting at someone's country home?"

"No. I've been called home. There's nothing more I can do here, and he has another job for me." The "he" Alyssa knew to be the President, to whom her father reported directly, even though he ostensibly worked for the Secretary of State.

"Oh, I see." Again she experienced the familiar, quickly suppressed sense of betrayal. "I'm sorry."

"So am I. I hoped for a little time together. However, it looks as though I'll be in D.C. for some time now. I can come up to New York to see you."

"I'd like that."

"Will you stay in Paris long?"

She had planned to stay two weeks, hoping for a nice, long visit with her father. But now there was little reason to remain. "I don't know. A few days, I suppose. I have fittings for some dresses I bought."

Grant smiled, and he looked less tired and old. "Following in the family tradition, I see. Your mother would have bought out the fashion houses here if she could." He shook his head reminiscently. "She looked so good in those clothes, though, it was probably worth the cost." He paused and studied his wineglass, twisting the stem between his fingers. "How is your mother?"

"Fine, last time I saw her. Still living with Gran." Grant look up questioningly, and Alyssa added, "Yeah. She's still drinking. On and off, as always."

He shook his head, and his voice roughened. "Such a waste. She was a beautiful woman. I loved her a great deal. Still do, I suppose."

"I know."

They didn't linger over dinner. Alyssa knew that Grant probably had a number of things to clear up before he left the next morning. They returned to the hotel early, and Grant escorted her inside the lobby, leaving the taxi waiting for him.

"I'll see you up to your room," he offered.

"That's all right. I think I can make it from the lobby to the room without mishap."

He smiled down at her. "If you're sure." Grant leaned down to kiss her on the cheek, and Alyssa threw her arms around him.

"Take care, Dad."

"You, too, sweetheart. I'll see you in New York."

Alyssa nodded, swallowing her tears. She watched him exit, then turned toward the elevators. As she walked across the elegant lobby, a man rose from a brocade chair and planted himself in her path.

"Philippe!"

*****

Philippe Michaude had spent a restless night alone in his bed after he parted from Alyssa. He awakened yesterday morning tired, irritable, and certain he'd been a fool. He realized from the beginning that Alyssa wouldn't be an easy conquest, but his pounding need for her had made him blunt and clumsy. He'd been off kilter from the moment he saw her and he made several amateurish moves before they arrived at her hotel room. Once there, he stumbled even more. He shouldn't have tried to follow her into her room. He should have waited for an invitation.

The worst outcome would have been that she offered none, but he at least could have managed to arrange another date. Instead, he rushed her, then compounded his sins by arguing with her. You'd think he'd learned nothing of sophistication since he escaped the streets of Lyons.

He knew he'd lost his chance with Alyssa, and he told himself to put it down to a lesson learned and forget her. But he found that was impossible. Two hours after he went to his office he ordered flowers sent to her room. Shortly after that he began phoning her. Clearly she had given orders not to accept his calls. Today he sent her another bouquet of flowers and when his calls went unanswered, he decided to talk to her face to face.

When he learned that she was indeed out of the hotel, not hiding from him, he sat down to wait in the lobby. He'd been here for over an hour, alternating between gloomy imaginings of what she was doing and with whom and astonishment that he was behaving in such an irrational fashion. He was not a jealous man nor one who pined romantically after a woman. Both those things had always seemed a fool's game. Yet here he was, wondering if she had come to Paris because of another man or if Kingsley Gerard had arranged some intimate 'business discussion' with her or…

She walked into the lobby, her arm entwined with that of a handsome middle-aged man, and Philippe's chest turned cold. Alyssa was smiling at the older man in a way she had not once smiled at him the other night. She sparkled in this man's company; her face was filled with warmth and love as she gazed up at him. The man kissed her chastely on the cheek, and she responded by throwing her arms around him and hugging him uninhibitedly in the middle of the lobby. How could she waste herself on such an old man?

She started across the lobby, and Philippe rose to intercept her, churning with resentment and desire. "Hello, Alyssa. Did you have a pleasant evening?"

"Yes, very. Thank you." She said nothing more, simply stood there coolly waiting for him to continue.

"Why haven't you answered my calls?" He blurted out, realizing even as he said it that this was not the way to woo a woman back.

"Was that you? The desk clerk said the caller wouldn't leave a message."

"I presumed you wouldn't call back if I had." He paused. "Would you?"

"I don't know. Perhaps not."

"Why didn't you tell me about him?" Another stupid way to go, but Philippe could hold it back no longer.

"Tell you about who?" Alyssa looked puzzled.

"Him!" Philippe nodded toward the front door. "The man you were with. Why didn't you tell me that you were already…"

"Already what?" Alyssa's eyes began to dance in that way he had found so bewitching just a few nights ago. "Already having an affair?"

He nodded shortly, surprised at how much it hurt to see her amusement.

"Monsieur Michaude, you have a lamentable habit of leaping to conclusions: I'm an actress, so I'm lacking in morals. I have dinner with a man, so I'm his mistress. In fact, he's my father!"

"What?" Relief swept Philippe, and he half laughed. "He's your father?"

"Yes. Grant Lambert."

Philippe grinned. He felt years lighter. Still smiling, he shook his head ruefully. "Obviously I have made a bad start again. I'm sorry. I didn't come here to display my bad temper. I came to apologize for my bad manners the other evening."

"You seem to be positively full of bad traits." Alyssa's tone was teasing.

"And, for some incomprehensible reason, they are appallingly evident when I'm near you." Philippe got an answering smile from Alyssa and it stirred something in his chest. "I came to persuade you to forgive me. I hoped we could have dinner together, talk. I wanted to ask for another chance."

"I've already eaten."

Her hedging pleased him. She wasn't refusing, she was negotiating. "We could have a drink. Go to a club—or the cinema. We have English-language cinema here."

"A drink would be fine. As long as I don't have to fight off advances all evening."

"I promise I will not so much as coax or cajole. All right?"

"All right."

He stepped closer, and his voice lowered. "At least, not tonight."

Alyssa felt the pull of his sexuality. Actually, he didn't need to coax or cajole. His mere presence was temptation enough. "I understand," she replied softly. "We're only calling a temporary truce."

"Please. Why must it be a battle?"

Alyssa smiled faintly. "I'm not sure. But somehow I think you're a threat."

"I wouldn't hurt you."

"Perhaps you wouldn't mean to."

Warmth stole through him at her words. She couldn't be afraid that he would physically hurt her; the only threat he could represent was emotional hurt. Heartbreak. So her resistance wasn't because she disliked him or was indifferent to him but exactly the opposite—because she feared she could like him too much.

"Did you really mean to apologize?" Alyssa changed the subject.

"For desiring you? No. I'm only human. But for upsetting you, yes. I acted badly; I should not have argued with you. I shouldn't have pushed. I'm sorry. Will you forgive me?"

Alyssa nodded. Forgiving him was alarmingly easy. She slipped her hand through the crook of his arm, and they started across the lobby.

Chapter 6

They went to a bistro not far from the hotel. It was small and quiet, and they were able to find a table in the corner where they could sit secluded from the rest of the patrons. They ordered drinks, and Philippe lit a cigarette. He settled back in his chair, arms on the table, careful not to touch her. Perversely, Alyssa found herself wondering what it would be like to touch him—to put her hand on his, to slide her fingertips along the straight line of his jaw, to tangle her fingers in his hair.

"So," she said, pulling her eyes away from him, "what do you do? You've told me little about yourself, you know."

He shrugged. "There's little interesting to tell."

"What sort of business are you in?"

"My company makes trucks and heavy machinery—among them army trucks, tanks, caissons for artillery."

"I see. You have a plant near here?"

"Just north of Paris. My offices are here; I have other interests as well. An electronics firm."

"Radios?"

"Among other things."

"Are you from Paris?"

"No. Lyons. Have you ever been there?"

Alyssa shook her head. "Just to travel through it. Does your family live there still?"

"I have no family."

She blinked. "None?"

"I never knew my father, and my mother died when I was fourteen years old. I had a younger brother, but he died as a child."

"How awful for you."

He shrugged. "And you? What about your family? Is your father vacationing with you in Paris?"

"No. I don't think he ever vacations. He's on business, as always, and he's leaving tomorrow."

"What kind of business does he do?"

"Something with the State Department."

"What is that?"

"Foreign affairs. Diplomatic matters."

"I see. Then you must have had a well-traveled childhood. Yes?"

"Part of the time. When I was younger, if Dad was posted to a particular country for relatively long periods of time, we went with him. But later he became something of a troubleshooter. He'd be sent wherever there was a problem, maybe only for a few days or weeks. Then, of course, I couldn't travel with him. I went to boarding schools a lot. First in New England and later in Switzerland."

"Boarding schools." He smiled faintly. "Doesn't sound like the flamboyant past of an actress."

"My family was horrified when I told them I was going into acting."

"I can imagine."

"It's a problem both ways. My grandmother and aunts and uncles all think I've blackened the Lambert name. People in the theater assume I'm just a debutante playing at acting, that I'm not serious and will grow tired of it and go back to marry some polo-playing heir. It's kept me from getting more than one job."

"No wonder you were—ah, touchy about being an actress."

"Does it change what you think of me, knowing that I'm the daughter of a diplomat as well as an actress?" Alyssa asked a little defiantly.

"Of course. It makes you even more fascinating. A puzzle. I want you more than ever. Sorry—I know I'm not supposed to say things like that tonight. But I couldn't be honest and not say it." He smiled. "It's very hard to keep my promise to you. I can't stop wanting you, can't stop thinking of what it would be like to be with you."

Alyssa felt the pull one felt standing atop a tall building, the curious mingling of fear and intrigue. She looked away from his eyes and tried to think of practicalities. "Are you married?" she asked.

He looked surprised, then chuckled. "Ah, you think I am the perennially unfaithful Frenchman. Sorry to disappoint you, but, not I am not married. I was once, many years ago, but she died."

"I'm sorry."

"We were young when we got married, very much in love. Solange was like spring, like sunshine. Completely frivolous—very pretty, always happy, never serious. She was not at all refined; neither was I. We were crude and lusty and very full of life. She died in a car accident when she was twenty-three. I was twenty-five at the time. I had always been ambitious and worked hard, but after that I drove myself. There was nothing for me but my work. Poor Solange; she would have had great fun with the money."

"And you never remarried?"

"No. At first I was too filled with grief; it was many years before I got over her death. By then I had gotten too old and cynical. My standards are too high, perhaps. I haven't met a woman I want to wake up beside for the rest of my life." *At least not until now.* Where had that thought come from? He wasn't interested in Alyssa in that way. This wild, intense feeling he had for her was only desire, greater than usual simply because she was an unusually desirable woman. Once he satisfied his desire, her attractions would fade. It would be as it always was. As it had to be. There could be no possibility of anything permanent between them.

"And you?" he asked, turning the subject back to her. "Are you married? Engaged?"

"No. Never have been."

"You haven't been in love?"

"A little, a time or two. But it never seemed to last. I've always been more interested in my career than in marriage."

"Other actresses marry."

"Yes. But it's hard."

"Tell me about this time or two."

"What? Oh, the men I was a little in love with?"

"Yes. Them." He lit a cigarette, watching her closely. He did not touch her or say anything sexual, yet sensuality hung thick on the air between them. Alyssa could feel the tension drawing out between them, taut and compelling; she was liquid inside.

Alyssa shrugged, trying to shake off the feeling. "I—nothing special, really."

"Did you sleep with them?"

Alyssa's eyes flew open wide. "Philippe!"

"Ah, is that forbidden, too?" A half smile touched his lips. "I am afraid I am not used to American mores. Tell me what I should say instead."

"Nothing. It's none of your business."

"The way I feel about you—"

"You can't possibly 'feel' anything about me."

"No?" His voice was wry. "You remember earlier when you told me that you were threatened?" She nodded. "It was because you thought I might come too close to you. Isn't that right? I might pierce your defenses?"

"Maybe," Alyssa admitted reluctantly.

"You have already done that to me. You conquered me two days ago when I first saw you. I have no defenses against you."

Alyssa couldn't look away from him. His eyes were deep; she felt as if she were being drawn into them.

"I don't want to seduce you to prove that I can seduce another woman. I don't want to add you to my 'collection.' I need you. My body is hungry for you. My soul. My heart. I want to see your hair spread out across my pillow. To feel you hot and pliant beneath my hands. To wake up beside you in my bed."

Alyssa found it suddenly difficult to breathe. "I—I don't know how to take what you say. You talk like a Frenchman. I'm used to plainer speech. I don't know how many grains of salt to take you with."

"Of course I talk like a Frenchman. I am a Frenchman. I say what I feel. I don't try to make it any less than it is or any sweeter. I am not afraid to let you see me as I am. It's not exaggeration, Alyssa. It's the simple truth."

"I don't think it's quite so simple."

Philippe took her hand in his and raised it to his mouth. Softly he kissed her palm, his lips moving across it in the lightest of caresses. His breath upon her skin was hot, enticing. "*You* make it not simple. Why should it be difficult?"

With his lips touching her like that, Alyssa wasn't sure anymore why it wasn't as simple as he said. She knew she ought to pull her hand away and remind him that he had promised not to seduce her, but she didn't want to. She wondered what his lips would feel like on her mouth… on the rest of her flesh. Philippe's eyes darkened as he watched her. Alyssa wondered what he was thinking. She suspected that it would make her thoughts pale in comparison.

Philippe released her hand and glanced away. He took a sip of his drink, and when he looked back at her, his face was carefully blank. "I would like to see you tomorrow. We could go to the Bois de Boulogne. It's lovely in the spring. Will you come?"

"Yes." She was fast losing all resistance to him.

He smiled. "Perhaps you don't distrust me so much any longer?"

"Perhaps."

They left the bistro and strolled back to the hotel in the enveloping night. Philippe held her arm tightly to help her across the treacherous dips and bumps of the dark sidewalk. Inside the hotel, however, he released Alyssa and politely walked her up to her room. When Alyssa took out her key, he took it from her and opened the door, but didn't make a move to come inside. Instead he leaned against the doorjamb, smiling down at her.

"Have I been a proper gentleman?" he teased, his green eyes a strange mixture of amusement, frustration, and desire.

"Somewhat." Alyssa returned with a flirtatious smile.

He bent his head toward her, and Alyssa realized that he was going to kiss her now. A sizzling excitement sprang to life in her chest. He hesitated for just a moment, giving her the opportunity to pull back. She raised her face to his.

Lightly Philippe ran his tongue along her vulnerable upper lip, savoring what had enticed him so from the moment he saw her. Then his lips caressed her lower lip. His mouth brushed hers with infinite lightness and returned to cover it fully, deeply. He pressed into her, his lips opening, opening hers. Alyssa's hand fluttered to his cheek and caressed him with a butterfly's touch. Philippe groaned, and his tongue went deep into her mouth. His arms wrapped around her, grinding her body into the hard bone and muscle of his.

His skin flamed. His mouth dug into hers, devouring, demanding. When at last he pulled away, both of them were breathing rapidly, their faces flushed and their eyes bright. Philippe spoke only one word, "Tomorrow."

*****

The day was bright and warm, with a soft breeze to stir the blossoms of the trees, and the Bois de Boulogne was filled with people. Philippe picked up Alyssa at the hotel in his low-slung convertible Bugatti. The car darted through the streets of Paris with a throaty roar that matched Alyssa's pulse. The wind tangled her hair and whipped new color in her cheeks. She wanted to laugh for no reason. She looked over at Philippe, smiling, and he smiled back slowly. He had a devastatingly sensual mouth, Alyssa thought. She was beginning to wonder exactly why she had been so set against him at first.

They passed the small lake in the Bois de Boulogne and stopped at the Pré-Catelan, a smaller park within the park, filled with huge and unusual trees. Philippe parked the car, and they strolled among the gigantic trees, pausing in the Shakespeare Garden for a moment. They left the path and walked until there was no sign of anyone else around.

Philippe stopped beneath an enormous tree and sat down, spreading out his jacket for Alyssa to sit on. They leaned back against the trunk and talked. Philippe told her about his youth in Lyons, the days of hunger, poverty, and fighting. "I'm not sure why I'm telling you this. It's not something that will win a woman over."

"No, I'm glad you did. I like learning something about you—the   real   you   beneath   the I-am-a-rich-and-powerful-Parisian role."

He huffed out a little laugh. "You left out handsome."

"Ah, well, that goes without saying."

"So you think what I am now is merely a role I play?" he asked.

"No." She drew the word out thoughtfully. "Not a role. It's a part of you, just as the other is still part of you, another layer. But it's the only layer you let show."

"And what layers do you not show?" he asked.

"I was raised to *not* talk about such things," she told him. "Diplomats don't engage in soul-sharing. One must be circumspect and tactful, ignore inconvenient truths, and conceal one's opinions. Even a diplomat's family must not make waves, not draw attention, not saying anything to upset others. Reticence is the by-word. It tends to seep into everything in one's personal life as well. And, of course family secrets must be hidden at all costs."

"And yet you chose to act. Something that is, by its very nature, all expression."

She nodded. "Yes. Perhaps that's why I chose acting. I am finally able to say things, do things, be emotional or silly or wicked, and it's all right because it's only a play. Or maybe it comes from a being an only child living in an isolated situation, with a father who was rarely there and a mother who drank away her loneliness. I was forced to play all the different roles of my friends; the people in the books I read were real to me. Playing pretend lives was natural to me." Alyssa glanced over at Philippe, whose gaze was intent upon her face. She gave a little shrug, feeling suddenly embarrassed. "I'm sorry; I must sound very ungrateful, complaining about a childhood spent in ease and comfort."

"There are other deprivations besides a lack of money or food," he said. "I am sorry that your mother was not…present? Is that the right word?"

"It sums it up," Alyssa told him.

"In that, then, we are much alike. My mother died; yours was there but not there. My mother didn't choose to die; perhaps it's worse to know your mother made that choice."

"Her drinking ruined Dad's career. That was one of the many things I used to blame Mama for. No diplomat can survive with a drunk for a wife. Divorce was out of the question, so they only separated, but even that was too much scandal for his career. No matter how well he did, how right he was for his job, everyone knew he could never become ambassador. Advising was all he could do. Troubleshooting. Correcting other people's mistakes, pulling them out of hot water, steering them away from trouble. All without recognition, of course."

"You said, you 'used to blame' your mother. Not any longer?"

"I idolized my father when I was young. I thought he could do no wrong. But the older I've become, the more I've realized how difficult he must have been to live with. He's completely dedicated to his job. Wife and child came in a poor second. But putting aside all that, Mama simply was not suited for life in the diplomatic corps."

"In what way was she unsuited?"

"She didn't like to travel; she wanted a secure home. Mama was under scrutiny all the time; there was no such thing as privacy. She was nervous meeting new people and rather intimidated by all the aristocratic foreigners. Mama was sweet and pretty, but she wasn't strong. She was a fluttery southern belle; my grandmother never approved of her as a wife for Father. Obviously Grandmama was right. But they loved each other very much. Still do, though they haven't lived together for years."

"You don't sound much like your mother, except for the beauty."

"You mean I'm not sweet?" she teased, widening her eyes and adopting her mother's breathy Georgia accent.

"Oh, I think you must be sweet." The glance and flash of a grin he sent her carried a subtle sexual undertone, but he went on seriously, "What I meant is that you have little weakness in you. You're a strong woman."

"What makes you think that?"

"It's obvious. The way you carry yourself, the way you talk. The way you defied your family to do what you wanted."

"Obstinate. That's what Grandmama called it. My other grandmother, being from Georgia, called it 'muleheadedness.'"

He chuckled and tried out the word. "Muleheadedness. What an expression. I shall have to remember it. But, still, I think it is really strength."

"I was raised by Grandmama and Father. They don't believe in weakness." Alyssa smiled, thinking of her two very different grandmothers. "In the summer I'd visit Mama and her mother. They'd tell me to be sweet and soft, and I'd be able to get a man to do anything." She fluttered her eyelashes in demonstration.

Philippe's eyes lit in response, and he placed a hand over his heart as if stricken. "They were right."

"Then I'd go back home to New England, and Grandmama would tell me to be strong. One didn't manipulate men; one set an example for them."

"So it was she who taught you to be prickly, no?"

Alyssa chuckled. "No. That came from experience." Her eyes danced as she cast him a sidelong glance that had felled more than one man. "Especially with Frenchmen."

"You wound me!" he protested dramatically. "What do you have against Frenchmen?"

"Their reputation."

"Undeserved."

"You mean they aren't the world's greatest lovers?"

His eyes went to her mouth. His lips softened. "We could test the theory."

"All in the name of science?" She told herself she shouldn't flirt with him. Philippe Michaude needed no encouragement. But today she felt very alive, giddy, even daring. The spring air must be infectious. She didn't really want to be safe.

Philippe reached out to touch her face; his thumb ran slowly along her cheekbone and down to her mouth. He traced the same line of her lip that he had sought the night before. Alyssa tasted the trace of salt upon his skin. She wanted to taste him more.

His hands tangled in her hair on either side of her face, and he went up on his knees, taking Alyssa with him. Their bodies were less than an inch away from each other. Alyssa imagined she could feel the material of his shirt, the heat of his body through her clothing. She swallowed. She was fast tumbling toward her fate, out of control. Philippe controlled the situation now, if anyone did. He held her head fast, gazing into her eyes. She couldn't move, couldn't look away. She didn't want to.

He kissed first her upper lip, then her lower, pulling it between his lips. Alyssa felt the nip of his teeth, his fingertips digging into her scalp with increasing pressure. She smelled his scent and the fragrance of spring—blossoms and earth and rain-washed air. His hands were hard and flat against her head;

his mouth was soft. He tested, tasted, explored. His tongue came into her mouth, and Alyssa released a tiny sigh of satisfaction. She hardly knew she uttered it, but Philippe felt it through every muscle and nerve of his body.

She was his.

He kissed her more deeply, more desperately. His hands clenched in her hair. Neither remembered moving, but now their bodies were pressed tightly together. Philippe felt the full mounds of her breasts pressing through her soft cashmere sweater, the hardening points of her nipples. His arms went around her, crushing her even closer to him.

He moved his head, changing the angle of their kiss, and hip lips dug fiercely into hers. His hands trailed down her back and caressed the curve of her buttocks. Alyssa could feel the full urgency of his desire, the stiff thrust of his manhood against her abdomen, and the passion within her bubbled up even higher.

Finally, reluctantly Philippe raised his head. He gazed down into her face, his eyes feverish, his face flushed. His chest rose and fell in rapid pants. "We have to leave. We can't—someone could come along." His voice was hoarse and barely coherent.

Alyssa wanted to melt into his arms, give herself up to him right here and now, mindlessly, brazenly. She wanted to stay. But he was already moving away, helping her to her feet, and she knew somewhere deep inside her heated brain that he was right. They had to be alone together. They walked back to the car, Philippe's arm pressing Alyssa close to his side.

He drove back to his apartment with great speed and concentration, never once looking at Alyssa or touching her. He didn't dare, for fear his desire for her would boil over. Philippe parked the car and led her upstairs to his apartment. It was spacious and pleasantly furnished, but Alyssa hardly noticed it. She was too eager, too nervous. Too excited.

Philippe led Alyssa into his bedroom. Her hand was chilly inside his. He took her into his arms and Alyssa looked up at him, her eyes wide and dark, half longing, half worried. The sight shook him. There was nothing of the sophisticated actress in her now, only a woman trembling on the brink, soft and vulnerable. "Don't look so anxious," he whispered, "I'll take care of you."

Alyssa's hands came up and curled into his shirt. She felt as if she were holding on for dear life, as if she could at any moment be swept away in the dark, rushing waters. It frightened her. At the same time she wanted to run into the danger. And, impossibly, Philippe was both her safety and her danger.

He ran his hands lightly up her arms and over her shoulders, his fingers reassuring her of his desire. He kissed her neck and nipped lightly at her earlobes. He buried his face in her hair. He twisted her hair back and lifted it up to kiss the nape of her neck. Alyssa moaned softly at that, moving a little to give him better access to the sensitive spot.

Philippe turned her and pulled her back against him, still nuzzling the side and back of her neck. He cupped her breasts in his hands, molding the plush sweater against them so that her pebbly nipples were outlined against the material. Caressing the turgid points with his thumbs, he mumbled in French against her skin, using words Alyssa had never learned in Madame Plauché's French classes, but whose meaning and urgency were clear.

Philippe undressed her, pulling off the soft sweater over her head and unclasping the delicate strand of pearls around her neck. He unzipped her narrow skirt and tugged it down and removed her sheer slip. He set her down on his bed and bent to unfasten her garters, raising one leg and sliding the gleaming silk stocking down her thigh and calf and off her foot. Alyssa's breath caught in her throat at the gentle caress of his fingertips. He kissed her instep, and Alyssa shivered. With equal slowness he smoothed the other stocking from her leg.

He undressed, his eyes never leaving her as he pulled off his clothes and dropped them on the floor. Alyssa stared at the lean beauty of his body, the graceful curve of long muscle and thrust of hard bone. Black hair roughened his arms and legs, but the skin of his chest and stomach was satin smooth, inviting her touch.

He came to stand beside her, reaching down to caress her face. His fingers drifted over the smooth skin of her neck and chest to the silk that covered her breasts and hips. His fingertips skimmed her flesh, faintly rough against her softness. Her skin was on fire wherever he touched, and she wondered if one could die from the sheer pleasure of a man's hands.

Alyssa moaned low in her throat. Philippe stretched out on the bed beside her, taking the last fragile wisps of her underthings from her. He kissed the thin line of her collarbone and the soft hollow nestled at its center. Alyssa's hands dug into the bedspread beneath her. She had never felt anything as exquisitely warm and soft and exciting as his tongue on her skin. She trembled as his mouth moved lower, laving the tender skin of her chest and coming at last, with aching slowness, onto her breast.

"Philippe!" she cried softly as his mouth found her nipple.

He did not answer. He could not. He was incapable of anything except feeling the riot of sensations pouring through him. He knew only the supreme softness of her breast and the thrusting fleshy button of her nipple, the hot ache that opened up within his gut, demanding more, the wild pleasure heightened by a prickle of pain as her fingers pulled his hair. He moved over her, his weight pressing her back into the feather bed. His mouth moved to her other breast. Blood pounded in his head, in his throat. He thought he could drown himself in her.

Alyssa's leg moved against his, sliding over his hair-roughened skin. His hand went to her leg, stroking up and down the length of her thigh, fingertips digging into its softness. He wanted to savor her breast forever, wanted to explore every inch of her skin and taste each exquisite pleasure. But desire drove him, wild and urgent. He had to have her. Had to sink into her welcoming warmth. His hand slid in between her legs and found the satin fold of her femininity. She was slick with desire, heated and waiting for him. He couldn't hold back any longer.

She opened her legs, and he came into her, fitting into the tight silken cocoon of her center. Again the knowledge came—*she was his*. And immediately an answering flash of realization—*he was hers*. Philippe began to move within her, no longer a man or an individual, but a fire that was part of her fire. A single soaring heat that grew past all bearing until at last it exploded, shooting them out of themselves and through an eternity of thundering, sparkling sensations so intensely pleasurable that the two of them felt as if they might die.

But then they were safely home, sinking down into the softness of the bed, bathed with the warm light of reality. Arms wrapped around each other, they slept.

*****

It was twilight outside when Alyssa awoke. The room was dim. She felt a little sore and tired and glowing. She smiled and pushed her hair back from her face, looking over at Philippe. He lay sprawled on his stomach, arms flung out above his head. A day-long shadow of beard darkened his jaw. His eyelashes lay thick and black against his cheek, softening the straight-edged planes of his face. Alyssa ran her hand lightly across his hair. It was thick and springy to her touch, and she tangled her fingers in it.

Philippe's eyelids fluttered open. The pale, vivid greenness of his eyes startled her. He smiled. "*Bonjour.*"

"*Bon soir,*" Alyssa corrected teasingly. "We must have slept for quite a while."

He rolled over onto his back and crossed his arms behind his head, looking at her with a certain male satisfaction. "You tired me out." His grin was full of meaning. "Besides, I haven't slept well the past few nights."

"Oh, really?" Alyssa arched one brow. "They say the wicked don't rest well."

"Wicked!" His eyes were alight with amusement. "I?"

"Yes, you. A man with wicked intentions of taking my virtue."

One of his arms snaked out and wrapped around her. He pulled her back flat on the bed and turned to rest on his elbow, looming over her, all in one smooth motion. "You're right. I'm happy to take your virtue." He kissed her ear. "And I'll take your sins as well." He kissed her forehead. "Your joys." He kissed her eyelid. "Your pains." He kissed her cheek. "I'll take all of you. That's all I want. All of you." He kissed her mouth.

There was little talking after that, and it was a long time before they rose from their bed. Philippe made love to her with the leisure he had wanted to before, exploring and experimenting, discovering each other's bodies with all the wonder that only lovers can attain. Afterward, as Alyssa lay sweetly tired and sated in his arms, she knew that she was in love. In love with a man whom only three days before she had disliked on sight. She must be crazy. Alyssa smiled. The thought didn't bother her at all.

They had skipped lunch, and it was past time for supper, so hunger finally pulled them from their bed. Philippe put on a dark silk dressing gown and handed another to Alyssa. It was ludicrously big on her, falling down to her ankles, but Philippe wrapped it around her, fastened the sash firmly, and rolled the sleeves up so that her hands emerged. Hand in hand, they padded down the hall and through the dining room into the kitchen. Alyssa pulled up short. There was a man in the kitchen.

Philippe didn't seem particularly surprised to see him. "Oh, hello, Georges. We're looking for some supper."

The man turned to him. He was short and bulky, with a square, rough face. His dark eyes swept over them without expression. "Very good, sir."

Alyssa blushed. She felt embarrassed to meet Philippe's servant in this way, obviously just risen from an illicit bed. She could well imagine what he must think of her.

"Alyssa, this is Georges, my valet—and most everything else as well," Philippe introduced her cheerfully, apparently not in the least embarrassed. "Georges, this is Mademoiselle Alyssa Lambert."

"How do you do, mademoiselle?"

Philippe frowned. "Is something the matter? You look rather long-faced to be meeting such a beautiful woman."

"I assume you haven't heard."

Philippe went very still, and Alyssa's heart picked up its beat. "Heard what?"

"Germany invaded Holland and Belgium today."

Philippe's hand fell away from Alyssa's waist. "*Mon Dieu.* It's begun."

Chapter 7

Alyssa felt as if the wind had been knocked out of her. The war wasn't phony now. German tanks were rolling into the Netherlands and Belgium, so much closer and more real than when they had invaded Poland or Norway. She had *been* to Holland and Belgium. She could imagine their roads choked with the German Army, their skies filled with the Luftwaffe planes.

"The Dutch are flooding the land to try to stop them, but, of course…" Georges shrugged his shoulders eloquently. What could the tiny country do against the might of Germany?

Philippe turned toward Alyssa. His face was suddenly years older. "You must leave France."

"What? Now?"

"Yes. Get the first train out."

She drew back, hurt by his sudden forceful insistence that she go away. "Why?"

"Why!" he repeated, his jaw dropping. "Because there's a war on. They're fighting. You can't stay; you could get hurt."

Alyssa almost smiled in relief at the realization that he only wanted to protect her, not get rid of her. She'd been on her own for so long and had always been able to handle whatever came to her that it hadn't even occurred to her that Philippe would be afraid for her and want to protect her. It engendered a warm glow deep inside.

"But, Philippe," she pointed out reasonably, "that's in Holland. We're in Paris. It's miles and miles away. A different country."

"You saw what they did to Poland. Denmark was taken without a fight, and Norway almost as easily. It will be sheer luck if Holland and Belgium last two weeks. Do you realize where they'll be when they conquer Belgium? Above the Maginot Line. Remember what Monsieur Gerard said the other evening? The line isn't of much protection to us if they simply go around it."

"But I'm an American. We're not at war with Germany. They wouldn't do anything to me."

"Bombs and bullets don't stop to ask for your passport."

"It's miles and miles to the border, and the French and English armies are in between. Surely they'll stop the Germans. Even if they don't, it would take months for the Germans to reach Paris. I'd be able to leave before then. Every American in France will be trying to get out tomorrow anyway. It will be easier to leave later."

"That is true," Philippe said, still frowning. "I have little faith in our ability to defeat the Germans; Gerard was right in what he said about the French military the other night. But still...there will be enough time to get you away. If it looks too chancy, we can retreat to my house in the country." He hesitated, his face torn. "Will you promise you'll leave as soon as it looks bad?"

"Of course."

Philippe pulled her close to him, wrapping his arms around her, and kissed the top of her head. "I shouldn't let you stay." Guilt pricked at his conscience. He knew he'd let himself be persuaded because he didn't want to part with her. Not just yet. Let her stay for a few days, even weeks. She would be safe that long, and when the time came he would see that she got to safety. Surely he could at least have this much.

*****

The prognosticators of gloom were correct. Holland surrendered in five days, and it was obvious that Belgium would not hold out much longer despite the French and English troops that rushed to their aid. The French established a line south of the Somme River and sent thirty-seven divisions to shore it up. The people of Paris looked at each other in shock. A line of defense *within* France? For so long they had lived secure in the knowledge that France was impregnable, safe behind its row of enormous forts. Now their security had been smashed. They waited, and fear rose.

Alyssa felt guilty for her happiness. In the midst of the fear and tension, she was head over heels in love, and every day sparkled with life and hope. Alyssa knew that she had at last found the magical love that had eluded her all these years. She had no thought except for Philippe; her entire spirit and being were wrapped up in him. And she knew why she had never loved this way before; she had never known Philippe before. It was obvious to her that there could never be any man other than Philippe in her life.

She was with him every possible moment, and when he was away from her at work, Alyssa did little but think about him. She had become the complete stereotype of a love-struck fool. And she didn't care. They talked and laughed and made love, learning about each other with the thirst only lovers have.

They went to the theater, to the cinema, to nightclubs. They dined at the finest restaurants in Paris and small cafes on the Left Bank. They strolled along the Seine, holding hands, aware of nothing but each other. They sat up till all hours, talking and sipping wine in a dark bistro. They danced, arms tight around each other, oblivious to the world around them. But most of the time they simply stayed inside Philippe's apartment, too content in each other's company to want anything more.

At first Alyssa retained her room at the hotel, but she spent little time there. One evening, as they sat curled up cozily on the couch, Philippe twining her hair around his fingers, he asked casually, "Why don't you move in here?"

"What?" Alyssa glanced at him, her eyebrows rising.

"I'd like for you to move out of the hotel. What point is there in keeping a room there?"

"I don't know. I hadn't really thought about it. I haven't been asked."

He smiled faintly. "Such a well-brought-up lady." He leaned over and kissed her eyelids, his lips soft and feather light. "You fascinate me."

"Do I?" Alyssa smiled up into his face. Just to look at him made her heart squeeze with such happiness and love that it was almost painful.

"You must know it." His mouth brushed her cheek, her ear. "You've played havoc with my life. I can think of nothing but you. My secretary is certain I've gone mad; she comes into my office and finds me staring into space." He nuzzled her neck. "Say you'll come to live here with me. I want to think of you at home in my bed."

"Such possessiveness," Alyssa retorted lightly, but her breath caught at the soft, sensual exploration of his lips.

"Mmm. That's true. You bring out the primitive male in me." There was no exaggeration there. Philippe couldn't think of any other woman who had aroused such feelings in him, such basic and intense desire. He wanted her every way imaginable—heart, body, soul—and he wanted her all the time. "Well, will you leave the hotel?"

He spread one hand out across her chest and moved it slowly downward to cup her breast. Her nipple tightened beneath his touch, and she drew in a quick, sharp breath. "Yes, I will."

She moved out of the George V the next day. It was wonderful to be there in the apartment when he left each morning, to lie in bed, deliciously sated from a night of lovemaking, and watch him shave and dress. When he was ready to leave, he would come over to kiss her, very proper in his suit and tie, and Alyssa would smile, remembering how he had looked in bed hours earlier, flushed and naked. Sometimes she would decide teasingly to test her powers when he kissed her good-bye, and then the suit and tie would be rapidly discarded, and it would be another hour before he made it to work.

During the day Alyssa had little to do. She went to fittings for the clothes she had purchased at the fashion houses. She and Lora made a few more halfhearted shopping expeditions and frequently got together for lunch or a bit of coffee at one of the many cafes all over Paris. Alyssa had been surprised when Lora and King didn't leave Paris, but Lora told her with a comic roll of her eyes that Claude Freret had at last agreed to go to the United States. King wasn't about to leave before Claude for fear the director would back out, and Claude was determined to sublet his apartment and sell or store his possessions before going, so Lora and King were cooling their heels, waiting for him.

King, Lora reported, was going crazy away from his beloved studio and spent most of his time sending and receiving telegrams. The rest of the time he harassed Claude. But Lora loved Paris and was happy to remain longer, even with the threat of war hanging over them. After all, it would be months before the German Army could get as far as Paris. Even King agreed with that.

It didn't take long to prove them wrong. One day, less than two weeks after Holland surrendered to the Germans, Philippe returned to the apartment early. His face was drawn in grim lines, and Alyssa gasped and rose to her feet when he came in.

"Philippe! What is it?" She hurried forward to take him in her arms.

He laid his cheek against her hair, breathing in her sweet fragrance. He knew it wouldn't be long now before he would never smell that scent again and feel Alyssa's softness against his body. "Belgium has surrendered."

"What? Already?" Alyssa drew back to look up into his face. There was a depth of sadness and resignation there that she had never seen before.

He nodded. "Yes. There's worse. They didn't even hold out long enough for their allies to get out their troops. The British Army and part of the French Army are trapped at Dunkirk."

"Oh, my God!"

"Almost four hundred thousand men. Four hundred thousand!"

"But the navy, the British Navy—can't they get them out?"

"That many? It would be impossible for all the fleet to get there in time to evacuate them. The navy can't even get close enough to load them. They need smaller ships for that. It will be a debacle." He ran his hands through his hair and walked past her into the room. "Now we can expect the Germans to pour into France."

Alyssa went cold. Philippe would want her to leave now. She had said she would when the danger drew near, and it was obvious that time was fast approaching. But she couldn't leave Philippe! Her heart ached at the thought. She tried desperately to think of a good reason why it wasn't necessary for her to leave.

"You better pack your bags," Philippe went on. "We're leaving for my country house tomorrow. It's in the Liore Valley, almost a hundred mile southwest of Paris. You should be safe there for a while." He looked at her, pain blazing in his eyes, and she knew that Philippe wanted her to leave no more than she wanted to go.

Alyssa sighed with relief and went to him. At least they had a little more time together. She slipped her arms around his waist and leaned against his chest, enjoying the security of his heavy, steady heartbeat. "All right. I'll be ready tomorrow morning."

*****

Alyssa went by the George V to urge King and Lora to come with them to Philippe's country home, where they would be safer. Now that Germany was poised to attack France, it was only a matter of time before the Luftwaffe began to bomb Paris. King was busy helping Claude, and Lora was certain he wouldn't leave until the director came with him. "You know him," she told Alyssa with a smile. "He's like a dog with a bone."

"Then you come by yourself. I'm sure King would rather have you safely away."

"Probably. But I don't want to leave him. Who knows what he'd take it into his mind to do next? Besides, I wouldn't do that to two lovers about to be parted."

Alyssa knew how Lora felt. If Philippe were remaining behind in Paris, she would have stayed, too. So she wrote down the name of the village near Philippe's house and the highways to take to reach it and handed the slip of paper to Lora. "Here. This is where I'll be. If you need to get out of Paris, just come and ask the way to Philippe Michaude's house."

"Okay. Thanks." Lora smiled. "Here's hoping we won't need it."

"Yeah." Alyssa hugger her, and Lora returned the embrace fiercely. Tears glistened on their lashes. It was impossible not to feel as though the world were coming to an end.

The next morning Georges left early with most of their luggage, taking the train. Philippe and Alyssa followed in the Bugatti. They whisked out of Paris and climbed into the foothills beyond. Philippe stopped the car on the crest of a hill, and they looked back at Paris, spread out before them in the sun, a jumble of buildings on rolling land.

Alyssa felt a pang of sadness. She had always loved Paris, and these past few weeks had made it very special to her. She thought of the tree-lined avenues where she and Philippe had strolled, the romantic small cafes and bistros where they had sat and talked and sipped their drinks, never tiring of gazing at each other or hearing the other's voice. She thought of their meeting at Maxim's, of dancing with him at Shéhérazade. Tears filled her eyes.

"*Nom de Dieu!*" Philippe muttered, scowling at the city, and slammed the car into gear.

They drove out of the wooded rolling hills and into the flat farmland of the Beauce, past stretches of broken dark dirt with fragile new plants beginning to shoot up. In the center of the fields stood narrow limestone farmhouses with charcoal-gray slate roofs, and clustering around them several other smaller houses and outbuildings, each farm a small community of its own.

They crossed the Loire River in the afternoon and drove alongside it for a time, passing small farmhouses and the wide, palatial châteaus of royalty and nobility in times past. The area was more heavily wooded than the region they had passed through earlier, with fruit orchards and dense stands of sycamore, oak, and poplar.

Philippe turned onto a narrow dirt lane lined with tall, thin poplars. At the end of it were a few outbuildings and a gracefully symmetrical château of white limestone and black slate. It was not as large as most of the palaces Alyssa had glimpse along the river, but, standing framed by the towering dark pines, it was impressive.

She turned to Philippe, eyebrows raised, and he grinned. "Too grand?"

"I was expecting something more like an old farmhouse or a cottage."

"Merely a hunting lodge," he assured her, stopping the car in the circular gravel drive and coming around to help her out.

"A hunting lodge?" Alyssa repeated in disbelief.

"Yes, for some nobleman. This region was a favorite for hunting. There are lots like this. It's considered rather small, really."

"Uh-huh."

"You should have seen it a few years ago when I bought it. It didn't look so grand then. I've had to renovate a good deal. I use only about half the house. The rest is closed off."

A woman and man hurried down the front steps to greet them, the woman smoothing down a starched white apron. She was middle-aged and rather stern looking, both taller and wider than her husband. Alyssa waited uneasily to meet Philippe's servants. She had come to like Georges and thought he returned the feeling. She had never seen disapproval in his eyes at her presence in his employer's apartment nor any sign that he thought less of her for it.

But Georges was utterly loyal to Philippe; no doubt Georges thought anything he did was acceptable. Alyssa was not so sure that these caretakers would be as tolerant. Surely here in the country they were more conservative. But as Philippe introduced her to his housekeeper and farm manager, she could see nothing but respect and liking for Philippe and polite interest in her in their eyes.

When Philippe had introduced Monsieur and Madame Dumont, and they had gravely exchanged hellos, Philippe took Alyssa's hand and led her up the steps into the house. "I'm surprised they're so...accepting of me," Alyssa whispered.

Philippe glanced at her in surprise. "What do you mean? Why wouldn't they be?"

"Well, I can't imagine my father or any other man I know having the nerve to take his mistress home."

Philippe's brows rushed together harshly. "Don't be ridiculous. To begin with, they know that it's no concern of theirs whom I bring home with me. But more than that, you are not my mistress. You're the woman I love."

Alyssa's eyes widened and she came to a halt, staring at him. "Philippe!"

He turned to her. "Surely you don't think I act this way about every woman for whom I have passing fancy."

"I don't know how you act."

His hands came up to cup her face. "When I met you, I wanted you with a great passion. You were beautiful, desirable. But it was more than that." His thumbs lightly caressed her cheeks as he looked down into her eyes, his usually cool eyes warm with feeling. "I have never wanted another woman as I did you, even a beautiful one. Even my wife, whom I loved."

A flicker of pain touched his face and Alyssa smoothed her fingers across his brow, wishing this small gesture could take some of his pain away.

"The more I've been with you, the more I've realized it was far more than desire I felt for you. I rush home at night to see you. I long to be with you every minute of the day."

Alyssa smiled, thinking of the long afternoons she'd spent impatiently awaiting his return.

"When I make love to you, I touch heaven. Your smile makes my soul lighter. It pleases me just to hear your voice." He paused, gazing into her as if he could see to the very center of her being. "I love you."

He pulled her against him, wrapping his arms around her and burying his face in her hair. "God help me, I love you so much I've been foolish and reckless. I knew I should have sent you home for your own safety long ago, when Germany invaded Holland. Certainly I should have put you on a train to Marseilles today. But I couldn't. I had to have these last few days with you. I had to fill myself up with your sweetness. It's insanity!" His voice was harsh with barely suppressed emotion. "I couldn't have found a worse time to fall in love. I want to ask you to marry me, stay with me."

"I will, I will," Alyssa whispered, holding him as tightly as he held her. "I love you, Philippe. Please, ask me to marry you. I want to."

"No!" He pulled away.

Alyssa watched him, frowning. "Why? I love you. I want to marry you. I want to be your wife and share a life together."

"It's not a good time. Let's not talk about it." He broke eye contact, rubbing the back of his neck.

"But—"

"Please!" He came back to her and took her hands. "Later. We'll talk about it after we've been here awhile. But right now, I don't want to talk." He bent to kiss her, his lips urgent and seductive, and any argument Alyssa might have made flew straight from her mind.

*****

The next week was the happiest Alyssa had ever known. She and Philippe rode horses across his land and picnicked by the lake. They strolled through the small formal garden and the trees beyond. She sat curled up in an easy chair reading a book while he worked at his desk. They explored the closed-off sections of the house. They kissed, whispering their love, and usually wound up making love in the huge, canopied bed in Philippe's bedroom. It was a brief piece of time disconnected from reality; for the moment there was nothing but each other, and they could ignore the war rushing down upon them.

Their moment of tranquility couldn't last long. The German Army swept into France, moving inexorably to Paris. Two prongs of the German Army rushed straight for the city. And the stream of refugees from the city began. Though Philippe's home was somewhat off the main road south from Paris, they saw the edges of the exodus—those taking the side roads to escape some of the congestion. There were trucks and cars, carts pulled by people walking, bicycles, even horse-drawn wagons, all piled high with possessions. People stopped by the estate, asking for water, food or shelter, even requesting permission to sleep in the stables. The manager's cottage was now stocked with packages of essentials for the travelers and there was currently a small group staying in the barn.

Alyssa's heart was wrenched by the frightened, confused people, unsure where they were going, only knowing they must flee the devil behind them. She kept thinking about Lora and King. Were they stuck in the flood of refugees—or, worse yet, still inside the city?

The only good news they received as the days passed was the report of the evacuation of the English army at Dunkirk, where hundreds of civilian vessels, from pleasure yachts to fishing boats, had ferried the British troops back to England. It had been an almost miraculous recovery and a shining example of the spirit of the British people. But even so, nothing could mask the fact that Dunkirk had been a tremendous defeat for the Allies.

One evening as Alyssa sat in the drawing room listening to the crackling radio report of the latest disasters for the French Army, a dark blue open roadster puttered up the drive and came to a halt in front of the door. Alyssa glanced out the window, mildly curious. Usually the refugees stopped at the manager's cottage rather than coming straight to the house. There were several people in the car. She saw a glimpse of glittering blond hair.

Alyssa jumped to her feet and pulled aside the sheer curtain, her heart beginning to race. Two men and a woman stepped out of the car. The woman wore sunglasses and a scarf, and she whipped the scarf off her head, shaking her hair out. Platinum blond. "Lora!"

Alyssa ran to open the heavy front door. "Lora! King!"

Lora looked up and smiled, taking off her sunglasses. "Hiya, kid. Thought we'd drop by for a visit."

Alyssa rushed down the steps to embrace her, then gave King and Claude Freret each a hug for good measure. "I was worried to death about you."

Philippe stepped out onto the porch. "Madame Gerard. Messieurs. Please, come inside."

The three travelers were dusty and wrinkled and exhausted. King managed a smile. "We left yesterday. It took us this long to get here."

"Oh, no."

"Oh, yes," Claude answered, waving an expressive hand. "It is madness, utter madness."

"Everybody's trying to get out," King went on.

"You can't imagine," Lora told Alyssa as they climbed the steps of the house. "People started leaving days ago. We thought we'd wait a while for the crowd to thin, but it didn't. The road was jammed. You could hardly move an inch. It took hours to go even a few miles. We had to sleep in the car last night."

"We'd heard it was bad but I didn't realize…" Alyssa searched for words.

"And that wasn't even the worst," Lora went on in a rush. "Outside of Paris, with all the cars almost at a standstill, the German planes flew over and started shooting at us! It was horrible!"

"What!" Alyssa gasped.

King nodded. "They were strafing the roads. No military purpose. Just to frighten and create even more chaos."

"Alyssa, I saw someone shot! Right there, two cars in front of us. We had to jump out of the car and run to the trees for cover." Lora's eyes were wide with remembered horror. "I'll never forget it till the day I die."

"How awful this all is." Alyssa felt like anything she could offer was inadequate. "I'll have baths drawn for you, and you can have a nice, long soak and a good sleep."

Alyssa linked her arm through Lora's comfortingly and led her up the stairs to the second floor, where the bedrooms lay. Claude followed the two women, but King lingered for a moment with Philippe.

"It is very bad, then," Philippe said, his voice low and drained of emotion.

"Yes. The road to Bordeaux is packed. We'll split off now to Marseilles, though; perhaps it will be better."

"Perhaps. You must stay and rest with us awhile."

"Thank you. Claude's car needs some work, too. I was afraid we weren't even going to make it here. When the planes strafed the road, a couple of bullets hit the engine. I managed to patch up the radiator, but it needs a more permanent repair, and there's other damage as well."

"I'll have the farm manager look at it. He works quite a bit with farm engines."

"Thank you."

"Are the Germans close to Paris?"

"Days away, I'd say," King replied. "The army's in a rout, and the government's expected to flee any day now."

Philippe sighed. "Alyssa must go home with you."

"Of course. We'll be happy to take her along." Gerard paused. "You might want to come with us, too," he said, in a rare tactful moment avoiding what they both knew: soon Philippe's country would be under the domination of Germany.

Philippe smiled thinly. "No. I'm afraid I must stay."

*****

Philippe lay quietly in bed, his eyes open, staring at the ceiling. He glanced over at Alyssa, who lay on her side turned away from him, sleeping peacefully. He eased out of bed, glancing back to make sure he hadn't disturbed her, and pulled his shirt and trousers from the chair where he had tossed them earlier. It took him only seconds to dress. Then he opened the door of the wardrobe and took out a pair of heavy work boots. Carrying them and his watch, he slipped through the door into the hall, gently closing the door behind him.

He crept down the hall past the closed doors where the Gerards and Claude lay. They had been here two days now; they would be leaving soon. Tomorrow he must tell Alyssa that she had to leave. He hoped she would let him drive her to Marseilles; he wanted even that extra day or two with her. But he was afraid she would fight so hard against going that they might come to an open rift. There was an ache in his chest at the thought.

At the bottom of the stairs, he sat down and pulled on his boots, then made his way by feel through the dark house and out the front door. Outside, it was only a little lighter; there was no moon. That was the reason for this excursion. He circled the house and cut through the trees. In the woods it was almost pitch black; he wished he could have carried a lantern or flashlight, but that might have attracted attention, and he couldn't afford that. He ran into a stump and barked his shin and let loose a low string of curses.

He left the woods and crossed a field. Beyond lay a road and another stand of trees. A dark car was parked at the edge of the road. Philippe moved past it into the trees and stood for a moment, trying to discern the shape of a man in the darkness.

There was a disembodied voice, "Hello, Philippe."

"Hello, Ian."

A man came forward, Philippe recognized the height and shape, though he couldn't see the sandy, balding hair or the grave, professorial look that always sat on the other man's face. Ian Hedley moved closer to Philippe and held out his hand. Metal glittered in his palm. Philippe reached out and took the heavy ring of keys from Ian.

"You got into the factory without trouble?"

"Yes. Your keys were a great help. Your factory's rubble now." He paused. "I'm sorry."

Philippe shrugged. "It's nothing compared to what I'm about to do."

"I know. It's more sacrifice than we have a right to expect from any man."

Philippe pocketed the keys. "When we began, I thought I wouldn't care what anyone thought of me. Now I find I do."

The other man glanced at him sharply. "Are you saying you're backing out?"

Philippe shook his head. "No. Of course not. I just kept hoping that somehow it wouldn't come to this."

"I've heard rumors about your personal life…"

Humor touched Philippe's face for a moment. His teeth flashed in the darkness. "Have you now?"

"Yes. I'm sorry. I never dreamed you would meet her; I would have tried to stop her coming here if I had."

"No. Don't be. I can't regret it, no matter how painful it will be. It will be…something for me to treasure in the months ahead. The years." He quirked an eyebrow at the other man. "Sorry. Am I being too French?"

Ian ignored his last words. "Are you sending her away?"

"Of course. You think I would allow her to stay in this hell? She will be across the ocean, safe at home."

"You will have to do it soon."

"I know. I'll tell her tomorrow."

Ian hesitated. "I feel there should be something else to say, but…" He shrugged. "I will hear from you?"

"Yes."

"Good-bye, then… your grace."

That brought a wry smile to Philippe's lips. "Good-bye, Pliny."

They parted. Ian climbed into the waiting car and was driven away. Philippe walked back across the corner of the field and into the trees, as he had come. Before long he was home again, climbing the stairs to his room. Alyssa lay on her back, her pale skin shining in the dark. Philippe shed his clothes quietly and came to stand over the bed, looking down at her. One arm was flung above her head. The sheet had worked down to Alyssa's waist, exposing her full, pink-tipped breasts.

Philippe sat down beside her, his hand reaching out to clasp her delicate hand. She stirred and her eyes fluttered slowly open. His hand slid over her arm and down her body, memorizing the feel of her skin. Alyssa smiled sleepily at him. He caressed her breast and she made a soft noise of pleasure. His fingers slipped between her legs and the noise became a moan. He bent to take one breast in his mouth, stroking the nipple into life. He moved to the other nipple and aroused it with the same gentle skill. He groaned and buried his face in her neck. "Alyssa, my love, my love."

His mouth turned fierce on her skin, hungry and searching. He kissed her wildly, desperately, as if he would consume her, and Alyssa responded with an uprush of desire. Her hands moved over his body; his skin was slightly damp and cool. A delicious outdoorsy scent clung to him. Her hands came between them to stroke the hard buttons of his nipples, then slid downward over his abdomen, lingering on the sharp points of his hipbones.

He moved down her body, his mouth touching her everywhere, and came again to her breasts. The suction of his mouth was hard, pulling at the very core of her being. Alyssa could feel warmth flooding her and a rising sense of urgency. She moved beneath him, urging him on.

He rose above her. "Say you love me." His voice was hoarse, barely under control.

"I love you," she whispered. "You know I love you."

He came into her then, filling her emptiness. "Love me always," he murmured against her neck.

"I will." She shivered at the uncontrollable pleasure of his movements, the rhythmic, hungry, urgent strokes of passion. She moved against him. He groaned, his fingers digging into the sheets beneath her, and began to thrust wildly, driving into her softness again and again. Alyssa felt the familiar urgent force building in her. She ached, she wanted. He trembled with need. Her arms and legs twined around him, and he pressed ever closer, as if they could break through their flesh and merge completely. Then, at last, poised on the abyss, he cried out and poured his seed into her, and the dammed-up pleasure burst its bounds, flooding out to every part of Alyssa's body.

Philippe collapsed upon her, burying his face in her hair. His hair brushed her skin, damp with sweat. His breath was hard and rasping in her ear. "I love you," he whispered huskily. "Never forget that I love you."

Chapter 8

They were awakened the next morning by Madame Dumont's discreet tapping at the door. When Philippe opened the door his housekeeper held out an envelope.

"Sorry to disturb you, monsieur, but this telegram arrived from Paris. I thought it might be important."

"Yes, of course. Thank you." He turned and walked toward the bed, slipping a thumb beneath the flap of the envelope to open it.

Alyssa sat up in bed, pushing back her sleep-tangled hair, watching Philippe's face. Telegrams usually meant urgent news, but his face remained impassive, only a slight flaring of his nostrils indicating that the news affected him. "Philippe? What is it?"

For a moment he didn't reply. Carefully he refolded the paper and slipped it back into the envelope. "My plant exploded last night and burned to the ground."

"What! How could it explode?"

He shrugged. "They suspect sabotage. Several small explosions in strategic locations, probably dynamite."

"My God, why?"

"A factory for trucks and heavy machinery is easily turned to producing military equipment. I imagine some of my countrymen decided they didn't want it to fall into German hands."

"Oh." A shiver ran through Alyssa. Somehow the news made the steady advance of the German Army seem frighteningly closer. "I see. But how terrible for you—a lifetime of work."

His face tightened, and Alyssa wished she could call back her words. What a clumsy thing to say—he was doubtless already aching at the loss. Philippe crumpled up the telegram and tossed it into the trash.

"It can be rebuilt," he replied shortly. He turned away. "Let's walk. I need to talk to you."

Alyssa scrambled into the first clothes she found and they went down to the formal gardens in back, not speaking. Philippe slipped his arm around Alyssa's shoulders and squeezed her close to his side as they went up the shallow steps into the small orangerie.

They sat down on a stone bench there, and Philippe took Alyssa's hand and gently rubbed it, watching the slow, circular motion of his thumb. Still not looking at her face, he rose and walked across the gallery to the lattice-framed window. He shoved his hands in his pockets and stared out the window. After a long moment, he turned back to Alyssa. His face was set in hard lines that made him look older than his years and the pale green eyes were carefully blank. "Alyssa, it's time for you to leave."

Alyssa drew in a shaky breath. She hadn't expected this. She had though his quiet and sorrow were solely for the ruin of his business. "No," she protested automatically.

"Yes. In a matter of days, the German army will be in Paris. It can't be long after that before they reach here."

"You think there's no hope?"

"None. I am so in love with you I've tried to pretend that it could be otherwise, that by some miracle the army would hold its ground. It was foolish. I knew before the Germans attacked that the military would collapse. It's run by blind fools. So is the government. France is about to become a German possession. You have to leave now. I don't want you caught in the last-minute panic as the Gerards were in Paris. You mustn't be on the road with the Luftwaffe strafing the cars. The Gerards will go this afternoon, I imagine. We will accompany them to Marseilles, and you can fly with them to Lisbon."

"No."

He glanced up at her sharply. "What? What do you mean? You have to leave."

"I'm not going without you." Alyssa shook her head as Philippe started to speak and held up her hand to stop him. "I've thought about this a great deal the past few days. In fact, I've thought of little else." She rose and went to him. "Darling, you must come with me."

"That's impossible."

Alyssa gripped his hands hard. "Listen to me before you refuse. You said yourself that all of France will fall to the Germans. But there will still be one country left fighting them—England. Perhaps soon the United States can be persuaded to come into it, too. We'll have to! The war won't be over when Paris falls. Come with me to England. The Poles who were able to escape are in England fighting alongside the British, and I'm sure there are Frenchmen in the same position—those who escaped at Dunkirk, if no one else. They'd welcome you, I know. They'll need all the help they can get in the next few months."

"No."

"Why not? There's nothing left for you here, especially now that your plant's burned down. But in England you could help win France back from the Germans. I'm sure there are hundreds of ways you could be invaluable. I've never told you, but I met a man in England, the uncle of one of my friends, who is working in secret. I'm sure he could use you, and I could do something, too. I've already gathered some information for him while I've been here. We'd be together and free and working for France's liberation! Don't you—"

"No!" Philippe's voice boomed out. "*Merde*! I don't want you working for him. Do you understand? It's dangerous. Don't go near that man again."

"What is the matter with you? So what if it's dangerous? It's necessary. Don't be so European. Just because I'm a woman doesn't mean I can't do anything. I have beliefs and principles too, and I'm as capable as a man of backing them up. Maybe I don't know how to fight, but there are lots of things I can do. I'm smart; I can learn what I don't know. I hate the thought of the Germans occupying Paris. They simply cannot be allowed to swallow up the world! Don't tell me I can't fight them."

"I can't bear for anything to happen to you."

"Then come with me." She smiled her most beguiling smile. "Be there to make sure it doesn't. Please, Philippe. Let's go back to England together."

"I can't. I won't leave France. Whatever happens to her, this is where I must stay."

"Then I'll stay with you.'

"Alyssa! You can't!"

"I can."

"I won't allow it. Don't you have any idea what it will be like, being ruled by the Nazis?"

"It will be less hard for me than for you," Alyssa replied reasonably. "At least I have an American passport."

"And what if America should come into the war, as you said?"

"It will be no worse than what you endure. I want to be with you, Philippe. I want to give you whatever aid and comfort I can. I know you. You're planning to fight them here, aren't you? You'll need someone to help you. To listen to you. To love you. I want to be that person."

For an instant Philippe's eyes flamed with light, and he reached up to cup her face. "You are so beautiful. So full of fire and strength. You'd give courage to any man." He bent and kissed her, his mouth sinking into hers desperately.

Then he jerked away, his face harsh. Not looking at Alyssa, he growled, "You don't know me at all. Believe me, you don't want to stay. You have a picture of me that's not true, one that is

colored with your own courage and ideals. I don't have them."
He swung back to her, facing her squarely, his jaw set and his
eyes hard. "Within two weeks you'd be cursing me. I don't plan
to fight the Germans, outside the country or in. I plan to get along
with them."

Alyssa's jaw sagged. She was as stunned as if someone had
bashed her over the head. She couldn't speak.

"I've traded with German companies the past few years,"
he went on. "I have several friends in Germany, some of them
rather influential. Some in the army. When I return to Paris, I'll
remind them of that friendship. With their help, I'll reopen my
plant. I don't intend to languish in poverty; I had quite enough of
that in my early life."

Alyssa managed to reach the stone bench before her legs
gave way. "You—you're going to cooperate with the Nazis?"

"Exactly. They've won, or they will have in a few days'
time. Whatever this country has been in the past, it will belong to
the Nazis from now on. The only sensible thing to do is to
recognize that. I don't plan to be on the bottom ever again, so I
have to join whoever's on top."

Bile rose in Alyssa's throat, and she pressed her hand
against her mouth to hold back the wounded cry trying to burst
forth. *It couldn't be true! It couldn't!* Yet it was. Philippe had
just told her, without any apologies or embarrassment. He cared
more for his wealth and position than for his country or anything
else, including her. Her love shattered around her like lovely,
fragile glass.

Alyssa rose jerkily and started toward the door. Philippe
took a step after her, then stopped. His face was bleak. "I'll drive
you to Marseilles."

"No!" Her shoulders stiffened. She didn't turn around. "I
couldn't stand to be in the same car with you."

His eyes closed briefly. When he opened them, they were as
hard and expressionless as marbles. "Very well. I'm sure

Monsieur Gerard will take you with them. I will speak to him about it."

Alyssa wanted to clutch her stomach and run to the house. She was sick and broken. But she forced herself to walk with her back straight, her shoulders up, relying on years of training. She walked out the door, then stopped and turned, one hand on the door frame to hold her steady. "I thought I loved you. Now I see that there was nothing there to love. I don't know how I could have been so blind."

She left the orangerie and strode across the garden. It wasn't until she turned the corner of the building and left Philippe that she broke into a run, tears streaming down her face.

Philippe looked after her, his hands clenched at his sides. *Only the first,* he reminded himself. The first rejection and contempt. The first cutting of ties. There would be many others. But he knew there could be none worse.

*****

Alyssa did not emerge from Philippe's room until Monsieur Dumont had taken her bags down to the car and everyone was ready to leave. When she reached the front door, she saw Philippe standing on the steps, chatting with Kingsley Gerard. She glanced at him once, quickly, then turned her eyes away and walked past him to the car. She climbed into the rear seat, tying a scarf around her hair. Lora looked at her, surprised. Alyssa's lovely skin was splotched, and her eyes were red-rimmed and puffy from crying. Lora glanced at Philippe curiously, but said nothing, simply got into the back seat with Alyssa. Philippe shook hands with the men and reached into the open car to take Lora's hand and politely bow over it.

"Good-bye, Madame Gerard. It's been a pleasure having you here."

"Thank you. You've been very kind." Lora's eyes were puzzled.

He spoke past her, "Good-bye, Alyssa."

Alyssa's chin came up. She didn't look at him. "Good-bye."

Claude started the car, and they drove down the driveway and out of sight past the stables. Philippe gazed down the empty drive for a moment, then returned to the house and climbed the steps to his bedroom. The fragrance of Alyssa's perfume still clung to the air. He looked at the dresser. Her small jewelry box and silver-backed brush and comb were gone. He glanced into the bathroom. The vanity table was empty of Alyssa's cosmetics and perfume.

Philippe opened the large mahogany wardrobe. There was a small vacant space beside his clothes. No feminine shoes on the floor, no frilly hats cluttering up the top shelf. She'd been at the house little more than a week, yet she'd left a huge hole behind her.

Two dresses hung at the end of the closet, light summer frocks she'd bought before they left Paris. They weren't the expensive creations she usually wore; she'd purchased them off the rack in a hurry because the weather had turned too warm for the clothes she had brought with her. They were plain cotton and linen in styles hundreds of other women wore. Yet she'd looked as beautiful in them as she had in a Jean Patou. Philippe imagined that Alyssa could wear a sack with style.

She probably thought they weren't worth taking with her—or perhaps she disliked them now because she had worn them only with him. Philippe ran his hand down the smooth, cool cotton finish. There was another hanger behind the dresses, and he moved them aside to see what hung upon it. A simple, pale pink blouse. He remembered it well. Alyssa had worn it that day in the Bois de Boulogne, when they had first made love.

Philippe jerked open the dresser drawers Alyssa had taken for her own. A pink cashmere sweater lay in the second drawer, neatly folded. Philippe crushed its exquisite softness between his fingers. He remembered how it had felt beneath his hands that day, how he had molded the soft material to her breast and felt the sweet response of her nipples to his touch. Tears glittered in his eyes. He brought the sweater to his cheek and rubbed it softly against his skin. Alyssa. Alyssa.

He had known how it would end from the very first, and it had been foolish to let himself care too much. He had thought he would indulge his lust with a beautiful woman, a final present of pleasure to himself... and instead he had wound up losing his heart. He wasn't a man who could afford to have a heart. Philippe threw the sweater back into the drawer and slammed it shut.

*****

It took Alyssa's party three days to reach Marseilles from Philippe's house. The roads were jammed with people fleeing their homes in all sorts of vehicles. Cars ran out of gasoline and were simply abandoned, often not even pulled off the road. Fortunately, the trunk of their car was half filled with extra containers of gasoline, so they didn't have to face that horror. Still, it was slow, uncomfortable, and aggravating.

Alyssa, numbed with pain and sorrow, hardly noticed any of it. She moved or sat as Lora and King directed, uncaring about what happened or what was said. The world was as flat and colorless as a movie, as disconnected from her. She had no feeling, no interest, no appetite or thirst. There was a vague pain in the region of her chest, but it wasn't enough to pierce the fog around her. She simply existed, unable to absorb the shattering of her world.

When they reach Marseilles, King managed to bribe his way into the best hotel, already stuffed to the exploding point. They were lucky to get in. Marseilles was swamped with the shocked, the desperate, the homeless. Red tape, confusion, and pain abounded. They were far better off than most, for they had American passports and King's huge wad of American dollars. But no amount of luck, bullying, or money could get them on an airplane to Lisbon. The daily flight was booked solid for days, and they simply had to wait. Claude, once so reluctant to leave his country, now grew more jittery every day because he couldn't escape it.

On June 14, the German Army rolled into Paris. There was no resistance offered, and the city seemed emptied of people. Even the Champs-Élysées was deserted, the shops closed and shuttered. Within hours the swastika flew at every major landmark in the city. Within two days the German Army had chased the French all the way to the Loire River.

Paul Reynaud resigned as Premier of France, and the aging Marshal Henri Pétain, the hero of the Great War, took his place. The government moved to Vichy. On the twenty-second of June, France surrendered to Germany.

The news set King into action again. He had been resigned to waiting, no matter how little he liked it, but with the country surrendering to the Germans, he decided that he better act quickly. There was no telling what regulations the new government might put on Jews now in order to please the victors. That afternoon he went to the docks and hired a fishing boat to take them to Portugal.

As they sailed to Lisbon, Alyssa's shock began to wear off, leaving behind a pain so fierce and consuming that Alyssa longed to return to the robotic tranquility of shock. Philippe had trampled their love. He had betrayed her as fully as if he had taken another mistress while professing to love her. He was a man without a soul, she thought, not worthy of love.

She had never really known him, Alyssa realized now. She had thought he was strong and principled, but he had been playing a part. He had not really loved her; he couldn't. A man who would be a friend to the Nazis could have no heart with which to give love. She thought of the horrors she had heard the Nazis were perpetrating, and she shuddered. A man who would join them could be nothing but cold. Worse, he must be actually cruel.

How could she have fallen in love with a man such as that? Why had she been so blind to his true nature? Somehow, because she had been so overcome with love and passion for him, she had managed to ignore what he was really like, and seen him only as she wanted him to be. She had given him qualities and principles he did not possess.

Alyssa felt torn and bleeding inside. She had never imagined that a broken love affair could bring such pain. Her world was shattered. She had loved Philippe with all her being, and with that love torn away there was nothing left of her except hurt.

When the boat arrived in Lisbon, King booked seats for them all on the first Clipper back to New York, but Alyssa refused to go. She was determined to return to England, and all their pleading couldn't change her mind. She had promised to bring whatever information she had garnered in France back to Ian. Heaven knows, it wasn't much—she had been too wrapped up in her love to talk to many people. And with France overrun by the Germans, she doubted that Ian could use anything she had picked up. Still, she had an obligation to report to him.

But more than that, Alyssa simply wanted to go to Jessica. She wanted to crawl in a hole and whimper with her hurt. She wanted comforting. New York and the theater would not provide her any of that. Nor could her mother, off in a hazy alcoholic world of her own, or her father, who was always busier than two men. Of all the people and places she knew, only Jessica and her home offered Alyssa solace.

She caught the first plane to Southampton from Lisbon. On the train to London, she gazed out at the English countryside, gloriously alive and green as it always was in June, yet nothing that she saw raised her spirits—or really even registered. She might as well have been in a tunnel.

It was late afternoon when Alyssa arrived at Jessica's house. She knocked at the front door and was surprised when Jessica herself answered it. For a moment Jessica stared at her in amazement, then opened her arms wide. "Alyssa! My dear. What in the world—"

Alyssa rushed into her arms, hugging her friend for dear life. "Oh, Jess!" She began to cry.

Jessica's arms closed around Alyssa, worry and fear twisting inside her. Alyssa looked thin and ghostly. What had happened to her? Jessica had been surprised when Alyssa did not return to England as soon as the Germans invaded Belgium and Holland, and as the weeks passed she had grown more and more worried. Alyssa's state seemed to confirm her fears. Obviously something awful had happened to her.

"Come in. Come in." Jessica urged her inside. "Dearest girl, whatever's the matter?" She turned and called down the hallway for her housekeeper. "Matty!"

Jessica steered Alyssa into the sitting room. Alyssa's sobs quieted gradually, and she released her friend, sitting down on the couch and shakily wiping away her tears with her handkerchief. Jessica's housekeeper appeared in the doorway, wiping her hands on her apron.

"Be a dear, Matty, and fetch Miss Lambert's bags, will you?" Jessica asked. Ordinarily she wouldn't have asked Matty to haul in bags from the steps. The woman was getting older and had more than enough to do trying to keep the house in order with the other servants now gone to work in the factories. But she could hardly leave Alyssa alone now. "And could you bring us a cup of tea, please, when you have a spare moment?"

"Yes, Mrs. Townsend." Matty's eyes went curiously to Alyssa, then back to Jessica. Jessica answered her housekeeper with a silent shrug, and Matty left the room.

Jessica sat down on the couch beside Alyssa, and Alyssa gave her a watery, apologetic smile. "Sorry to cry on your shoulder."

"Nonsense. Now, what's all this about? Where have you been? What happened?"

"I was in Paris. We got out of France only a few days ago—took this bucket from Marseilles to Lisbon. We were probably lucky we didn't drown."

"But why did you stay till the Germans got there? And why were you crying?"

"I fell in love."

Jessica stared. "What! In love? In two months?"

"Actually, it took about three days, I think."

"But what—who—"

"Philippe Michaude."

"A Frenchman?"

Alyssa had to chuckle at Jessica's amazed expression. "There are other men in the world besides Englishmen."

Jessica smiled. "It isn't that. It's just so—startling." She had never known Alyssa to be truly in love. Besides, Jessica figured when it did happen, the only heart in danger would be the one that Alyssa had stolen.

"Yes. It took me by surprise, too. It took me even more by surprise when I asked Philippe to come back with me and fight the Germans from here, as Ky is doing, and he replied that he hadn't any plans to fight the Germans. He intends to get along with them."

Jessica's eyes widened. "You mean help them like that fellow in Norway? Quisling?"

Alyssa nodded. "Yes. He's traveled on business to Germany frequently and has friends there. He has friends in the German Army. He told me that he wants to continue his business, even though the Nazis will use it for their own ends. The only thing he loves is money and his own comfort." Alyssa's voice was laced with bitterness.

"I'm so sorry."

Matty bustled in with a tray of tea and cups. Alyssa smiled wryly. "The English cure. A cup of tea."

"That's exactly right," Matty replied stoutly. "You drink up, and you'll feel better."

"I wonder if that will ever happen."

"Of course it will." Jessica poured a cup of tea and dosed it with cream and sugar. "I'll make sure of it. You'll stay right here with me, and I shall coddle you."

"Sounds heavenly." Alyssa strove for a light, teasing tone, but Jessica could see the tears glistening in her eyes. Jessica took her friend's hand, and Alyssa squeezed it tightly. "Thank God for you, Jessica."

Jessica set Alyssa up in the guest room and proceeded to mother her. She made sure Alyssa ate all her meals and took a turn around the square every day. She listened when Alyssa wanted to talk and was silent when Alyssa was withdrawn. She talked of ordinary, everyday things, and she talked of the war. She tried to think of things for them to do to take Alyssa's mind off her troubles.

Alyssa was grateful for her friend's care and understanding. She hoped that somewhere inside it was helping her to heal, but she could see no signs of that. She still felt sliced to ribbons. It was an effort to get up each day and go through the motions of living. If Jessica hadn't been there, she wondered if she would have even tried.

Jessica and Alyssa went out rarely now, in contrast to the time Alyssa had been here only two months before. Alyssa preferred it that way. But she did attend a dinner party where she knew she would meet Ian so that she could report to him on the information she picked up in Paris.

She apologized for the small amount she had gleaned, but Ian waved away her words. "Nonsense," he told her. "You did splendidly. I couldn't ask for anything better than what you picked up from that diplomatic party." His eyes gleamed for a moment with a speculative light, then he made a slight negating movement with his head and went on. "I'm simply sorry I placed you in danger by having you in Paris when the Germans attacked."

"I chose to stay in Paris," Alyssa replied shortly and changed the subject.

The party was an agony to sit through, and after that Alyssa stayed at home even on the few occasions when Jessica went out. Claire came to visit often. She was as worried about her husband in the RAF as Jessica was about Alan, and each tried to shore up the other's courage.

Alan came home on leave from his RAF station a time or two, but his visits were rare these days, for now the RAF waited daily for the expected attack of the Luftwaffe. There had been a few dogfights over the Channel, brief, sporadic forerunners of the gigantic battle building up. But most of the time the pilots and crews waited, half bored, half on edge, for the German attack.

They weren't the only ones who waited for the attack. The whole country was in a feverish rush to defend the island. Factories went on around-the-clock shifts, trying to turn out the steel, rubber, uniforms, and guns that the country so desperately needed. There was no longer unemployment, and servants streamed out of their employers' houses, all finding work in the factories or in some auxiliary service. Women ran the factories and even the farms. They volunteered for the auxiliaries. Suddenly uniforms were everywhere, worn by both sexes.

Government officials sent urgent messages to the United States, begging for arms. Along the coast, citizens scattered old cars across the fields as barriers to invasion, and trenches were dug. Signposts were turned around or painted out in order to make it difficult for the German Army to find its way when it landed. Concrete posts were planted in fields the Luftwaffe might try to use for landing strips. Watches were set up for an invasion of German parachutists.

However, the military activity had started much too late, and everyone knew it. They had wasted all the time given them in the "phony war," and now they were in grave danger and much too far behind.

Alyssa knew her family and friends would tell her that she ought to leave England as soon as possible. Yet she couldn't bring herself to do that. She couldn't leave Jessica to face the terror of the Nazi air raids and invasion by herself. Somehow this war had become her fight, too, and she didn't want to scuttle off to safety in the United States.

The precious days slid by. The country seemed to hold its breath, waiting. Then, in August, the Luftwaffe swept over the Channel.

Chapter 9

Alan Townsend stretched his long legs out in front of him and leaned his head back against the wall of the Rochford operations rooms. He was in gear, ready to fly at a moment's notice—which was usually all they had. His eyes closed, and, drifting for a few minutes in a dreamy world that was not quite sleep, he thought of Jessica. He was exhausted.

The Luftwaffe had come at them full tilt for almost a month now, bombing the coastal towns, airstrips, and factories. The RAF was stretched to its thinnest point. Some days they scrambled as many as four or five times, and there had been moments when almost the entire air force was in the air at one time. Had another wave of Germans come then, they would met no opposition.

The chair beside him creaked as someone sat down, and Alan opened an eye. It was Geoffrey Raglin, a Canadian. He was chewing gum rapidly, his eyes darting around the room, his face tight. He folded and refolded a gum wrapper. Alan thought the man looked about ready to snap. That wouldn't be surprising. It was probably more surprising that so few of them did. One thing Alan was certain of was that a man who had flown against the Luftwaffe this past month would never be the same again. It did something strange to one's insides.

Either you got so jumpy you cracked, as Raglin was on the verge of doing, or your feelings died inside you. One couldn't afford to indulge in emotions in this constant flirtation with death, except perhaps to feel the relief at escaping again or the joy of seeing your tracer bullets rip through a Messerschmitt and send it plummeting to the ground. And surely it wasn't normal, wasn't right, to feel such fierce pleasure at causing death. He tried to think of Jessica often, clinging to the love that was the only thing alive left in him, but there were times when he could hardly remember her face.

"You see Holcomb?" Raglin asked, popping his gum.

Alan shook his head. He had no desire to talk about the gut-shot man who'd flown back to the station earlier this afternoon, dying minutes after he'd landed. Holcomb had known he was dead, of course, but he'd wanted to get the Hurricane back. Every airplane was precious.

"I did," Raglin went on, uninvited. "I took his plane back to the hanger. I sat in his blood—never get it out of my uniform." He would never get the smell or the sight out of his mind either, Alan knew, but he didn't say it. "Don't know how Holcomb made it back. Do you?"

Again Alan shook his head. He wished the man would be quiet.

Raglin started to speak again, and Alan had to set his teeth to keep from shouting at him to shut up. Then the red warning light flashed on, and the *woop-woop* began.

"Scramble!" A voice came over the loudspeaker.

Alan was on his feet and out the door on the run, moving by instinct long before his mind began to operate on a conscious level. He ran for his Hurri and clambered into it, cramming on the headset, his hands automatically running through the routine. Routine. That's what you concentrated on. Never think about what you are really doing.

Instructions crackled over the radio as they taxied and took off: "Seventy Bandits approaching Calais, Yorker red leader. Twenty plus at Angel 6, remainder Angel 12, over."

They settled into formation. One section would dive to a lower level to attack the German bombers, and Alan's section would take on the higher-flying fighter escort of Messerschmitts. He wiped his hand against his pants leg; it was slippery on the stick. One of the most important regulations was to wear one's gloves and googles at all times. Alan and most of the other pilots disregarded the regulation. A glove slowed down the fingers on the gun buttons and the controls; goggles hampered peripheral vision. But the lack of them left a man more vulnerable if fire broke out in the cockpit, the horror of every pilot.

They were over the Channel in minutes, and the German escort came into sight, heavily outnumbering the British Hurricanes and Spitfires. The other section dived to intercept the bombers, and the Messerschmitts started after them. Alan took aim on a Messerschmitt and flew in, tracer bullets spitting out red fire. The German rolled, and he followed. The German banked, returning fire. The bullets shooting out looked like little red blinking lights. Alan banked to escape them.

They turned and dived and rolled in a deadly dance. Another Messer streaked in on him, and Alan fell away. He pulled back up, firing, and hit the Messerschmitt's cockpit. It exploded into fire, and for an instant he saw the terrified face of its pilot. Then it plunged, spiraling, to the sea. A ghastly grin spread across Alan's lips, but he hadn't time to watch the plane hit, for the other plane was still dogging him.

Alan peeled away, heading out across the Channel. His pursuer followed, and another German broke away to join him. Alan's Hurricane climbed steeply, then dived, firing. A Hurri moved to intercept the second Messerschmitt. The RAF airplane was hit, and as Alan dodged and ran, from the corner of his eye he saw the pilot parachute out. The second Messer shot the dangling pilot on his slow descent.

Alan zipped away from his pursuer and engaged the second plane, catching him by surprise. But the first Messer was not to be denied. He came after the two, who were now dogfighting. Bullets ripped one of Alan's wings. They were already low, the gray water of the Channel clearly visible below them, but Alan dived lower still to escape. He pulled back up. The aircraft wouldn't respond. He jerked back with all his might, grimacing from the effort. His engine sputtered and stalled, and suddenly the choppy gray water came rushing up to meet him.

*****

Jessica trotted lightly down the stairs to answer the thudding of the door knocker. She opened the door, and the messenger on the doorstep held out a cable to her. Jessica stopped dead and stared at the small envelope. Everything around her went perfectly still, perfectly silent. She wanted to step back inside and close the door. Instead she stretched out a hand, moving as woodenly as if it didn't belong to her, and took the cable. The boy pulled at his cap and turned away. Jessica turned back to the hall. Her fingers were numb on the envelope. She moved away from the door, leaving it open behind her.

Alyssa appeared at the top of the stairs and started down. She stopped when she saw the open front door and her friend's expression. "Jessica?" She focused on the paper in Jessica's hand. "Jessica!"

Alyssa ran down the remaining steps and shoved the door closed, turning back to squeeze her friend's shoulder. "What is it?"

Jessica finally looked at her. Her face was drained of color, her eyes huge. She wet her lips. "Cable."

"Do you want me to open it?" Alyssa asked gently, and Jessica shook her head. She tore at the envelope with shaking fingers. It slipped from her hand and hit the floor. She stared down at it. Alyssa reached over quickly and picked it up, ripping it open and pulling out the paper. She handed it to Jessica without reading it.

Jessica read it. She swallowed. Her eyes moved over it again. "Missing," she murmured. Her breath caught, and she glanced up at Alyssa, a flicker of hope warring with dread. "What does that mean? 'Missing in action over the Channel?' What does that mean?"

Jessica held out the piece of paper to Alyssa, and she read it. "Probably that his plane went down. But he might have lived. Maybe he parachuted out. They must not know exactly what happened."

Alyssa took a firm grip on her friend's arm. Jessica looked as if she was about to faint. Alyssa led her to the first chair inside the sitting room. Jessica sat down mechanically, shivering.

"Oh, God, Alyssa, what am I to do? I've never been without Alan." She looked up at her friend pleadingly. She was beginning to shake. "What if he's dead? What if he's dead?"

"We'll find out more," Alyssa promised, kneeling down beside Jessica's chair and taking her cold hands between her own. "We'll talk to somebody—his commanding officer. I'll call him."

"I must tell his parents."

"Later. Right now, you just sit there. I'm going to get you a blanket." Jessica looked in shock. Her face was paper white, and her skin was freezing. Alyssa hurried back upstairs and came running down again with a comforter from her bed. She wrapped it around Jessica and called to Matty to bring tea quickly.

Alyssa sat on the sofa with Jessica, holding her hand and watching her as she drank the tea. Gradually color began to come back to Jessica's face, and she returned the pressure of Alyssa's hand. Her eyes were big and full of turmoil. "I'm so scared," Jessica whispered, and her voice broke. "I'm just so scared." She burst into tears.

Alyssa put her arms around her friend and held her. It felt strange to hold a woman for anything longer than a greeting embrace. She could smell the faint scent of Jessica's face powder mingling with talcum and a gentle, flowery perfume; she could feel Jessica's hair against her cheek. Jessica's bones felt fragile, like those of a child or an old woman. Her fingers dug into Alyssa's dress in the back. The world Alyssa had lived in all her life seemed suddenly very far away and as unreal as characters in a play. Tears filled her own eyes. What a sad, sad place the world had become.

*****

Discovering what "missing in action" meant turned out to be more difficult than Alyssa had imagined. She placed several calls to Alan's commanding officer at Rochford Field, but she was unable to reach him. She pulled every string Jessica knew of in an attempt to speak to someone who would know the facts of Alan's disappearance, but to no avail.

Jessica's tragedy pulled Alyssa from her own sorrowing lethargy. She took up the shopping and most of the house-cleaning that Matty was unable to do. She talked to Jessica's friends and family, shielding her from everything she could. In comforting her friend, she was able to forget, at least for the moment, the pain which had festered within her for over two months.

The acid of anger replaced her pain. She hated Philippe. She hated the Germans. Jessica's loss fueled that anger. Every evening they listened to the radio, hearing the news of the war, the details of English losses in the dogfights over the south of England and the Channel, and that stoked her anger, too. The Nazis were destroying everything and everyone, and Alyssa couldn't remember ever before feeling such hatred.

About a week and a half after they learned that Alan was missing over the Channel, Jessica received a letter. With shaking fingers, she tore it open and scanned it. "It's from Alan's squadron leader."

Alyssa, who had been trying rather clumsily to mend a small rip in one of her slips, dropped her work and looked up. "What does he say?"

Jessica's hands fell back into her lap, still holding the letter, and she looked at Alyssa bleakly. "He's dead."

"What? Is that what he says?"

"As good as." Jessica's voice trembled. "One of the other pilots saw him go down. Alan was flying low and dived and apparently couldn't pull out of it. He crashed into the channel. The other pilot said he didn't parachute out. Didn't have time to. He says it might just be possible that he could have gotten out after the crash and swam to shore. They weren't too many miles off the coast of France, and Alan was a good swimmer. If his name shows up on the rolls of prisoners the Germans send, they'll notify me. But it's obvious that he doesn't think it will."

"Oh, Jessica." Alyssa went to her friend and slipped an arm around her shoulders. "I'm so sorry."

"I'll have to write to Alan's parents and tell them what the pilot said. I'm sure his mother will cling to the hope that he swam to France. He was a good swimmer, but…" Jessica's voice faltered. She couldn't bear to say the rest aloud, so she silently shook her head. After a long, shuddering breath, she blinked away her tears and patted Alyssa's hand where it lay on her shoulder. "You've been such a help to me."

Alyssa gave her shoulder an extra squeeze. "I'm just glad I'm here. We'll help each other."

Jessica rose to her feet a little unsteadily. "I think I'll work in the garden." It was her favorite way to ease pain and she felt an intense urge to get out of the house. As though if she could only put some distance between herself and the walls that were closing in, she could distance herself from the emotions that threatened to collapse her very being.

Jessica headed into the kitchen with Alyssa trailing behind her uncertainly. She set down the letter on the table but before she could fetch her workbasket, the piercing sound of sirens split the air. Alyssa and Jessica both froze, then swung to stare at each other. "Air raid," Jessica breathed. They ran for the back door. "Matty! Come on! Into the shelter."

Jessica held open the back door for Matty and Alyssa and dashed out after them. Alyssa shielded her eyes and looked up. She turned to the east, and her face went slack. "Oh, my God!"

Jessica, opening the door of the shelter, glanced back at her, then in the direction where Alyssa stared. Jessica stiffened, and a fear far greater than that induced by the siren sliced through her. The late afternoon sky east of London was thick with planes. She'd never seen anything like it, never imagined anything like it. As they watched, black objects dropped from the bottom of the planes. Seconds later fires erupted from the ground. "Oh, God." Jessica's hand shook on the door. "Oh, God."

"Let's get in." Alyssa broke from her trance and shoved open the shelter door. She helped Matty down into the shelter and thrust Jessica in after her, then went in herself, closing the metal door.

They stood in darkness. Only the faintest line of light shone from around the upper rim of the door. Outside, the world exploded into noise. As long as she lived, Alyssa knew she would never forget the thundering explosions.

Jessica took her hand, and Alyssa squeezed it. She wondered how close the bombs were falling. They sounded horribly loud; they must be nearby. Matty edged closer to her, too, and Alyssa reached out to put her other hand around Matty's.

They waited for what seemed hours, their ears assaulted by the noise. Alyssa felt sweat trickling down her scalp and neck, running down her sides. It was hot and airless inside the shelter. She wished it weren't so dark, but she was too frozen by the sounds of devastation outside even to think of the kerosene lamp Jessica had put out here.

The explosions moved from continuous thunder to single, distinguishable hits, then dwindled away altogether. Now there was only the sound of sirens.

"Is it over?" Jessica whispered, her voice cracking.

"I don't know." Alyssa waited a few minutes longer. She had never been able to stand not knowing. She opened the door a slit and peered out. She saw only a garden at dusk. She opened it wider and climbed out. The garden and the houses beyond it looked perfectly normal. Her head turned toward the east.

Black clouds billowed up to the sky, and flames illuminated the growing darkness. The whole East End must be on fire.

Jessica and the housekeeper scrambled out after Alyssa, their eyes riveted on the eastern horizon, too. "My sister lives in the East End," Matty said softly.

They returned to the kitchen, and Matty sat down heavily at the table where the letter from Alan's commanding officer lay. The open letter stared up at Jessica, a reminder of how quickly and completely her world had fallen apart. She laid a hand on Matty's shoulder, uncertain how she could offer the woman comfort when things looked so dire.

"Would you like to call your sister? I'm not sure if the lines will be working, but you are more than welcome to try."

"My sister doesn't have a phone." Matty was pale and stared blankly at the letter, unseeing. It was worse than if she had started crying; at least then Jessica could embrace her. Instead Matty sat stock-still, looking like a ghost.

"I'm afraid it wouldn't be safe to go look for her right now." Jessica frowned. "Would it be all right if Alyssa and I accompanied you to the East End tomorrow?" There was no guarantee what they would find there and Jessica was terrified of the prospect of seeing all the carnage close up, but if she had been able to search for Alan herself after she had gotten that first telegram, she would have been there in a second. They had to be strong for Matty. And maybe this time the news would be happier than her news had been.

Matty seemed to see the letter then with its official RAF seal; she pulled her head up and finally made eye contact with Jessica. Seeing the young woman's tears, Matty forced a weak smile. "That's so kind of you, dear heart, but are you sure you're up to it?"

Jessica realized she was. After everything that the Germans had taken from her, things she could never get back, she'd be damned if she'd let them take let them take away her humanity and love for a woman she'd known since she was young.

"Of course. I'm not sure why I phrased it as a question. I won't take no for an answer." Jessica bent over to hug Matty and she returned the embrace fiercely.

"I'm so sorry about Mr. Townsend, ma'am." Matty whispered, her voice breaking a little.

"Thank you." Jessica gave her another squeeze, then stood up and straightened her shoulders. "I'm going to check on Alyssa."

Alyssa was upstairs in the front guest room, looking out the window, and Jessica joined her. They could see the East End. The whole dock area was an inferno.

"They must have decided to start bombing the cities instead of the strategic targets. They're trying to break the people's backs," Alyssa guessed.

"They'll never do that." Jessica's voice was so cold and fierce that Alyssa turned, startled, to look at her friend. Jessica's face was pale, her eyes huge, but the small jaw was set and the eyes blazing with determination.

Alyssa looked back at the flames licking the distant sky, and the anger within her grew harder, icier, larger. She had to do something, she thought. She had to do something to stop the Nazis. She had been frightened by the air raid, but strangely excited, too. She felt exhilarated, flooded with the adrenaline of danger faced and passed. If there had been an enemy in front of her, she thought she could have picked up the first weapon handy and waded into him, swinging. She wished there were an enemy there.

They gazed at the distant fires for a few more moments, then went downstairs to listen to the large brown console radio. It crackled with static as the announcer reported major fires and devastation around the dock and East End.

A little after eight o'clock, the hideous sirens began again. Jessica and Alyssa stared at each other in amazement. "Again?"

They hurried for the back door, taking a shaken Matty with them. As they ran to the shelter, they could see the approaching formations of planes, the larger bombers below with the fighters above them. It was almost completely dark, and the great beams of the searchlights probed the sky, highlighting the planes for the antiaircraft guns below. Quickly the three women scrambled into the shelter.

This time they didn't wait by the door, clutching each other in fear. Alyssa turned on the electric torch she had brought with her. Its beam illuminated the small room weirdly, casing a bright circle of light against one wall, but it enabled Alyssa to find the old kerosene lamp and matches on the shelf, where Jessica had stored them some time ago. She lit the lamp and turned off the torch.

They looked around at the little room. It was narrow, with two small bunk beds on either side. A shelf on the wall at the back between the bunks held the lamp and matches, as well as several tins of food and an opener. A large bottle of water sat on the floor beneath it. In front of the bunk bed sat a small stool and an old chamber pot.

Matty perched on one of the bunks. Alyssa sat down on the stool, and Jessica sat on the bunk close to her. Outside, the bombs crashed through the city. "I wonder if they're closer this time," Alyssa mused aloud.

"Are you frightened?" Jessica asked, rubbing her arms.

Alyssa thought for a moment. "Actually—no. I feel a bit of fear, but it's not that bad. I'm a little ashamed to admit it, but it's kind of exciting, too."

Jessica gave her a wan smile. "I might have known you'd feel that way. It sounds as if the world's ending to me."

"You're scared?"

Jessica nodded her head. "Yes. I hate to be such a coward."

"There's nothing wrong with being scared. If you think about it, it's really a greater proof of bravery to stick it out here in London if you're frightened by the bombs than if you aren't."

Jessica smiled faintly. "Thank you."

The raids continued throughout the night, ending, then starting again an hour or two later, so that after a time they elected simply to spend the night in the small shelter. It wasn't a comfortable night. The beds were narrow and hard, and they were jolted awake whenever a new raid began.

The next morning they crawled out of their shelter, stiff and sleepy. Jessica turned on the radio again, and they listened to the grim statistics: Woolwich Arsenal, the docks, Beckton Gasworks, the West Ham Power Station, the City, and Westminster had been bombed. A few bombs had fallen in Kensington, close to the area where Jessica lived, but the major portion of the damage had been confined to the East End, near the docks and the business center of the city.

It was the poor section of the city, and the destruction of its buildings had left thousands homeless, including Matty's sister, Sarah. Luckily, she was not one of the hundreds believed dead, and after searching the large crowds of displaced citizens, they finally found her. Sarah had grabbed what little possessions she had that were not destroyed and Alyssa and Jessica took them from her, insisting that they would carry them back to Jessica's house. Matty thanked the women profusely for letting her sister stay, but Jessica just said firmly, "Matty, you are family, so it follows that Sarah is family. And we don't need to be thanked for helping our family in a time of crisis."

No one could deny that this was truly a time of crisis. Fires still burned, and the fire brigades struggled all day to put out the blazes so they would provide no illumination for the enemy bombers when they came again that evening—for everyone expected them to come again.

And they did. At dusk, later than the evening before, the sirens sounded again. It was to be the second in twenty-three consecutive nights of bombings. Sometimes there was only one raid, other nights several. First a wave of bombers would drop incendiary bombs to explode and burn, giving illumination for later bombers to see their targets. The Luftwaffe came at different times and in different strengths to unnerve the citizens below, for the primary aim of the bombing raids was to break the spirit of London's people.

But this they were unable to do. The four women banded together in Jessica's shelter. When they weren't tucked away in the bunks they played card games or talked to pass the time. And they were always there to comfort each other when it got to be too much. Londoners without shelters moved below ground at night, taking bedrolls, water, and food with them into the deep underground tube stations, preferring them to the public shelters that the government had built.

Volunteers watched for the fires set by incendiary bombs so that the fire brigades could douse them before they provided light for other German planes. Volunteers manned ambulances, driving through the streets, dodging craters made by bombs and toppling buildings, to reach the wounded. By day, crews worked to dig out the rubble of the bombed buildings, searching for signs of life. Stubbornly they refused to let the nightly raids bring the huge city to a standstill.

Bombs soon fell all over the city, no longer just in the East End but in the fashionable West End as well, hitting even Buckingham Palace. But the buses ran through the raids; it was a matter of pride to maintain their schedules. Workers reported to work each morning despite lack of sleep the night before. The rubble was cleared away, and businesses reopened.

It became a routine every night for the four women to go down to their shelter when they heard the first wail of sirens. After a while they almost became accustomed to the sound of explosions and they were able to read and sleep much more easily than they had been able to at first. The next morning they would go to Stepney as usual, where they worked for a volunteer canteen, handing out food and drink to the battered, homeless victims of the air raids.

Matty and Sarah worked as tirelessly as their younger companions, fueled by the knowledge that if it weren't for Jessica they could have well been one of the crowd they served. Destruction lay all around them, and sometimes Alyssa thought her heart would break to look at the children, hungry and without shelter, and often without parents as well.

Sometimes Claire came to visit Alyssa and Jessica. She had quit her job with her uncle and had become a volunteer ambulance driver. She spent her nights speeding through the destruction to pick up the wounded. Thin and pale, she was obviously exhausted by her work, and she could talk of little but the horrors she saw each night.

With every day, Alyssa's hatred and bitterness grew toward those who were wreaking this destruction. She ached to do more than she was doing now. She wanted to fight back directly, to do something to actually hurt the enemy. If she were a man, she would have joined the RAF. Alyssa thought she would relish meeting the enemy face-to-face in the sky. She wasn't made to stand around and watch.

Jessica wasn't usually as headstrong as Alyssa, but she now had a fire inside that drove her each day. She immersed herself in the work she was doing so that each night she was so tired that even the uncomfortable bunk beds lent themselves to a dead sleep. The chaotic schedule kept her from having to think too much about what she'd lost.

Letting Alan's parents know what had happened had been heart- wrenching for Jessica, and his mother swore she would not hold any memorial for her son because she refused to believe he was actually gone. Alan had been everything to Jessica for as long as she could remember, and now she didn't even have a headstone where she could go to feel close to him.

One day Jessica did not go to work with Alyssa, mysteriously refusing to talk about what she was doing. That evening when Alyssa came home, Jessica told her that she had decided to go to work for Ian Hedley. "I'm going to a school in two weeks to become a radio-telegraphist. Ian says he'll need quite a few of them, and I'm certain I could learn it."

"A radio-telegraphist? You mean, one of those people who sends Morse code?"

"Yes, as they do on ships." Jessica went on, "I simply couldn't bear doing no more than I was. When I think of

Alan—all the destruction—well, I just have to fight back. Handing out food in Stepney isn't enough. And Ian will let me work, really work for him. He won't shunt me off into something trivial just because I'm a woman. That's one area, at least, where women are considered competent to do the job."

Alyssa looked at her friend for a long moment. Why hadn't she thought of Ian herself? She'd been wishing she could do something more direct, yet she hadn't thought of the obvious possibility. Why would Ian want telegraphists? Who would he be contacting at a distance secretly? The answer was obvious: people in occupied Europe. People who were fighting from within the Nazi empire.

Alyssa's stomach began to flutter with excitement. She could do that. Once she had laughed at the idea that she could be a spy. Now it didn't seem so absurd. Death no longer scared her. There had been times the past few months when she would have welcomed it. She was colder now, harder, older in a way that had nothing to do with age. She knew now that she could spy for Ian, that she could risk death and danger. That she wanted to.

The next morning she told Jessica that she wanted to see Ian herself. Jessica chuckled. "I don't know why I'm surprised. The only unusual thing about it is why you didn't join up before I did."

Jessica telephoned Claire and arranged for Ian and her to come over that afternoon for tea. "After tea, Claire and I will discreetly slip out to look over the garden or something."

Work crawled by that day, and by teatime, Alyssa was jumpy with nerves. When Claire and Ian arrived, the four of them sat down for a superficial chat. Jessica poured tea, and they nibbled at the sandwiches on the plate. There were no cakes. Teatime, like all meals nowadays, was skimpy. With the strict rationing, it was almost impossible to get sugar and eggs, as well as any number of necessities.

Afterward Claire and Jessica drifted away, as Jessica had promised, and Ian turned to face Alyssa. His expression gave away nothing.

Alyssa wet her lips. "I want to work for you."

Ian said nothing, merely waited.

"You must plan to have some sort of… operation in France, don't you? I'd like to help."

He gazed at her appraisingly. "Why?"

Alyssa frowned, surprised. "Why? That's obvious, isn't it? I want to stop the Nazis. I want to help end this destruction and pain. There must be something I can do."

"Yes, there is. But you have to be willing to sacrifice to do it."

"I'm willing."

"Willing to set aside your career?"

"Yes. I'm already doing that."

"Your father is in Washington, D.C., isn't he?"

"That's what he planned when I talked to him in Paris."

"His daughter, if she were living with him in Washington, would be in a position to hear all sorts of things which I would have difficulty finding out. She could go to diplomatic functions, flirt with young men on the staff of the German embassy. The South American embassies. Talk to wives and daughters."

"You mean you want me to go home and go to parties? Ian, no! That's not what I mean. I want to do something real, something important."

"You said you wanted to work against the Nazis."

"I do! But I don't want to go back to the United States and sit out the war in safety while all of you are risking your lives."

"Tell me, Alyssa, are you interested in really helping or in presenting a romantic and noble picture of yourself?"

Alyssa's cheeks flamed. "I'm not trying to appear noble. But I have skills you may not have thought about. Skills that would make me valuable in France. I'm an actress; I'm good at pretending to be something I'm not. And I can speak French well."

"I have other people who speak French."

"Like Englishmen," Alyssa retorted.

Ian smiled. "We're working on that. My dear, I fully realize your skills. I might be able to use you in France. But the fact is that we have almost nothing set up there yet."

"Then make a beginning—with me."

"I don't question but what you are willing to risk the danger. More than that, I think you *want* to risk the danger. I don't think you much care whether you die. You've been badly hurt, and you're reckless. That makes you dangerous—to us. We need careful people, those who are concerned with protecting themselves and their fellow workers. Not people who are concerned with derring-do. Not those who are hurt and enraged and trying to get back at what's hurt them."

Alyssa bit her lip. She didn't like the way he described her, but she had to admit there was some truth in it. Perhaps her emotions would make her careless. Still… how could she bear calmly to return to a nation that was not only not at war, but determined not ever to be, a nation that didn't even want to help Britain when the country's back was to the wall?

Ian went on calmly, "Besides, you have something that none of the other people who work for me do—an entrée into diplomatic circles in a neutral nation. Working there might not seem as brave as sneaking about an occupied country, but, frankly, at the moment you'd be far more useful to me. It will no doubt be harder for you. You will have to keep silent about your sympathy for Britain. You will have to smile at the Germans despite your dislike. Flirt with them and feed their egos. You will have to be cheerful and pretend that your mind isn't on the suffering over here. It won't be an easy task, but it is most definitely an important one. Men have looser tongues around beautiful young women, particularly when they've had a little to drink. You could find out a great deal for me."

Ian paused, watching Alyssa. Alyssa stared back at him. This wasn't what she wanted to do, but she realized the truth of his words. It wouldn't be easy. She would hate the inactivity and having to present a smiling face to the enemy. But she could do it. Her chin thrust out a little. She could do it *well*. It would be fighting back in the best way she could.

"All right," she said quietly. "I'll go to Washington."

Chapter 10

Three days later Alyssa left for the United States. Jessica knew better than to ask why she went. Alyssa hugged Jessica tightly, and her heart ached at the separation from her friend. During the past few months, they had helped each other through the worst period of their lives, giving unstinting support and friendship when it was most necessary. They had cried together and listened to each other talk without criticism or advice, only sympathy. They had endured the Blitz. For years they had been good friends, but they were far closer than that now. Alyssa felt like a traitor, leaving Jessica to face the bombs and the misery of Alan's death by herself.

It was odd to be back in New York City. Much as she had always loved New York, she felt a stranger to it now. At nights there were lights everywhere; she'd never noticed before how many there were, nor how bright. She found herself waiting for the frightening screech of the air raid siren, and she had to remind herself that she would not hear it again. After the months of rationing in London, it was strange to walk into a grocery and find bins full of oranges, apples, and grapefruit, or to see butcher shops loaded with meats. There were no buildings in ruins, no homeless, hungry children, no lines of fear etched on the faces of the people. Alyssa felt sick with guilt at being in such comfort and safety.

She stayed in New York only long enough to pack several trunks of clothes for her stay in Washington and to contact her agent. He clucked over her long absence, bewailing the multitude of plum parts she had lost. When she told him she planned not to act for a while, he argued and protested. At last he accepted her decision grudgingly and promised to check around for someone to sublet her apartment.

Alyssa sent a telegram to her father, telling him that she was coming, and the next morning she boarded the train to Washington, D.C.

She was waiting in her father's Georgetown home that afternoon when he came in from work. Three large steamer trunks and several suitcases sat beside the staircase leading to the second floor. Grant Lambert eyed the pile of luggage curiously, but managed not to mention it as he went forward to kiss Alyssa on the cheek. "Thank God you're home. You have no idea how worried I was about you. When you telegraphed me that you were in London, I was sure you'd taken leave of your senses."

"No, I was just... I wanted to see Jessica again before I came home."

"Was it terrible?" He sat down on the couch beside her and took her hand in his. "You look paler, thinner. When I think of you living through that bombing..." He shook his head, unable to express the enormity of his fear for his child.

"I wasn't hurt. Jessica and I always went into the shelter. I was caught out of the house only once—during a daylight raid—but I went down into the Aldwich Tube Station." She managed a teasing smile. "As for being pale, you try living in London for several months and see how much color you have!"

"I don't know. You look different... almost ill."

"Thanks a lot. Don't you know you aren't supposed to tell a woman she's not looking her best?"

This time he accepted her playful dismissal of the subject. "My dear girl, even not looking your best, you outshine any other woman." He paused and glanced toward the baggage in the hallway. "Have you come for a long visit, or do you plan to wear all that this weekend?"

"I've come to live with you."

"What!"

"You said you would be posted in D.C. for several months, didn't you?"

"Well, yes, maybe longer, but—"

Alyssa grinned. "Don't look so dismayed. I'll think you don't want me to stay."

"Of course I do! You know it isn't that. I'd love to have you here with me all the time."

"I can be your hostess, and you'll have someone to escort to parties without causing gossip."

"You'd be a great advantage to me. There's no question of that. But what about you? Why do you want to do this? Is there something wrong? What about your career?"

Alyssa shrugged. "My career has been at something of a standstill the past year or so. I've gotten stuck in the same kind of part. Lately I've begun to wonder whether the stage really holds any future for me. So I've decided to take a break from acting."

Her statement was the farthest from the truth in all of what she told her father, Alyssa was to discover. Over the course of the following months, she used her acting skills more than she ever had before. In the privacy of her father's home, she worried about England and Jessica and scanned the newspaper for every bit of news about the London Blitz. But when she emerged from her house, she appeared frivolous and carefree. At night she often cried herself to sleep, heartsore over Philippe. She was interested in no man. Yet every evening she put on makeup, slipped into a beguiling dress, and went forth to entrance every man she met.

She started attending parties with her father and giving them as well, and she was quickly the social hit of the season. Alyssa was invited everywhere; her presence was said to "make" a party or dinner. She listened carefully to every conversation, committing it to memory—her former script memorizing skills enhanced by the importance of her new task—and, when she returned home, she wrote it all down in a notebook.

After a week, she began to wonder what she was supposed to do with all this information. Ian had told her that she would have a contact in Washington, an agent to whom she could give the material she gathered, but so far she hadn't seen a sign of him. One evening, at a dinner party given by a senator's wife, a young English attaché took an interest in her. He was a handsome man, though his forehead was deeply scored by a wide, flaming scar that his hair only half hid, and he walked with a pronounced limp. He seemed a brooding sort who made small talk only with effort. Alyssa was surprised when he drifted over to the group with whom she was conversing and even more surprised when he outstayed everyone else. She made no effort to encourage him; she had no interest in any man except for the information he could give her, and there was no likelihood of an Englishman giving her the kind of information she needed.

However, he stubbornly stuck to the group through the cocktails and jumped in to escort her to the dinner table, beating out the other single man in the group. Alyssa gave him a perfunctory smile as she took his arm. They walked across the hall into the formal dining room. The man, who had been introduced to her as Everson Blakely, bent his head to hers and murmured, "Ky sends you his regards."

Alyssa raised her head, surprised. "Ky? You know Claire and Ky?"

"Yes. He and I flew together in the RAF—for a while, at least. I was shot down in August." He gestured toward his bad leg. "They won't let me fly anymore."

"I'm sorry." Alyssa had been around Alan enough to know that was the fate every pilot dreaded.

He smiled bitterly. "Got me a cushy job in Washington."

"If that's what you want…" Alyssa replied neutrally.

"What I want and what I do have little in common," he replied. They were almost at the table, and he changed the subject swiftly. "I'd like to see you again. Perhaps lunch tomorrow?"

"I'm afraid that won't be possible," Alyssa demurred.

He interrupted her softly, "My mother raised lavender in her garden."

Alyssa was too good at her job to change her expression, but inside her nerves stood on end. Blakely had uttered the sentence she had been waiting to hear since she arrived in Washington, the code phrase that would establish her contact's identity. "I see," she replied smoothly. "I'd be happy to meet you, Mr. Blakely."

He smiled and seated her, then went to his own place at the table. Alyssa poked down some food and tried to listen to the conversation of the men on either side of her. Suddenly, what she was doing seemed a great deal more real than it had before.

Alyssa successfully hid her impatience when Blakely didn't seek her out after dinner. She suspected that he was testing her to see if she gave away her interest in him or any anxiety. As he was leaving, Blakely stopped to say good-bye to her. Alyssa turned to him, taking a step or two away from the man with whom she had been talking, and Blakely smiled down at her. He looked at her with undisguised admiration, as most men did, but it was relaxing to know he didn't mean it.

"Do we have a date, Miss Lambert?" he asked, and Alyssa gave him a dazzling smile for show.

"I believe we do, Mr. Blakely."

"One o'clock? In the restaurant at the Mayflower Hotel?"

Alyssa nodded her agreement.

The next day she dressed for her date and ripped the filled pages from her notebook, folding them and tucking them into her purse. She ate a pleasant luncheon with Blakely and discreetly slipped him the folded notes. They arranged to meet a week later at a particular party, and he gave her a telephone number where she could contact him if she had something to impart that was too important to wait for their regular meetings.

As the weeks passed, Alyssa pursued her acquaintance with the members of the German, Italian, and Vichy French embassies. She grew more and more skillful at meeting the men who could give her information, deciding who could be manipulated, and milking them for information. She assessed each man, then acted in the way she thought would most appeal to him. With some she was wildly flirtatious and empty-headed. With another, she was a sultry siren. And to others she appeared a perfect lady, calm and beautiful, or a woman of great style and dash. But with each, her goal was the same: to coax information from them.

Alyssa hated every minute of it. There were times when she despised herself almost as much as she despised the men she deceived. Yet she knew she had to do it. Everything she learned could help England in its struggle—and perhaps her own country, eventually.

She met Blakely every week or two, always in a casual way at a party or an accidental meeting on the street, and gave him the material she had gleaned from her sources. Blakely and his superiors soon became aware that Alyssa was excellent at her job. She was cool, intelligent, and an adept actress. Blakely began to direct her toward specific areas of interest to them, and Alyssa began not only to listen to her enemies, but to dig out information.

She flattered a German military attaché into revealing how effectively the Vichy French government was gathering information in the United States for the Nazis. With another member of the Germany embassy staff, she used the opposite approach—pricking his pride by undervaluing German achievements in science—to lead him to talk about the strides Germany had made in radar aboard their U-boats.

She was most adept at discovering the weakest link, the person who could be duped or bribed into giving information, the person who had something to hide and upon whom pressure could be put. Alyssa was a seasoned people watcher, studying mannerisms, looks and emotions to use as an actress. She put these observational skills to use now in analyzing the people she met at parties. She picked up on every stray bit of gossip that floated around, often finding the women's room at such functions a veritable gold mine of information. Alyssa also discovered that men were quick to drop disagreeable bits of information about possible rivals for her affections.

What she found hardest was encouraging men to talk to her without letting them into her bed. She was sickened when she had to allow her various suitors to kiss her or steal a caress. Since Philippe she had had no interest in any man, let alone any of these. She flirted and teased, yet remained eternally elusive. She knew she was at best acquiring a reputation for being a shocking flirt, a 'fast' woman, or a 'tease.' At worst, she knew gossip circulated that she was having an affair with one man or another. It didn't bother her. Being an actress, she was used to such speculation, and there was no one here about whom she cared enough to worry what was thought of her.

Except her father. Alyssa caught him looking at her strangely from time to time, and once he commented that he had heard some unpleasant rumors about her. Alyssa flashed him a smile. "Now, Father, you shouldn't listen to gossip."

He frowned. "It isn't just the gossip. There's always plenty of that about everyone around D.C. It's the changes *I've* seen in you that worry me. You seem... almost hard. Cold."

Alyssa glanced away to hide the flash of tears in her eyes. "Sometimes I feel hard and cold," she admitted.

"Why? What happened?"

Alyssa shrugged, keeping her face turned from him. "Maybe it was what I saw in France and London—the death and fear. I don't like myself for being here in comfort while they're dying and suffering over there."

"Just be thankful for being an American."

Alyssa swallowed and summoned up a smiling, sophisticated mask for her father. "Maybe a man made me the way I am," she went on lightly. "That's what usually is to blame, isn't it?" Alyssa started toward the door. "Sorry, I have to run.

I'm due at a coffee at Teresa Brugman's house in thirty minutes."

Christmas passed, and soon it was the dead of winter. Alyssa snuggled into her long, mahogany mink coat, fully aware of how it set off her dark beauty, and continued her social whirl, struggling to keep her mind only on her job. Trying not to think about London and how Jessica was faring. Trying not to think about Philippe.

That was almost impossible. Hardly a day went by that something didn't remind her of him or that she didn't feel a spurt of longing. She cried less often now; time was slowly soothing the sharp pain of loss. But its passing left behind only dullness and apathy. There was no happiness for her. They had been so close, she had loved Philippe so deeply that it was as if a piece of her was gone.

The first time she met a man from the Vichy French embassy, it was all she could do not to turn and run, so heartbreakingly familiar was his soft, slurred accent. It was an agony to deal with the French, but as the weeks passed, it was precisely that embassy on which she had to concentrate.

"We must prove that the Vichy are working for the Germans," Blakely told her emphatically at a tête-à-tête in an empty hallway of a Washington hotel while hundreds of people whirled in the ballroom beyond them. "Both in Canada and here in the U.S. They're passing information on British ships in U.S. harbors and putting pressure on Canada through French descendants there. They're using French money and French business to influence American businessmen, threatening to cut off their trade if the U.S. continues to aid Britain. Their spies and sympathizers are everywhere; we have to find out who they are and be able to prove it to the Canadian and U.S. governments."

"I'm not sure. I—"

"Alyssa, this is extremely important. We also need Vichy visas, documents, blank passports, rubber stamps, etc., to give validity to the people we send into France. You have to establish a line into the Vichy staff."

Alyssa closed her eyes. Obviously she would not be able to avoid this. "All right. I met a young man a couple of weeks ago. Paul Chermé. He seemed interested in me. I'm not sure what he does."

"Follow him up," he ordered brusquely.

A door into the ballroom opened behind them. Blakely's back was to it; he frowned. "Damn! Who is it?"

Alyssa smiled at him, pretending not to see the woman who had just stepped through the door. "Annette Lowry. We might as well put an ad in the paper as have her see us together."

"Oh, hell. Well…" He raised Alyssa's hand to his lips and kissed it softly. "Is she looking?" he murmured.

"Of course." Alyssa flashed him a sizzling look, but removed her hand coquettishly.

"Why, Alyssa!" a high-pitched voice sounded behind Blakely. "What a surprise. Whatever are you doing out here in the hall?"

Blakely turned and fixed Mrs. Lowry with a black gaze. "I should think that would be obvious, even to you."

"Now, Everson…" Alyssa gave him a light, admonishing tap on the arm. "Actually, we were just about to return."

She slipped neatly past Blakely and started off down the hall with the other woman. "I'm so glad you came out," she whispered. "That man is getting to be such a bother." It was the cover they had agreed upon if people began to notice them together at functions—that Blakely was pursuing Alyssa but she was not interested. It would account for their being together for brief periods of time now and then without being seen together regularly.

"Oh, really?" Annette asked, eager to hear more. "What has he been doing?"

"Well…" Alyssa launched into her planned stories with the enthusiasm such gossip required, but inside she felt nothing.

*****

The next morning Alyssa dug through her invitations for a party at which she was likely to meet Paul Chermé again. Finally she came upon one for the next Friday at Betty Haskell's. Betty considered herself very sophisticated, and as part of her image, she was slavishly devoted to anything French. That would be the place where Alyssa would be most likely to see Chermé. She had planned to go to the theater that night, but she would simply cancel.

Alyssa was lucky. Paul Chermé was at the party. As soon as she stepped inside the door, he spotted her and crossed the room to speak to her. This time Alyssa didn't turn a cold shoulder as she had before. Instead she smiled and flirted, and before the evening was through, she had accepted a date for the following evening.

Her efforts were worthwhile. Once she'd made herself ignore Paul's accent and French gestures, all achingly reminiscent of Philippe's, she realized that she might have a real find on her hands. After a few more evenings of his company, she was sure she did.

Paul was an ambitious man, the son of a good family but one that had always struggled on the edge of poverty. A wealthier relative had paid for his university education and had arranged to get him into the diplomatic service, but Paul found that his poverty put him at a disadvantage. He had not risen as quickly or as far as he had hoped; and because he had to spend so much of his salary on the social life that was part of the diplomatic service, he was continually in debt. Most important, on probing gently into Paul's job at the embassy, Alyssa found that, while he was a loyal Frenchman, he disliked the Germans, calling them boorish and crude, and resented the fact that his government was under their heel.

He was perfect, Alyssa thought, exactly what they needed to be turned into their own agent inside the embassy—so perfect, in fact, that Blakely wondered at first whether he might be a plant by the Germans for the purpose of feeding the British false information. Because of Blakely's doubts, they proceeded cautiously at first, Alyssa pursuing nothing more with Chermé than a light romantic relationship.

Then, gradually, she began to talk about the Germans, feeding his dislike and distrust, emphasizing how they had conquered France. She hinted that she was not friendly to the Germans without telling him what she did. He seemed interested, but Alyssa continued to play the game out, letting her secrecy increase his interest while she elicited vague promises of help from him. One day she hinted that she could use blank Vichy French passports. The next evening, when Paul arrived at her doorstep to escort her to an embassy party, he pulled a stack of blank passports out of one pocket of his overcoat and several rubber stamps out of the other.

"You did it! Paul!" Alyssa threw her arms around him in a spontaneous hug.

"Ah, for that I would steal anything—would you like the ambassador's desk, perhaps?" His brown eyes twinkled down at her.

Alyssa thought of green eyes smiling at her, and her stomach knotted. She stepped back out of his arms and forced a little laugh at his joke. "No, I don't think so. But there is more you could do. I'd understand if you didn't want to; it could be very dangerous."

He fell immediately for that appeal to his masculine pride. "Dangerous? That wouldn't stop me. Actually, I found it exciting."

The heightened color in his face and the sparkle in his eyes confirmed his words. Alyssa smiled and worked her way slowly into the conversation, reminding him of his loyalty to the *real* France, of his dislike of the Germans, skillfully using her voice and words to paint a picture of him as a brave patriot who would be honored and loved later when the Germans were defeated and it was revealed how he had helped to do it. She mentioned that he would be rewarded financially now for his effort, subtly slipping in that fact as though she must mention it but knew it was of little importance to him. By the time she finished, he was hooked.

She arranged for them to accidentally run into Everson Blakely the next day, and after that Paul Chermé went to work for them. He continued to bring out passports and documents and the Vichy visas with the special mark that showed they were real and not counterfeit. Blakely asked Chermé for proof that the Vichy government was supplying the Germans with information, and he showed up with copies of telegrams which the embassy had sent to the Germans, giving information about British ships docked in the United States. Later Paul brought them carbon copies of correspondence filched from a secretary's desk that confirmed the presence of Vichy spies and sympathizers in New York City.

Over the next few weeks, Paul funneled out huge amounts of information. To cover their frequent meetings, he and Alyssa dated heavily. He was the first man in whom Alyssa had shown any long-term interest since she moved to Washington, and the gossip circuit had a heyday with it. In private, their relationship was purely platonic. Personally, Paul would have liked nothing better than to have an affair with Alyssa, as everyone assumed. He found her beautiful, and her cool, standoffish ways intrigued him. But he was a practical man, too. Alyssa was firm about not wanting anything but a working relationship, and he realized that there was nothing to be gained by pushing her.

Early in March Paul invited her to a formal dinner at the French embassy. It was to be given in honor of a group of visiting French businessmen who were in the United States to apply pressure on American businessmen to work to prevent the pro-British Lend-Lease bill from passing Congress. It was a raw, blustery evening despite its proximity to spring, and Alyssa wore her mink coat against the chill wind. As she and Paul stepped inside the embassy, her cheeks had a high color and her hair was tossed by the wind. She smoothed her hair with her fingers, glancing around the room, as Paul came up behind her to remove her coat. She shrugged out of it, the fur sliding off her bare shoulders in an unconsciously sensual gesture, just as she looked across the room at the receiving line and her gaze locked with a man standing there.

Philippe Michaude.

Chapter 11

Alyssa's knees began to buckle, and for a moment she thought she would fall, but Paul's hand on her arm steadied her. "Alyssa? Are you all right?"

"What?" She turned an unnaturally pale face to him; her eyes were huge.

"I said, are you all right? You look…"

"Like I've seen a ghost?" Alyssa offered, her mind beginning to function again. "Something like that." She was afraid she would start shaking all over.

"Who did you see? What is it?"

Alyssa shook her head. "Too long to explain. I'm all right now. Really."

He checked her coat, and they started through the long line waiting to greet the ambassador's guests. In the minutes they waited before they reached the ambassador, Alyssa struggled to talk courage into herself. She didn't look at Philippe again. She didn't need to; his image was clear in her brain. He was slim and tall in his tuxedo, as sophisticated, male and appealing as ever. The thick black hair fell across his forehead in the same way; his eyes were as piercing a green. Alyssa found herself wishing she had worn a different dress, that stunning black Chanel, for instance. Then she was disgusted with herself. Why should she care what she looked like for *him?* It was absurd. Pride—that was all that it was. She didn't want Philippe to see her looking bad, as if she'd been pining away for him.

They reached the ambassador, and Paul introduced Alyssa to him and his wife. The ambassador presented Alyssa as if she were a great prize to the man beside him. Philippe.

Philippe took her hand. She hoped he didn't feel the quiver that ran up her arm at his touch. Alyssa forced herself to look into his face. He seemed a little tired, as if the journey had been too long, and there were new lines on his forehead. He looked more than a year older. He also looked incredibly good to her.

Alyssa felt the familiar warmth spreading through her. Just from seeing him, from feeling his hand on hers.

"Ah, but Mademoiselle Lambert and I have met before, haven't we?" His voice was calm and light, with none of the nerves that affected her. He raised her fingers to his lips and kissed them lightly.

"Yes," Alyssa managed to get out. "It's nice to see you again, Monsieur Michaude."

The line moved on, and he released her hand. She and Paul walked into the large reception room where drinks were being served. "You know Philippe Michaude?" Paul asked, surprised.

"Yes, we met in Paris last year. I was there visiting my father."

"He makes you nervous?"

Alyssa nodded. "A little."

"Why?"

Alyssa shrugged. "Would you get me a drink, please? I'd really appreciate it."

Paul quirked an eyebrow at her abrupt change of subject, but said only, "Of course. What would you like?"

"Anything. Gin and tonic. Tom Collins."

Paul moved off to get her a drink from the bar. Alyssa rubbed her bare arms. It was drafty inside the huge, high-ceilinged room. But the cold she felt came from nerves. Never in her wildest dreams had she imagined that she would see Philippe again. It had been a shock, like meeting someone you thought was dead. But what had frightened her most had been her response. Everything in her had leaped up with joy at the sight of him. She wanted never to let go of his hand. She wanted to feel that well-remembered mouth on hers, those supple fingers on her skin.

She shivered. This was insane. How could she feel this way, knowing what he was? She had battled her love for him for months now and thought she was winning. Yet in one instant, all her hard months of work fell to pieces.

She couldn't love him, Alyssa assured herself. She couldn't love a man like that. What she felt when she saw Philippe was nothing more than shock and a sudden rush of desire. Even that was bad enough. She felt cheap and debased at her undiminishing longing for a man she should despise. Whom she *did* despise.

Long masculine fingers grazed her bare shoulder and arm. Alyssa stiffened. She knew the touch even before he spoke. "Hello, Alyssa. You are as beautiful as I remembered."

Alyssa was careful to arrange her face into haughty, unwelcoming lines before she turned to look at Philippe. She slipped away from his hand. "We haven't anything to say to each other."

"Probably not. I confess I wanted only to look at 'you again."

Her knees melted at the sound of his low, seductive voice. How could she have thought that other Frenchmen sounded anything like him? Her lips were dry, and she longed to wet them with her tongue, but she was determined not to let him see that he made her nervous. Alyssa glanced toward the bar, hoping to see Paul coming to her rescue, but he was still caught in the crush.

"Who is your friend?" Philippe asked, following her gaze.

"Just someone I've gone out with a time or two."

"You have lost your aversion to Frenchmen who deal with the Nazis?"

His remark sent a new kind of fear through her. What if he became suspicious of Paul, knowing how she felt about the Nazis and those who helped them? Philippe might tip off his German friends to what Paul was doing.

She shrugged, careful to keep her manner cool and unconcerned. "It's different when you think yourself in love with the person. Now I know better. I'd never lose my heart to another one like you. I use Paul to occupy my time."

His mouth quirked. "And is he aware that's his place in your life?"

"I've never asked him." Her voice indicated vast unconcern.

"I could almost feel sorry for the man."

"I'm sure that would be a most unusual feeling for you." She wanted to gaze at him forever, to slide her finger across his chin and jaw. She knew exactly how his skin would feel, smooth from a recent shave. Alyssa looked away to hide the desire in her eyes, and her glance fell on Betty Haskell.

She made a motioning gesture toward the woman, and as Betty drew near, reached out to take her hand. "Betty! I was just telling Monsieur Michaude how interested you are in French architecture."

"Oh, yes." Betty glowed at the chance to talk to the handsome Frenchman. "And French furniture."

"French clothes. French art," Alyssa added lightly.

Betty chuckled, and Philippe managed a smile. "Yes," Betty confessed, smiling. "I'm quite a Francophile."

"If you'll excuse me," Alyssa put in quietly. "I'm sure you two will have a thousand things to talk about, and I must find Paul. He promised to bring me a drink, and now I've lost him."

"Of course," Betty agreed happily.

"Mademoiselle Lambert." Philippe inclined his head slightly toward her. His eyes followed her as she made her way across the crowded room.

Philippe had felt a jolt clear through his body when he'd seen her enter the door on Paul Chermé's arm. Alyssa was a vision, her hair wind-tossed, her cheeks flushed, the fur collar turned up to frame her face softly. He'd wanted to sink his hands into the luxurious fur and pull her to him, to kiss her until neither of them could think anymore.

"Lovely girl, isn't she?" Betty prompted.

"Yes, indeed." Philippe flashed the woman—what the hell was her name?—a charming smile. "As it seems all American women are."

Betty dimpled in acceptance of his compliment, and they watched Alyssa reach Paul and tuck her hand into his arm. Paul turned to her, and they smiled at each other. Philippe's stomach knotted. She didn't smile at Paul as if he meant nothing to her.

But she couldn't have fallen in love with someone else so soon, could she? Philippe had seen the hint of sadness in her eyes, the sorrow he knew he'd put there. It made him hate himself, yet he couldn't deny the bittersweet flood of relief to know that she had truly loved him. Perhaps she loved him still. He would be a kinder, more noble person if he wished she was over him. He should hope that she found a new love, one worthy of her. But nobility was poor comfort when he saw her smile at Paul Chermé. He didn't want her to love anyone but himself.

"Mademoiselle Lambert also seems to favor the French," he commented to Betty, hoping his voice was light.

Betty chuckled. "So it seems. Before Paul came along, she played the field. She's left a trail of broken hearts all over Washington. But now Paul is the man she's seen with most often—although I would say that two or three others are not *completely* out of the running."

"She is a flirt, then?" He smiled as if he found the subject amusing.

"Yes…" Betty answered slowly. "Personally, I like Alyssa. I ignore the gossip I hear. Ugly rumors—this city is always full of them. But I think she's what you say—just a flirt."

"Rumors?"

Betty made a dismissive gesture. "Well, you can imagine what they say. That she does more than flirt. There are even people who point out that she has an excessive fondness for the Germans, Italians, and French. As if she were secretly a Nazi. I think it's just that she avoids the British embassy because that young man there pursues her so. Everyone knows she's not interested in Blakely—except him, of course. Who can blame her for liking European men better than Americans? I have a certain fondness for European men myself." She glanced up at him archly, but her expression was wasted on Michaude, who stared straight ahead, his jaw clenched.

At dinner Philippe was not seated near Alyssa, since he was one of the honored guests who sat with the French and German ambassadors, while Alyssa was relegated with Paul to the area of the junior embassy employees. But he watched her, paying scant attention to his companions, and thought about what Betty Haskell had said.

Later, when the interminably long meal was over, he kept watch over Alyssa's date, waiting until at last Paul left Alyssa talking with a group of women and wandered over to the bar. Philippe eased himself in behind Paul, and struck up a conversation with him. Paul, obviously flattered by an important guest's attention, was eager to talk. After a few minutes, Philippe saw Alyssa break away from her group, which gave him the opportunity to introduce her into their conversation.

"I think your lovely companion is looking for you." Philippe nodded his head in Alyssa's direction.

Paul followed his gaze and smiled.

"She is a beautiful woman," Philippe went on, his eyes now on his companion, who was gazing at Alyssa. He could see the desire spark in the other man's eyes.

"Yes, isn't she?" There was the smugness of possession in Paul's tone, and Philippe had to clench his teeth to keep from jerking the young man up by his lapels and warning him to stay away from Alyssa.

"She is your mistress?" he asked pleasantly. "Or is she free?"

Paul glanced at him sharply, then grinned in a very male way. "She wouldn't like the term. But, no, she isn't free."

"Pity." He gave the younger man a friendly smile. "Perhaps you'd better go to her."

His impassive face as he watched Paul make a beeline to Alyssa belied the writhing jealousy inside him. So she was sleeping with Paul. And the others? The Germans and Italians Betty had hinted of? No, not them; she would never—unless she had to. Would she go that far in this dangerous game he suspected she was playing? She was harder now, more cynical; he had only himself to blame for that. But Ian, damn him, was responsible for using her this way.

Throughout the rest of the evening, Philippe kept one eye on Alyssa. It was easy enough after the dancing started, for she was on the floor every dance. Finally, after she had danced with several other men, Philippe went over to her and asked her formally for the dance. She was standing with several other people and could hardly refuse without causing talk, as he had planned.

She smiled stiffly. "Of course."

He took her hand and led her onto the smooth wooden dance floor. She was like a mannequin in his arms. "Relax," he said. "I don't plan to ravish you right here on the floor."

"I didn't think you did."

Alyssa had felt him watching her all through dinner and afterward. She managed not to even glance at him, but it hadn't helped. She could picture him in her mind as clearly as if he stood right in front of her, and it made her stomach curl with excitement and helpless anger. Why did she let him affect her so? Why couldn't she control her trembling, aching emotions?

She couldn't bear being in his arms as they danced. He was too close. It made her think of all the other times they danced, closer still. She could smell the familiar scent of his aftershave, feel the warmth of his hand through her dress. His body was so close to her, it would take very little for his arms to encircle her. Alyssa trembled, knowing that was exactly what she wanted him to do. She refused to look at him, knowing her eyes would roam to his mouth and he would see the hunger in her face.

She wasn't aware that if she had looked, she would have seen the same hunger stamped on Philippe's face. In a low voice, he said, "I want to talk to you."

"Then talk."

"Alone."

"No."

"Why? Are you afraid of me?"

She raised her head defiantly at that, as he had known she would. "No, I'm not afraid of you. I just can't stand to be near you."

He did his best to stay impassive, but his mouth thinned ever so slightly and his fingers tensed on her waist. "Perhaps you would rather I talk to the French Ambassador about the games you and Chermé have been playing."

He admired her acting skill, her calm. There was no hint of alarm on her face, only a faintly puzzled raising of her eyebrows. "I haven't the slightest idea what you're talking about."

"No? Then there's no need for you to worry, is there?" The dance stopped, and slowly his arms fell away from her. He looked at her for a moment silently, then started to turn away.

"No, wait!" Alyssa hissed. "I'll talk to you."

He took her arm and led her off the dance floor and down a hallway. Finding a small, empty waiting room, he pulled her inside and closed the door after them. He turned to face Alyssa. She crossed her arms and stared back at him defiantly.

"What do you think you're doing?"

"I don't know what you mean."

"Alyssa Lambert, girl spy," he went on scornfully. "This is serious, Alyssa. It's not a game, not a play."

"I didn't say it was."

"Leave it alone."

"I don't know what makes you think that I—"

His mouth twisted. "I heard a lot of things about you tonight. Such as that you're having an affair with Paul Chermé. That you have a decided preference for Germans and Italians.

That the only Englishman you speak to is some man named Blakely who pursues you diligently despite your repeatedly giving him the cold shoulder."

Alyssa did not answer, and his eyes burned even more brightly.

"I'm not a fool. I know your opinion of those people. I know why you're socializing with them. Why you might feel compelled to—damn it, Alyssa." Jealousy twisted up and through his fear for her safety, so that the two became impossibly entangled. "Was Chermé lying? Are you sleeping with him?"

"I'll sleep with whomever I choose. It's none of your business."

Philippe grabbed her arms, and his eyes bored into hers. "Don't you realize what a dangerous game you're playing? What they might do to you if they suspect you're spying on them? What it will do to your soul to consort with them, to beguile and charm and smile into their faces?"

Alyssa jerked away from him. "You're being ridiculous. I'm not spying on anyone. I can't imagine what it would accomplish, anyway." She whirled to face him, her face cold and hard. "No one cares. England is doomed; Americans can't be bothered. Everyone is like you—chasing their own interests. No one values honor or goodness anymore. And neither do I. I'm not the naïve, idealistic woman you knew. I should thank you for waking me up to reality. The world as I knew it is over. We are sinking into oblivion, and I intend to grab every bit of life I can before we go down."

He made a derisive noise. "Nice little bit of acting, but I don't believe you. You don't give up without a fight."

"No? Well, I do now. I learned, Philippe; I learned it at your hands. Never count on anyone; they will always let you down. Everyone can be bought; the only difference is the price it takes. I'm not playing the fool anymore. Not for you, not for anyone. Least of all for some pie-in-the-sky ideal. I'm looking out for *me*." She slapped her hand against her chest. "*I* am going to have fun, and to hell with you and to hell with the rest of the world."

"And that is why you're sleeping with Chermé? To show the world how tough you are?" He drew closer. "To show me how little I meant to you?"

"You *don't* mean anything to me." Alyssa snapped, moving back.

"Ah, I see. That must be why you daren't be close to me. Because I am nothing to you." His voice dropped. "It cannot be because you fear what you'll feel if I touch you." He raised his hand to touch her cheek.

Alyssa stiffened. "I don't feel anything for you but loathing."

Phillipe leaned closer, gazing down into her deep blue eyes. He heard the soft catch of her breath, but she didn't move away. This was madness. He knew it, and yet he could not resist. He kissed her.

Softly, tenderly, he opened her lips to his with a teasing tongue. She shuddered and melted against him. Philippe groaned, and his arms slid around her. It had been so long since he had felt her softness in her arms; for months his body had ached to feel her again. Among all the other agonies, that had been the sharpest.

His mouth was avid on hers, as if he could consume her, and her mouth answered with equal hunger. He felt her breath in his mouth, against his face. He felt her heat against his skin. It seemed to him as though he could feel her very blood inside his veins. His hands roamed her body.

Her fingers dug into his shirtfront. She pressed up into him, her breasts flattening against his chest. He ran his hands over the curve of her buttocks and down her slim thighs, bunching up the fabric of her dress, blindly aware of nothing but the need to feel her skin beneath his fingertips. His fingers slid up the smooth silk of her stocking and onto the flesh above, and his hand trembled on her skin. He parted her legs with one of his and

Alyssa pressed herself against him, her fingers digging into his hair.

For the first time in months, Alyssa felt alive, awash with desire, pure hunger without mind or memory. She ached to hold onto the moment. It could have been a day in Paris almost a year ago. The room could have been Philippe's, the long window open to the sounds of Paris and the gentle May breeze, instead of a waiting room in an embassy in Washington, the windows closed against the chill of a March wind.

But it wasn't. She knew it wasn't. It was here and now. And she and Philippe were not lovers any longer but people fighting on the opposite sides of a war. He was a man without scruples. A man she *hated*.

Disgust flooded her, and Alyssa twisted sharply out of his hands. Philippe's eyes opened dazedly, his arms suddenly empty. "What? Alyssa."

"No!" She turned away, hastily tugging at her skirt. Tears filled her eyes. How could she have given in so easily? How could she have responded to him like that? Like an animal, a mindless animal.

"Please." His voice shook a trifle. It was husky and rich with desire. He came up behind her, his hands reaching out to touch her shoulders. "Let me love you again. Just for tonight. No one will know. There's no one and nothing we'll hurt. One time, for a memory to keep me human."

She jerked away from his touch. Her voice was raw with tears. "Leave me alone. I don't want anything to do with you. Just leave me alone!"

Alyssa ran from the room, slamming the door behind her. Philippe started after her, but stopped at the door. He sighed and leaned his head against it. She wanted him as much as ever, but she hated him, too. She would never make love to him again. She was lost to him. He had lived with that knowledge for almost a year now, and he would simply have to continue to live with it. His hand clenched into a fist, and he crashed it against the door.

The door shook in its frame. He wanted to smash something, to destroy the room around him. But he knew that what he really wanted to destroy was the prison he had built for himself. And there was no way he could.

*****

Alyssa fled to the women's powder room to hide from Philippe and compose herself. Shakily she washed the tearstains from her face and combed her hair as best she could with her fingers. There was nothing she could do to hide her flushed cheeks or the swollen look of her passion-bruised lips. She'd left her handbag in the ballroom, so she had no makeup to help hide the results of Philippe's kisses. She smiled a little at the attendant; she hadn't a coin to give her either. Alyssa left the restroom and went to find Paul.

When she told him she wished to leave, he was immediately concerned and accommodating, and they left as soon as he retrieved their coats. Alyssa was quiet all the way home, confirming his assumption that she wasn't feeling well. He chattered on about her health and springtime colds and the cures his mother had used until Alyssa thought she would scream. All she could think about was Philippe. The magic of his touch, the fire of his kisses. No other man could arouse a spark in her, but Philippe had only to kiss her to set off a conflagration. Why was she like that? Why did she let him have such power over her? What was the matter with her that she couldn't feel that way about someone decent? She felt low and cheap.

Philippe had guessed immediately what she was doing, dating Paul and the others. If he told the French Ambassador or, worse yet, the Germans, it would mean the end of Paul. She had no doubt that Philippe would be happy to get rid of Paul. He had obviously been jealous at the idea of Paul's sleeping with her. But surely he could not have become that hard, that wicked. He had warned her about the danger to her—would he really turn around and give up Paul to the enemy, knowing that it would reveal her part in it, as well? After the way he had kissed her?

She said good-bye quickly to Paul when their cab reached her door, and was grateful that for once he didn't try to come inside. She slipped inside the darkened house and turned on the hall light. Her father was out this evening, probably working late at the office. She started up the stairs.

Suddenly a shadowy figure loomed up in the doorway from the kitchen, and Alyssa froze.

"Don't worry," a soft English voice came down the hall. "It is I. I thought it better to enter by the rear door."

"Ian!" Alyssa cried out and ran to throw her arms around him. Surprised, he stumbled a little, but hugged her back. Alyssa stepped back to look at him. "What are you doing here?"

"Business. A rather important conference I had to attend. I won't bother you with the details."

Alyssa grinned. "You mean you wouldn't *trust* me with them. Come in. Sit down. But what were you doing in the kitchen? How did you get in?"

"I let myself in, I'm afraid. Sorry to frighten you, but I thought it best that no one see me calling at the front door. I picked the lock on your back door and waited for you in the kitchen. Why don't we return there? No reason to have the drawing room lights on."

"Yes, of course. Could I get you anything to drink? Or eat?"

"A spot of tea would be nice, thank you."

"Coming right up." Alyssa linked her arm through his, and they walked back into the kitchen. "I'm so happy to see you. Tell me, how is Jessica? And Claire and Ky? How is London? I read about all the destruction every day in the papers, and it wrings my heart."

"London is surviving. There are signs up now on the walls of collapsed buildings reading 'London Can Take It.' And apparently she can. As we all seem to be able to. Jessica is holding steady. She finished top in her class and now works with us. Ky is alive and in one piece, which means that Claire is happy. She continues to drive an ambulance, and there are times when I think she means to save the entire city by herself. She never gets enough rest."

"What about Alan? Has Jessica heard anything?"

Ian shook his head sadly. "No. His name hasn't appeared on any list of prisoners from the Germans. That's not conclusive, of course. His name could have been omitted, or he could have been picked up by a friendly French fisherman and be hiding out in France. But it's not likely, and the longer the time that passes, the less likely it seems. Jessica accepted Alan's death a while ago, but there will probably always be some small glimmer of hope."

"Poor Jessica." Alyssa sighed and lit a match, turning up the knob on the stove to light the burner, and set the teakettle atop it. She came back to sit down at the small table across from Ian. She studied him in the overhead light. He looked older and more tired. She supposed they all did.

"How are you?" he asked, surprising her.

Alyssa shrugged. "All right. Everson tells me I'm getting rather good at digging out information."

"I didn't mean your job; I've seen the results of your work, and it's most impressive. But I meant you, personally."

Alyssa shrugged and didn't meet his eyes. "I'm okay." She sighed. "No, actually I'm not. Not professionally either. Something happened tonight that worries me. I don't imagine you know, but when I was in France, I met a man. He was—well, I fell in love with him. But when France fell, he stayed and cooperated with the Germans."

"I had heard some of the story from Jessica."

"I saw him tonight. He's part of a delegation of businessmen the Vichy government has sent here to talk to American businessmen. Apparently he heard I was dating Paul and had been seeing a lot of German and Italians. Of course, he knows my views on the war, so he became suspicious. I spun him a tale about just having some unbridled fun, but I doubt he believed me. What if he tells the ambassador about Paul?"

Ian's brows rose. "Do you think he will?"

"I don't know. He's. . .not the man I thought I knew. He may tell somebody, but on the other hand, he may hold it over me. And I don't know what to do in either case."

Ian sighed. His eyes were sad as he reached over to pat Alyssa's hand. "I wouldn't worry about him. We'll take care of him, I should think."

Alyssa's head snapped up. "Don't kill him! You wouldn't do that, would you?"

"No, no. We won't do anything like that. What I meant was that he's probably open to a bribe. After all, it's profit that put him with the Nazis, not principle. Correct? I imagine a bit of money will keep his mouth shut."

Alyssa looked doubtful. "You think so? He's not a poor man."

"I suspect he won't object to being slightly richer. He thinks only of himself; he has no cause or beliefs."

"You don't seem very concerned about it."

"I'm not. I think you will be safe from this particular man. With everyone else, though, you watch your step."

"Yessir." Alyssa smiled and gave him a snappy salute. The teakettle went off, and she jumped up to pour the boiling water over the leaves in the teapot.

Ian watched her. There were times when he hated himself. He played with people's lives. Separated them, hurt them. He knew it was for the general good. For everyone's survival, in fact. What was important was that England and democracy survive. Still, there were times when the sacrifices seemed too hard. He shook his head. He couldn't sit here feeling sorry for himself or the people who worked with him. He had countenanced worse things than what had happened to Alyssa Lambert and Philippe Michaude. He imagined he wouldn't hesitate to do worse things yet.

*****

The following afternoon, a frail old gentleman made his slow way down the street. A plain wooden cane supported his steps, and he was stooped over. He had bundled up against the brisk March wind with an overcoat, a hat pulled low on his head, and a heavy muffler wrapped around his throat. Above his mouth was a small white mustache, and white hair peeked out from under the hat at the temples. Wire-rimmed spectacles perched on his nose. He turned the corner and shuffled through the entrance of a small, modest downtown hotel. He took the elevator to the third floor and stepped out, carefully bracing a hand against the elevator door. Slowly he walked down the hall and around the corner, stopping at the room directly across from the doorway to the side stairs. He bent to unlock the door and went inside.

Straightening, he stretched his back and strode across to the window, tossing the cane onto the bed as he went. The hat, muffler, and coat joined the cane on the bed, revealing a head that was covered with reddish-blonde hair everywhere except the temples, and a face and form that were more middle-aged than old. The room had been rented the day before by a Mr. Cranston, a young man with a Midwest accent who was neither the old man nor the middle-aged man hidden beneath.

Ian sat down in a straight chair beside the window. He knew it could be awhile before his visitor showed up. It was impossible to judge exactly when the other man would be able to slip away. Ian pulled a small leather-backed notebook from an inside pocket of his suit jacket and opened it, removing a pen, and began to jot down notes. Ian Hedley was not a man to waste time.

About an hour later he heard the sound of a key in the lock, and the door opened to admit a tall, slender man. He was dark-haired and handsome, with sharp, light eyes, and he was dressed in clothes of a distinctly foreign cut. All in all, he was a much more noticeable person than the old man who had ridden up in the elevator, which was why he had slipped in the side door of the hotel and taken the stairs.

He closed the door behind him and Ian rose. "Hello, Philippe. It's nice to see you again." He extended his hand, and the younger man shook it with a quick, hard grip.

Philippe looked thinner to Ian; the skin of his face seemed stretched to tightly across his bones. His pale eyes were coldly furious. "What the hell do you think you're doing?" he began without preamble.

"About what?" Ian returned mildly.

"Do you know what Alyssa is doing? Or is she acting on her own?"

Ian sighed and sat down. "The less you know about our other operations, the better it is for both you and us."

"It's plain what she's doing! Anyone who knows her would realize why she's consorting with Nazis and collaborators."

"This doesn't concern you."

"*Merde!* It very much concerns me." Philippe slammed his fist down on the desk beside Ian. "My God, what else do you expect me to sacrifice? I have given up everything! My reputation is shattered. Alyssa despises me. I live everyday among people I hate and I have to smile at them. And now you expect me to idly stand by while the woman I love is in danger?"

"I *expect* you to do your duty," Ian retorted. "Just as Miss Lambert will do hers."

"Then she *is* working for you?"

"You know she is."

"Why? How could you put her into this? If I could work out her scheme, so will others. She's a wonderful actress, but anyone who has spoken with her in the past would see the inconsistencies in her views. What happens then? Have you thought of the peril she could be in?"

"Everyone that helps us is aware of the potential risks." Ian sidestepped Philippe's question.

"And how clearly do you believe she was thinking when she agreed to do this? After all that happened in Paris? Would she even have considered putting herself in this position if it weren't for the wrenching her heart just received? How could you do it? You knew how she felt, how wounded and angry she was, and you took that pain and twisted it to your advantage. How could you ask her to seduce dangerous men to obtain secrets for you!"

"Alyssa does this of her own free will. I didn't coerce her. She wanted to do whatever she could to fight the Germans, and this was where she could be the most useful."

"Seducing Nazis?" Philippe sneered.

"I asked Alyssa to gather information for me by returning to Washington and acting as her father's hostess. I never asked her to seduce anyone. I don't inquire into Alyssa's personal life. She does a job extremely well, and that's my only concern. It's all I can afford to care about. None of us can put his or her personal wants first right now; you should know that better than anyone. How Alyssa accomplishes what she does isn't really my affair. If she has sacrificed more than a human being ought to sacrifice, it has been her decision to do it for the good of this world. She hasn't been alone in making that kind of decision. And whatever she has done, to me she is and will remain a lady."

"Of course she's 'a lady.' Do you think I'm worried about her reputation? That I am acting out of jealousy? Whatever she has done won't change her essential goodness any more than it will alter my love for her." Philippe sighed and for the first time sank down into a chair. "It's what it will do to her inside. I know how it feels to smile at these snakes and pretend not to care, to stand by while people are being murdered and carted away. You can tell yourself that you are selling your honor for the better good, hold onto the fact that it's all a lie and pretend that inside you are still the same. But you aren't. It stains your very soul. It slices the humanity from you, strip by strip." Philippe sighed and closed his eyes, his face unaccustomedly vulnerable. "I never want Alyssa to feel as I do when I look at myself in the mirror."

"I know." Ian's voice was kind. "I'm sorry. For all of it."

Philippe's eyes opened, and he gave the older man a half smile. "I know you are."

"Alyssa is strong. She's handling it very well. And at the first hint of suspicion from them, I will pull her out of it."

"Will you promise that?" Philippe stared intently into the other man's eyes. "Will you swear to it?"

"I swear it."

Philippe nodded. "Then that must do. Now... shall we discuss how you plan to steal the French hoard of gold in St. Martinique?"

Chapter 12

Alyssa had difficulty sleeping that night after Ian left. For a long time she had managed more or less not to think about Philippe, but seeing him tonight had broken her carefully constructed barriers, and memories rushed in. She remembered dancing with him, walking through the Bois de Boulogne, sitting beside him at a sidewalk café. She thought of the night she had met him, when she had struggled not to let him seduce her. She hadn't done a very good job. But then she had thought he was dangerous just because he was a wolf—if only that had been his worst quality.

She thought of his green eyes and thick black hair. She remembered his hands upon her body. His lips. Why did she still find him so damned desirable? Why was her heart so rebellious? She ought to hate him. She *did* hate him. He had killed her love. What he inspired in her was nothing but desire. It seemed wrong that desire should be so strong.

When she did at last drift off, she slept lightly, fitfully, with dreams about Philippe that were by turn sensual and scary. The next morning when she awoke she felt drained, as if she hadn't slept at all. She picked at her breakfast, then simply sat, staring into space. What was she to do?

She dreaded the idea of seeing Philippe again. Her heart couldn't stand it; just the thought of him made her ache. She was afraid that if he kissed her again, if he trailed his hands over her body as he had last night, she would succumb to him. The only way she could be sure she would not do so was to remove the temptation from her path. She must not go where she might see him. That meant breaking her date with Paul tonight, for he had planned to take her to Betty Haskell's party, and Alyssa was certain Betty had invited Philippe.

She wondered how long Philippe would be in Washington, how long she would have to avoid him. Some perverse instinct in her made her yearn to be with him as hard as she longed to run from him. Perhaps she should go to visit her mother for a few days. It would be warm in Georgia, the trees bursting into bloom. She could rest; it had been a long time since she'd taken a good rest. It would be a pleasant break—and, far from Philippe, her wayward heart wouldn't have any chance to lead her astray.

Alyssa went upstairs to pack, pausing only to phone her mother to tell her she was coming and to dash a note off to Paul, canceling their date. Her packing was disorganized and jumbled and took far longer to do than usual, but by late afternoon she had finished. As she was fastening the clasps of her suitcase, the doorbell rang downstairs, and moments later the maid stuck her head in the door. "Gentleman downstairs to see you, Miss Lambert."

"Thank you." Alyssa's chest tightened. She told herself it wasn't necessarily Philippe. The odds were that it was not he. Yet somehow she knew it was. On shaky legs she walked down the stairs and into the formal parlor.

Philippe stood by the mantel, studying a Lalique vase. He turned at her entrance, and Alyssa felt the familiar jolt of love and eagerness that she couldn't quite suppress. "Hello, Philippe."

"Alyssa." He simply gazed at her for a moment.

Alyssa remained standing, curling her hands over the back of a chair to hide their trembling. How could he do this to her from clear across the room? He made her want him simply by being. She thought of his hard, lithe body against hers last night, and her breath quickened. "Why are you here?"

Philippe cleared his throat and glanced away. "I came to apologize for what I said last night."

It was the last thing Alyssa had expected him to say, and she stared at him in amazement.

"I shouldn't have said what I did; I had no right to tell you what to do or who to see. I have no claim on you—other than loving you." He looked at her then, his eyes boring into hers. "Even the most despicable of people can love. And I love you. I never lied about that."

Pain sliced through Alyssa, leaving her heart torn and bleeding. "What do you want from me?"

"You know what I want. What I'll never be able to have again. Your love."

"Oh, you have that," Alyssa flung bitterly. "You have that. You broke my heart, destroyed every illusion I had about you. But somehow I can't stop loving you." Tears choked her voice, and she whirled away.

"Alyssa." Philippe came up behind her and put his hands on her shoulders. He kissed her hair, resting his cheek against it for a moment. Alyssa could fell his breath against her scalp, the warmth of his skin, and she longed to lean back against him, melt into his arms. "I love you. I love you every second of every day. From the first moment I saw you. All these months I didn't stop loving you, or wanting you. I'll never stop."

"No! Philippe, no." Tears streamed down Alyssa's face. She wanted desperately to turn in his arms and hold him, give herself to him. "I can't. If you loved me, you'd stop saying this. You wouldn't ask me to—"

"I'm not asking you for anything!" His fingers tightened on her shoulders, then he released her and stepped back. "I know how you feel about me. Being with me would leave you feeling… soiled." His voice dropped on the word. Alyssa turned to look at him. His face was bleak, his mouth harsh. "I hate myself for what I've done to you. I never meant to cause you pain. I swear it. If I could take it back from you, I would. But, please, no matter what I've done, don't ever believe that I didn't love you."

He bent to kiss her. His lips were hard and searching against hers, but he broke away quickly. He turned and walked through the door. Alyssa wrapped her arms around herself, trying to hold back the sobs that beat at her chest. She trailed after Philippe into the hall and watched as he opened the front door.

He paused, hand on the doorknob, not looking at her. "You needn't worry about Chermé. I won't tell anyone what I suspect." He started out the door.

"Philippe!" Alyssa cried, and he turned back to her. Feelings she could not express boiled up in her. "I'm not having an affair with Paul Chermé."

Something sparked in his eyes, and for an instant Alyssa thought he would come back and sweep her into his arms. But he only nodded and walked out the door. Alyssa burst into sobs, leaning against the wall for support. Slowly she sank to the floor, crying. Philippe was gone. Again.

*****

During the months that followed, Alyssa's work was her only refuge, and she clung to it with grim determination. Nothing was too small, too dangerous, or too boring. She tackled each task as if it alone might win the war, and she wasn't satisfied until she turned up the answer to any question Blakely asked. Yet she never felt as if she was doing enough. There must be more. Something more difficult, more important, more immediate.

On December 7, over a year since she had returned to the United States, the Japanese bombed Pearl Harbor. Within days the United States was at war with Japan, Germany, and Italy. The United States was now allied with England, and the Axis embassies in Washington, D.C., were closed. Alyssa knew her job here was over.

Days after Pearl Harbor, Alyssa requested a meeting with Blakely and told him that she wanted to work more actively against the Germans. He tried to discourage her. He had come to like Alyssa over the months of working with her, and he hated to think of what might happen to her if she became any more involved in the clandestine warfare going on between England and Germany. But finally he promised to send her request back up through channels to Ian, now referred to only as Pliny.

Three weeks later, Alyssa received her last visit from Blakely. He was being reassigned to a South American embassy, where he would be more useful to "the organization." And, he went on somberly, he had received instructions that Alyssa was to fly back to England the following week to meet with Pliny.

Alyssa flew the secret northern route, squeezed into the gun turret of a Ferry Command, accompanied by one small suitcase of durable clothes. Her feet were encased in sensible heavy socks and shoes, her body in woolen slacks, a flannel shirt, and sweater, with her long mink coat over it all. Even so, she thought that she would freeze to death before they landed. These northern Ferry Command flights from Canada were so secretive that not even the RAF knew about them, and as sometimes happened, the RAF itself fired upon Alyssa's plane as it approached Scotland. One engine was damaged, but the pilot managed to land safely. They need do nothing more, Alyssa thought, to test one's courage and determination than to send a person across the Atlantic on a northern flight.

She didn't pause to rest in Edinburgh, but took the night train to London, eager to see Jessica again before her meeting with Ian Hedley.

*****

Jessica Townsend sat at her desk in Evington Court, an old manor house a little southwest of London which "the organization" had taken over as their headquarters. She waited patiently, headphones on her ears. She was one of the best radio-telegraphists at Evington Court. She had worked there for over a year now, and in all that time her job had been the only thing in her life. Though she was supposed to work in three-day shifts, each one followed by a leave of thirty-six hours, in truth she spent almost every day there, working longer than normal shifts and rarely taking more than a day off every two weeks.

She straightened, adjusting her headphones slightly. A message in code was coming across. Quickly she jotted it down. "From the Duke," it began, and excitement began to jump in Jessica's stomach. The Duke was the code name for the most important agent in occupied France; no one knew his identity, and his messages were always of the utmost secrecy, reported only to Ian himself. Jessica's fingers flew, taking down the message. It was a listing of military movements—numbers, times, and places in precise detail. The familiar fist of the operator finally stopped, ending with his code name "Fire."

Jessica ripped off her notes from the pad and quickly typed the message. It had been a valid transmission. That was always the greatest worry—the fear that the operator might have been captured by the Germans and forced to send false messages or that the Germans themselves were using the transmitter. To safeguard against that, all messages must end with the operator's code name, and a meaningless word—changed every month—had to be inserted into the message. If the word "brandy" was in the message, it meant that the operator, known as a "pianist," had been captured and was being forced to transmit. Also, Jessica could identify most of the telegraphists' individual styles, or "fists," so that she recognized it if the message was sent by someone other than their own operator.

When Jessica had finished typing up the message, she took it down to Ian. His office was a damp little cubicle in the basement of the house, where Ian sat hunched over his papers, bundled into an extra sweater and suit coat to combat the chill.

He smiled at seeing her. "How are you, my dear?"

"Very well, thank you. I have a message from the Duke."

He reached for it silently and read it, frowning. Jessica didn't linger, but immediately climbed back up the stairs to her attic post. It was a long night, with several messages, and when dawn came, she was glad to retire to the bedroom on the floor below, which she shared with three other radio-telegraphists. She sank down on the narrow iron-frame cot and was soon asleep.

A gentle hand shook Jessica's shoulder, and she flew up, instantly alert. Ian's secretary stood beside her cot. "Viv?" she asked, puzzled.

"He wants to see you." There was no need to ask who. Viv handed her a cup of tea. "I thought this might help."

"Yes. Thank you." Jessica took a sip of the strong, sweet liquid. Standing up, she ran her hands through her hair and straightened her wrinkled skirt. She thought of what her grandmother would say, seeing her setting off for a meeting looking like this, and the thought made her smile. She picked up the teacup and followed Viv, drinking as she went. She wondered why Ian wanted to see her. Perhaps he had a question about the message she'd received from the Duke. Her mind went scurrying back to it, trying to remember any hesitations, unclear words, or inconsistencies.

But she knew as soon as she stepped inside the office that Ian was not going to question her about a message. He gave her an odd, sad smile. Fear clutched at Jessica's heart. What could have happened?

"Please, my dear, sit down." Ian tried to make his face reassuring. He came around his desk and looked down at her. "I hardly know how to begin." Ian had grown very fond of her over the past years, probably as fond as he was of her friend Claire, his own niece. He hated to hurt her, and he knew this news would. Yet it would ease her, too, for it would end the uncertainty with which she had lived for so long. "Jessica, my dear, I have news about Alan."

Jessica's head snapped up. "Alan!" That was the last thing she had expected to hear. Her mind couldn't adjust for a moment. Then a trace of optimism flared in her. "Is he—"

"No," Ian cut in quickly. "No, I'm sorry. He is dead, just as we feared."

"Oh." The anticipation beginning to dawn on Jessica's face faded. "But you have proof now that he is dead."

"Yes, and… his body is here. You'll be able to give him a proper burial."

"What happened?"

"I can't give you all the details. It involved one of our operations. The rescue of a scientist who foolishly enlisted in the army and was captured at Dunkirk and whose expertise is now most desperately needed. A couple of our best men went into Germany to the POW camp and released him—along with several others to help confuse the trail. Alan was one of the officers in the camp."

"Then he was alive!"

"Yes. Apparently he didn't die in the crash of his plane. For some reason, his name wasn't listed on the rolls of prisoners that we received. At any rate, Alan escaped with the other men. They split up into groups. It was vitally important that the scientist escape, of course, and he and one of our men separated from the others. Many of the men just fled wildly on their own. Our other man, a chap named Marek, took several officers with him, including Alan. The fellow's a damned good escape artist; almost made it. They got as far as Belgium, but they were discovered there, and Alan was shot. He was bleeding quite badly, I understand, but Marek wouldn't leave him. He almost literally carried Alan—despite his own wounds—to the fishing boat that took them across the Channel. The fisherman says Marek wrapped his own coat around Alan and held him the whole journey, trying to keep him warm. It was no use. Alan was dead almost from the time they left Belgium."

Tears glistened in Jessica's eyes. "Poor Alan. I—it's so odd. I've believed he was dead for so long, and to find out that he was alive all that time but is dead now—it's—I hardly know how to feel." She stared at her hands. "What about the other man? Mr. Marek? Is he all right?"

"He's alive. He's in the hospital, suffering from exposure, wounds, and near starvation. Still, the doctors are optimistic about his chances. He's a strong man."

"I'd like to see him."

"What?" Ian looked startled, then frowned. "I don't know, Jessica. He's being kept very secluded."

"Ian, I want to see him. I have to thank him for not leaving Alan there, for bringing him back to me. Maybe he could tell me about Alan—what he said, what he looked like, what his last days were like."

"I'm not sure you'd want to know."

"Please, Ian, I'm not a child or a silly, fragile lady to be coddled. You think that working here I don't know about the harsher realities of this war? I don't expect a pretty story; I don't need to be told one. I simply want to know." When he hesitated, she said sharply, "What do you think? That I will reveal this man's identity or tell anyone what he did? Of all the people in the world who might visit him, you know that I'm one of the most trustworthy. A great many more important secrets have been passed through me."

"Of course I trust you. As much as anyone in the world. But Marek is very sick. I understand that he's being difficult. Half the time he's babbling nonsense, and the rest of the time he won't say a word to anyone including our agents."

"Perhaps he would talk to me."

Ian looked thoughtful. "From what I've heard the man is having strange delusions about Alan's death. I suppose Alan's wife might be able to reach him when others cannot. But… are you sure you're up to it? Emotionally?"

"Yes. I *want* to. Please. I'd feel much more at peace. In a way, it would be like saying good-bye to Alan."

"Yes. I understand." Ian sighed. "All right. He's at Long Grove. His name's Stephen Marek. As I said, he's being kept in seclusion—only one physician and one trusted nurse attending him. Delirium talk, you see."

"Yes, of course."

"There's an officer guarding him. Captain Fletcher. I'll let him know you're coming."

"Thank you."

"You'll need several days to make arrangements about the funeral. I want you to take a week off."

"All right." Jessica stood up slowly. She was still stunned by Ian's news.

He took her hand and squeezed it gently. "I'm so sorry."

Jessica managed a faint smile. "I know. Thank you."

She collected her things and boarded a train into London. She sat in her compartment on the train, staring blindly out at the rows of houses flashing past. Alan was dead. She'd known it over a year, had accepted it long ago. She thought she had cried out all her tears for him, but now fresh tears rolled down her cheeks. Jessica didn't want to cry. She had almost begun to feel again, to live again. She woke up nowadays without the heavy grayness clouding her world. She could laugh. She had begun to actually enjoy a few things—a conversation with friends, a crisp, wintry afternoon, a pretty song. She didn't want to sink back into the morass of sorrow.

But the tears came, regardless of her wishes. She tried to remember what Alan looked like; it was harder all the time. She could summon up a picture of him in her mind, but she knew it was really a memory of the photograph that stood on her dresser, not the real, breathing, living man. He had been alive the past year, had lived without her knowledge, without knowing about her. Somehow that seemed the saddest thing of all. She had mourned him, and he hadn't even been dead. Now that he was dead, her mourning was past; she didn't know how to act.

At home she trailed up to her bedroom and opened his wardrobe. His suits still hung there; shoes sat on the floor, hats on the shelf above the clothes rod. The highboy in the corner held his shirts and sweaters, handkerchiefs, pajamas, underclothes. She had been unable to put them away, as if doing so might make his death a fact. She had hoped that somehow, someday he might come home.

That was impossible now.

Jessica ran her hand down a tweed jacket, remembering the times she had seen him in it. Her grief for Alan, reduced to a small, soft ache, like a half-forgotten bruise, now twinged to life again. She pulled the jacket from its hanger and cradled it against her chest as if it were a baby. The faint smell of Alan clung to it—a woodsy cologne mingled with the scent of pipe tobacco. She lay down on the bed, cuddling the coat to her, and began to cry.

*****

Alyssa got off the train from Scotland at the ornate St. Pancras Railway Station, a huge Victorian gothic building that looked more like a palace than a train station, and walked through it to the tube. Brightly colored posters reminded her that "Careless Talk Costs Lives" and that she should refrain from taking the underground trains for any but long distances. She took the tube to the station nearest Jessica's house and walked from there. The streets were empty of vehicles except for the red city buses and a few military or government cars. Everyone else walked or rode bicycles, dodging around the gaping craters left by the bombs.

The city was much the same as it had been when she left it. There were more buildings destroyed, more holes in the ground. But clearing away the debris, and rebuilding, was constantly in process, just as it had been a year ago. The looks on the faces of the people she met were the same, too—still determined not to give in. That fact gave her a lift despite her weariness. England had held out against the Germans all alone for over a year. Hitler hadn't been able to defeat them. Now that the United States, with its vast resources, was in the war, too, it would soon no longer be a question of just holding on. They would be able to turn and fight the enemy. Alyssa smiled, and a woman she passed smiled back at her.

When she reached Jessica's house, no one answered her knock. Disappointed and a little surprised that not even Matty was at home, she was about to turn away when the front door opened. "Alyssa! I can't believe it."

Smiling, Alyssa whirled back around. "Jessica! I was just about to give up." Her smile died on her lips. Jessica had obviously been crying. Her eyes were swollen and red rimmed, and her face was blotched with tears. "Darling, what's the matter?"

"I can't believe you came just when I needed you." Jessica held out her arms, and Alyssa quickly stepped inside the door to hug her. Arm around her friend, she guided her into the sitting room. She was reminded vividly of the day that Jessica had received the news that Alan's plane had been shot down.

"Is it Alan?"

Jessica nodded. "He's dead. He's actually, truly dead."

"Oh, Jessica." Alyssa released a long sigh. "I'm so sorry." She had hoped against all reason that somehow her friend's husband would return to her unharmed. It seemed unbearably wicked that something like this should happen to Jessica.

They sat down on the couch and Jessica briefly told Alyssa what had happened.

"What are you going to do now?"

"They're shipping… the body home to Chilton Dean for the funeral. I must go down there this afternoon and tell Alan's parents."

"I'll go with you."

Jessica smiled faintly and shook her head. "No. You must have something to do or you wouldn't be here."

"I'm going to see Ian, but I can put that off."

"No. Go ahead. Have Claire call Ian and tell him you're here. Claire should be back soon; she's living here now. Her flat was bombed, like Matty's sister, and she moved in, too. There's so much room here and as little as any of us are home nowadays, it seems foolish to keep multiple residences. So we've just retained the arrangement. It helps a bit with the loneliness."

"But wouldn't it help if I were with you in Chilton Dean?"

"Come for the funeral if you can. But I have to see Alan's parents alone. You understand."

"Of course."

"They're the ones who will need the help," Jessica went on. "Poor Cecily, she's always maintained Alan was still alive; this will be very hard on her." She paused, staring into space. "You know, it's strange…this morning I cried and cried about Alan. But I felt a kind of curious release. As if after all these months of wondering and hoping and telling myself not to hope, now, at last, it's over. And I can go on."

Jessica wiped the tears from her face with a handkerchief. She sighed. "Well. I'd better pack and be on my way."

Alyssa watched her friend start up the stairs, tears stinging her eyes. Poor Jessica. It seemed as if no love could survive this war.

*****

Before she traveled to Chilton Dean, Jessica had a stop to make; she must see this man Marek at Long Grove Hospital. From what Ian had said, Stephen Marek might be too ill to talk to her, but she needed to see the man, and she didn't want to wait several days to thank him for what he had done.

She reached Long Grove in the middle of the afternoon. The front desk gave her Marek's room number, and when she found the proper wing, a nurse showed her to his small private room. A captain in dull army green sat beside the door to Marek's room, and he rose at her approach.

"Sorry, miss. No one's admitted in here."

"I'm Mrs. Alan Townsend. I believe I'm expected.'

"Oh. Yes." He looked at her disapprovingly. "They did ring up to say you were to be let in." But he didn't move away from the door. "I must tell you that I don't think it's a good idea to see

Mr. Marek. He's not quite right. It won't be a pleasant experience for you."

"I didn't come here to be pleased," Jessica retorted, irritated by the officer's attitude. "I came to see how Mr. Marek is doing and to thank him. Now, if you'll excuse me..."

He shrugged as if to say it was her mistake. "If you insist. But he's rather surly and, well, a little 'off' acting." He paused, then added as if that explained it, "He's American, you know."

"No. I didn't." Jessica waited for the man to move aside.

Instead, he opened the door and walked into the room before her. Jessica followed him, her irritation with the captain growing. She hoped he didn't plan to stay with her the whole time she was here. She wanted to see Stephen Marek alone.

A man lay in the bed, asleep, one arm flung across his eyes to shut out the afternoon light. The sheet was pulled up to his waist, and above it he wore only a white T-shirt. His collarbone stuck out sharply above the T-shirt. He was too thin, and his skin was pasty. There was a stubble of beard on his chin.

"Marek!" the captain said loudly.

"Oh, no! Don't wake him!" Jessica protested in a hiss.

But the man in the bed was instantly awake. His arm flew away from his eyes and he sat bolt upright. Fierce black eyes focused on the army officer. His upper lip curled with contempt. "You son of a bitch. Get out." His voice was no less vicious for the fact that it was low and hoarse. He flopped back onto the bed and closed his eyes.

"I say! That's no way to speak in front of a lady," the officer reprimanded him.

The dark eyes opened again, and his head turned toward Jessica as he growled, "I don't want any damn woman in—" He stopped, his eyes widening. "Jessica!"

It was eerie. She had never seen the man, yet he had recognized her, had spoken her name as if she were an old friend whom he was surprised to see. But, of course, he had been with Alan in close quarters all through their escape. Alan had probably talked about her or shown Marek her photograph. Alan had always carried her snapshot with him.

Jessica smiled at Marek. "Yes, it's I." She stepped past the obstructive captain. "How are you feeling?"

He shook his head as if that was of no consequence. His eye darted back to the army officer. "Get out of here."

"I can't leave Mrs. Townsend—"

"Please," Jessica cut in, putting her hand on the captain's arm. "It's all right. You may leave us."

"I'm not sure it's safe."

"I'll be all right. I'm positive. Go ahead." Jessica smiled encouragingly.

He cast another doubtful glance at Marek, then at Jessica, but he pivoted on his heel and walked out the door. Jessica turned back to Stephen Marek. He was a dark man, his hair and eyes black, but illness had turned his skin sallow. His eyes seemed too bright and fierce for the pale face, and his bones pressed against his skin.

His dark eyes bored into Jessica. She gazed back, not knowing what to say. She had hoped to feel some connection with Alan through this man, but she did not. She felt nothing except a faint pity because he was obviously unwell.

He spoke, his flat American voice shooting out suddenly and startling her. "Where's Alan?"

Jessica stared, thrown by his words. "Pardon?" she asked finally, feebly.

"Where is he? Do you know where he is? These bastards keep telling me he's dead. He's not. I know he's not. I don't know why they're lying."

Jessica felt as if the wind had been knocked out of her. No wonder the captain and Ian had spoken of Marek's not being quite right. He though Alan was still alive!

"He was shot, sure," Marek went on, not waiting for her answer. His breath rasped in his lungs, panting as if he'd been running. "But he wasn't dead. I put my coat on him to keep warm; it was cold out there on the ocean. He was warm enough. He had to be. I held him. And we talked. I remember talking. He couldn't be dead. He couldn't."

Jessica's heart went out to him, and the faint, cold fear left her. He was simply sick and a little feverish, and he didn't want to admit that Alan was dead. It wasn't insanity or anything close to it. She remembered after Alan's fighter had crashed into the Channel that she had denied that he was dead. "He couldn't be," she had said because she had wanted so badly for the words to be true. Stephen was doing the same thing, although in his weakened state he was confused enough to really believe Alan hadn't died.

"Mr. Marek." She came forward and laid a hand on his arm. His other hand clamped down on it fiercely. "I'm afraid it's the truth. Alan is dead."

"No!" His face contorted with revulsion, and he jerked away from her, sitting up. "You're lying, just like all the others!"

"No, truly I'm not. I wouldn't lie about that. I love Alan. I wish he were alive as much as you do. More. But it's the truth. His commanding officer identified the body. I'm traveling to Chilton Dean to Alan's parents right now."

"No! He was alive! He was warm. I held him right here." He looked down at his arms as if they would somehow prove his words. His head snapped up. His eyes were razor sharp. "You're an imposter."

"Really. Now why would I pretend to be Jessica Townsend?" Jessica asked indulgently, almost smiling.

"I don't know! I don't know what you're trying to pull. It's some trick. You're—"

His hand lashed out and gripped her arm with a strength that was surprising, considering his weakened state. He jerked her closer to the bed, his black eyes blazing into hers. His other hand clumsily unbuttoned her sleeve at the wrist and he rolled it up. Jessica gasped, frightened now, but too stunned to pull away. He revealed the soft flesh of her inner arm. There was a dark, almost heart-shaped freckle there, a mark she had had from birth and which Alan had always called sexy. Marek stared at the mark. Slowly his fingers relaxed, and he rolled the sleeve back down. He released her arm.

"You *are* Jessica." She could see the knowledge growing in his eyes. "Oh, God. Oh, God. He's dead." Marek looked at her. Tears sparkled in the dark eyes. He shook his head. "Christ!" His hands came up, palms digging into his eyes, and his shoulders shook.

Answering tears welled in Jessica's eyes. She had no thought except for his pain, a pain she had known for a long time. She put her arms around Stephen and pressed his head down onto her shoulder. His arms went around her, hard and hurting, and he cried against her.

Chapter 13

The telephone rang, and Alyssa jumped to answer it. She had been waiting to hear from Ian since yesterday evening. A male voice asked for Alyssa, and when she identified herself, he told her to go to an office building not far from St. James's Park and take the elevator to the fifth floor.

Alyssa threw on her coat and hurried over to the building. Inside, a glance at the directory on the wall beside the elevator told her there was nothing listed above the fourth story. She frowned, wondering if the caller had been wrong or had used the American system of numbering floors for her convenience. As she hesitated, a man rose from a bench by the door.

"Miss Lambert?"

"Yes."

"I'm to take you up." He led her into an elevator and told the operator to take them to the fifth floor. Alyssa realized that the entire fifth floor must be secret.

Her escort took her down a hall past several closed doors and knocked on the last one. Ian's familiar voice called to them to enter.

"Hello, my dear." Ian rose and came around his desk to take Alyssa's hand. "How are you?"

"Fine." Alyssa glanced around. "Is this where you work?"

He shook his head. "No, they have me in the basement of an old house outside the city. But this is a better place to meet people."

When he remained silent after that, Alyssa prodded, "You know why I'm here."

"Yes. Blakely recommended you highly, though he added that he disliked sending you into certain danger." A thin smile touched his lips. "That caused some stir here, for Blakely is generally regarded to be lacking a heart."

"And what did you think about it?"

"I think he's right. It's too dangerous a task to ask of any woman, although I'm sure you would be good at it. I won't put you through another list of objections. No doubt you heard quite enough of that from Blakely. Frankly, I don't want you to go."

"But why? I don't understand—if Everson praised me—"

"It's not a question of your abilities; Blakely's words only confirmed what we had already learned about you. Nor is it a question of my refusing to let you do the job. It is my *preference* that you not go. Sometimes I think that I have asked too much of people, that I have sent too many people to their deaths. And you have already given up a great deal."

"I *want* to go."

"I know. And if you are absolutely positive that it is what you want to do, I shall send you to the three people who make the decision on your suitability."

"I'm positive that I want to do it."

A smile escaped him. "Don't you even want to hear what the job is first?"

"I wasn't sure you would tell me."

"I don't think I need be quite that secretive with you. Your security has been well established. What we need is a 'pianist.'"

Alyssa stared at him, confused. "A what?"

"Pianist. A slang term we use for a radio operator."

"Like Jessica?"

"Yes, like Jessica. But Jessica operates here at our base. She receives the messages of operators stationed in France. They're associated with groups of French fighters who are clandestinely working against the Germans. That is what we are talking about for you."

Alyssa drew in a sharp breath. At last what she had wanted for so long dangled before her, and it both excited and terrified her. "Working inside France?"

"Yes. You would be flown in and would hook up with one of the resistance networks. Then you would send back their messages to headquarters."

"I want to do it."

"Don't jump in so quickly," Ian cautioned. "Think about it. This is a dangerous job. The resistance groups suffer terrible risks. They're open to the infiltration of informers and spies. The Germans monitor radio transmissions, trying to find the illegal transmitters, so that sending radio messages is in itself dangerous. A transmission that lasts too long could bring the enemy straight to you and blow your cell, or even an entire network. There's always the chance of discovery, and for someone who isn't French, the chances are even greater. A slip in the accent, a lack of knowledge of a place, an incorrect idiom—any little mistake could betray you. Capture means death, or, worse, unspeakable tortures. It's something I cannot urge anyone to do, and I don't advise a person to do it if he or she has any doubts. That's why I ask you to think about it carefully."

"All right. I will." Alyssa's stomach fluttered at the things he described. She would have to be insane not to be frightened by the prospect, she thought. Even so, she was determined to do it.

"Good. Then, if tomorrow you are still convinced you want to do it, go to this address." He handed her a slip of paper. "It's a residence near Berkeley Square. Be there at nine o'clock, and you will talk to a woman code-named Athena. She is one of the three people who must approve you for the program. If you're accepted, she will work with you on much of your preparation. Answer all her questions openly. She and the others know of your record." He paused. "Quite frankly, I hope they decide against using you."

"One would almost think you didn't like me," Alyssa remarked lightly, standing to take her leave.

"No," he replied, his cool gray eyes a trifle sad. "No, it's that I like you too much."

Alyssa did as Ian directed and spent the rest of the day thinking over the opportunity. The prospect frightened her, and she felt a few qualms over whether she could do it, but neither of those things were enough to squelch her determination to go to France.

The next morning, promptly at nine, she rang the doorbell at the address Ian had given her. It was a small, pleasant house in a nice neighborhood. She doubted that anyone would suspect that it was a meeting place of spies and saboteurs. A tall, spare woman opened the door. Her features were thin and sharp, her eyes shrewd as they swept over Alyssa. She stepped back from the door and motioned for Alyssa to enter.

Alyssa followed her into the small parlor. "Please, sit down." The other woman motioned toward a chair and sat down herself beside the tea cart. "Tea?"

"Yes, please."

"I have coffee, if you'd rather."

"This is fine."

"I am Athena, as I suppose you've guessed. Milk? Sugar?"

"Yes, to both. One lump."

Athena gave Alyssa a carefully measured smile as she handed her the teacup. "One feels a trifle awkward using these names, but it's a necessary precaution. Much better all-around not to know actual names."

"Yes, of course."

They sipped their tea, and the dark, thin woman studied Alyssa. Alyssa was careful not to betray any nervousness under the steady gaze. She knew that her looks would work against her in this situation; the last thing one wanted was to stand out for any reason. So she had left off all her makeup and dressed her hair in a plain roll. She had worn her dullest dress, a simple dark blue wool, and had borrowed from Jessica's closet a tweed coat whose dark mix of colors was not complimentary to her complexion.

After a moment Athena smiled. "You've done a good job of hiding your looks. I'd like to see you in makeup and attractive clothes, just to see how different you appear. Still, it's hard to completely cover up natural beauty. It would be a problem." She switched to French, continuing, "What abilities do you have that will make up for that negative feature?"

"I have experience in secretive work from my days in Washington. I am less likely to betray myself by speech or actions than most Englishmen or Americans," Alyssa answered in a French far better than Athena's own. "I learned to speak French as a child, when my father was stationed in Algeria, and my knowledge was strengthened by attending a Swiss boarding school, where we spoke French in all my classes. Most of all, I am an actress—a good one, I assure you. I am adept at accents." To demonstrate, Alyssa switched to French spoken in the tones of Lyons, something she had picked up from listening to Philippe's valet, Georges. "I am accustomed to playing a role, and I have learned to control any display of nerves."

"Most impressive," Athena admitted.

"I think I could fool many Frenchmen, and I certainly can speak French well enough to deceive a German."

"I distrust an actress," Athena went on in a hard voice. "You have too much need for praise and applause. You will seek recognition, even though unconsciously. That will be disastrous for your network. We can't have anyone playing to the gallery."

Alyssa masked her quick, angry reaction to Athena's words and answered calmly, "I'm not seeking glory. If I wanted recognition and praise, I would have spent the past year onstage, not ruining my career and my reputation doing the work of this organization. I could get glory right now stumping for war bonds in my own country, safe from German bombs."

Athena's narrow face hid any reaction she had to Alyssa's words. She continued to question Alyssa about her reasons for wanting the job, ending with a long and sickeningly detailed depiction of the terrors that would probably await her at the hands of the Nazis.

Alyssa knew she couldn't prevent the sudden whitening of her face, but her voice didn't tremble as she replied, "I realize that. I would have to be crazy not to be scared by what will happen to me if I'm captured. Naturally, I don't wish to be killed or tortured, but I wouldn't think it's any less frightening to the other people who have done it. I have to take the risk. What I could accomplish in France is more important that my fears."

"I'd like for you to talk with someone else, if you don't mind."

"Of course."

The someone else turned out to be a short, thickly built man called Stiletto. His eyes were dark and bright, and they flicked over Alyssa, then away, as they talked. The movement of his eyes gave him a furtive look at odds with his stolid appearance. He talked to Alyssa about all manner of things, very few of which had anything to do with France or the war or resistance groups. Yet, after an hour he exchanged a glance with Athena, then turned to Alyssa. "Are you positive you want to do this?"

"Yes."

He gave a short nod. "You have to go to school first to become a radio operator. Then you'll have two months intensive training by Athena and me."

"You mean I'm accepted?" Alyssa asked cautiously.

"Yes. Didn't you expect to be?" he countered.

"I wasn't sure."

He shrugged. "We could hardly afford to pass you up, now, could we?"

"But what about the third person? I thought there were three who had to approve me."

"You already have the third approval."

"I see." So it was Ian himself who ruled on her suitability. It warmed her that he had already accepted her, despite his words yesterday.

"Are you ready to begin the telegraphy school?"

"Right away."

"Good. There's a new class starting next week. First you have to become a member of the FANY. Athena will see to it."

"FANY?" Alyssa repeated, a little dazed at the sudden acceptance.

"First Aid Nursing Yeomanry," Athena explained. "They're a volunteer organization, rather antiquated, but at least they have a uniform and aren't stuffy about women taking part in military operations. The RAF, army, and navy won't allow it, although the RAF will give you an honorary commission when you finish training. Becoming a member of the FANY gives you a credible explanation for where you are and what you are doing while you're going through training. Also, it will allow you to claim to be a member of the armed forces if you're captured and receive treatment under the Geneva rules. I've never known it to make any difference to the Nazis, though."

Stiletto rose and stuck out his hand to shake Alyssa's. "I'll see you in training camp. Good luck."

"Thank you." She was in. She was finally in!

*****

The next day Alyssa traveled with Claire to Chilton Dean for Alan's funeral, and later the three friends sat up much of the night together, talking, reminiscent laughter mingling with their tears. Early the following morning, Alyssa took the train to Yorkshire to begin her training.

Jessica remained in Chilton Dean another day, trying to support Alan's mother through her stunned grief. With relief she boarded the train that would take her back to Evington Court and her work, carrying her away from the miasma of grief and regret that enveloped Alan's home.

As the train chugged along, she thought of Stephen Marek. After crying in her arms the other day, he had turned away abruptly, embarrassed by his display of emotion, and Jessica hadn't had a chance to express the thanks she had gone to the hospital to give him. Now, thinking of him, she decided to detour by Long Grove Hospital on her way back to Evington Court. This time she would tell him how grateful she was that he had brought Alan back. And maybe this time he would talk to her about Alan.

The same army captain was seated outside Marek's door, and he looked no happier to see Jessica than he had been before. However, he didn't try to stop her. A nurse was leaving the room just as Jessica walked in, and she smiled at her. "Oh, a visitor! How nice.'

"Hello, Sister."

The nurse turned back to Stephen, saying brightly, "Captain Marek, there's someone here to see you. Isn't that nice?"

Stephen sat in a chair by the window, wrapped in a blue robe. He turned his head to look at Jessica and frowned. He turned back to the view. The nurse made a small apologetic gesture and whispered, "Please stay. It will do him good."

Jessica nodded, and the woman left the room. Jessica went over to Stephen. "How are you?" What a stupid thing to ask! It was obvious that he was still quite sick. Though the signs of fever were gone, he was thin almost to the point of emaciation, and his color was poor.

His only response was a shrug, and he continued to stare out the window, ignoring her. Jessica stood uncertainly. The nurse had suggested she stay, but it seemed foolish since he obviously didn't want her here. She wet her lips and tried again, "I see they're letting you up and about now. You must enjoy that."

His head swung around, and he fixed her with a flat, dark stare. Finally he asked harshly, "What is it you want?"

Jessica's lips thinned. "I simply wanted to see how you were doing."

"Why?"

"Why! What a bizarre question! Why shouldn't I? I hoped you were feeling better." He said nothing, and she went on, "I wanted to thank you."

"For what? Bringing you home a corpse?"

Jessica's telltale skin flushed. "You are an excessively rude man. But, then, I suppose that doing something heroic doesn't necessarily make one a decent human being, does it?"

"Heroic?" His mouth curled into a sneer. "I wasn't heroic, lady, just trying to save my skin."

Jessica frowned. He was trying to anger her, she realized, to force her away. "Captain Marek, I don't understand why you're doing your best to make me dislike you. Or why you'd like to think that you are less than you are. But I happen to know what you did. You rescued Alan from a prisoner-of-war camp, and you tried your best to save his life. They told me how you put your own coat around him to keep him warm. How you carried him to the boat and pulled him on. You could have left him there for the Germans to pick up. *That* would have been saving your skin."

"Well, it didn't do much good, did it?"

"It did *me* quite a bit of good. And his parents as well. At least we were able to bury him. At least we know that his body wasn't left lying in a foreign country at his enemy's mercy. That means a great deal to a family." She squatted down beside his chair. This close she could see the ache that dulled his black eyes. Jessica laid her hand on his arm, wanting to comfort him. His skin jumped beneath her touch, but he didn't pull his arm away. "I meant it when I said I wanted to thank you. You see, I thought Alan died over a year ago when his plane was shot down in the Channel. All that time I've thought his body was lost in the water, and that was very painful to me. But I no longer have to live with that. You brought Alan home, and we were able to bury him in the family plot at St. Crispin's. We can go to visit his grave. He's no longer lost to us."

Stephen stared at her for a long time. Slowly his other hand came up and covered hers. They remained in that position for a long moment, neither one speaking.

Marek removed his hand and said gruffly, "You're a kind woman. Townsend said you were."

"Did he?" Jessica smiled. "I'm glad he thought so." She patted his arm. "I know you're tired. I shan't stay any longer. But I would like to come back to see you. May I?"

He nodded.

"Thank you. I'll be over my next free day. Perhaps in a week." It was clear to Jessica that Stephen was suffering as much mentally and emotionally as he was physically. He needed something to bring him back to life, and visitors were the only thing Jessica could think of that would help. She owed him that.

"Could I bring you anything to read? Puzzles? Cards?"

He shook his head. "They have stuff like that here. I'm not interested."

"You're a hard case." She smiled at him. "All right, then. I shall simply bring my sparkling conversation. But in the meantime you must get better so that you can enjoy it properly."

For the first time, a faint smile crossed his face. "Yes, ma'am."

"Good-bye, then, until next time."

"Good-bye." Jessica was halfway to the door when Marek spoke again. "Mrs. Townsend?" She turned inquiringly. "Thank you."

Jessica smiled. "You're very welcome. And you must call me Jessica."

"Jessica."

*****

He wouldn't have admitted it, but Stephen woke up each morning hoping that Jessica might come that day. He told himself it was crazy. She had said it would be a week—and that was presuming that she'd meant it and wouldn't forget. He didn't want to think about it. He didn't want to feel the tingle of anticipation.

On the third day, early in the afternoon, his door opened, and instead of the heavy rubber-soled tread of the nurse, he heard the light tap of a women's shoes. He whipped around in bed to look at the door, an uncontrollable smile already forming on his face. "Jessica!"

"Hullo." She smiled back at him. She wore a simple tweed coat and a small hat over her thick, curling hair.

"I didn't expect you this early." But he had hoped it. Stephen turned, swinging his legs out of bed. He had started wearing a robe all day the past few days, not wanting to be caught awkwardly without one—just in case she did come.

"I work not far from here," Jessica explained, "and I realized it wouldn't take much time to pop over to see you."

She walked farther into the room, making a negating gesture as he started to get out of bed. "Oh, no, don't get up. It's quite all right. I'll just move one of these chairs closer."

Stephen started to protest that he wasn't too weak to sit in one of the chairs by the window with her, but he realized that it was probably better if he kept this much distance between them. The two chairs together were too casual, too close. They bespoke familiarity, and she wouldn't want that. *He* wouldn't want that. She was Alan's wife and only paying a duty call. He preferred it that way.

Jessica moved the lighter chair closer to the bed and sat down. "Well, you're looking better. Sister told me you were on the mend."

He shrugged. "I don't feel like a drowned cat anymore."

"I'm glad."

A silence fell between them. Stephen tried to think of something to say. He shouldn't feel happy to see her, he told himself, shouldn't have this effervescence bubbling in his chest. She was Alan's *wife*, damn it. Her husband had died in his arms, for Christ's sake.

"I've seen you before," he said abruptly, simply to break the silence and his thoughts.

Jessica looked surprised. "Really? Where did we meet?"

"We didn't meet. I saw you from across the room. Almost two years ago at the Savoy. You were eating lunch with Alyssa Lambert and another woman."

"You know Alyssa?"

He shook his head. "I used to be in New York some. I've seen her a couple of times onstage."

"Of course. You are an American, after all." Jessica frowned, trying to recall the lunch about which he spoke. Her brow cleared. "Oh, I remember! It was just before Claire got married. You were the man who was staring at us."

His grin was a little sheepish and utterly endearing, like a small boy found out. "Yeah. That was me. Finesse was never my strong suit."

She smiled. "It's all right. I've been Alyssa's friend long enough that I'm used to men staring at us when I'm with her."

Stephen wanted to tell her that it hadn't been Alyssa Lambert he'd been watching that day, but he let it slide. It wasn't the sort of thing you said to a grieving widow. Instead, he went on, "I recognized you then when Alan showed me your picture." Stephen glanced away as he said it; he still had difficulty saying Alan's name, particularly to her. He'd wronged her, failed her, even worse.

"Did he talk about me?" Jessica asked almost shyly.

Stephen gave a soft grunt of amusement. "He talked about almost nothing else." It was true. Alan had hung onto her picture as if it were a talisman and talked about her constantly, almost as if his love for her would insure his returning to her safely. He had told Stephen about her ladylike demeanor and the hidden sense of mischief, her engaging laugh and the beauty of her wide, grave eyes. He'd even spoken of more intimate things, thought Stephen wouldn't tell Jessica that. He doubted any woman would want her husband describing the beauty of her breasts, covered in a light dusting of freckles, or the softness of her skin, or the little sigh she made when she reached satisfaction—no matter with how much love it had been revealed.

But, looking at her now, Stephen remembered the things Alan had said, and the thought tightened his loins. Not for her particularly, he told himself. It was just that it had been a long time since he'd been with a woman, any woman. But he knew that wasn't true. He was trying to convince himself because he knew he shouldn't want her. Must not want her. She was Alan's wife.

"How was he? How did he look?"

Stephen gave her a quick glance, and she straightened, generations of breeding suddenly showing in her. "Was it bad?" she asked quickly. "You can tell me; I won't cry or faint."

"I didn't imagine you would." He smiled. He'd found out a long time ago how tough English women were under their porcelain exteriors. "It wasn't bad. He hadn't been tortured or anything. He was just thin—they're poorly fed. And jumpy."

"He wasn't the sort of man who would take well to being locked up."

"No, he wasn't. But he had survived it. He was very eager to come home to you."

They talked some more of Alan, of how his plane had crashed and he had survived, his yellow inflatable 'Mae West' keeping him afloat until he washed ashore in Brittany. Alan had tried to get back to England, but the Germans had caught him almost immediately and sent him to a stalag. Stephen talked a little about the escape from the prisoner-of-war camp, but that was a topic he tried not to think about, and Jessica was astute enough to let the subject drop.

"Tell me, how did you get involved in all this?" she asked. "Being an American, I mean. You must have joined before the United States entered the war."

"I was a foreign correspondent for a New York newspaper, covering the war, and I was with the British Army when it was trapped at Dunkirk. I was rescued along with the others—by an old scow that looked as if it couldn't have made it across the Channel, let alone get back. The skipper was a tough

white-haired man from Essex. His grandson was in the navy."
He shrugged and offered her a deprecating smile. "I suppose his
example must have inspired me. When we got back, I decided to
join up."

Jessica smiled at him. "For my sake, I'm glad you did." She
glanced at her watch and sighed regretfully. "I must get back to
work. But I've really enjoyed getting to talk to you. Is it all right
if I come again?"

"All right! Are you crazy? Of course. I'd like it very much."

"Good. So would I." She smiled again. He felt as if the sun
had bathed him in warmth. "Then I'll see you in a few days.
Good-bye."

"Good-bye."

Jessica's step was light as she left the hospital and walked
toward the train station. She looked forward to coming back
here. The chat had been a pleasant break in the grim routine of
her work and… well, there was something very nice about
Stephen Marek.

*****

Alyssa spent the next six months stuffing so much
knowledge into her head that sometimes it made her dizzy. First
she attended radio telegraphy school, the basis of all her work in
France. Alyssa, who was used to excelling in all her endeavors,
worked long, hard hours on her telegraphy skills, both learning
and practicing them. But when she had mastered that, she found
that it was only the beginning. She moved on to a camp buried in
Hampshire and there, with ten men and two other women, was
taught the arts of "ungentlemanly warfare" by Stiletto himself.
She was shown how to use a knife—delicately, as Stiletto
described it—to kill a man. She learned to slip it between the
ribs and upward into the heart or to thrust quickly down inside
the protective bone ring of the collarbone or to draw it in a sharp,
deep arc from ear to ear, killing without a sound. She learned to
knee an enemy in the groin as she smashed her hand, palm up

and flat, into the man's jaw. Every day she practiced at the pistol range until her aim was perfect.

She and her group were taught to parachute from an airplane in case the plane carrying them to their destination was unable to land, using stationary balloons to practice their jumps. Then they progressed to "blind drops"—jumping from moving aircraft in the frightening darkness of the night.

Stiletto described ways to fashion a weapon from anything at hand and how to act under interrogation—to subdue their nerves and remain calm, to keep themselves from being rattled, and to stick steadfastly to their stories. Time after time he ran them through drills of dummy Gestapo questioning. At the end of the camp, he tested them by putting each one through a long and arduous grilling, lights blazing in their eyes and questions barked at them in rapid, harsh succession. Alyssa excelled at this part of the training, yet she and everyone else knew with uneasy certainty that these fake interrogations held nothing of the terror of a real questioning by the Gestapo.

The physical training was grueling, but it was not all Alyssa had to learn. Though she was well grounded in the basic radio telegraphy skills, she also had to be able to transmit quickly and with accuracy, even under conditions of stress. The German detection devices could zero in on the radio signals with incredible swiftness, and even the slightest mistake in transmitting could lead to disastrous errors.

Alyssa learned coded abbreviations for commonly used signals, since these took up less time to transmit. There were definite, inflexible rules regarding how she was to make contact with other agents, networks, and home bases, and Alyssa had to know them by heart. She memorized each regulation, each code, and had to spout them back whenever questioned, even after a day spent in rigorous field exercises or a night spent without sleep.

At last, one day late in May, Stiletto called her into his office in the main building and said, "Pack your bags."

"What?" Alyssa's breath caught. Were they booting her out? Or was it...

"You're leaving for London tomorrow. It's time; you're ready for the final step."

Chapter 14

Jessica visited Stephen often at the hospital. At first they talked about Alan and the war, but soon they moved on to themselves and their pasts. They discussed their families and where they had grown up, their likes and dislikes, and the thousands of bits and pieces that made up a person. Jessica found out that Stephen liked Humphrey Bogart movies best and that Katherine Hepburn was his favorite female star, whereas she adored Laurence Olivier and thought Hedy Lamarr the most beautiful woman in the world. He told her that he was from Chicago, and she laughed and asked if he knew any mobsters. She described her parents' comfortable old country home in Kent and her swarm of sisters, and he chuckled over her stories, as she had meant him to.

She brought him books, magazines, games, and jigsaw puzzles. She wheeled him into the solarium. As he grew stronger, she walked with him up and down the halls until it seemed that they had explored every inch of the hospital. It warmed her to see him growing better almost daily, and it made her proud to know that her visits had helped—though she enjoyed the visits so much that there were times when she wondered whether she came for Stephen's sake or for her own.

Soon it was apparent that Stephen had recovered sufficiently that he no longer needed to be in hospital, although he wasn't well enough to return to duty. Jessica knew he would improve more quickly away from the hospital if he had someone to care for him. She would have volunteered for the job herself, but she was bound to her work. Then she struck upon the happy idea of sending him home to her parents in Kent for a few weeks of recovery.

"No, I couldn't impose," Stephen protested at first.

"It wouldn't be an imposition. They'd love for you to come. My family's all girls, and Dad would adore having another man around to talk to. The house is awfully lonely for my parents—only my youngest sister, Lizzie, is there now, and they're used to a whole houseful of children. And don't worry, Mum won't smother you. She's a dear, but quite eccentric. An artist, you see; she writes and illustrates children's books. She lets everyone go his or her own way and never fusses or pries."

"It's not that. I'm sure I'd enjoy it. But they couldn't want to have a stranger foisted on them."

"Don't be silly. They're dead bored down there, with so many people gone to the war. They'd be delighted. You must go!" she ended fiercely.

Stephen smiled. He probably would have done anything when she looked at him like that, her cheeks high with color and gray eyes bright. Not for the first time he wanted desperately to kiss her. But, as always, he shoved the impulse down to the secret, locked-away place inside of him and said only, "All right. If you're that set on it."

"I am."

So he went down to Chilton Dean on the train, wearing the uniform that now hung awkwardly on him. Jessica's mother greeted him at the depot and drove him home in their great old Bentley, using up most of their ration of gas for the week. Stephen stayed with them for two weeks. Jessica's mother wrote her that he had charmed her father by listening to his tales of farming with grave attentiveness, that he teased and flirted with Liz, who now adored him, and that she herself thought him a thoroughly handsome young man. Jessica understood him to be practically a member of the family now, and it made her chuckle.

When she saw Stephen again on his return to London, it was obvious that the rest in the country had been good for him. He was a bit less lean, and the sallowness of ill health was gone. His stance was straighter, his face less scored, and he moved with a new strength and agility. She hadn't realized that he had such power and grace, Jessica thought with some amazement. And though she had seen the good looks that were latent in his bone structure and vivid dark eyes, she hadn't been able to guess how very attractive he would turn out to be. She noticed that when they went out, more than one woman turned to look at him. Even Claire, normally so wrapped up in Ky and her ambulance work that she could see nothing else, remarked that he had that sort of sexy American look, a little tough and deliciously illicit. For some reason, Jessica felt a sort of pride, as though Stephen Marek were one of her pet projects.

He wasn't yet physically up to resuming the dangerous rescue operations he had been involved in before, so headquarters gave him a temporary desk job in London, acting as a liaison between the British organization, for which he had worked for two years, and the new clandestine American operation, the OSS. He was set up in a charming old house in Kensington, where several of the American officers working with him were housed.

Often when Jessica took her day's leave, they went out together to the cinema or dancing at Hammersmith Palais. Other times they simply walked through the cold, fog-bound streets of London, talking.

The bombing raids still came, the incendiary bombs crashing into flames, the land mines floating down on the end of a huge parachute and sometimes tangling in trees or electric wires. There weren't as many raids as in the beginning, nor were they usually as heavy, and not as many people ran out to their shelters as they once had. At the Palais, most of the couples simply kept on dancing, yet Jessica still felt a clutch of fear when the sirens sounded and the heavy thud of bombs began. Stephen soon learned that and was quick to take her to an air raid shelter when the bombs were close. One night they sat with others in the crypt of St. Martin in the Fields, by Trafalgar Square, and another time they went down into a deep tube station, where many families spent the night, bringing down bedding and food.

But usually the bombs weren't close, and Jessica and Stephen felt no need to move to the shelters. The flare of bombs in the distance, the shriek of sirens, the probing beams of the searchlights through the night sky were hardly noticed.

Jessica saw Stephen almost every week, and it gave her something pleasant to look forward to in the midst of her intense, grinding work. He wasn't an easy man. Sometimes he was moody and silent, and often she would turn to find him watching her with a dark expression she couldn't fathom. But at other times he made her laugh. He told her stories about his family and friends and the things he had done, all far removed from the war, and he had a dry, witty delivery, usually unsmiling, that caught her unawares and was all the funnier for its surprise.

It was fun simply to have a masculine presence beside her after all this time. He would putter about her house, fixing up all the little things that had broken or come undone. Matty and her sister had gone to work full time at a munitions factory and had gotten a flat near there, and with Alyssa away on training, the house had grown lonely. It was far less lonely with Stephen there. She would brew him a cup of the strong black coffee he liked, and she would sip her own tea, watching him, and think how marvelously contented she felt.

It seemed almost a sin to feel this happy, this pleasant, with Alan dead and the world a shambles around them. But she wasn't willing to give up her friendship with Stephen because of a few vague twinges of guilt. One thing she had learned in this war was to savor the moment as it came, not regretting, not thinking ahead, for the moment was all that any of them really had.

*****

Alyssa returned to London, where she stayed with Athena, and Athena led her through the last-minute preparations for landing in France. She gave Alyssa a packet of pills, with careful instructions on how to use each kind. One sort would keep her awake and another would make a person fall asleep. Another kind would make her temporarily ill if she needed to pretend to be sick. Most important of all was the potassium cyanide capsule which she could carry inside her cheek and which would not dissolve in her mouth or in her stomach, if swallowed. But if she chewed the pill, the deadly poison inside would kill her in a matter of moments. It was to be used in case of capture so that she could die instead of facing the Gestapo interrogation, if she wished.

Athena brought in an expert in French to work with Alyssa on her accent. The rest of the time Athena, who had lived in Paris for many years, used pictures and a map to familiarize Alyssa with the city, so that she would appear to be a native. She told Alyssa of local regulations, habits, gestures, and mannerisms. She provided Alyssa with a set of clothing, all actual French clothes taken from refugees. She even added verisimilitude in the form of a subway token from the Métro in the pocket of a dress and a receipt from a Paris restaurant in Alyssa's handbag. For days Alyssa walked, talked, and dressed the part, with Athena and the voice teacher watching her like a hawk, correcting her if she stood wrong or let slip an Americanized vowel or poured out her coffee incorrectly. And all the time Athena checked her on the codes, the map of Paris, the rules, the best responses to all sorts of situations.

Then, at last, one afternoon in early June, Athena came into the room where Alyssa was conversing with her dialect coach and asked Alyssa to join her in the parlor. Alyssa's heart began to beat faster. There was something different in Athena's manner. She followed the other woman into the parlor, closing the door behind them. Athena turned to face her.

"You have been assigned to the Paris network known as the Rock. Your code name will be Cleopatra. You are flying into France tonight."

*****

"Cora will sing in February."

This phrase, inserted after a Tchaikovsky concerto in the regular BBC programming, notified a small group of people in Paris that they would be receiving a radio-telegraphist the following evening at a certain secret field two hours' walk from the city.

The next night a heavy British Lysander touched down on the short, rough landing strip lined with lanterns for the pilot's guidance. The plane bounced and jolted to a halt, and Alyssa crawled out without looking at or even speaking to the pilot. It was standard practice for the pilot to know nothing about the peculiar nighttime missions he was called upon to make or the passengers he dropped off and picked up. He waited only until Alyssa was far enough away before he took off again.

Two people waited at the edge of the clearing for Alyssa, dark lumps silhouetted against a slightly lighter sky. One held a lantern, which he now extinguished. They hurried to put out the other lanterns along the landing strip. The fewer strange lights around at night, the better for everyone concerned. Alyssa joined them. As she grew closer, she could see that one of the figures was a woman and the other a man, but even a foot away she couldn't clearly discern their features. The man reached out a hand to shake hers and introduced himself as "le Chêne." The Oak. Alyssa replied that she was "Cleopatra." The woman volunteered nothing. The man made a movement of his head and said for Alyssa to follow, then set out across the field, carrying the lanterns. Alyssa followed, and the woman brought up the rear.

They reached a copse of trees and stowed the lanterns in a hiding place in the midst of several bushes, then continued silently onward. Alyssa stumbled along behind the man as they tramped through fields and trees, never using a road and rarely even a path. This almost moonless night was the best time for flying because the plane would not be outlined against the sky. It was also a good night for creeping about among the shadows, but not as good for walking, especially on unfamiliar ground. Alyssa kept thinking about what would happen in she stepped in a hole or twisted her ankle. Would she become next to useless before her real work had even begun?

She was relieved when they reached the outskirts of the city. She was more sure of herself on pavement, although she knew that the city was more dangerous than the open country. A curfew was in effect and Germans soldiers patrolling to enforce it—and there was less room to hide.

Alyssa and her guides walked quickly now, staying to the inside of the sidewalks, close to the buildings, and taking narrow, winding back streets. Alyssa had spent a good deal of time in Paris over the years, and had had many hours of instructions with the Paris street map, but already she was hopelessly lost.

When they turned a corner and spotted two German soldiers on patrol a block in front of them, they slipped back around the corner and ran down the block on their tiptoes to avoid noise. They continued cautiously up another street.

A few blocks later, the woman vanished into the dark night, and Oak beckoned Alyssa to follow him. He led her down a narrow alleyway, and at the end of the block stopped and peered out at the cross street. A military car roared past them, and they flattened themselves against the wall, mingling with the shadows. Oak stuck his head out again and motioned to Alyssa. They darted across the street. Two blocks later they turned down yet another small street. Alyssa was beginning to wonder if they would reach their destination before dawn when at last they climbed a small hill and stopped in front of a door.

Alyssa's companion pulled out a key to unlock the door, and they climbed the stairs on tiptoe to the third floor, where he opened a door and motioned her inside. A middle-aged woman slept on the couch. Oak pointed down the hallway and Alyssa tip-toed past him into a small bedroom. In the dim light she could see only a window and the rectangular shape of a bed. Gratefully she slipped off her shoes and lay down atop the covers. Within seconds she was asleep.

*****

The rattle of pans in the kitchen awakened Alyssa. She slipped to the door and opened it a crack to peek out. She could see nothing, only a small hall and a portion of the living room beyond. Suddenly the door across from her opened, and a man stepped out. He nodded at her, smiling, and Alyssa thought he must be the man who had escorted her last night. "My wife is preparing breakfast. Come." He nodded toward the kitchen.

Alyssa joined them in the kitchen, and the man introduced Alyssa to his wife. "I am Jules Roffignac. This is my wife, Odette. You are to be my wife's cousin up from the country to seek work. We are the only ones whom you will know by anything but a code name. But since you are to live with us, we cannot have you calling your cousins 'Oak' and 'Lace,' now can we?"

Alyssa smiled and shook her head. Last night he had seemed a grim man, but this morning he was pleasant. There was even a slight twinkle in his eyes. "The name on my identification papers is Yvonne Pitot," Alyssa said, bringing out her papers to show them. Jules studied them carefully, nodding his head in approval.

"Very good papers. Very good. The first one they sent us had papers so bad they looked as though a child had made them. The man would have been picked up in minutes if anyone had seen them. We had to steal him some new ones."

Alyssa didn't ask what had happened to 'the first one.' She didn't want to know.

Odette set down a pot of coffee on the table and a plate of buttery croissants. Alyssa's stomach rumbled hungrily at the smell. She had had almost no supper last night; she'd been too nervous. "Are you French, mademoiselle?" Odette asked shyly.

Alyssa smiled. "No, but thank you for thinking it."

"You speak very well."

"Thank you."

Jules soon left for work, and Odette suggested that Alyssa accompany her to the market. A frisson of fear ran up Alyssa's spine at the thought of walking out into Nazi-held Paris in broad daylight. But she squared her shoulders and replied that she would be happy to go along. The sooner she became reacquainted with the city, the better.

They walked four blocks to the market and Alyssa watched Odette buy vegetables and fruits. As they made their way back, Odette stopped to purchase a long, thin loaf of bread. Alyssa unobtrusively observed everything around them. She had seen no German soldiers yet, but as they started to cross the street to their apartment building, an open car drove past them, two men in gray uniforms inside it. Odette and Alyssa waited on the curb for it to pass, eyes lowered. Alyssa's stomach was a tangle of nerves. She wondered if she would become less frightened with time.

Alyssa's transmitter, hidden in a small suitcase, and her bag of clothes were dropped that night, and Oak retrieved them. The next evening at twelve midnight, she made her first transmission to "Mother," the code name for headquarters in England: She had landed safely, and the Rock network needed money and guns.

*****

Jessica rose and stretched wearily. It had been a long night; several messages had come in, and her back ached from sitting in the chair. She had received her first message from Cleopatra, which had given her heart a special lift. Unfortunately, the message she had received from the Duke a few hours later had brought her down swiftly. He reported that there was a traitor within the Rock network, which meant Alyssa was in danger already.

Jessica left the old house and walked the mile to the train station. The lovely June morning lifted her spirits. It was the beginning of her thirty-six-hour pass after three straight days of work, and she was returning to her house in London. Jessica smiled. She would see Stephen tonight.

Stephen arrived at the house that evening, handsome in his army uniform. A smile broke over his face when Jessica opened the door, and her spirits soared. She was more than ready for an evening of fun.

She took his hand. "I'm so glad I know you."

He glanced at her in surprise. "What brought that on?"

"I don't know. The evening's pretty and warm, and I'm awfully happy to be going out." She gazed at him more seriously. 'I'm happy you're my friend."

An odd look flitted across Stephen's face. "Jessica…"

"What?"

He hesitated, then shook his head "Nothing. I'm happy to be your friend, too. Now we better hurry, because I managed to find us a taxi and he's waiting."

They spent the evening at the cinema and returned to the house before midnight. Claire was in the sitting room reading when they came in, for once off duty from the ambulance service. Stephen chatted with the two women for a few minutes, then left. Jessica saw him out the front door, and smiled a good night to him.

She returned to the sitting room to find Claire watching her with an air of puzzlement. "What's going on between you two?"

Jessica's brows shot up. "What do you mean?"

"Well, you've been coming home on leave a lot more lately, and every time you do, you see Captain Marek." Claire spread out her hand and began to tick off points on her fingers. "He wines and dines you. He takes you dancing. You two go to the theater. The cinema. You take long walks in the afternoons."

"He's my friend."

"So I've noticed. I was beginning to be happy for you, thinking that at last you'd started to live again. That you were interested in another man, maybe even in love. But when I saw the way you two acted together tonight, I knew that couldn't be the case. He didn't kiss you when he left, didn't even hold your hand. What's his problem?"

"Nothing!" Jessica shot back, rising quickly to Stephen's defense. "You have it all wrong. We're just friends. Nothing romantic."

"Why not?"

"Why should there be? He tried to save Alan, and I visited him in hospital, and we grew to like each other. Like any friends. Like you and me."

"I don't have wide shoulders and dark mysterious eyes."

"Just because he's good-looking doesn't mean he can't have a platonic relationship."

"He's the first Yank I've met who wasn't trying to get a girl 'into the sack,' as they so quaintly put it."

"Claire! He's different. He's not some farm kid from Ohio who's never been abroad before and has nothing on his mind but sex with a foreigner."

Claire chuckled. "Maybe not, but he's still a man. And when a man sees as much of a woman as he does of you, it usually means he's interested in more than just her witty conversation."

"That's not it at all. Stephen sees me as Alan's wife, a woman who was kind to him when he was ill and weak. He stayed with Mum and Dad and Liz for a while, you know, and he was like part of the family. I'm something of a sister to him."

Claire's face expressed some doubt, but she conceded the point. "Okay, let's say that is the way he feels about you. But what about you? Is that the way you feel about him?"

Jessica blinked. She hadn't thought of it before. She hesitated for a moment, then quickly said, "Of course. He's a friend. What else could he be? Alan's been dead only a few months."

"But you believed he was dead for almost two years. Your heart and your mind adjusted to his death long ago. Come on,

Jessica, there's nothing wrong with being attracted to a man again."

"Honestly, Claire, that's all you think about since you met Ky."

Claire laughed, her eyes brightening. "Not quite all," she demurred jokingly. "Now and then I spare a thought for the war."

She began to talk of Ky and the last brief note she had received from him, and the subject dropped. Still, when Jessica went up to bed later, she couldn't keep from thinking back to what her friend had said. Was it possible that Claire was right? Could it be that she felt more for Stephen Marek than just friendship?

*****

Alyssa spent her first week in Paris reacquainting herself with the city. It was greatly changed—and not for the better. Everywhere she looked was the bleak gray of German uniforms. Military trucks and cars moved through the streets, soldiers sitting or standing with their weapons at the ready, the butts of the heavy rifles resting against their thighs. The French citizens were hungry, poorly clothed and frightened. Happiness was in as small supply as material things, it seemed; only the invaders had an ample quantity of any of it—they and their French collaborators.

But it was summer, and Paris could be nothing but beautiful then. It was the same time of year as when Alyssa left France two years ago. The warmth of the sun, the dappled shadows of the trees' foliage upon the sidewalks, the buoyant air—it was all as it had been, eerily transporting her back in time. Her weeks with Philippe might have happened yesterday.

She couldn't stop thinking of him. After their meeting in Washington last year, she had struggled to put him out of her mind and thought she had succeeded fairly well. During her months of rigorous training in England, she hadn't the time or energy to think of him. Her days were so filled that there was no room for anything but what she was doing, and at night she was so exhausted she fell asleep as soon as she tumbled into bed. She had come to believe that she was over Philippe at last. She had forgotten him.

Until she came to Paris. Now Alyssa couldn't stop remembering. Wherever she went there was something to remind her of him—a café where they sat, holding hands and sipping apéritifs; a boulevard they strolled along; an open-air-market stall of fruits and vegetables like the one where they purchased food. Alyssa thought of what they said to each other, the things they did. She remembered the long, sweet nights of lovemaking, the quiet, sleepy breakfasts. She remembered sitting on the couch beside him one evening while he worked on papers he brought home from the office, his arm draped around her shoulders with the casual possession of love. She held his hand in both of hers, teasing him by running her thumb slowly over his palm and fingers and kissing the back of his hand. He pretended not to notice her, but the same letter lay before him for ten minutes and Alyssa felt the skin of his hand flush with heat. She had wriggled closer to him... and the next thing she knew his papers were lying on the floor and they were stretched out full length on the couch, his hard body pressing into hers.

Alyssa wished she could stop thinking about it. Sometimes she caught herself smiling, recalling something he had said or a certain look on his face that she had loved. At other times her blood ran hot and she trembled with desire under the hot seduction of her memories. It wasn't right. It wasn't fair. She'd worked so hard to be rid of her love for him! How could the man still haunt her after all this time?

Alyssa walked past Philippe's apartment building, knowing even as she did it that she shouldn't. What if he happened to emerge just as she passed by? He would recognize her—and he was sitting in the Germans' pocket. Even more foolishly, she went to one of their favorite cafes along the Champs-Elysées.

Not only was there a possibility that Philippe might come along and see her, but she realized after she sat down that she no longer belonged here, an ordinary girl in a shabby dress. She was a ladies' maid, according to her identification papers. She took a few gulps of her cup of coffee and left.

Oddly enough, with the silly risks she took visiting places where Philippe might be, it was at none of them that she chanced to see him. Jules began to give her errands to run for him, and one day he sent her to set up the signal informing his group of a meeting the next day. She stopped by a flower vendor's cart and bought a single deep red rose, then strolled along, casually twirling it between her fingers and now and then taking a sniff, a woman enjoying the lovely day and the romantic flower. She sat down at a small, inelegant café for a croissant. A pair of daisies stood in a bud vase in the center of the table. Whimsically, Alyssa added the rose to them. She ate her croissant without haste, paid her bill, and walked away, leaving the rose in the vase.

Her job done, she walked home less aimlessly, though she was careful not to hurry, trying, as always, to appear as unobtrusive as possible. A man and woman stepped out of a house a few yards in front of her. Alyssa glanced at them, and her steps faltered. The man was Philippe.

Chapter 15

Alyssa started to turn around and walk in the other direction, but just then she noticed a long black car parked on the street in front of the house. A chauffeur waited beside it, his eyes ceaselessly studying the street around him. Alyssa was certain he waited for Philippe, and he looked as much bodyguard as chauffeur. The man would notice if she did something as suspicious as turning around and walking away. She decided to risk walking past Philippe. He was looking down at the woman, smiling. Perhaps he wouldn't notice a plainly dressed woman on the sidewalk.

The woman with him was pretty, and her face glowed as she gazed up at him. Philippe's arm was hooked casually around her waist. Alyssa walked past them, keeping her eyes in front of her, neither looking at Philippe nor keeping her face obviously averted. Philippe kissed the woman lightly on the mouth. Alyssa's stomach knotted with jealousy. Although it was very early in the morning, Philippe was dressed in evening clothes; they were slightly rumpled, as if they had been worn for a while. He had spent the night with the woman. Alyssa hated herself for caring that he had.

Philippe raised his head from the kiss and chuckled at something his companion said. His eyes lifted, and he looked straight at Alyssa.

His face didn't change expression, and he looked back down at the woman with him. Alyssa managed not to hurry. The chauffeur hardly glanced at her. She turned the corner and almost ran the rest of the way home.

*****

Alyssa! It was all Philippe could do not to run after the woman and spin her around so he could stare into her face. Could that really have been Alyssa? No makeup, plain clothes. Her hair was the wrong color. But those eyes! He couldn't mistake those eyes, even after this long, nor the sweet vulnerability of her short upper lip. *Enfer et damnation!* What was Alyssa doing in Paris? They must have gone mad in London.

Geneviève glanced up at Philippe, surprised by the sudden tightening of his grip. He forced a smile and kissed her again. Geneviève took the lapels of his coat between her fingers and smiled up beguilingly at him. "Is something wrong?" she asked in a soft voice.

"No. It's all right. I just had a thought. Thank you for last night."

"You're welcome." They both knew he referred to the information safely stowed in an inside pocket of his jacket. "I am seeing our friend tonight," Geneviève continued.

"Good."

"A threesome. I'm borrowing a boy."

"See if you can get anything about the informer." Philippe bent to nuzzle her neck. She smelled of expensive perfume. Had he told her everything? Asked everything? Philippe raised his head. "Good-bye."

Geneviève went on tiptoe to give him a light peck on the lips. "Until next week."

"Yes."

Philippe turned and walked to the car. The chauffeur jumped to open the door for him, then got into the driver's seat and started the car. As he drove to Philippe's home, Philippe stared out the side window, his face unreadable. He thought of Alyssa. It had to be her. He couldn't mistake her face, even in that brief instant, even with the precautions she had taken to subdue her looks. What idiocy had brought her to Paris? Rage surged in him. They were asking to have her killed—and worse.

He could imagine what would happen to her if she fell into the hands of someone like Dieter Gersbach.

Once inside his apartment Philippe went straight into his bedroom and shut the door. Locking it, he whipped out a piece of paper from his inside pocket and sat down at his desk. After studying the paper, he jotted a note on the bottom and tucked it back into his pocket. He removed the jacket and tossed it onto the bed, and left the room, his bedroom door open behind him.

He showered and washed his hair, working up a thick lather all over him. Sometimes he felt as if he would never get clean; he took at least two showers a day now. The filth round him stained him until sometimes he was surprised to see that his fingers didn't leave a trail of black on everything he touched. He wondered how long a person could live in dirt and not become it.

After the shower he returned to his bedroom to dress. Georges was there picking up Philippe's discarded clothes and taking them away to be cleaned and pressed. Philippe knew that somewhere in the process the slip of paper inside his suit jacket would be transferred to Georges' pocket. Later this afternoon Georges would go for a walk, as he did every afternoon, and he would sit on a park bench, reading a newspaper. When he left the bench, he would leave the newspaper behind with the message carefully folded inside it. The newspaper would be picked up and read by the stranger occupying the other end of the bench, and later he, too, would walk off, leaving it behind. But the slip of paper would be inside the jacket pocket of the stranger—Dragon, the one man in Paris who knew the identity of the Duke.

Philippe could imagine what Georges would think when he read the last line of the message: "Duchess here?" It was the only brief way he could think of to describe Alyssa to Pliny, and he was sure Georges would also know immediately to whom he referred. He wished he could have talked to Georges about it, but nowadays that was too risky. When they began, it had been easier; he and his valet had been able to speak freely. But as his circle of German friends had grown to include a Gestapo agent, Albrecht Schlieker, Philippe had been presented with first a chauffeur, then a housekeeper, both German. And Philippe and Georges had stopped talking about anything of importance inside the house or in the car.

The presence of his new servants smothered him. There was almost no time now when he could relax and be himself; the charade must always be carried on. He wasn't sure whether Schlieker suspected him or was simply a very cautious man.

Philippe sat down by the window and closed his eyes. He remembered Alyssa lying on the bed, her soft white body naked to his eyes, distracting him as he dressed for work. She had known the effect she had on him and had purposely not pulled up the sheet to cover her full, pink-tipped breasts. Instead she smiled at him bewitchingly, and he had gone over to the bed and sat down, burying his face in the sweet-smelling valley of her breasts.

His body tightened at the thought. He could feel the creamy perfection of her skin, smell her perfume and the scent of him upon her skin. Philippe wet his lips, tasting her on them again. He shook his head to clear it of the treacherous thoughts and stood up. Why was he letting himself think this way? He had realized long ago that dreaming about Alyssa would drive him crazy. She could not be a part of his life, even in his thoughts—thinking of her only made him despise his life more.

Walther, the chauffeur, waited downstairs on the sidewalk for him, arms folded, his eyes never missing anything around him. Sometimes Philippe thought that he had wronged Albrecht in assuming that he had set Walther to spy on him. Perhaps Walther really was there to protect him; he was always on the alert and quick to shield Philippe if there was any danger. He had jumped in to save Philippe's life when the three assassins had attacked him a few months ago. Perhaps Schlieker had only wanted to help his friend, not keep tabs on him.

Or perhaps Schlieker was doing both.

Walther drove Philippe to the factory. It was completely rebuilt and producing again. About a year ago one of his army friends had requisitioned slave labor from Poland for his factory. Philippe hated going to it now and rarely stepped outside the office area when he was there. The few times he went into the factory and saw the workers there, he wondered whether what he did for the organization could possibly be worth it. He wanted to blow up the place again and flee to England.

But he knew that if he fled the country, the slave laborers would be sent somewhere else, would build trucks and cars and tanks for the German Army in another factory. And England would lose the secrets he provided. So he stayed—and avoided the factory.

He had abandoned his electronics business as well; there was too much in that field that could be discovered and used to Germany's advantage. Instead he devoted most of his time now to his newer business interests—Geneviève's place, the club, his dabbling in black market goods. They were more pertinent anyway, since they gave him contacts through-out the German Army. They gave him friends and favors. And information.

He left the factory a little before noon. He had a luncheon date with Albrecht, and it would never do to be less than punctual. Walther drove to Gestapo headquarters on Avenue Foch, a wide, tree-lined boulevard centered by a green swath of flowering bushes and small trees. It was a beautiful street, a perfect setting for the graceful large houses on either side. The idea of the darkness of the Gestapo residing on this lovely avenue was incongruous, like a huge spider hiding in a bed of flowers. But it wasn't surprising—the Nazis, particularly the Gestapo, always seized the finest for themselves.

Walther stopped in front of number 84, a large, pale beige building with ornate black wrought-iron balconies. A tall black iron fence stretched across the front of it, and two gray-uniformed guards stood outside the gate. Another pair guarded the front doorway. One of the guards glanced suspiciously at the car, but Walther stepped out, and the soldier looked away again, recognizing him. Philippe waited inside the car. Albrecht would appear at twelve on the dot.

He watched the gate, wishing a miracle would occur and he would see a Frenchman slipping in or out of the headquarters building without a Gestapo escort. An informer. God, how he wanted that informer! It had been obvious from the way the Diamond network had been smashed that a traitor had been at work on the inside. Now cells of the Rock network were falling, too. Schlieker had let it slip in one of his rare confidences that his spy was at work again. He had predicted that the Rock network would soon be completely blown, too.

Philippe couldn't let another resistance network be smashed. The name of the Nazi infiltrator was the most important information he could obtain right now. That was the reason he had been concentrating on the Gestapo lately. He'd even introduced Schlieker's junior officer, Dieter Gersbach, to one of Geneviève's girls, hoping that the rougher, louder, cruder officer might be more likely to let the information slip. But nothing had come of that except that the girl had wound up with bruises and several loose teeth from the "games" Gersbach like to play. Philippe had decided that Gersbach, in fact, didn't know who the informer was. The informer was Schlieker's tool and jealously guarded by him. It was common knowledge that Gersbach despised Schlieker as an effete intellectual and would love to take Schlieker's job away from him. But Schlieker's informant gave him an edge Gersbach couldn't possibly overcome.

The front door opened, and a man stepped out, dressed in a crisp dark pin-striped suit. The fact that he wore no uniform when all the other Germans in Paris did immediately identified him as a member of the dreaded German secret police, the Gestapo. The man's eyes ran automatically around the small yard and over the guards, checking for mistakes or anything suspicious. Schlieker was a very careful man.

He walked across the yard and out the gate as the guards saluted him, and climbed into the back of Philippe's car. He smiled. "Philippe."

"Albrecht." Philippe thought that Albrecht Schlieker had as much liking for him as he did for anyone. Schlieker enjoyed conversing with him, often remarking that it was his only opportunity for intelligent discussion. When it came to art and music, he dismissed his Gestapo compatriots with a sneer. Philippe had once heard him joke that Dieter Gersbach understood nothing more refined than beer-hall polkas. Philippe cultivated Schlieker carefully, maintaining a charming, friendly, but unservile attitude with him. Schlieker was used to everyone fawning over him because of his power, and while he accepted it as his due, he despised the people who did it.

Walther drove them to an expensive restaurant where a table sat waiting for them. Schlieker never sat at a sidewalk café, and his preference was for a table in a corner, where he could have his back against a wall and survey the entire room. Since the assassination attempt on him a few months ago, Philippe could understand Schlieker's precaution; he found he was no longer as fond of sidewalk cafes himself.

Schlieker spent a good deal of time and effort choosing their wine, and Philippe offered no suggestion. It was a point of pride with the Gestapo officer that he knew wines, and he enjoyed thinking that a Frenchman relied on his expertise in choosing wine. The sommelier brought the wine, and they savored it for a moment. Only then did they begin to talk.

"How is our lovely Madame Geneviève?" Schlieker asked, smiling faintly. Philippe wasn't surprised at his bringing the woman into the conversation today; he liked to remind Philippe that he always knew where Philippe was and what he was doing.

Philippe managed to look astonished. That was another thing Schlieker liked—amazement at his knowledge and skill. Philippe's stomach curled in disgust at playing Schlieker's games, but the feeling was so long-standing he no longer paid it any attention. "As lovely as ever. I saw her last night." He paused. "Does that bother you?"

Schlieker laughed. "God, no. She is just a tart. I'm happy to share her with a friend."

Philippe had suspected that would be his answer. Schlieker would never allow a prostitute, no matter how lovely, to come between him and a male friend. Besides, he imagined Schlieker used Geneviève more as a cover than anything else, a woman to be seen with. From what Geneviève had told him about the man, he was more given to young men than beautiful women.

"Speaking of Geneviève…" Philippe began, frowning a little.

"A problem?"

"I'm not sure. But I am a little concerned about one of her girls."

"Yes?" Schlieker's eyes lost interest, and he lit a cigarette.

"From what Geneviève tells me, I think she may be a spy."

Schlieker's head came up, his interest revived. "Why?"

"She asks too many questions. She is always talking to the other girls about the men they service—and as you know, nearly all Geneviève's customers are German officers. She seems much too interested in what the customers say. And Geneviève has found her once or twice where she should not be."

Philippe and Geneviève had indeed discussed the girl last night. As usual on the evenings when he stayed at her place, Geneviève gave him the information her girls gathered throughout the past week. This exchange of information was all that occurred between them; the pretense of an affair made a good cover-up for their real relationship.

Philippe had known Geneviève for years; she had grown up in the slums of Lyons with him, and long ago they had been lovers for a brief time. Later she moved to Paris and became a dancer in a club, supplementing her income with the money she received from men. The sideline became more lucrative than the job, and before long, she had established herself as one of the most beautiful and talented courtesans of Paris, a city famous for such women.

After Philippe began his secret work, he thought of her. His German 'friends' seemed insatiable for the company of lovely Frenchwomen. Setting them up with women seemed a perfect opportunity to supply their needs, thus earning their gratitude and friendship, while at the same time gathering more information from them. Philippe approached Geneviève cautiously, but it hadn't taken long to realize that she was in agreement with him on the subject of Nazis. At first he simply introduced her to various officers, and she gave him whatever information she gleaned from them. Later they decided to expand their operations, and he set her up in a brothel.

Only two of the girls besides Geneviève were aware of her activities and actively participated in them—though even they had no knowledge that Geneviève's sometime lover, Philippe Michaude, was actually the ultimate receiver of the information. The other girls were there simply to earn money in the manner easiest for them, but Geneviève and her two co-conspirators were able to pick up information from them in conversations.

But now there was a new girl, hired a month ago to replace the woman Gersbach had damaged, and she asked a great many questions of the other girls about the officials they serviced. One of Geneviève's employees had seen her meeting a man secretively in the alleyway early one morning. Philippe and Geneviève suspected she had been set to spy on them by the Gestapo.

Questions to headquarters brought back denials that the woman worked for the Free French or the British, and after that Genevieve kept a closer eye on her. It was soon clear that she was regularly meeting the same man in the alleyway or at the market or a cafe. Worse, Genevieve recognized him as a man who worked at Gestapo headquarters.

They had to get rid of her; a Gestapo spy would cramp Geneviève's activities. There were several ways to do so, the easiest being simply to fire her, but doing so might fix the Gestapo's attention even more on Genevieve's house. Turning her in to Schlieker, however, served the double purpose of disposing of her and proving their loyalty to the Germans at the same time. The subtle twist pleased Philippe.

"What is her name?" Schlieker whipped out a flat little notebook and removed a small pen.

"Lisette. I don't know her last name. A rather flamboyant redhead." He watched Schlieker jot down the information and return the notebook to his pocket. It went against the grain to inform on anyone, even a German spy. But Schlieker wasn't one who would wreak vengeance on one of his own. He lacked Gersbach's sadistic delight in torture. That didn't mean he was any less likely to torture suspects, but he did it only with reason. It was merely a job to him, and in a way that was even more chilling.

Philippe thought of Alyssa and what Schlieker or someone like him would do to her, and his insides turned cold and liquid with fear in a way that they had never done when he considered the danger to himself.

Surely that woman he had glimpsed on the street hadn't been Alyssa. Pliny couldn't have been so foolish as to send a woman with her distinctive good looks. It was merely a woman who somewhat resembled Alyssa, and Philippe thought about her, dreamed about her, so constantly that his mind had turned her into Alyssa. That was all.

But he thought again of those vivid blue eyes, and he knew it couldn't be anyone but Alyssa.

The waiter arrived with their first course, escargot swimming in a buttery herb sauce. Philippe could hardly force it down.

*****

Alyssa returned to Jules and Odette's apartment, thoroughly shaken by her encounter. Philippe had looked straight at her. Was it possible he hadn't recognized her, given her unflattering clothes and new hair color? No, he knew her too well to be fooled by that. More to the point—having recognized her, would he turn her in?

They had been so close once, so intimate. He had loved her. A year ago in Washington, he swore that he loved her, and she believed him. It was difficult to reconcile what he was doing with any ability to feel love, but he clearly held some strong feeling for her. Still… she reminded herself that he had no moral fiber. Even if he had once cared for her, that had been two long years ago. And who knew how low he might stoop to ingratiate himself with his Nazi friends? It would be foolish to rely on his silence. She must be very cautious, very alert to any danger.

The next evening after curfew, one by one, three men came to the apartment. Jules introduced them to Alyssa as "Green," "Blade," and "Unicorn." Green and Blade were both dark, one quite tall and slender and the other short and heavyset. They made Alyssa think of Mutt and Jeff from the comic strip. Unicorn was a small man with sandy hair and eyebrows and reddish-brown eyes. He smiled at Alyssa, and there was hint of a devilish twinkle in his eyes.

"Cleopatra has heard from Mother," Jules began without preliminary. "They told us where the Germans are storing the torpedoes. In the sewers. Here and here." He pointed with a blunt pencil to the two locations on a map. "Now it's up to us to destroy them."

"I don't understand it," Blade marveled. "How is it that people in England know so much when we who are living right here can't discover it?"

Jules shrugged. "That's not important. What's important is getting rid of the torpedoes. That's our job. Giving us the information is theirs."

"They must have a spy," Unicorn surmised. "Probably a German."

"Why a German?" Green seemed offended.

"Because he has access to so much information. Who else would?"

"A clever Frenchman. A man who sneaks in and steals the documents."

Unicorn shrugged. "I doubt it. It must be a German."

"Perhaps it's more than one man," Odette suggested.

"I've heard rumors about a man named le Duc. Now who could he be but a Frenchman?"

Jules frowned. "You're no better than a bunch of gossiping old women. It's not important who it is, and it's better for everyone that we not know. Now, let's get down to planning this."

They talked for several minutes about times and methods and escapes, eventually settling on the following Friday for their raid. Jules turned to another matter. "Blade, what do you have to report?"

"On Operation St. Patrick?"

"Yes, of course."

"I followed Cobra to a house in Montmartre."

"A mistress?"

"I think so. He visited the house twice last week. Another time he went back to Avenue Foch. Twice to parties, and two nights he stayed at home."

Jules sighed. "I had hoped for more regularity."

"I think morning would be the best time."

"I don't know. We're not in charge of the morning watch. I'll have to wait to hear from their leader. In the meantime all we can do is keep following him. Maybe his visits to the mistress's house will prove to have a pattern; maybe he goes there on the same days each week."

"Why waste our time following him?" Blade grumbled. "Why don't we just kill the bastard as he leaves his house in the morning?"

"Because Cobra isn't worth a suicide mission," Unicorn replied with some sarcasm.

"Right. If we can catch him without his guards, we can get away without being killed or caught ourselves."

Alyssa spoke up a little timidly, "Excuse me. Who is Cobra?"

"Albrecht Schlieker. Gestapo. A pig. He's killed more good Frenchmen…"

"I say we ought to go after his friend. That bastard Michaude," the man named Green stuck in fiercely.

Alyssa's heart began to thump wildly. Her hands clenched in her lap. No, oh, no, she cried inside. Please don't let them kill him!

Jules shrugged. "He's a worm. He's not important."

"He's an insult to France! He fawns on the Nazis, eats with them, drinks with them, brings them French women. Once he seemed a true Frenchman, a patriot, a leader. He was a man I respected—and now he owns a brothel that caters to German soldiers. He helps them in every way he can. God knows how many loyal Frenchmen he's sent to the Gestapo torture chambers. We should make an example of him, show other collaborators how the citizens of France will deal with them."

Alyssa's stomach twisted; she felt sick. Philippe brought the Germans women. She thought of the woman she had seen Philippe with yesterday. Was she one of the prostitutes he provided to the Nazis? Alyssa burned with anger; she hated him; she felt dirty to think that he had ever touched her. And still she prayed that they would not decide to kill him.

"He is dirt," Unicorn agreed. "But do you remember what happened to the last team that tried to assassinate him? He and that Nazi chauffeur of his fought them off. He came away with a scratch, but our people died inch by inch in the Place des Saussaies."

"I am not afraid."

Jules frowned. "No one doubts your courage. But Philippe Michaude is not worth getting you or anyone else killed for. He is a traitor, but it is Cobra who is killing and torturing our people."

"Right. Now let's get back to Cobra," Blade urged.

Alyssa sagged with relief. The others continued to discuss Operation St. Patrick, but it was time for her to make her transmission to England. She edged away from the group and went into the bedroom, closing the door behind her. She pulled the small suitcase containing the transmitter out from under her narrow bed and opened it. Quickly, efficiently, she set it up and contacted headquarters. She identified herself, then waited for whatever message Mother had to send her. It was somehow comforting to know that it was Jessica on the opposite end, replying to her. The message from headquarters was quick and to the point: "Traitor in network. Unknown. Caution."

Alyssa's blood chilled. A traitor from within—the worst, the deadliest thing that could happen to them. Alyssa wanted to jump up and run into the other room to tell Oak and the others. It took all her discipline to remain where she was and send back her own message to Mother. She was near the end of transmission when she heard shouting at the door of the apartment. Alyssa froze. A fist hammered against the door. Her heart skittered and set up a hard, racing beat. Hastily she discontinued transmitting, using the special code for such situations, and closed up the transmitter just as her bedroom door burst open. Unicorn darted into the room, his eyes wild. "Gestapo!"

Chapter 16

Jessica pondered Claire's comments about her relationship with Stephen. She remembered the way his face lit up when he was amused, the brooding darkness of his eyes when he was quiet. Was Claire right? Could it be that Jessica was attracted to him? She thought of how she looked forward to her days off from work because she would see him. How carefully she dressed and arranged her hair for their evenings out. How her stomach jumped as she hurried down the stairs to open the door when he knocked.

The thoughts left her feeling vaguely guilty, as if she were betraying Alan. Could she possibly have turned her interest to another man already? But it hadn't been quick at all, really; it had been almost two years since she lost Alan, a long time to be alone. He was dead, and she had mourned him. There was no reason to feel guilty if she did have feelings for another man now. Alan would have wanted her to be happy, not close herself into a shell, missing him. Still, it felt wrong somehow.

Besides, there was nothing to indicate that Stephen had any interest in her except as a friend. He'd never made a move to kiss her or even to hold her hand, except to help her over a puddle or up a high step. Perhaps he was more familiar in his manner than others, but that was simply the American way. He didn't flirt with her as that American major had last weekend. She thought of the gaze Stephen had turned on the major and the man's hasty retreat. She hadn't thought anything of it at the time, but now she wondered if it had been jealousy that spurred Stephen, not just an escort's duty to protect a lady.

And what about his smile—did his eyes light up like that with everyone? Did he lean forward, listening with the same attentiveness, with others? Was it more than companionship he sought, more than his friendship with her husband, that brought him back at every opportunity?

Such thoughts plagued her all week, and when the next day of leave rolled around, the train couldn't get to Victoria Station fast enough for her. She loitered around the telephone, and when at last it rang, she jumped on it. Her heart executed a peculiar little leap at the sound of Stephen's voice on the other end. They arranged to go out to eat, then dancing at Hammersmith Palais. As soon as she hung up the receiver, Jessica ran upstairs to draw a bath, humming as she went. She was glad Claire was out, or she would have teased her unmercifully.

When Jessica opened the door to Stephen an hour later, happiness surged up in her and spread over her face in a grin. Was she always this happy to see him? Was he always this handsome? Stephen smiled, his eyes dark and glowing, and she tried to judge whether more than friendliness lay behind his gaze. When he politely helped her with her jacket, his fingers brushed her shoulders, and Jessica's skin tingled at the touch. Had his touch been on purpose? Or was she making too much of every little thing?

They went to the Savoy for supper and talked and laughed all through the meal. Jessica had never really thought before about how much she enjoyed Stephen's company, but now she realized that she felt happier with him than with anyone else. Their conversation seemed unutterably clever, their silences warm and intimate. His eyes were full of interest, with never a hint of the disapproval that Alan had sometimes shown when he thought she was being a bit too outrageous. Jessica realized suddenly that she had always felt as if Alan were somehow her superior. She supposed it was because they had grown up together, and he, being older and a boy, gave the commands and she followed. But now, with Stephen, she felt an equal. She found she liked it.

She was very aware of him physically—the width of his shoulders beneath his uniform, which he was beginning to fill out again nicely; the dark intensity of his eyes; the hard, sculpted beauty of his facial bones. Her eyes went to his hand across the table from her, long and thin, sensitive, but saved from weakness by the masculine cords of strength across the back and the sprinkling of fine black hairs. She could imagine those hands on her skin, and the thought gave her shivers, but of heat, not cold.

Stephen watched Jessica, the familiar bittersweet ache gnawing at his loins. She looked unusually beautiful tonight, sparkling and flushed, her red-gold hair glowing in the dim light. He wanted nothing more than to take her in his arms and kiss her until she was breathless. Hell, what he really wanted was to whisk her away to one of the rooms upstairs in the hotel and peel away each scrap of clothing, then make slow, shattering love to her.

He didn't know why he tortured himself like this. He knew he wouldn't take her, now or ever. He wasn't going to seduce her with hot caresses and sweet kisses in the dark, his hands sliding beneath her dress to explore and arouse. Not that it was likely she would let him. She was a widow, still in love with her husband, and she thought of him only as a friend. But more than that, he knew he wouldn't even try. She was Alan's, and because of him Alan had died. To make love to his widow seemed yet another betrayal of him. Guilt swamped Stephen whenever he was near Jessica, knowing how much he wanted her.

The crazy thing was that he continued to see her. It would have been far kinder to himself to stay away, because every moment he was with Jessica made him want her more. Now, sitting across from her in the pristine elegance of the Savoy, he kept imagining her naked. His mouth was dry, and he had no idea what she was saying, but he kept on smiling gamely, glad for the concealment of the table.

Stephen wondered what her perfect ladylike face would look like in the throes of passion. Would she whimper, cry out? He could imagine her bright hair darkened with sweat around the edges of her face, hear her murmuring his name, feel those long, graceful legs wrapped around him.

Stephen clenched his fists and forced himself to think of anything but Jessica. He ought to give up seeing her. It drove him mad every time, and he always went home flushed and hard, aching for release. But there was none. He could have found another woman who would have taken his passion, but he wasn't interested in cold sex with a stranger, all the while thinking about the woman he truly wanted.

He called himself all kinds of a fool for continuing to take her out. He was only increasing his pain. But he knew he wouldn't stop. He didn't think he could bear not to see those wide gray eyes light up with laughter again, not to hear her soft, cultured voice. For he felt much more for her than desire. He was afraid he'd fallen in love with her. It was a wild, curious combination of pain and joy to be with her. And he couldn't stay away from that tumult of feeling.

When they left the restaurant, there were no taxis, and they walked, wisps of fog floating in front of them like scarves and dissolving as they walked through them. Stephen's body was large and warm beside Jessica. She shivered a little, and he put his arm around her in a friendly gesture to provide her with warmth. Jessica thought how nice it would be to stand together, pressed up against his chest with his heavy coat pulled around them both.

When they danced later, she was very aware of his hand on the small of her back and her hand in his, bare skin against bare skin. Jessica kept her other hand correctly on his shoulder, but she kept wondering what it would feel like to glide across to his neck, to trace the line of his hair and feel the prickle of his short hair at the base of his skull. Heat flooded her cheeks, and she knew a curious mingling of excitement and frustration.

Claire was right. She *was* attracted to Stephen Marek. Somehow it had crept up on her, overtaking her without her noticing it. She wanted suddenly to hear endearments from his lips and the quickening of his breath that spoke of desire. More than that, she had the funny feeling that she was more than halfway to falling in love with him.

The awful thing was, she had to admit that Stephen obviously felt none of the same things for her. She had watched him carefully tonight for any signs of interest. He was polite and friendly, but he wasn't lover-like. He touched her no more than courtesy dictated—taking her arm as they walked or helping her on with her coat. He'd said nothing remotely suggestive. Indeed, he didn't allude to sex in any way. Nor had those deep dark eyes glowed with interest. She had lingered with him on the doorstep, just to see if he might make a move to kiss her, but he had not. It was apparent that he hadn't the slightest interest in her as anything but a friend.

Jessica returned to work at Evington Court the next evening in a blue mood. The evening started out slowly, and her mind kept returning to Stephen, despite all her best efforts not to. A call came through from Cleopatra, and Jessica began to jot it down. Alyssa's first request was for supplies, specifically an explosive known as "marzipan" for its faintly almond smell. Suddenly there was a break, an unexpected pause of seconds. Jessica stiffened, sensing danger. Messages were usually quick and without hesitation. Then came the dreaded signal: QUO—"forced to stop transmitting because of imminent danger."

*****

When Unicorn burst into the room, hissing "Gestapo!" Alyssa acted without hesitation. She crossed to the window in a single step and shoved it open. Behind her she could hear Unicorn closing the door and dragging a small chest across it. It was a long drop down below the window, offering at best a broken limb, so Alyssa looked to the side. Less than a foot from the window on the right was a sturdy metal gutter pipe. It was bolted into the wall and appeared to be able to hold a person's weight. Of course, if it didn't hold her, she would wind up dead or broken on the pavement of the narrow alley below. Nor was she at all sure she could climb down the wall holding on to the pipe, even though she had done the same sort of thing holding onto a rope at the training camp in England.

She hesitated for only a second. Something heavy crashed against the outer door of the apartment. She shoved her arm through the handle of the transmitter case and slid out of the window, grabbing the gutter. She felt a clutch of fear as she swung free, but she had done this often enough in training. She braced her feet against the wall and started down. The metal was cool and slippery beneath her hands, not burning like rope, but not as good a handhold either. It was more awkward than her practice climbs, but this time she was impelled by fear, and she raced down. Above her, Unicorn swung out of the window and began to follow her.

She jumped the last few feet, landing in a crouch. She could hear the splintering of wood above them. They must be breaking in the door to her bedroom now. Unicorn was slower than she, not having had her professional training, and when he jumped, he landed awkwardly and rolled over in a sprawl. In the window above a capped head emerged and looked around, then down. He stuck his gun out the window and fired at Unicorn, but the shot went wide. By the time he got off a second bullet, her companion was up, and they melted into the deep shadows of the wall. The bullet smacked into the wall several feet from them.

"This way," Unicorn said softly. Alyssa ran in the direction he pointed, sticking close to the wall, and he followed closely. Behind them the soldier fired, but the steep angle and the darkness made it impossible to aim with any accuracy, and the bullets ricocheted harmlessly off the walls.

They ran to the end of the alleyway and peered out. There was no sign of a soldier along the cross street. Unicorn motioned to her, and they darted across the street into the alley beyond. They ran lightly but quickly, no longer keeping to the sides of the narrow pathway. At the next cross street Unicorn turned right and ran, Alyssa on his heels.

They ran for what seemed like hours, twisting and turning, ducking down alleyways and darting across streets. Alyssa's heart pounded with exertion and fear, and her breath rasped in her throat. The transmitter case banged against her leg. She was tiring now that the first burst of adrenaline was past. She stumbled on a piece of buckled pavement and barely saved herself from falling, but a pain shot through her ankle. Unicorn angled across the street. He, too, was slowing down. Alyssa followed him as he ducked into a space between two buildings. It was pitch black and so narrow they could walk only single file. Alyssa kept her eye on the faint glimmer of the man's fair hair and stretched out her arm to touch the wall beside her. They were moving at a fast walk now.

Suddenly the wall beside her ended; her hand touched only air. Unicorn stopped abruptly, and she bumped into his back. He turned, whispering, "In here."

He led her into the empty space. It seemed to be a sort of box, enclosed on three sides, and it was even darker than the passageway had been. Alyssa could see nothing. She leaned against the wall and closed her eyes. It was a place to hide, to rest. That was all she needed to know. Thank heavens she was with someone who knew the area. She would never have found anything like this on her own.

Beside her, Unicorn slid down to the ground. "It's all right. You can sit," he told her in a low voice. "It's a little dirty, that's all."

Alyssa sank to the ground. Gradually her breathing slowed, and she whispered, "Where are we?"

"It's a recessed doorway. You couldn't see it at night from the street, even if you shone a light down the walkway. A nice little hidey-hole. I think it's best we stay here till dawn. It's risky to walk around after curfew. And it's not a good idea to go to anyone's house yet. We don't know who they might have rounded up tonight."

Alyssa swallowed. He was right. They could arrive at one of the safe houses Jules had told her about only to find the Gestapo already there or pounding on the door a few minutes later. She sighed. "There's a traitor in the network."

"Not necessarily. Someone could have given Oak's address under torture. Or maybe the Gestapo was spying on one of us and followed him to the meeting place tonight."

"No. It's a traitor. That was the first message Mother gave me when I made contact tonight. But before I could finish my transmission and tell Oak, they were breaking down the door." Alyssa chewed at her lip. A traitor was the worst danger of the resistance. It was horribly easy for one to get in. They had no way of checking out those who wanted to join; there were no credentials. They had to rely on trust and instinct, and it the traitor was skillful, it would be difficult to weed him out in an initial interview. Their only safeguard lay in keeping their identities secret, thus the use of code names, and in keeping the fighters as separated as possible, with cut-outs and small cells. Unfortunately, the latter often created confusion, duplication, and even some working at cross-purposes. Still, at least it meant that the whole network wasn't blown just because one person or one cell was.

She felt more than saw Unicorn turn toward her. "You mean they knew in England that we had a traitor in our network? How on earth—"

Alyssa shrugged. "I don't know. But that's what she said."

"Surely if they found out that much, they must know who it is."

"Apparently not."

"I'd give my left arm to know his name," he went on in a low, savage voice. "I'd like to take care of that bastard myself."

"I'm sure they'll tell us if they find out."

They fell into silence. Slowly Alyssa's lungs ceased to ache, and her pulse slowed. She leaned against the wall and angled her legs, settling into as comfortable a position as possible, given the hardness of the wall and pavement. It would be impossible to sleep, she thought, but after a time she dozed off. She slept fitfully through most of the night, twisting, floating just below the surface of consciousness, now and then jerking awake.

It was a relief to awaken at last and be able to see Unicorn's face. It was dawn. As if he felt her gaze upon him, Unicorn's eyes flew open. He stared at her blankly for a moment, then recognition touched his eyes, and he straightened and glanced around. "It's getting light."

Alyssa nodded. He stood up slowly and stretched, and Alyssa did the same. Her bones cracked and popped. The running last night coupled with sleeping on the hard ground in an awkward position had left her sore and stiff. "Where should we go?"

He shook his head. "I'm not sure. Perhaps the safe house on Rue de l'Assomption. It's closest. Why don't we walk past it and see if it's been discovered? If it has, I know one or two others we could try."

"All right." They brushed the dirt from their clothes as best they could. Alyssa straightened her skirt and combed through her hair with her fingers in an attempt to look like an ordinary citizen going to work in the early morning.

They slipped along the narrow passage out to the street. There was almost no one about, and the light was gray; it was very early in the morning. They forced themselves to walk at a normal pace, not rush as they wanted to. They kept to the less traveled streets. Finally they reached the Rue de l'Assomption and approached the safe house. The narrow street was quiet and empty. They glanced at each other. It looked perfectly innocuous, but there was no way of knowing whether a Gestapo soldier waited inside to trap anyone who sought refuge there.

"I don't see anyone watching it," Unicorn rubbed the back of his neck tiredly. "I'll go in while you wait here. If I don't return in two minutes, take off."

Alyssa started to protest, but stopped. He was right. There was no sense in both of them getting captured, and the radio transmitter and its operator were vital to the survival of the network. She nodded.

Unicorn strolled across the street and up the two shallow steps to the front door. He tried the door and found it locked. He reached above the door and took down a key, then opened the door and went inside. Alyssa waited, her heart pounding. Two minutes, he had said. She glanced at her watch, then looked back at the door. It seemed like forever. She kept glancing at her watch. Finally the minute hand had crept two spaces. Alyssa glanced around. Should she take him at his exact word? It might take him longer than two minutes to search the house and make sure no one was there.

She tensed, poised for flight. Her hand was sweaty on the handle of the small suitcase. Unicorn appeared in the doorway. Alyssa let out a sigh of relief and crossed the street to him.

"It appears safe," Unicorn said as she slipped inside. He locked the door, and they dragged a heavy bench across it. "At least that'll give us notice if the Gestapo comes."

There were no other doors. They checked the windows for an escape route, but there was no easy way to get out of the house except through the front door. The only other possibility of escape lay in the attic, where a trapdoor led onto the roof. Alyssa hoped fervently that they wouldn't have to face departing that way.

They ate a filling meal of canned meats and vegetables in the kitchen; the place was well-stocked with imperishables. Afterward they went up to the second floor and chose their bedrooms. Alyssa lay down on top of the covers, fully clothed, still too jumpy to risk taking off her dress and crawling beneath the sheets. Almost instantly she was asleep.

*****

A faint tapping penetrated her brain. Alyssa's eyes fluttered open, and she glanced around. The noise came again, soft and persistent. Alyssa went to the window and edged aside a corner of the curtain to look down at the front door. She saw the foreshortened figure of a plainly dressed woman. She could see nothing of her face. Now and then the woman glanced around her, then resumed the quiet rapping.

Alyssa started out into the hall and saw Unicorn already slipping quietly down the stairs. She followed him to the front room where he peered out through the curtain. His body relaxed, and he turned to smile at Alyssa. "It's all right. She's one of us."

He opened the door narrowly, and the woman, who had once again turned to look down the street, whirled back, her face fearful. When she saw Unicorn, she sagged with relief. "Thank God," she said, slipping inside the door.

"Hello, Faith." He nodded toward Alyssa. "This is Cleopatra. New pianist with our group."

Faith glanced at Alyssa and gave her something resembling a smile. "Did they get you too?"

"Four of us. We escaped through a back window. How about your group?"

"I don't know. I went by Silver's house this morning to pick up a gun. When I got there, it was deserted. The landlady said the Gestapo had come and taken him. I was supposed to leave the gun for Thunder at a little café in the Montmartre, so I went there to tell him what had happened, but he never showed up. I'm afraid they've gotten him, too. I didn't know what to do! I was so scared. I was afraid to go home. Finally I decided to come to this safe house. When the key was gone, I hoped someone else had gotten away and come here."

Grimly Unicorn described to the other woman what had happened to them. They fed her, and Unicorn gave up his bedroom to her, moving up to the third floor, so that the two women could share the floor. Alyssa was more clearheaded now after her sleep, and she decided to make an unscheduled transmission to let headquarters know they had escaped.

She rigged up the transmitter in the bathroom, using the long chain from the cistern to the toilet bowl for an aerial. Rapidly she tapped out a message to Mother: "Escaped. Unicorn, Faith, Cleopatra hiding, safe house. Oak, Lace, Green, Blade, Silver captured. Maybe Thunder." The reply from headquarters was swift. Alyssa could almost feel Jessica's relief coming through the wire. Mother informed her that much of the network was smashed, and they knew little about who had been captured or what cells were compromised. They advised that Cleopatra return home immediately.

Alyssa's hand trembled. Nothing seemed better than getting out of this mess, fleeing to safety. But she couldn't do it. She could be of too much value here, helping the remnants of the groups get together and reconnect with their base. She typed back a simple message: "I will stay."

*****

At the quiet tap on the door, Albrecht Schlieker crossed the room to answer it. Good. Bousquet was on time, even a little early. Schlieker disliked tardiness, and he disliked even more waiting in this miserable hotel room for his informant. It was unfortunate that it was too risky for Bousquet to meet him in Schlieker's own elegantly furnished office on Avenue Foch.

He opened the door, and Bousquet hurried inside. He was a small man with dark blond hair, ordinary in the extreme. That was an advantage in his profession; people rarely suspected him of anything.

"We had a very successful evening, thanks to you, Herr Bousquet," Schlieker related with a cold smile. "Almost thirty arrests."

"Good. Then you must have my payment." Schlieker could see the fear in the man, however much he tried not to show it. Good. That was the way he liked it.

"Of course." The German officer picked up a small drawstring bag from the dresser top and tossed it to the other man. Bousquet caught it and poured the contents into his hand. Diamonds sparkled up at him. Pulling out a jeweler's eyepiece, he examined the stones. Schlieker's lip curled. The man was crude and common—checking the diamonds as if he, Albrecht Schlieker, would try to cheat him. "None of the ones we picked up has told us about the spy. Their ignorance seems to be genuine on that score."

"I told you that. No one *knows* anything. There is nothing but rumor. Some say he's a German officer, others that he's French. One even told me he's sure it's a woman. It's all speculation. Most don't even know his code name; the very fact that he exists is a secret. All I've learned is that his code name is le Duc. I think it is only one man, not a whole ring of spies."

"Why do you say that?"

"It's too secret. If there were more than one, someone would be bound to know something. There'd be more talk, more gossip, at least."

"Still, even one man can't operate in complete secrecy, can he? There must be others who know of him. He has to have some kind of backup. How does he get the information to England?"

"He could radio it himself," Bousquet suggested.

"Not likely. A transmitter is too easily caught, and that would blow his whole operation. He must give the information to a messenger or a radio-telegraphist."

"Probably. And no doubt there's a go-between between him and the telegraphist, so the telegraphist couldn't identify him. As you say, pianists are too easily caught."

"You're right. There must be another person or two who know of his existence."

"They're very close-mouthed."

"I have to have him!" Schlieker's normally controlled face contorted with anger, and he slammed his fist down on the dresser top. "This man is dangerous. He's making fools of us all!" Schlieker turned and jabbed his forefinger at the informant. "Find him! And give him to me."

"I will do my best."

"That's not good enough. He is worth ten of these little cells you've brought me. He is worth more than any information you've given me. I don't want your best. I want him!"

"I understand. I will infiltrate another group; there's still a great deal of the Rock network intact. It won't take as long to get in this time. I have a passport now."

"What is that?"

"A radio-telegraphist. Everyone wants one."

"All right. You may go now." Schlieker nodded toward the door. "Good-bye…" he smiled thinly. "Unicorn."

*****

Alyssa and her companions left the safe house the next day. With so many of their friends captured, it was likely that someone would be forced to tell the Gestapo of the existence of the safe house. They decided to try an address that had been given to Alyssa before she left England.

It lay on the Rue Raynouard. They walked to it, Unicorn carrying Alyssa's little suitcase with the all-important transmitter inside. As they neared the number of the house, Unicorn, who was walking abreast of Alyssa with Faith slightly behind them, suddenly gripped Alyssa's arm. "Walk on," he murmured, and they continued down the street without pause. Unicorn turned at the next corner and, out of sight of the house, picked up his step.

"What is it?" Alyssa asked.

"There was a man in a doorway across the street from the house. I didn't like the way he looked."

"You think he was watching the house?"

"He seemed out of place. He didn't look French. I'm not sure, but I'd hate to test the theory. Let's find someplace else."

"I have a cousin," Faith offered. "We could spend a night there, but no more than that. I don't want to endanger her."

"That'll do."

They stayed two nights with Faith's cousin. During that time Unicorn came up with phony identification papers establishing him as René Dupree, Alyssa as his wife, Madeleine, and Faith as her sister, Louise Fabre. Under their new names they rented a small two-bedroom apartment on the Left Bank.

Alyssa dyed her hair back to its original black and wore it in braids to give her a more youthful appearance, so that she would not be as recognizable from a description that might be forced from someone with whom she had worked. Unicorn, or René as they now called him, went back to his old job, reasoning that there was nothing to fear since no one in the resistance had known his real name or where he worked.

Faith and Unicorn left each day for work, while Alyssa stayed home and did their shopping, cooking, and cleaning. She grew increasingly frustrated; hiding in an apartment and being domestic was hardly what she had come to France for. However, it was safer for them all for her not to try to find a job; she was much more likely to be found out, and besides, she had few marketable skills. And she could do nothing of the work she was trained for until they found another resistance group.

In the evenings they visited the small cafes along the Boul' Mich' and the larger ones on the Saint-Germain-des-Prés that were favorites of the resistance. But they had little luck. Faith and Unicorn saw no one they recognized from the organization, and any questions they asked were met with blank stares. On her next transmission home, Alyssa asked for help in locating a new group, but Mother could give her nothing. Headquarters was still groping in the dark, unsure which groups had been compromised; any group they gave Alyssa could in reality be under the operation of the Nazis.

Finally one evening Unicorn came home, his face gleaming with barely suppressed excitement, and announced that he had found a man who belonged to another cell of the Rock network.

The man, though somewhat suspicious of him, had agreed to let them meet his cell's leader the following night in the Catacombs.

Late the next evening Unicorn, Faith and Alyssa slipped down an entrance to the underground chambers. When they reached the bottom of the steps, Alyssa gasped and shivered, not entirely from the cool temperature of the place. The Catacombs had addressed two problems in Paris: the overflowing cemeteries inside the city, and ancient quarries beneath the Montparnasse area that had been plagued by buildings collapsing and mine cave-ins. During the eighteenth century the city officials had shored up the subterranean holes with skeletons taken from the crowded cemeteries. Alyssa had known the history of the place, but it hadn't prepared her for the macabre tunnels.

The walls of the tunnels were made of solidly packed bones, placed side by side with the ends pointing outward. Rows of skulls, spaced a few feet apart, ran between the other bones like morbid decorative borders. It was cold, dark, and damp, and the light of Unicorn's flashlight didn't alleviate the gloom, only added eerie shadows.

They walked along the walled pathway and turned into another. The place was a haphazard collection of intersecting tunnels, and Alyssa was soon hopelessly lost. After a time they came to a well, and here Unicorn stopped. He switched off his light to conserve the battery. The darkness was total. Alyssa found the utter blackness less frightening than the rows of bones and grinning skulls.

Finally the bobbing of a lantern approached from a different direction. As they came nearer, Alyssa could see two men. Unicorn stepped forward to greet the one in front, who carried the lantern. They talked briefly, and Unicorn came back to the two women. "He wants to blindfold us so that we can't identify their leader and the other nor find their meeting place again."

Alyssa and Faith agreed, though they dreaded it. At least it indicated that if the group decided not to accept them, they wouldn't kill them to keep their identities secret. The men stepped forward and bound their eyes tightly with black bands of cloth. One of the men took the two women by the arms, and the man with the lantern led Unicorn. They walked for a long time, twisting and turning. Finally they stopped, and their guide told them to sit on the floor. Alyssa heard a faint shuffling, a cough, a whisper too soft to be understood.

"Why do you want to join us?" A harsh, grating voice came out of the darkness near Alyssa.

Unicorn explained what had happened to their own group, and another voice sneered, "How do we know you aren't the ones responsible? They say it was a traitor. How do we know we can trust you?"

"How do we know we can trust you?" Alyssa retorted. "It may be your game to trap those who wish to fight the Nazis."

"Ah, but you are the ones who want to join us, not the other way around. You must prove yourselves to us."

"How can we do that?" Alyssa identified Faith's voice across the pathway from her.

"This man says one of you is a pianist from England. Is that true?"

"I am."

"When did you come here? Tell us about your training in England."

"You must know I can't give information like that to anyone. But if you like, I can send a message. Will that prove it?"

"It would prove you're a telegraphist, but not that you're from England."

"You speak very good French for an Englishwoman."

"I have spent some time in France, and I'm good at languages. Anyway, I'm an American."

Another man's voice spoke, "I have spent time in America. I stayed at the Plaza Hotel on Park Avenue."

Alyssa smiled. "It's on Fifth Avenue."

"Ah, yes, that's right. And where is Louisville?"

"Kentucky."

They asked a few more questions of them, then the main speaker told them to remove their blindfolds. Alyssa looked around at their questioners. There were four men of various shapes, sizes, and colorings. The leader, a large, beefy man, stuck out his hand to shake theirs. "My name is Allegro. You are welcome to join us."

Chapter 17

As soon as Jessica stepped inside the door of her house, she heard Ky and Claire laughing upstairs. Ky was home on leave this weekend. Claire's laughter was a breathless giggle, and his was low and deep, and there was something obviously, intensely sexual about it. A quiver raced through Jessica's abdomen. It didn't take much to awaken the barely dormant sexuality in her these days, apparently. It had been two weeks since she had discovered the amazing fact that she was attracted to Stephen—indeed, it seemed like a very weak word to describe the bubbling longings within her—and since then she had done little but think about Stephen and her desire for him.

Why wasn't he attracted to her in return, she wondered. As Claire had pointed out, he spent a great deal of time with her. Of course, there was nothing to say that he didn't spend even more time with other women; after all, she saw him only one day a week usually. But when she was in London, he spent all his free time with her. He liked her, she was positive of that; she would even go so far as to say that he liked her very much. But looking back over the months they had known each other, she couldn't recall a single touch or kiss or even look of desire for her. Did she simply not appeal to him? Or was his heart given to someone else, perhaps someone back home in Chicago? Either possibility sent a slice of pain through her.

Tonight, she told herself, she would somehow find out what it was that made Stephen so indifferent to her. Even if she had to ask outright.

She took the box where she and Claire kept their ration coupons and shuffled through the different colored books—crimson, olive, magenta—for the ones she wanted. She could get a joint of meat, the coffee Stephen and Ky both loved to drink, four ounces of margarine, and even two precious ounces of butter. Adding the potatoes that she had in plenty, she could make a decent meal out of it, especially considering her real prize: two Hershey's chocolate bars given to her on the train today by an American daylight bomber, who gravely assured her he'd fallen in love with her on sight. Jessica had laughed and tried to give them back. She started to tell him she was married and hold up her wedding ring as her usual defense, but she realized that she had taken it off last week and put it away. So she simply said that she already had a date the evening. The flyer just laughed good-naturedly and insisted she take them anyway.

Jessica stuck the coupons into her purse and hurried to buy what she needed, then spent most of the rest of the afternoon whipping together a presentable meal. When she was done, she searched the bathroom cabinet and found an aging bottle of bath salts stuck way at the back. She took a long, soaking bath and styled her hair in a fashion she'd never tried before, swept up and pinned, with the top a riot of curls.

She was pleased with the results, so she dressed in a frock she hadn't worn since before the Germans conquered France, a beautiful black silk Molyneaux. No stockings, of course, for anything but silk would have looked ridiculous, and she hadn't seen silk stockings in over a year now. But with a bit of powder and lipstick, and the briefest touch of her precious supply of French perfume—now down to the bottom of her last tiny bottle—she decided that she'd do well enough. Perhaps Stephen Marek wouldn't find it so easy to ignore her tonight.

In fact, when she answered his knock and Stephen saw her framed in the doorway, her hair a saucy cap of curls that invited his fingers, her lips glistening, the black dress softly outlining her breasts and hips, he almost turned and walked away. He didn't think he could stand to be around her tonight and not kiss her. But neither could he bear to leave, and it would be too absurd anyway, so he came inside, gritting his teeth and looking absolutely thunderous.

Jessica stepped back a little before his look. "My goodness, what's happened?"

"What? Nothing particularly. Why?"

"You look so black, as if you'd like to put your hands around someone's throat."

And so he would, though not to choke, but to glide up Jessica's neck and cup her face, or down her shoulders and arms, feeling the cool smoothness of silk overlying her even softer skin. He cleared his throat. "No. Just tired of being stuck here, I guess, playing diplomat between a bunch of green Americans and another bunch of rigid Englishmen."

Her heart clenched in fear. "You're wanting to get back into action?"

"Yes. I've never liked trying to smooth things over. A loner, that's me." He sighed and tried to summon up a smile. "But I don't think headquarters wants me back in the field, after the way I fouled up the last mission."

"Don't be nonsensical. You didn't 'foul' it up. You and your partner got the man you went for, didn't you? And both of you managed to return yourselves as well. That's quite an accomplishment."

But we didn't save your husband. He didn't say it, but he knew it was in both their minds.

Jessica frowned. "If there's a reason they haven't given you another assignment other than because you needed the rest and are handy as a liaison to the Americans, it's probably because they believe you're not in the proper mental condition for it. It's you who think you failed in your mission, and as long as you believe that, you haven't the confidence to take on another one. I imagine they know it."

Stephen stared at her in some amazement. He'd expected them to send him out again and had been half surprised, half worried that they hadn't. But he hadn't realized until this moment that he was dreading the time when they did. Not getting wounded or caught—he'd long ago learned to live with those common fears—he dreaded making another mess of it. How had Jessica known when he hadn't even known it himself?

Jessica and Stephen walked down the hall to the kitchen. Once, she thought, she would have reached out and taken his hand to lead him there, but now she was too self-conscious to do that. She wanted too much to feel the touch of his skin.

"Mmmm." He sniffed the air appreciatively and sneaked a peek in all the pots. "Mutton?"

"Yes. Do you like it?"

He chuckled. "I've acquired the taste over the years. Hard for a boy from Chicago. I didn't know there was any meat besides beef until I was a grown man."

She laughed and made a face at him, as he intended her to, and he thought, as he thought each time he saw her anew, how lovely she was. How infinitely precious. How far away from him.

"Shall I set the table?" he asked to break the train of his thoughts. "I'm good at it. My older sisters always pushed it off on me."

"Already done. You just sit there and relax while I check on the meat."

He looked down blankly at the bare oak kitchen table. "You call this table set?"

Jessica laughed. "We're not eating in here, silly. Quite fancy tonight—we're using the formal dining room down the hall." She nodded in the direction of the dining room, and Stephen stepped down the hall to look at it.

"I've never seen this," he commented, glancing around the elegant room, softly lit and furnished with heavy pieces that looked centuries old and terribly grand.

"Mm-hm. I seldom use it nowadays. Seems a waste with just me and Claire. And too much trouble, with no servants to clean it. Besides, you're always whisking me away to eat out."

He glanced at the blue and white Wedgwood dishes and heavy silver utensils arranged on the table. "Four places? Is someone coming?"

"Claire and Ky Dubrowski, her husband. He's home on leave for a few days."

"Where are they?"

"Upstairs, where else?" Jessica rolled her eyes. "When Ky is home, they hardly come up for air."

For a moment everything seemed to stop—the clock, their breathing, the very world itself—and the air was alive with sexual tension. Jessica blushed, appalled at her bluntness. She'd only meant to be light and amusing, but somehow she had brought the heavy scent of sensuality right into the room with them. She could think of nothing now but naked bodies and clinging skin, harsh, panting breaths, eager mouths. And she knew that the knowledge was in Stephen's mind, too. She could see it in the sudden tautness around his mouth, the flare in his dark eyes.

"I—I'm sorry. You must think I'm terrible, not a proper British lady at all."

"Don't be silly." Stephen gripped the back of a chair, trying to collect his thoughts. He noticed that there was the faintest tremor in his hands. Lord, but what she said rocked him, driving everything from his mind except the vision of torrid lovemaking. He was intensely aware of Jessica—the sheen of her hair, the seductive scent clinging to her, the whiteness of her skin, her long, narrow hands. He wanted her so much he could hardly think.

After that, neither of them was able to shake the overwhelming atmosphere of desire. No matter what was said, no matter what they did, they could think of nothing else. Jessica dished up the meat and potatoes, and Stephen watched her, his eyes following her capable hands and imagining them on his skin. She tore off a bit of meat and tasted it, and he wanted to feel her mouth, her elegant little white teeth. She moved from the kitchen to the dining room, setting out the food, and he saw nothing but her body moving beneath the slick dress. He wondered what she wore underneath the slinky black gown, and how long it would take to strip it all off.

He hoped that when the other couple joined them, it would lighten the situation, but instead it grew even worse. Claire and Ky came down, flushed and damp from bathing, exuding a satisfied sexuality. They were dressed casually, Claire in a simple housedress and Ky in his shirtsleeves, collar unbuttoned. They looked drained, weary, and utterly happy. Eyes shining, a soft curve to their lips, the sharp edges of strain missing from their faces. The couple chatted with Stephen and Jessica, but their eyes continually strayed back to each other. They were never far apart, hands reaching out to touch or to smooth back a stray piece of hair or to adjust an imaginary misalignment of a sleeve or collar. After dinner, as the foursome talked over coffee and the bits of luxurious chocolate, they scooted back their chairs from the table, and Ky hooked his arm proprietarily over Claire's shoulders. There was something stirringly elemental about their pose; Ky might as well have said: "This is my woman and she pleases me."

Stephen felt envious and hungry. He glanced at Jessica. Her eyes were dark, the pupils large and black. He wondered what she was thinking, if she, too, felt the sizzle of excitement that lay in the room. He wondered what she would do if he kissed her. He wondered if she had ever thought of his touching her.

Claire helped Jessica clean the dishes while Stephen and Ky conversed. Then the married couple smilingly climbed the stairs to Claire's room. There were only the cups and saucers left on the table, and Stephen helped Jessica carry them back to the sink. As Jessica began to wash the dishes, he set the last of the cups into the sink. He looked down at her, unable to make himself move back and pick up a towel. Jessica's skin was rosy and inviting; he could see the tops of her breasts in the V of the dress, jiggling a little as she moved the cloth over the cup.

Stephen hesitated for a moment, his mind thick and slow with passion. He leaned closer, breathing in the subtle fragrance of her perfume. He knew he shouldn't. He was afraid she would hate him. But he couldn't stop. He bent and touched his lips to the soft white skin where her neck joined her shoulders. His mouth was as light as a butterfly's wings.

Jessica let out a breathy little sigh, and her eyes fluttered closed. His mouth pressed deeper, sinking into her softness. His lips slid upward, tasting the faint bitterness of her perfume, the sweetness of her skin, until he came to her ear. He nuzzled it, and his tongue came out to trace the rigid whorls. His teeth closed over the sensitive, plump lobe, worrying it gently.

Streaks of pleasure darted through Jessica, so intense she was scared to move lest it stop. She thought she might melt and flow down into a puddle at his feet. Stephen pressed closer against her, and she felt the hard bone and muscle of his lean chest and legs, the thrusting hardness against her buttocks that told so clearly how much he wanted her. His breath was hot and fierce against her ear; she could hear its ragged cadence.

He put his hands on her shoulders even though they were still wet and smoothed them slowly down her front to cup her breasts, leaving a damp trail behind. The water glistened on her bare skin and made her dress cling. His thumbs circled her nipples, and they burst to life, suddenly hard and pointing. With the tip of his tongue Stephen licked the dampness from her shoulder. The antique Wedgwood cup Jessica was washing crashed into the sink and broke, unheeded.

Jessica whirled, her arms going up to encircle his neck, and Stephen wrapped his arms around her, crushing her to him. At last he kissed her mouth. His lips were hard and demanding, but they asked no more than Jessica wanted to give. She pressed up into him, her mouth moving against his in hungry response. His tongue filled her, ravaged her. She couldn't get enough of him. She twisted up, feeling the pressure of his manhood through her clothes and wanting to position herself where she ached most to feel it. He knew what she sought, and his hands went to her hips, lifting her up and into him, grinding his hips against her.

Jessica wanted him with a wildness she had never known. Stephen was driven, aching, primitive, almost mindless with desire. His lips left hers and roamed down her neck, and she whimpered, moving her leg restlessly against his. His mouth reached the top of her breast, and Stephen thrust down her bodice, delving into her slip and freeing her breast. The soft globe nestled in his hand, pure white against his brownness. His eyes darkened, and he bent to take her breast in his mouth, almost shaking in his eagerness, starved for her taste.

Jessica groaned, her fingers digging into his shoulders. Stephen's mouth seemed to pull at a cord that went straight down to her abdomen, and each tug sent the hot moisture of desire flooding between her legs. She almost cried at the pleasure, so intense it tasted of pain. She wanted him inside her, wanted the full measure of his strength and hardness.

But some small remnant of her mind reminded her that they were in the kitchen and that she didn't want their love-making to happen in this public, mundane place. "Please," she murmured. "Not here. Not here."

He heard and understood, though he said nothing. Sweeping her up in his arms, he carried her up the back servants' stairs and into the hall above. Jessica motioned to her room and he went inside, nudging the door closed with his shoulder. Slowly Stephen let her slide to the floor, enjoying the sensation of her body against him, thinking of nothing, aware of nothing, but Jessica and his desire for her. She looked up at him. His eyes were wild and black as he glanced around, seeking the bed. Suddenly he stiffened and stared across the room as though struck to stone. Jessica whirled, looking where his eyes did, and she saw the picture of Alan that sat on her dresser.

Stephen turned to her, his eyes stricken, like an animal in pain. "Oh, God, Jess. Jess. I'm sorry."

"No, wait!" she began, but he had already rushed from the room. Jessica darted after him, still overcome by his caresses and dazed. "Stephen!"

He clattered down the front stairs, and by the time Jessica reached the top of the stairs, he was already opening the front door. "Stephen, wait! What's the matter? Please." She hurried down the stairs. "Please, tell me."

He shot her a look that was dark with despair and self-hatred. "You're Alan's wife, that's what's the matter."

She gaped as he opened the door and went out into the night. "I'm his widow!" she protested.

But he was already gone.

*****

Allegro's group did not need a pianist at the moment, but he promised that he would find a group that did. In the meantime Alyssa worked for Allegro as a courier, much as she had done for Jules.

One afternoon Alyssa left a message at a bookshop, hiding it in a book of short stories by Balzac. She found a scrap of paper already there, waiting for her. She slipped it into her pocket and left, not reading it until she was safe within the walls of her apartment. It said little, only her code name, the time 18:00, and the word "Dome," which she knew to be a small café in the Montparnasse area. When she showed the message to Unicorn, he frowned and insisted on coming with her to the meeting, concerned that it might be a trap of some kind. Alyssa agreed, for the message made her a little uneasy, too.

She and Unicorn were at the café early, and they had to wait thirty minutes before Allegro arrived. He frowned when he saw Unicorn. "I didn't ask for you."

Unicorn shrugged. "I was afraid it might be a trick. I'm more experienced at these things than Cleopatra."

"She does well enough by herself." Not for the first time, Alyssa sensed a bit of animosity for Unicorn in their new leader. From things Allegro had said and the way he looked at her sometimes, Alyssa had begun to wonder whether the group's leader was becoming romantically interested in her. If so, he might think her relationship with Unicorn was more than platonic and resent it.

"Why did you want me to meet you here?" Alyssa asked, drawing Allegro's attention from Unicorn.

"I have a new job for you." Allegro couldn't conceal the light in his eyes. "You are very lucky."

"What is it?" Excitement began to stir in Alyssa. From Allegro's manner, this was something special.

"The leader of the network has lost several people in his group. A freak accident. They were supposed to meet someone near the university, and they got caught in a student demonstration. The Gestapo rounded them up. Hopefully, the Germans won't realize what an important catch they've made. One of the people lost was Dragon's pianist."

"Dragon?"

"Yes. He's the leader of Rock. A very important man. He wants to meet you."

"All right. Where?"

"He's coming now."

Alyssa looked up. A tall, inordinately thin man, fortyish and balding, was walking toward them. When he sat down at the table with them, Alyssa could see that his small brown eyes were hard and sharp, like those of predatory bird. He glanced at Unicorn.

"Who is this one?" He talked in a peculiar husky whisper.

"Unicorn. He was a member of Cleopatra's original cell and is with us now."

Dragon turned his eyes to Alyssa. "You are very pretty, my dear. How have you managed to escape the Nazis' notice?"

Alyssa smiled. "I try to stay out of their way."

She had thought he would ask her questions, but instead he only studied her for a long moment, then said, "I have a message which must be sent now." He laid a book down on the table between them. "Tell Mother what happened to my pianist. Meet me tomorrow at noon at Brasserie Lipp to give me their reply."

"I want to join your group, too," Unicorn said boldly. "Allegro told us you were short on men."

Dragon's cold, bright eyes flickered over him, assessing. "I do have need of more men. But you are part of Allegro's cell now." He looked toward Allegro inquiringly.

Allegro shrugged. Alyssa suspected he would be happy to get rid of Unicorn. "It won't hurt my group, Cousin. They were extra anyway."

"All right. I will be in touch with you about it." Dragon downed his drink in one gulp and left as abruptly as he had come. Moments later Alyssa and Unicorn also left. Alyssa was eager to get to her message, and she ground her teeth in frustration when they stepped inside and found their landlady visiting in the parlor with Faith.

But Alyssa managed a cheerful smile for the woman and excused herself for a moment. She set down the book Dragon had given her in the bedroom she shared with Faith, then returned to the front room to chat. She envied Unicorn; being a man, he wasn't expected to do more than exchange a pleasant greeting with the woman, and he retired almost immediately to his bedroom. It took over thirty minutes of nerve-fraying small talk before the landlady finally left and Alyssa was able to escape to her bedroom.

She picked up the book and flipped through it, stopping when it opened to a page where a thin piece of paper had been inserted. On one side was written the name of a café, Brasserie Lipp, and a time of twelve noon the next day. She turned the paper over and her breath caught in her throat. The message began "From le Duc." Quickly she ran her eyes over the message, which was a long rendering of information about Nazi movements. Dragon was the Duke, the spy for headquarters whose name was mentioned with hushed reverence.

Alyssa sat down abruptly. Allegro had been right when he had said it was an important job. Probably even he didn't realize how important. She wanted to jump up and run in to tell Unicorn, but she stopped herself. Such information was too important to reveal to anyone. A man might tell anything under torture.

Instead, she pulled out her transmitter case and set it up to send the message.

*****

It was the middle of the night. The apartment was hushed and dark. Unicorn opened his door and slipped into the hall, padding to the front door and easing the lock open. Stepping outside, he moved like a wraith down the stairs and out the front door. Outside, he paused to slip on his shoes, then scurried along the sidewalk to the nearest public telephone.

Inside the phone booth, he pulled a scrap of paper from his pocket and dialed the telephone number written on it. The phone rang over and over before it was finally answered by a sleepy male voice. *"Ja?"*

"I must speak to Herr Schlieker."

"Don't be insane," The speaker switched to heavily accented French. "It's two o'clock!"

"I realize that," Unicorn replied acerbically. "But I wouldn't be out telephoning him at this hour of the night if it weren't something important. Get him."

"Give me your name and the message. I'll tell him when he wakes up."

"Nom de Dieu! You idiot, get Schlieker on this phone, or it may be the last time you answer it."

There was a hesitation on the other end of the line, then the servant said, "One moment."

Two minutes later Schlieker's voice was on the phone, as crisp as if he'd never been asleep. "Yes? This had better be as important as you said."

"Is knowing the identity of the Duke important enough to awaken you?"

"Mein Gott!" For the first time since he'd met him, Unicorn heard excitement in the German's voice. "Are you serious?"

"Never more so."

"Then tell me, you fool! Who is it?"

"Where's my payment?"

"Don't try to bargain with me. You'll regret it. Tell me."

"My friend was asked to send a message tonight by a man known as Dragon. I sneaked into her room and read the message. It was a listing of information I'm sure you would rather be kept secret, and it was signed le Duc."

"This Dragon. You think he is the one?"

"Possibly, though I suspect he is more likely the go-between we talked of. But he should know the spy's identity."

Schlieker chuckled. "And I presume you know where we can pick him up?"

"Yes, he'll be at the Brasserie Lipp tomorrow with my friend. You can take them both; she is of no more use to me."

*****

Alyssa was late to her meeting, and she hurried, ashamed that she should be tardy at her first assignment with Dragon. She had set out in plenty of time, but a Nazi checkpoint had made a detour necessary. Though she had false papers, it was better not to expose them to scrutiny if she could avoid it.

Dragon was waiting for her when she arrived, and she slipped into the seat across from him breathlessly. Her cheeks were flushed from her haste, and she looked unusually pretty. Even Dragon, who was known for his somber nature, had to smile.

"I'm sorry I'm late. I had to make a detour; they were checking ID's."

"It is no problem. I have been enjoying the sunshine. Very pleasant today, don't you think?"

"Yes." Alyssa opened her large handbag and took out the book Dragon had given her last night. She laid it down on the table just as the waiter arrived to take her lunch order. Dragon had already ordered, and his meal lay on the table before him. He had eaten little of it, and now as he and Alyssa chatted, he poked the food around on his plate, not eating.

"You aren't hungry?" she asked, thinking of how very thin he was.

He shook his head. "I have developed a stomach condition. An ulcer. I was not made for intrigue, I suppose."

"Were any of us?"

"Yes, some. Allegro loves it. My cousin is a man for danger; he has been so since we were boys growing up. I sense that about your Unicorn as well."

"Perhaps that's why they don't like each other?"

He smiled. "I think it may have more to do with you."

Alyssa returned the smile, shaking her head in modest denial. She wondered if Dragon was really the Duke; she had realized last night that he might be only a messenger for the spy. She glanced toward the sidewalk, past Dragon's shoulder. Her smile froze. Four Gestapo soldiers were walking through the tables toward them. "Gestapo!" she breathed.

Dragon's head snapped up, and by the expression on his face Alyssa realized that there were more soldiers behind her. They looked at each other, their eyes flaring first with fear, then a shocking realization. Only two other people know of this rendezvous: Allegro and Unicorn.

"Allegro is my cousin," Dragon said softly. "I trust him above all others."

They both knew. Alyssa's stomach contorted in icy pain. Unicorn was a traitor.

A heavy hand clamped down on her shoulder. "Get up, and come with us."

Alyssa stood, unsure whether her legs would support her. Eight booted, heavily armed soldiers stood around them. Escape was impossible. They were escorted to a large gray car and shoved into the back seat. A soldier sat down on either side of them and two in the front. The driver crossed the river and maneuvered the Étoile. Alyssa realized they must be going to the Gestapo headquarters on Avenue Foch.

Only important prisoners were taken to 84 Avenue Foch, and Alyssa knew she was not that valuable. It was Dragon they were after. But did they realize how very vital Dragon was? Did they think only that he was the leader of a cell... or did they know that he was the liaison for le Duc? Whatever happened, she must keep that knowledge to herself.

The car pulled up in front of the classic white stone building on Avenue Foch, and their captors pulled Alyssa and Dragon out of the car. They were marched through the back iron gateway and into the house. Alyssa's knees were watery. She was afraid she might suddenly drop to the floor, unable to walk. She prayed she wouldn't disgrace herself.

Half the soldiers left them once they were inside the building. Two on either side of Alyssa took her down the hall and up the stairs to the second floor. Dragon walked in front of her with his escort. The soldiers stopped Alyssa before a door while Dragon and his escort went on. One soldier opened the door and shoved Alyssa inside, following her.

The room they entered was an office. A male secretary sat behind a desk. Seeing her, he rose and walked through a door in an inner wall of the office. A moment later he returned and spoke to the guards. "Herr Gersbach will see her now."

One of the soldiers poked Alyssa in the back. "Walk."

Alyssa went into another office, larger and more luxuriously furnished than the secretary's. A chunk of a man sat behind the desk. His face was round and pasty, and his eyes were so pale a blue they were almost white. His eyes flicked over Alyssa, and she shivered as though a snake had run across her skin.

"Well," he said, standing up. "You are certainly an improvement over our usual crop."

He jerked his head at the two guards, and they left the room, closing the door behind them. Alyssa held herself stiffly as she watched him approach, willing courage into her icy body. She thought of the L-pill hidden inside the hem of her dress. She had always been afraid she would not be able to withstand torture and had counted on being able to die quickly if ever she was faced with it. But what if she wouldn't be able to remove the pill and place it in her mouth before they started in on her?

She stared straight at the man, her jaw thrusting out a little, determined not to let him see the fear that ate at her insides and chilled her skin.

Gersbach stopped less than a foot away from her, and again his eyes traveled slowly over her face and form. "It would be a shame to ruin that face." He ran his forefinger across her cheek. "The slice of a razor here. Or there. No longer such a pretty girl." He smiled. His hand moved heavily down her body, across her breast and stomach and poked vulgarly between her legs.

Alyssa had been determined not to move, but at his intimate gesture, she recoiled involuntarily. He chuckled. "Don't like that, eh?" His hand splayed over her breast and squeezed painfully. "That is nothing. You will be begging for something that pleasant before I'm done with you." He twisted her nipple between his forefinger and thumb. "I am very successful at getting information from prisoners. Especially women. I like my work, you see. You might want to save yourself the agony and simply tell me what I want to know."

Alyssa answered him with her haughtiest look.

Again he smiled. "Oh, yes, I shall enjoy my session with you a great deal. I'm glad you won't tell me right off."

He reached out and hooked his hand in the neck of her dress and casually tore it downward, exposing one pale breast. Alyssa stepped back and came up against the wall. He made no move toward her, simply gazed at her breast and wet his lips obscenely. Alyssa shivered and pulled the material up, holding it over her bared skin.

"You will be taken to the Cherche-Midi prison, and there you can think about what will happen to you tomorrow. Two of my men will bring you to the Place des Saussaies and take you to my special chamber. There they will strip off your clothes." In horrible detail he described what he would do to her, and bile rose in Alyssa's throat. It required every bit of will she possessed to breathe naturally and keep her face placid, not betraying the terror inside her.

Gersbach called to the guards, and the same men entered the room and marched her out of the house. They walked through the black iron gate and past a sleek black limousine to the gray military car which had brought Alyssa there.

They drove across the city to the dark, looming walls of the women's prison of Cherche-Midi. There the guards released her to a stern-looking female in the gray uniform of the Nazi female auxiliary. The woman led Alyssa deep into the prison to a small, damp, windowless cell. Alyssa had a brief impression of a dirty stone floor and a small bare cot before the matron left, locking the door behind her and leaving Alyssa in utter darkness. There was a scurrying noise, and Alyssa shuddered. Quickly she crossed to the cot, scraping her shins on it, and sat down, curling her legs up under her. It was cold, and she wrapped her arms around herself, shivering. She thought of Gersbach and wanted to vomit.

But at least she had been given extra time. Alyssa reached down and grasped the hem of her skirt, feeling along it for the small bumps that were her pills. When she found them, she carefully picked the threads from her hem, moving slowly in the dark, and pulled out the pills. She fingered them to determine which was the capsuled L-pill and which the other two tablets. She stuck the tablets back in her hem and curled her fingers around the suicide capsule. Tomorrow morning when the Gestapo came for her, she would put the pill in her mouth.

And she would have the last laugh on the sadistic officer, for she would rob him of his victim. Soon after she entered the torture chambers of the Place des Saussaies, she would be dead.

Chapter 18

The door opened with a clank, and Alyssa's head snapped up. She had thought she would never go to sleep, but somehow she had, even cramped in this curled-up position. The female attendant barked an order at her and motioned for her to come out of the cell.

Slowly Alyssa straightened out her legs and stood up. One of them had gone numb, and she could barely walk. She stumbled toward the door, pushing her hair out of her face with one hand while grasping the top of her dress with the other hand, holding it closed. It was torn badly and she hadn't been able to do anything with it to make herself feel less exposed. It was now also wrinkled from sleeping in it, and the odor of the cell clung to her.

She felt horribly dirty and bedraggled, and it surprised her that it should bother her at a time like this. But it did. She desperately needed her pride. They had given her no comb, no water, no mirror. They had brought her no food or drink, either, and hunger and thirst added to the twisting agony of nerves in her stomach.

Alyssa followed the gray-clad woman up several steps and down a long, poorly lit hall, surreptitiously slipping the pill into her mouth and moving it carefully to lodge safely between her teeth and cheek. When she got outside, she would flick it with her tongue onto her teeth and crunch it open. She could have done it here and now, but she didn't want to die in prison. She wanted to see the outside and daytime again.

The guard led her into a small reception room. "Here is your prisoner, sir."

Alyssa kept her head down. She couldn't bear to look at the guards—or had Gersbach himself come for her? She waited. And then a familiar voice said impatiently, "Very well, come along."

Alyssa's head snapped up, and she stared straight into the eyes of the elegantly dressed man across from her. "Philippe," she whispered. Her knees sagged, and he caught her arm, his fingers digging in and compelling her to stay upright. "What are you doing here?"

He cocked an eyebrow, his tone mocking as he answered, "Why, coming to rescue you, my dear. So England's reduced to sending minor actresses out to play spy? It's no wonder they're losing the war."

Alyssa glared at him. He was clean and handsome, his clothes expensive. The crease in his trousers was razor sharp. Alyssa was humiliatingly aware of how she looked, and she hated that he was seeing her this way. She hated his arrogant, smug words. Most of all, she hated that her heart leaped like a crazy thing when she saw him.

Philippe nodded at the woman who had brought Alyssa to him. "Thank you, Fraulein. I will be sure to tell Herr Schlieker of your efficiency." He strode from the room, pulling Alyssa along with him.

She almost had to trot to keep up with his long strides, and she stumbled a time or two. He walked her out of the prison and across the street to a shiny black limousine. A muscular chauffeur standing beside the car jumped to open the door for them. Philippe thrust Alyssa into the back seat and climbed in after her. The chauffeur closed the door and started the car.

Alyssa glanced over at Philippe. "Have you sunk to this now? Joining the Nazis in torturing prisoners?"

There was a flash of fire in his eyes, and she was gratified to see her barb go home, but then his face switched to that same smug amusement, and he said, "I've always found that pleasure is more effective than pain in getting what one wants."

She flushed at his words, but before she could think of anything wounding enough to throw back at him, his cold voice stopped her. "Good Lord, you smell like a peasant. I can see I shall have to clean you up before you're of any use to me."

Up front she could hear the chauffeur smother a snicker. Alyssa scooted as close to the opposite door as she could, and Philippe turned his indifferent face away from her, watching the passing buildings. Nothing else was said the rest of the trip.

Alyssa thought of the pill in her mouth and wondered what to do. She hoped that Philippe's arrival meant she would not be forced to use it—surely, however despicable he had become, he would not turn her over to be tortured—but she didn't dare get rid of her suicide pill or let him see it. If she was lucky, she would be able to slip it back into her hem when they reached wherever he was taking her.

The limousine stopped in front of his apartment building. Alyssa clutched her torn dress tighter to her. She didn't want to face the memories she knew that seeing his home would bring. But she had little choice. Philippe got out of the car and stepped aside with mocking courtesy for her to precede him into the apartment building. The place was unbearably familiar; tears welled in her eyes, and Alyssa struggled to hold them back. Philippe unlocked the door to his apartment and ushered her in, calling out, "Frau Heuser!" Alyssa glanced around. It was very much the same, and she was swept with sorrow. It was so dear. So lost to her.

A slender middle-aged woman entered the room, dressed in a starched gray-and-white servant's uniform without frills of any kind. "This is Frau Heuser, my housekeeper," Philippe told Alyssa, and Alyssa wondered what had happened to Georges. She had always liked the man; perhaps he had been unable to stomach working for a traitor.

Philippe turned back to the German woman. "Take the prisoner and make sure she has a bath. Then give her something else to wear and burn those rags. Be sure to rid her of whatever fleas and other vermin she's picked up as well."

"Yes, *mein Herr*." The older woman came up and grasped Alyssa's arm, surprising her with the strength of her grip.

"Oh, and Frau Heuser—" Philippe's voice stopped them as they left the room. "Make sure she doesn't have a chance to flee or pick up any sort of weapon, either."

"Yes, Herr Michaude." She tugged Alyssa's arm and marched her down the hall to the bathroom. Alyssa thought the woman seemed more like a soldier than a housekeeper.

Frau Heuser entered the bathroom with Alyssa and closed the door behind them. She began to prepare the bath, turning on the taps and dumping in fragrant salts, before turning to Alyssa and saying brusquely, "Take off your clothes and get into the tub. I will be back with your new clothes."

The housekeeper marched out of the room, and as soon as the door closed behind her, Alyssa reached into her mouth and removed the L-pill. She picked up her dress and pulled the other two tablets from the hem as well. Philippe had told the terrible woman to burn her clothes, so she must find some other place to hide the pills. Quickly she glanced around the room. But where could she put them that Philippe might not stumble upon them? She opened the drawers beside the sink, and in the last one she found what she needed: a roll of white adhesive tape, such as one used on a bandage. Quickly she ripped off a piece and stuck the three pills to it, then opened the top drawer and taped the pills to the underside of the counter above it.

Her heart pounding and palms sweaty, she moved away from the drawers. She had seen no straight razor, scissors or nail clippers in her search, nothing that could be used as a weapon. It was doubtless why Frau Heuser felt comfortable leaving her in here alone. Hopefully Alyssa wouldn't need any of those things. However hard Philippe had become, she could not believe that he would hurt her. She drew a deep breath and sat down on the edge of the tub.

Reaching over to turn off the faucets, she cast a longing glance at the water, filled with sweet-smelling bubbles. How long had it been since she'd had a scented, frothy bath? Months and months, not since she'd left the United States. It seemed wicked to accept Philippe's luxury, but she longed so to be clean. She felt filthy and contaminated from the odorous dirt of the prison, the vile touch of Gersbach's hand.

She hesitated for a moment, then rose and began to undress. After all, if she didn't, Frau Heuser was likely to put her in forcibly. Alyssa sank down into the soothing, scented water and leaned back, resting her head against the rim of the tub. For a long time she simply lay there, soaking. There were three little roses of soap, pink, blue, and yellow, sitting in the silver soap tray.

Alyssa picked one up. She'd had nothing but the roughest of soaps since she'd come to France. She sniffed the rose and closed her eyes, remembering other days, other long soaks in the tub. There had been times when Philippe walked in while she bathed and knelt beside her, rolling up his sleeves, and soaped her body all over. Then, with equally close attention, he had rinsed every vestige of soap from her skin.

Just at the thought her abdomen tightened. Alyssa straightened, blushing, and dragged her mind away from her treacherous memories. She scrubbed the soap harshly over her skin, trying to rub away the stench and grime of the Cherche-Midi and to subdue by force the emotions that plagued her.

When she had finished soaping and rinsing her body, she dipped her hair back in the water and washed it. To her surprise, the door opened, and Frau Heuser came in, carrying a bottle. Alyssa gasped and tried to cover her nakedness. "What are you doing in here?"

"I will wash your hair."

"I've already shampooed. Please leave."

The older woman shook her head. "You haven't washed it with this." She poured some foul-smelling concoction into her hand and began to rub it into Alyssa's hair and scalp.

"No! Stop it! What is that?"

"Herr Michaude said to. He wants no lice or fleas in his bed." Frau Heuser continued imperturbably with the scrubbing.

Alyssa's cheeks burned with humiliation. She wasn't sure which was more embarrassing—the idea that she was infested with vermin or the woman's assumption that Alyssa would share Philippe's bed.

Finally Frau Heuser stopped the torturous scrubbing of her head and rinsed out Alyssa's hair with a pitcher full of clean water and pulled the plug.

"I take it my bath is through," Alyssa commented dryly, rising. Frau Heuser held out a large, sinfully soft towel to her, and Alyssa took it, quickly wrapping it around her. As she dried off, Frau Heuser left again and returned with a filmy blue garment over one arm. In her hands was a mirrored cosmetics tray, bordered with silver. On it lay a silver-back brush and comb, two atomizers and a tiny bottle of perfume, several lipsticks, various pots and bottles of cosmetics.

Alyssa took a step toward the tray, drawn by the display of feminine luxury she had known all her life until the last few months. She hadn't realized until that moment how much she missed them—the scent of expensive perfume clinging to her skin and clothes; the rich smoothness of creams, the beauty-enhancing touches of mascara and lipstick, the glossy shine of painted fingernails against a smooth hand.

Surely it wouldn't hurt, she thought, to style her hair attractively and put on makeup and perfume. After all, there was no more reason to hide her looks; the Gestapo had found her. Frau Heuser held out the pale blue peignoir she carried, a soft confection of gleaming satin and delicate lace. Alyssa slipped her arms into it and pulled it closed, tying the soft belt that was the only fastening. She looked at herself in the mirror. Her hair tumbled to her shoulders, wet and tangled. Her skin was dewy and flushed, her eyes bright. The robe caressed her skin, not quite clinging, but lovingly outlining the rich curves of her body. The V of the neckline cut across her white skin and tantalizingly showed the shadowy cleft of her breasts. She looked like a woman of wealth, beauty, and sensuality. Like a woman kept by a powerful man.

Alyssa's expression hardened. There was no way she would be that. Philippe still wanted her physically; he had proved that a year ago in Washington. No doubt that was why he had brought her here from the prison, thinking her gratitude would put her in his bed. That was what the peignoir and the enticing tray of cosmetics were for—to look good for him, to enhance the prize he had captured today. Well, she'd be damned if she would play along with his game. The cosmetics could stay right where they were. She wouldn't go a step out of her way to appear pretty for Philippe Michaude.

Alyssa grabbed the comb and brush from the tray and worked the tangles out of her hair, then left it wet and hanging. She dismissed the rest of the tray with a contemptuous glance, not even applying lipstick to give color to her mouth. She glanced down at the seductive peignoir. "Isn't there anything else to wear?"

Frau Heuser shook her head firmly. "Herr Michaude put that out, and that is what you will wear."

"Of course," Alyssa blew out a short breath. "Then I suppose I'm ready."

The housekeeper led Alyssa out of the bathroom and down the hall into Philippe's bedroom. Everything inside Alyssa quivered when she entered the familiar room. She walked over to the window, crossing her arms across her chest and fighting the sweet memories that flooded her. Velvet dark nights in the bed; lazy, sultry afternoons; the faint breeze through the open windows; the scents and sounds of loving; Philippe's skillful fingers on her skin.

She sat down, then realized she was sitting on the bed and jumped up again immediately, as if she'd been burned. She glanced at Frau Heuser, who observed her with indifference. Alyssa lowered her arms to her sides and faced her, chin thrust out pugnaciously, determined not to let the woman witness the signs of her distress.

The door opened, and Philippe entered, carrying a tray, which he set down on a large lamp table. He dismissed Frau Heuser with a nod, and she left the room, closing the door after her. Alyssa glanced at the tray. There were two plates, each adorned with a yellow, fluffy omelet flecked with green herbs, a plate of light golden croissants and small pats of pale yellow butter pressed into rosettes, a pot of deep red strawberry preserves, and two steaming cups of aromatic, sweet French coffee, laced with cream. She turned her head away quickly so she wouldn't have to look at the tempting food, but she couldn't escape the delicious odors. Her stomach rumbled, and her mouth watered. It had been over twenty-four hours since she'd had anything to eat—and months and months since she had eaten food this delicious.

Philippe pulled over two chairs. "Come and eat. This is bound to be an improvement on prison fare." When Alyssa stayed stubbornly where she was, he added, "Georges made this omelet especially for you. His feelings will be hurt if you don't eat it."

So Georges was still here. Alyssa remembered the last time Georges had whipped up one of his special omelets for them, the night after they had first made love. She set her teeth against the bittersweet memory. "If he still works for you, I doubt he is capable of feelings."

Philippe sighed. "Come! Even martyrs are allowed to eat, you know."

Alyssa sat down. She did have to eat, after all. The food would build up her strength, make her think better. But she also knew that such kindness was often another trick used by the

Gestapo. First fear and intimidation, excruciating pain, and then an officer who was kind, who fed one and healed one's wounds. With such a person even the strongest-willed people were apt to talk, especially about their childhoods or some unimportant thing in the past. And that sort of innocent remark was often what the Germans needed, the kind of thing that headquarters asked about when they tried to establish whether a transmitter was being used by the enemy.

But Philippe already knew thousands of things about her; he wouldn't have to seduce her into taking about her past. Alyssa dug into the meal, ashamed of the way she was cramming down the food, yet unable to slow down. It was too good, and she was too hungry. She kept her eyes lowered, embarrassed to look at Philippe, watching his hands instead. His fingers were curled around his coffee cup, and Alyssa saw with a jolt that they trembled slightly against the eggshell-thin china.

Her eyes darted to his face, fear sweeping through her. Was he ill? Philippe was watching her, an expression of infinite sorrow and pain on his face. Alyssa laid down her fork. Was he ill? Her eyes ran over him. When she first saw him at the prison, she had noticed only how clean and handsome he appeared. But now that she looked closer, she saw that his face was thinner, and there were faint dark circles beneath his eyes. Two deep permanent lines slashed across between his eyebrows, and grooves that had not been there before were etched around his mouth and eyes. There were even touches of gray hair in his temples.

"Philippe!" Alyssa started to rise from her chair, in that instant the war and their relative positions driven from her mind. She knew only a woman's instinct that the man she loved was in pain, that he needed her, that she wanted to soothe and heal him.

Philippe's nostrils flared, and he jumped to his feet, his chair shooting back. "Sit down and eat!" he ordered roughly and strode away to the window, pulling out a pack of cigarettes.

It had been getting harder and harder for Philippe to do the work he'd sworn to do even before he'd discovered Alyssa was in France. Ever since he'd first caught a glimpse of her in Paris, it had been nearly impossible. And that was before she'd been captured. Now... now it was pure agony.

Yesterday, when he was sitting outside the Gestapo headquarters waiting for Schlieker and saw Alyssa being led to the car in front of him, his heart and lungs had stopped. He knew what would happen to her, what might already have happened to her, and he'd been cold and sick with dread. It had taken every ounce of willpower he possessed to regain his calm and coolly remark to Schlieker later that he thought he knew the girl and could perhaps ease from her the information they desired.

There had been murder in his heart today when the prison matron led Alyssa out. She had looked so pitifully dirty and unkempt. He knew how the humiliation must have scored her soul, particularly with him witnessing it. He'd wanted to scoop her up in his arms and smother her with kisses, assure her that he would protect her, but that would have ruined any chance she had of escape. Instead he'd had to be harsh and cool toward her; it wouldn't do to have Walther or Frau Heuser reporting that he was smitten with the woman.

He had to keep Alyssa at arm's length in order to save her life and preserve the fight that meant so much to both of them—whether she ever knew it or not. He could do it; he'd done far worse things. But the one thing he could not endure was her compassion.

Alyssa plumped back down in her seat, flooded with shame. How could she have felt concern for him? How could she have let him see it? It was no loss to her if he was sick or plagued by conscience. He was as much her enemy as the Germans and she should be glad if he was in any way debilitated.

Keeping her eyes down, Alyssa attacked the food left on her plate, shoveling it in. When she was finished, Philippe laid a hand lightly on her wrist. "Would you like more?"

Alyssa looked at him; his touch was soft, almost a caress. He didn't appear to be mocking her now. She put down her fork, knowing she would make herself ill if she continued to eat. Pulling away from his touch, she folded her hands in her lap and gazed down at them. Philippe continued to stand over her. "Were you treated badly in prison? Did they—do anything to you?"

Sarcastically Alyssa retorted, "Why, no, it was just like the George V."

"This is not a game, Alyssa, where your good looks and snappy repartee will get you out of any difficulty. You're facing death and torture! *Nom de Dieu!* Don't you realize what Gersbach would do to you? What if I hadn't happened along yesterday and seen you?"

She didn't reply, just glared up at him, struggling to think of a sufficiently venomous reply. But before she could speak, the door to the hall burst open. Alyssa jumped, and Philippe whirled around. The doorway was filled by a squat man stuffed into a dark suit. Gersbach. Alyssa tightened all over, her stomach squeezing in fear. He looked furious, and behind him loomed two large, armed men.

Chapter 19

"Well, Herr Gersbach," Philippe said pleasantly. Alyssa noted that he moved slightly in front of her, and she was grateful for his presence, however cowardly the urge was. "Come in. What brings you here this morning?" He made a gesture toward the remains of the meal. "Would you care for breakfast? I'll ask Frau Heuser—"

"I don't want any breakfast," Gersbach interrupted impatiently. "I came for the girl."

Philippe perched on the arm of Alyssa's chair and looped an arm around her shoulders, casually possessive. Alyssa stiffened, embarrassed at the flood of sensations that swept through her at Philippe's touch. Even after all that had happened, even with her mind railing against it, her body wanted him. And his gesture was clearly meant to state to the other man that Philippe intended on keeping her for himself. "My guest?" he asked lightly. "I'm afraid that's impossible."

Gersbach's face congested with rage. "Impossible! How dare you say that to me? How dare you take her? She is mine!" The German's eyes ran down Alyssa's body, taking in the soft satin that curved over her breasts. Alyssa was glad she was sitting down so that the table covered everything but her upper torso.

She felt the almost imperceptible stiffening of Philippe's body, but his voice was breezy as he responded, "Ah, but you see, I know the lady from some time back. We are old friends, and Albrecht agreed that I would be able to get more information from her than anyone else." Philippe's forefinger ran a lazy circle down her shoulder, grazing the upper part of her breast and

Alyssa was humiliated by the way her body responded to his touch.

"And I can get it in a much shorter period of time," Philippe went on smugly.

Gersbach's tongue crept out and wet his lips as he stared avidly at Alyssa's breasts. "I will get it out of her. She's mine."

Philippe pulled a slip of paper from a pocket and extended it to the other man. "As you can see, Albrecht has given her to me. Now, unless you care for an omelet, may I suggest you leave so that I can begin, ah, retrieving information from our prisoner?"

Gersbach glared at him, and Alyssa thought he would have liked to crush Philippe between his meaty fists, but obviously Philippe's paper was more powerful than he was, and he backed down grudgingly. "You better get something from her quickly," he growled. "I'll talk to Schlieker about this. If you don't have the information from her by tomorrow, it will be my turn with her."

Philippe smiled and replied carelessly, "Oh, I'll get the information all right, but then she's yours. You know I don't mind sharing with my friends."

Gersbach cast a last, lascivious look at Alyssa before he turned on his heel and left the room. His men followed. Philippe closed the door and returned to Alyssa. She began to tremble all over. Philippe pulled her up from the chair and wrapped his arms around her. He bent his head, and Alyssa felt the soft rush of his breath against her ear as he whispered, "It's all right. I won't let him have you."

Alyssa clung to him, warmed and strengthened by his hard body and powerful arms, for a moment floating in a delicious haze of security. Suddenly she realized what she was doing, that she was holding on to Philippe as if to a rock, believing him, *trusting* him. She broke out of his arms, aghast at her own actions. "Oh, really? Until you decide to 'share' me with your friends, at least."

Philippe grimaced and moved toward her, but Alyssa backed up quickly. "Is that part of your plan to get me to talk? Did you arrange for that brute to charge in here so that I would feel grateful and trusting?"

"Don't be absurd."

"You're the one who's absurd if you think you can get information out of me with sweet words and lovemaking. I got over you a long time ago."

Philippe cocked an eyebrow, and his voice registered mild amusement. "Did you now?" He shrugged off his jacked and tossed it across the chair, then loosened and stripped off his tie. It followed the coat onto the chair, and he sat on the bed to remove his shoes and socks. He stood and folded down the covers of the bed before he unfastened his cuff links and tossed them onto the bedside table. He unbuttoned his shirt, his eyes fixed unswervingly on her, and took it off. Alyssa looked away. His body was lean and powerful; she still felt an elemental pull of desire at the sight of him. But she would *not* let that affect her. He was her enemy.

She glanced back at Philippe and saw that his eyes were ablaze with the familiar heat of his desire. He wanted her. She knew what he would do, how he would touch her. Kiss her. Take her to the trembling heights of passion. Alyssa felt herself begin to melt, but that was more dangerous than any threat. She knew, with a sick hunger, that she had never really gotten over Philippe, hard as she had tried for two years. It would take very little to bring her back under his spell, to fill her up with love for him. If that happened, he would have an unholy power over her. She couldn't risk that. She simply couldn't.

An almost unbearable hunger rose in Philippe as he looked at Alyssa. He wanted to go to her, to take her in his arms and feel her warmth seep into all the dark, cold places that had grown in him these past years. He ached to tell her everything and see the love for him that had once lain there shine again in her face. But that was the most dangerous thing he could do.

He couldn't let her know how much she meant to him, couldn't show her what lay beneath the cold façade he'd built around himself. The slightest change in her demeanor toward him, the least suggestion that she knew he was not the man he pretended to be would arouse the suspicions of the guards and spies who posed as his servants.

At the very least, if they guessed she was important to him, it would place him firmly under their thumb; any threat to her would keep him in line. An even worse possibility was that it would set Schlieker to wondering whether Philippe was truly the man he pretended to be. Schlieker was a suspicious bastard to begin with. They would torture Alyssa to get the truth from her. Hell, they would torture her to get the truth from *him*.

If he let down his guard with her, he would put not only Alyssa and himself in danger, he would jeopardize the entire operation for which he had sacrificed his love. It was imperative that Alyssa continue to believe he was the enemy.

He turned away. "Undress and get into bed."

"Wh-What?" Alyssa's voice faltered, and she moved further away from him.

He hated the fear and disgust in her eyes, but it would ruin the entire charade if Frau Heuser walked in to find his captive not naked and in bed. He cocked an eyebrow and said, "It's nothing I haven't seen before."

But he turned his back to her. Behind him he could hear the soft slide of her belt untying, the silky swish as her dressing gown fell to the floor, the creak of the springs as she climbed into bed. It was almost as torturous as watching her.

He went to the door and flipped the lock, then turned back to the bed, where Alyssa lay, covers pulled up to her chin, glaring at him. Her fierce expression made him smile. "What a fire-eater you are."

He stood at the foot of the bed for a moment, looking down at her. He gazed at the soft bow of her mouth, the curve of her cheek, the shadow of her lashes against her skin. How beautiful she was. More than beautiful. She had wit, character, courage. She infuriated him. She delighted him. He wanted to bury his face in her hair and tell her how proud he was of her, how much he loved her.

What he said was, "Go to sleep. I imagine your night wasn't too restful."

Philippe walked around to the other side of the bed and messed up the pillow and sheets with his hands. He had to at least make it look like he had been in bed with his captive. Taking a smoking jacket from the wardrobe, he pulled it on and went to the desk on the far side of the room. There, he turned on a low light and picked up a notebook and pen.

Alyssa shot straight up in bed. "You never meant to take me, did you?"

He twisted around in the chair to look at her. She seemed almost disappointed, and he couldn't keep a smile from his lips. "Did you want me to?"

"Of course not! I'd rather sleep with a… a snake than with you. But you were cruel to make me think that."

He wanted to tell her that he had to behave this way. That things had to appear just so or the whole operation would fall apart. But he couldn't. "It was the only way I could think of to get you to shut up and get in bed."

"Then how do you plan to get information from me for your friends? Don't think that kindness will make me talk."

"Heaven forbid that kindness should influence you." Philippe laughed. "Now, please, go to sleep."

Alyssa lay back down and rolled over onto her side, facing away from Philippe. Within moments her breathing had slowed to such a pace that Philippe knew she was asleep. He turned his mind to what he had to do. He must send Mother the message that anything from Alyssa was phony. Knowing Ian, he'd manage to turn that to his advantage.

Philippe jotted down a few things he could give Schlieker, pretending they came from Alyssa. There was some false information he'd been wanting to feed them. He could intermingle it with bits of information that were real but relatively unimportant or which Schlieker would soon discover anyway.

He could provide more authenticity by giving them Alyssa's history. Georges was already on his way to the country today to set things up, and she'd be far out of their reach before Schlieker could use the knowledge. Besides, Philippe wanted the Gestapo to know all about Alyssa, for then headquarters wouldn't even consider sending her back to France.

Philippe rose and walked over to the bed to gaze at Alyssa's sleeping form. He desired her with all the aching hunger he'd ever known. She was the one real, pure thing in his life. He wanted desperately to hold her, to feel her skin and mouth pressed against his, hoping that making love to her would wash him clean. Afraid that it would stain her with his dirt. If only he could have her love again… If only she would look at him in the same shining way she once had. Move her hands lovingly across his flesh. Murmur joyous sounds of pleasure at his touch. Then, perhaps, he could be whole again.

But it would never happen. Philippe bent and brushed his lips against her forehead and walked away.

Chapter 20

Jessica didn't see Stephen for a fortnight after they almost made love. When she went to London on leave the next time, he neither called nor came by. She was lonely and hurt, and she didn't understand what had caused his sudden desertion. He'd wanted her; she knew she couldn't be mistaken about that. But when he saw Alan's picture in her bedroom, he ran away, his only reason being that she was Alan's wife. Did her passion for another man only months after Alan's death disgust him? Did he think her cheap because of that? Or was Alan's memory so close to him that he felt he was committing adultery, even with Alan dead?

It was unfair! She had loved Alan, and she had cried bitter tears over him. The past two years her world had been gray without him. But at last she started to feel again, to be happy and alive. To love again. Yet Stephen seemed to want to keep her immured in her widow's weeds, locked in the dreary suffering of mourning. But she was more than just Alan's widow. She was a person in her own right, a woman with the same needs and feelings anyone else. Why couldn't he accept her as herself instead of as an appendage of Alan?

She told herself to forget Stephen, that there was no possibility of anything between them. She would have to start to live again on her own, perhaps find someone else who wanted her without connecting her to her dead husband. But even at the idea, her tears would start, and she realized with a kind of horror that she was grieving again—this time over Stephen Marek. She missed him; she wanted him; life was lonely and bleak without him. She had fooled herself when she thought she was only halfway to loving him. She was already there. She loved him, and already she had lost him.

But Jessica had never been one to give up. She remembered how she had had to jolt Alan into acknowledging his love for her, and the memory made her smile through her tears. Perhaps she was doomed to want men who required a push.

She wiped away her tears and sat down to think, her chin thrust forward in determination. It wasn't all that bad, really. Nothing to cry over. Stephen wasn't completely lost to her as Alan had been. He was alive, and it was possible to bring him back to her. It would simply require some effort on her part.

After a few moments of thought, Jessica went downstairs and called the house in Kensington where Stephen lived. Another American answered the phone and was inclined to linger talking to her himself, but at last she laughingly persuaded him to bring Stephen to the phone. She could hear the trepidation in his voice when he answered, but she started out blithely, as though nothing had happened between them. "Stephen. It's Jessica. How are you?"

"All right." He hesitated, then went on almost as if against his will. "How about you? Are you okay?"

"Perfectly all right. I called to issue an invitation. I have a three-day leave next weekend, and I thought I'd run down to Chilton Dean to see my parents. Perhaps you'd like to come. They'd love to see you again; Mum always mentions you in her letters."

On the other end of the line, Stephen gripped the phone so hard it turned his knuckles white. He shouldn't go. He shouldn't expose himself to the temptation. She was Alan's wife. She would hate him if she knew what really had happened. *I can't.* That's what he should say, and then it would be over. Jessica was too much of a lady to call him again.

But he had almost gone crazy the past couple of weeks without seeing her. He thought about her constantly, and the only way he had avoided calling her when she was on leave last week was to go with one of the men in his house on a sightseeing jaunt to York. He'd hated every minute of the trip, and all he could think of was Jessica and how she must be hurt at his avoidance of her. He ached to see her; just hearing her voice across the telephone wire made his pulse race.

"Stephen? Are you there?"

"Yes. Yes, I'm sorry, just working out my schedule. I'd love to come."

Jessica broke into a grin, but kept her voice carefully steady. "Good. Shall we just meet there? You know the way."

"Yes, that's fine. Tell me when your train gets in, and I'll meet it."

"Friday afternoon, three forty-five."

"I'll be there." They said good-bye, and Stephen hung up, calling himself a fool and feeling happier than he had in two weeks.

It didn't take too much maneuvering to obtain an extra day off the next weekend, and Stephen managed to catch an earlier train than Jessica so he could be there waiting when she arrived at the station. Jessica saw him standing on the platform as the train pulled in, handsome and dark in his olive-green uniform, and her heart gave a leap. She wanted to run from the train straight into his arms. She wondered what he would have done if she had.

Instead, she exited demurely, crisp in a pale blue suit, a cunning straw hat with a half-veil shadowing her eyes. She smiled at Stephen, extending her hand to him. He could have shaken it and let it go, but instead he curled his hand around hers, holding it, and grabbed her small bag with his other hand. If Jessica had had any doubts about his interest in her, they were resolved by the bright flame in his eyes and the broad grin that covered his face.

They walked toward the stairs up to the depot. Stephen couldn't make himself let go of her hand nor could he stop his thumb from caressing the back of her hand in lazy circles. He felt as if he could consume her, just looking at her. "How are you? How was the trip?"

"Fine—to both."

Upstairs he retrieved his duffel bag and carried it as well as her suitcase, but he managed not to let go of her hand. Jessica laced her fingers through his and smiled sunnily. They started home to Malthouse Farm on foot, enjoying the walk on the sunny summer day and enjoying each other's company even more. But a short distance out of the village, a Land Army girl driving a horse-drawn wagon stopped to give them a ride. Jessica was amazed to see that she was the local solicitor's daughter.

The girl laughed when she saw Jessica's expression. "Yes, it's I. Things have changed here, just as they have in the City."

Stephen helped Jessica into the high old wagon, and they rumbled off slowly. "How do you like doing this?" Jessica asked.

The girl smiled. "I'm quite enjoying it, actually. Terrible thing to feel the war's done you a favor, but, frankly, I've always wanted to farm. Of course, it was out of the question before. Now even Father accepts it because it's patriotic. Don't know what I'll do when it's over."

She set them down at the narrow lane leading to the farmhouse. They only walked a short distance before the front door opened and Jessica's sister tumbled out, running toward them.

"Stephen! Jessica!" Jessica suspected her name was an afterthought. Lizzie clearly had a crush on Stephen. She was fourteen and as gangly as Jessica remembered being at her age, all arms and legs and no shape to speak of yet. Her fair hair was in braids, wisps escaping around her face, and she wore a faded blue cotton frock, belted tightly to her thin form. Her skin was as fair as Jessica's and showed her excitement in its high color. A line of freckles crossed her nose and cheeks.

Jessica smiled. Liz was the baby of the family, dear to them all, a madcap, a forgetful rusher, but kind of heart. If it hadn't been for the war, she would have been leaving soon for boarding school in Switzerland, as Jessica had, to acquire some polish. Jessica wondered what would happen to Liz. Because of the war, she would be knowledgeable in ways Jessica had never thought of being and lacking much of what had been considered so important before the war.

Jessica hugged her sister, and Stephen delighted the girl by picking her up and swinging her around before planting a kiss on her forehead. Liz talked and laughed excitedly as they walked to the house, where Jessica's mother, Vivian, stood waiting to greet them. Again there were hugs all around, and Stephen took their bags up to the second floor, bending his head on the stairs to avoid hitting the ceiling. Their home was a fifteenth century half-timbered farmhouse without a level floor or straight door in it, and on the stairs and in some of the upper rooms anyone taller than Jessica couldn't stand upright.

The family was with them the rest of the day, buffering them as Jessica had planned they would, so that she and Stephen were able to be together with little of the tension that would have sprung up in a more intimate setting. What she hadn't planned on was that watching Stephen here with her parents and sister, she would fall more in love with him by the minute. Patting the aging Irish Setter, teasing Lizzie, carrying in the meat platter for Mum, playing checkers with her father before the fire—he was such a perfect part of the picture that it made her heart ache. It was amazing to think how many thousands of miles apart they had grown up, yet how easily he fit into her life.

That night, as she dressed for bed in the room that had been hers from childhood, she thought of Stephen in the room next door. Removing his clothes, slipping into bed. She thought of his skin gleaming in the low light, his firm chest and long, slender legs. She had seen him once or twice in hospital in only his T-shirt and pajamas but never in less. A warm, steady throbbing started low in her abdomen as she imagined how he would look completely naked.

In the guest room, Stephen thought of Jessica amid the chintz and frills of her girlhood, pulling on her nightgown. Would it be cotton and chaste, sprigged with flowers and buttoned to her neck? Or satin and lace, cupping her breasts and hinting of the shadowed nipple and the triangle of hair below. And would the curls that tangled there be the same bright red-gold as the hair on her head? He bit back a groan and jerked the covers up over his head. It was going to be a long night, he could tell. He should never have come. He wouldn't have left for the world.

*****

When Alyssa awakened, she was alone. The light through the window curtains was fading; she must have slept several hours. There was a sheer gown spread across the foot of the bed, as well as the satin robe. Alyssa slipped on the gown. It was made of blue satin trimmed in fine champagne-colored lace, and the front of the bodice was almost entirely lace, which did little to conceal her breasts. Rather, she thought, the hint of concealment made them more alluring.

Quickly Alyssa covered the gown with the matching peignoir. She wondered what woman had left the set of nightclothes here or whether Philippe had simply bought them to accommodate whatever woman chanced to be in his apartment on any particular night. Alyssa didn't know which idea made her feel worse. Clearly, for all his avowals last year in Washington that he loved her still, he hadn't stayed away from other women.

Alyssa padded to the window in her bare feet and opened the curtains. The windows were open in the afternoon heat, and she leaned out and looked down. It was a two-story drop that would be sure to break her legs at least and no handy fire escape or even a rain gutter, as there had been at Jules's apartment. She sighed. The only possibility of escape was through the front door, and she suspected the chances there were none.

Alyssa walked to the door and tried it; to her amazement, the knob turned. She stuck her head out into the hall and saw why there was no need for locks. Philippe's chauffeur was seated in a straight-back chair on the opposite wall. He jumped to his feet as soon as the door opened.

Alyssa smiled half-heartedly and explained that she needed to use the bathroom down the hall. He nodded and watched her as she went into the bathroom and closed the door. A cursory examination was enough to tell her that there was no chance of escape here, either. There was one transom-type window high in the wall, but it was too small for her to squeeze through. Sighing, she opened the drawer where she had put her pills and reached into it. There was nothing attached to the underside of the counter above.

Frantically, she ran her hand all over it, then pulled the drawer out and scrabbled through it to see if the pills had fallen into the drawer. She checked the top again, and finally she had to accept the obvious truth: Her pills were gone. Philippe must have found them and taken away what little weapons she had. She sagged against the counter, fighting the waves of hopelessness that swept through her. Now she didn't even have the comfort of ending her pain if it got bad enough. It was all she could do not to cry.

Alyssa returned to the bedroom and locked the door. It was pointless, of course, for they could get the door down one way or the other, if necessary, and she had nowhere to go. Still, it made her feel safer and more in control of the situation. She went the large easy chair in one corner of the room and sank down into it.

She couldn't give up, she told herself. It was imperative that she escape. She must let headquarters know that Dragon had been captured. If Dragon was not the Duke himself, he must be the liaison to the man—there would, after all, be an extra layer of concealment between their informer and the members of the network. That made his capture just as dangerous to the operation, for Dragon would know who the Duke was, perhaps the only man in France who did so. At the very least, he knew enough about how the Duke gave him the messages that the

Gestapo soon would be able to ferret out the identity of that all-important spy.

Then there was the matter of the traitor. Unicorn. It had to be him. Dragon could have been betrayed by someone in his group who had been arrested by the Nazis the other day. But, while one of them might identify Dragon as the leader of the Rock network, none of them could have known when and where he would be meeting Alyssa. Dragon hadn't even been aware of Alyssa's existence until after that raid.

There were a few members of Dragon's group left, but it seemed unlikely that Dragon would have revealed his plans to any of them, given that those captured might reveal the other members of the group. After all, he had turned to his cousin Allegro, a trusted family member, when he needed a new radio-telegraphist.

Only Allegro and Unicorn were with Alyssa when Dragon told her where and when he would meet her the next day. And Allegro was Dragon's cousin. A family member could, of course, betray one, but how much more likely was it that a stranger would?

But, no, surely Unicorn couldn't be a traitor. He was her friend; he'd helped her escape when the Nazis broke in and captured Jules and the others. But, looking back on it, wasn't it suspicious that Unicorn had been with the others in the living room but was the only one who had managed to run away? The Gestapo could have let him escape so that he would be free to join and entrap other resistance groups. Yes, he had taken Alyssa along, but he more or less had to if he didn't want to reveal his betrayal. Besides, two of them escaping would raise less suspicion among the freedom fighters.

It all made a terrible sense. A radio-telegraphist would have been a valuable asset for Unicorn; they were in great demand. Any group would jump at the chance to get one. Because she was an American and a telegraphist, her identity was easy to verify, and once she was accepted as genuine, her companion would be more or less taken on faith.

Just as important, Alyssa would trust him. She thought of how insistent Unicorn had been that he accompany her to that first meeting with Dragon and how easily she accepted his excuse that he wanted to protect her. She hadn't even thought about how unusual that behavior was among the secretive freedom fighters. Working separately was one of their firm beliefs.

And her trust would make it far easier for him to discover the vital information a radio-telegraphist received. She thought of Unicorn going to his bedroom the other day while she talked in the parlor with Faith and the landlady. Dragon's book had been lying in her unlocked bedroom. It would have been easy for him to read the message and realize he had stumbled on the Duke himself, or the person closest to the Duke.

Alyssa shivered. Dear God. She had betrayed England's brightest hope in France!

Guilt swamped her. It was all her fault. Because of her, Unicorn had been easily allowed into Allegro's group. She had let him come with her to that meeting. Worst, her carelessness with the book had exposed Dragon to the traitor. How could she have been so easily deceived? That Unicorn was obviously practiced and had deceived many others besides herself was no excuse. She had been around him almost constantly, she should have noticed something! After all, she was an actress; you'd think that would make her more qualified to recognize another's acting.

But sitting here and bemoaning what had happened would not help anyone. What would be of value would be to escape Philippe and warn headquarters. But how, with no exit possible out the window and either Philippe or the chauffeur watching over her all the time? Her strength wasn't a match for either of them. Perhaps she could find some sort of weapon in the bedroom and use it against Philippe when he returned, but then she would have to make it out the front door past the housekeeper and the chauffeur. And she would have to at least hurt Philippe with the weapon—could she do it?

If by some miracle she made it out of the apartment, where would she go? What would she do? She was sure that the Gestapo had seized her transmitter from their apartment, so she would have to find a resistance group who would believe her and let her use their transmitter. She knew from experience how long that could take. It seemed impossible.

Still, she had to try. Alyssa began to search the room for a weapon. She could find nothing, not even a letter opener in Philippe's desk. The best she could do would be to hit him over the head with a heavy object such as an ashtray or one of the lamps, but it seemed unlikely that she could take him by surprise with one of them. And could she do it? How could she pick up something and smash it into Philippe's head, even to escape?

The doorknob rattled, followed by a loud knock.

"Who is it?" Alyssa called. She certainly wasn't going to open it if it was Gersbach standing outside.

"Frau Heuser!" came the irritable answer. "Open this at once. Herr Michaude will not like you locking the door."

Alyssa opened the door, and the housekeeper puffed in indignantly, carrying a large tray of food. She set the tray down on the table and marched out without another word, pointedly leaving the door open. Alyssa made a childish face at the empty doorway and sat down at the table. Suddenly she was hungry again. The food was lacking in style and too heavy, but it was plentiful and tasty, and Alyssa ate eagerly.

When she was finished, she set her tray down outside her door and returned to the large easy chair across the room. There, with nothing to do or think about, it was hard to keep the memories at bay and harder still to deny the longing that filled her at the thought of Philippe. She wondered where he was and when he would return. She wondered if he would try to seduce her. She couldn't give in to him. She tried to gird herself to face him, to thwart him. She laid elaborate, doubtlessly impossible, plans to incapacitate him and slip out of the house in the night.

Rather anticlimactically, the hours crept by and Philippe didn't return. Boredom, coupled with days of tension and lack of sleep, weighed on her, and she went to bed. But she found she could not sleep; the thought of the bulky chauffeur lurking in the hall kept her too on edge. Finally, she heard the sound of the outside door opening and closing, then the low murmur of voices. Philippe had returned. It shouldn't have been reassuring, but strangely, the knowledge made her relax, and she slipped into sleep.

*****

Alyssa drifted awake from a warm, contented sleep. She lay with her cheek against smooth skin—the feeling, the scent, the warmth sweetly familiar. Philippe. He must have joined her in bed sometime during the night; she could hardly believe it hadn't awakened her. Her head was nestled on Philippe's shoulder, her arm thrown across him and their legs intertwined.

Alyssa's eyes flew open as their position registered in her brain, and she jerked up to a sitting position. Philippe awoke and smiled at her, his face drowsy and unguarded, in that moment so much the man she had fallen in love with. He curled a hand around the back of her neck and pulled her down for a kiss.

His lips were warm and soft. It wasn't a demanding kiss or a passionate one, but one of gentle affection. It shook Alyssa more than anything else could have. She drew back shakily and stared at him, not knowing what to do. He gazed at her for a moment, then his face shifted and changed. He pulled inside himself, and the lined world-weary mask was in place again.

Philippe swung out of bed and stood up. He was naked, and Alyssa's eyes ran involuntarily, hungrily down the muscled curves of his back, buttocks, and legs. She sucked her breath in when she was the long swoop of a reddish scar across his lower back.

"What's that!" She gasped.

Philippe turned and looked at her with mild questioning. "What? Oh. The scar? A few of your friends gave that to me about four months ago."

"What?"

"Some loyal Frenchmen tried to assassinate me for my sins." He pointed to a small puckered pink scar on his right arm. "This was a present from a poor marksman. It's fortunate that those who hate me are amateurs." He pulled on his dressing gown, covering the scars.

Alyssa swallowed. She was suddenly cold as ice. She had known that he was hated, even that there had been an assassination attempt on him, but the sight of his scars made it real. She didn't care, she told herself. She shouldn't care. The fate of Philippe Michaude should be nothing to her. But she couldn't deny the fear that clutched her insides.

Philippe left the room. When he returned sometime later, his hair was wet and there was a damp towel flung around his shoulders. His chest and feet were bare, but his legs were now encased in blue trousers of the finest silk. He carried a pitcher of steaming water, which he poured into the bowl of the antique shaving stand near the window. He preferred to shave here, looking out on Paris, and Alyssa couldn't count the number of times she had lain lazily in bed and watched him shave. It had been an intimate ritual between lovers. Just the sight of Philippe lathering his face started a hot little ache between her legs.

Alyssa moved restlessly, crossing her legs beneath the sheets. Damn him! Why did he still have to be so appealing? Why did her treacherous heart ache at the signs of care upon his face? To cover her emotions, she commented lightly, "Your traitorous dealings seem to be telling on you. You look older."

"Perhaps I've been pining away for you."

Alyssa frowned and got out of bed, pulling her robe on over the flimsy gown. When she looked up, she caught him watching her, and she blushed. Though he didn't move, his eyes were avid, hungry; she felt almost as if he had touched her. Alyssa glanced away quickly.

"Don't you have any other clothes for me to wear? Surely you keep a more extensive wardrobe for your female visitors than this."

"I have no female visitors in this room," he responded quietly and turned back to his shaving.

Alyssa glanced at him, startled. "You can't expect me to believe that," she retorted, her eyes narrowed.

He shrugged. "Believe what you like."

"What about the women you procure for your German friends? Surely you try out the merchandise first. What about the woman I saw with you that day?"

Philippe frowned as he set down his razor and wiped the remains of the lather from his face. "Who? Oh. Geneviève?"

"I suppose. The woman you were kissing on the steps in front of a house."

"Jealous?" He raised one eyebrow mockingly.

"Don't be absurd. I don't envy any woman sleeping with filth."

"Yet you once slept with the same filth and seemed to enjoy it." Philippe crossed the room with long, quick strides, stopping only inches away from her. "Or have you conveniently forgotten that?" His voice was harsh, and his eyes flamed.

"I only wish I could forget it!"

"Do you? Do you really, Alyssa? Do you hate to recall how my skin felt on yours?" He laid his hands on her shoulders, sliding across the glimmering satin with the lightest of caresses.

Alyssa felt the shock of his touch all the way through her. She wanted to speak, to stop him, but her mouth was too dry to utter a sound, and her limbs were heavy and weak.

"How my lips touched yours? How you responded to me?" Philippe's hands slid down her arms, and he pulled her slowly to him. His head bent, and Alyssa stared into his eyes, unable to look away. His mouth touched hers, hot and sweetly familiar.

She smelled the faint scent of his shaving soap, felt his arms sliding around to enclose her; his chest hard against her breasts. It was forbidden. It was heavenly.

She made a soft noise of confusion and regret—and surrender. She pressed upward, opening her mouth to him, seeking the joy she had lost long ago. At her movement, he shuddered, and his arms tightened convulsively around her. He was suddenly, fiercely out of control. Desire, long pent up, pounded in him, thick and hard and unreasoning. Time and place were gone. Gone, too, all gentleness and savoring. There was only hunger—immediate, craving, insatiable.

His lips ground into hers, and his tongue plunged into her mouth. His hands slid over the slick satin, moving it against her skin. He wanted to tear the garment from her, wanted to sink into her softness. He changed the angle of their kiss. His every breath was difficult, shallow. He couldn't get enough of her. He couldn't have her quickly enough.

Alyssa moaned and twisted against him. She yearned to feel his hands upon her naked flesh. She couldn't think, only feel. And she wanted him. The sky could have fallen in, and she still would have had to have him. Like a relentless wall of water, her passion swept her onward. She clung to him, scratching her nails down his back in silent urging. She moaned his name, and felt his answering groan against her mouth.

Philippe shoved down her robe and gown, not noticing the slight sound of ripping, not caring. Her breast were bared, and his hand came up to claim them. Her nipples hardened and pressed against his hand, pebbly in contrast to the silken smoothness of her breasts. He lifted her up and took one nipple into his mouth, stroking it with his tongue. Alyssa writhed and dug her fingers into his still-damp hair. She moved her legs restlessly against his, encountering the frustrating cloth of his trousers.

"Please," she cried softly. "Please."

His mouth went to her other breast, loving it with the same devouring haste. Alyssa felt as though she were burning. Dying. She wrapped her legs around him, squeezing him to her, and felt a primitive satisfaction at the great tremor than ran through him. Philippe raised his head and let her slide slowly down so her feet touched the floor, their bodies touching at every point. His hands went to the fastening of his trousers, and he quickly removed his clothes.

His eyes never leaving her, he trailed his fingers down her stomach and into the cleft between her legs, touching the thick moisture of her desire. Alyssa twisted and thrust against his fingers as they renewed his knowledge of her. She moaned helplessly as he found the hard morsel of flesh that was the center of her passion, and the sound stirred him past all reason and restraint. He lifted her, his arms beneath her buttocks, and braced her against the wall. He came into her.

Alyssa wrapped her legs tightly around him. The wall was hard behind her back; his shaft was hard and piercingly sweet within her. Philippe groaned and buried his face in her neck, his hips thrusting, pouring out all the suppressed longing and love within him. Alyssa twisted, sinking her nails into his shoulders, a great explosive force building within her, shoving out everything inside her except this hunger, this need…

Their climax thundered through them, and Philippe cried out. Alyssa shook and held on to Philippe as to the only solidity in a whirlwind.

Slowly they returned to sanity. Slowly Philippe's arms eased around her and allowed Alyssa to slide down until her feet touched the floor. His breath rasped above her head. His skin was hot and damp against her. Alyssa stood for a moment within the circle of his arms. She could feel the throbbing of her own tender flesh, the liquid, boneless luxury of fulfillment.

She realized what she had done. And she cried.

*****

Philippe held Alyssa as she sobbed, and she clung to him. He stroked her hair and back, murmuring soft words of love and comfort. "My love, my love, please don't cry. Shhh. Beloved, please. I never meant to hurt you."

He felt drained and replete, physically satisfied as he hadn't been since he had last lain with Alyssa. But the satisfaction was bitter, robbed of joy. Alyssa hated him, and now she hated herself for making love with him. He knew that she probably felt as if she had betrayed herself and all that she believed in. Why hadn't he been able to control himself? He had not meant even to kiss her.

Philippe carried Alyssa to the bed and set her down on it, wrapping the peignoir around her. He looked down on her dark, satiny hair and ran his hand down it tenderly. "There's been no other woman in this room since you left. The clothes are yours. I bought the gown and robe for you, but I never had the chance to give them to you. If you want to dress, there are some of your clothes in the wardrobe."

He paused. She said nothing and kept her head averted. He turned away and dressed quickly, heartsick and grim. He glanced back at her. She hadn't moved from where he placed her. "I'm going out for a while," Philippe told her. "Please don't do anything foolish. When I return, we'll drive down to the country house."

After he left the room. Alyssa continued to sit on the bed, staring dully at the floor. She had failed at everything. Dragon—and who knows how many others—were in jail because she had foolishly trusted the wrong man. While they suffered unspeakable torments, she was in the arms of their enemy, returning his kisses with fervor, begging for the fulfillment only he could bring her. She lay down on the bed, weak and drained, wrapped in her misery. Frau Heuser brought her a tray of food, but she didn't even see her.

She hated herself. She wanted to die. She had betrayed herself, her friends, her principles. All out of weakness. She loved a wicked man, and she had let her heart rule her.

But as she lay there, her thoughts began to reach past her misery. Philippe's parting words were that they were going to the country house. Surely in the country it would be easier to escape. She knew a few people there from her earlier stay; if she could find someone who would take her to a resistance group, she could let them know about Dragon's capture and Unicorn's betrayal.

And that was the important thing, not weeping over the weakness of her body. Alyssa wiped away her tears and went determinedly to the wardrobe. She searched through Philippe's clothing and at one end found a couple of summer dresses and a skirt and sweater set that she recognized as hers. She remembered leaving them at Philippe's country house when they parted. There had been too many painful memories attached to them.

Thoughtfully Alyssa ran her hand down one of the dresses. Why had Philippe kept them? Had he told the truth when he said that no other woman had been in his bedroom since Alyssa? Did he really love her still?

Alyssa jerked a dress out of the closet and slammed the door shut. What if he did love her? It didn't change anything; it meant nothing except that even a collaborator was capable of love in some form or other.

She bathed and dressed and slipped into the silk-and-lace underthings which sat on the counter in the bathroom, still wrapped in tissue from the store. There were new, more comfortable shoes, too, and when she was dressed, she looked more like the woman she had been two years ago than the plain girl who had lived in Paris the past couple of months. But it was an illusion, she thought, as she looked in the mirror. That woman had died long ago, when the Germans marched into Paris.

Chapter 21

Philippe did not linger at 84 Avenue Foch. He handed Schlieker the information supposedly given to him by Alyssa, and Schlieker ran his eyes down it, his brows rising. "Most impressive." He commented, giving Philippe an approving nod.

"Thank you. Now I have a favor to ask of you."

Schlieker leaned back in his chair, steepling his fingers and resting the tips lightly against his chin. "Certainly."

"I would like to keep the woman a few more days. Take her to my country house."

A genuine smile spread across Schlieker's lips. It was the first time he had detected a real weakness for anyone or anything in Philippe; he enjoyed discovering it. "For pleasure?"

Philippe gave him a smugly male smile. "Of course. Although I think with added time I can entice a few more secrets out of her."

"Perhaps you would like to have her permanently?"

Philippe was startled. "But I thought she was promised to Gersbach…"

Schlieker shrugged. "If you don't want her. But Gersbach can be satisfied with someone else. He's not particular. Most women bleed and scream about the same."

Philippe's stomach twisted. "It might be amusing to keep her for a while." He smiled and let his eyes light with amusement. "But I don't know that I would want *any* woman permanently, not even one as beautiful as she."

"Why don't we leave it indefinite?"

"Of course. Thank you."

"My pleasure. Will you stay for lunch?"

"No, if it's all the same to you. I'd like to get an early start on the drive to the country."

"Ah, yes." Schlieker smirked. "I can see you must get back. Just as well. We picked up a large number of prisoners along with your woman, and I must get back to questioning them. Very stubborn, some of your countrymen."

Normally Philippe would have done a little subtle questioning to try to discover whom Schlieker had brought in. But today he was concerned only with Alyssa. He wanted only to get out of town before Gersbach had a chance to protest his superior's decision. So he shrugged indifferently in response to Schlieker's statement. "Some men are fools."

"Yes." Schlieker bid Philippe good-bye and watched him leave the office. How very interesting. Michaude seemed quite taken with the girl. Men often made idiots of themselves over a woman; he had seen it many times before. But until now Michaude had shown no signs of falling prey to such madness; Schlieker had begun to think the man as immune as he was himself. But now the little spy had seized his fancy. She wasn't particularly important, though Schlieker could certainly use the information Michaude had obtained from her. But she could turn out to be very valuable where Michaude was concerned. You never knew when you might need some leverage in dealing with anyone, even a friend.

Schlieker rose, dismissing Michaude from his mind for the moment, and opened the small door inset in the rear of the room. It opened outward onto a small terrace, and there a man sat on a stone bench, waiting for him. "Come in, Bousquet."

The man rose and followed Schlieker into his office. He held his hat in his hand, turning it nervously. Bousquet hated coming to the headquarters building. He was certain that he would be seen there and that it would eventually lead to his discovery. He avoided the Avenue Foch building assiduously, but Schlieker had more or less commanded him to appear there this morning.

"What can I do for you, sir?" Bousquet asked, always more obsequious inside the headquarters than he was on his own ground. The place made him nervous—and not just because of the risk of being recognized going in or leaving the building.

Schlieker smiled to himself. He knew how Bousquet reacted to number 84 Avenue Foch. That was why he called him down here periodically. "Please, sit down, Herr Bousquet. I have a slight problem with one of the prisoners. The Dragon. He is very stubborn; he's told us nothing."

Bousquet wondered if Schlieker was blaming him for that. He felt like pointing out that getting a prisoner to talk was the Gestapo's job, not his. He was responsible only for turning them in. But he said nothing and waited politely.

"I don't think he is the Duke himself, but I am positive he knows him. I have to find out his name!"

"But how can I help?"

"He is almost through. I am afraid that with more questioning, he will die, and then I will never discover it. He has been completely alone, seen no other prisoners since he was brought in. He has no idea whom we have picked up. I thought if another prisoner were put in the cell, he might confide in him. If he is the only one who knows the Duke's identity, he might feel it important that another of his kind know who the man is and contact him."

"It's a possibility. But he wouldn't tell me. He must have realized that it was I who betrayed him."

"I wasn't suggesting that you go as yourself. But the man's sight is not the best right now. And you are a man accustomed to playing a role. Perhaps there is someone in Allegro's group he might know. Someone you could resemble enough to get by him."

Bousquet pursed his lips, thinking. It sounded rather unlikely to him, but he supposed he must play along with Schlieker. "Not Allegro himself. He is too big. Perhaps the one who had been to America. They call him 'Midnight.'"

Schlieker sneered. "Such romantic names. Well, this Midnight. Could you imitate him?"

"If Dragon can't see well, perhaps. The man is about my size, though his face is narrower. His hair is dark brown; I could dye mine. He has a thin mustache, like this." He ran his finger across his upper lip. "I can cut my hair a little and comb it over to the side in the fashion he does." Bousquet closed his eyes, remembering the man. "He has a distinctive walk. I can imitate it. He throws one foot out."

"That's close enough. We will make your face look battered and bloody; that will take care of any differences. How much time will you need to change your appearance?"

A frisson of fear ran through Bousquet. Exactly how would they make his face look battered? But he kept his voice steady as he answered, "A few hours, that's all."

"Good. Do it." Schlieker smiled in a way that chilled the other man's blood. "I will have that name."

*****

The next morning Jessica awoke in a sparkling mood. Yesterday she had lulled Stephen into a feeling of safety with the presence of her family. Today it was time to put the rest of her plan into action. She decided not to change from the cotton nightgown in which she had slept, and pulled a light robe over it. The combination wasn't exactly sexy or revealing, but just the fact that it was nightwear made it somewhat suggestive. She bounced down to breakfast, smiling.

Stephen sat at the kitchen table by himself, sipping a cup of coffee, as she had suspected he would be. She knew her family's habits. He looked up when she entered, and Jessica saw the quick darkening of his eyes before he pasted on a friendly smile. "There's a pot of oatmeal on the stove. Your mother left it when she and Liz went to town."

Jessica made a face and poured herself a cup of tea. "Why did they go to town?" she asked innocently.

"Volunteer work. Apparently they spend every Saturday rolling bandages or knitting socks or something like that. She said you'd throw together some lunch for us."

"I expect I can manage." Jessica sliced a piece of bread to toast. "Dad out in the fields?"

"Yeah. Up with the chickens. He was already gone when I came down, but I was awake in time to help Lizzie bring in the eggs."

"And no doubt ate them all, too," Jessica joked. They were alone in the house, just as she'd hoped. She glanced at Stephen and saw the same knowledge in his eyes. He looked away quickly.

Jessica swallowed and turned back to her toast. She had set up the situation, everything was going according to plan… now it was time to seduce him.

The only problem was, she hadn't had any practice at this sort of thing.

She cleared her throat. "More coffee?"

"Yes, please." Stephen handed her his cup, and Jessica made sure their fingers grazed each other as she took it. She walked to the counter to pour the coffee, feeling his eyes on her as she moved. Purposely she made her steps slow and languid, prolonging the moment. She returned and leaned over to set the cup down on the table, and she saw his eyes flicker to the neck of her robe, where her shadowed breast were barely visible. She felt her nipples tighten at his gaze and knew that that too, was visible through the soft material.

They sipped their drinks, looking at each other. Jessica's eyes were wide and misty, full of promise. He kept thinking about the night he had kissed her and the way she had reacted. Her pleasure. Her eagerness. How she had arched up into him, hot and sweet and hungry. If he reached for her now, would she come to him the same way? Would her mouth open under his and let him drink his fill?

Slowly, thoughtfully, Jessica ran the tip of her forefinger across her lips. Stephen's hand open on the table, curled up into a fist. His loins were on fire.

She reached across the table and ran her thumb across the tight knuckles of his doubled-up fist. "Are you angry with somebody?"

"I ought to be." His voice was low and thready. "You're doing this on purpose, aren't you?"

"What do you mean?"

"Touching me, swaying across the room, coming down here wearing a robe that clings to every curve. You're working at being sexy."

Her smile was an invitation and a dare. "How am I doing?"

"Real well, if what you want is to drive me crazy."

Jessica was scared and excited and filled with hope. Her hands shook, and she clasped them together in her lap. Her voice was low, almost a whisper. "What I want is for you to finish what you started two weeks ago."

He looked away. "Jessica, please..."

"If you aren't interested, you only need tell me. I won't press you. If you don't want me—"

"Don't want you!" Stephen's voice was explosive and raw with barely suppressed desire. "My God, of course I want you. I can't think of anything except touching you, kissing you. Last night I couldn't go to sleep for thinking about you lying in your bed in the next room. I could see your hair all over the pillow, your skin in the moonlight, your body in some very ladylike nightgown that would reveal just enough to make me sweat. It seems as if the only way I can keep from taking you is to stay away from you altogether."

"Why do you have to keep from it?" Jessica returned bluntly.

"You're Alan's wife!" he bit out, the lines of strain around his mouth and eyes deepening.

"That's all I am to you? Alan's wife? Not a person in my own right?"

"No, of course that's not all you are to me."

"What am I supposed to do? Quit living because Alan died? Would you like for me to immolate myself on my husband's bier?"

"For God's sake, Jessica!" He ran a hand distractedly through his hair.

"Am I not entitled to my own life?"

"Yes!" he burst out. "I want you to have it! But I'm not the man to live it with you."

Jessica rose and went around the table to him, her heart aching. He looked so troubled and torn, and she couldn't understand the depth of his misery. Softly she ran her hand across his hair and down his cheek. "I don't have any choice, Stephen. I love you."

"Jessica!" The word was a low cry of pain. His arms went around her tightly, and he buried his head in her breasts, wanting her comfort, wanting her. "Oh, Jess, I love you too."

She kissed the top of his head. "I don't understand. Why—"

"*Because*, damn it!" He jerked away and jumped to his feet. Shoving his hands in his pockets, he crossed the room. She was forcing him to reveal it, making him say why he was riddled with guilt each time he looked at her, why he was the man she should hate instead of love. The thing he'd been too cowardly to tell her—too hungry for her friendship.

Finally Stephen turned to look at her. His eyes were tortured. "Because I killed your husband."

Jessica's breath stopped. Her mind was blank. She felt as if everything had frozen. She sat down in the chair Stephen had just vacated; her knees were too shaky to stand. "What?" Her voice came out thin and remote.

"I killed Alan."

"You shot him?" Her mind was a jumble; she couldn't deal with it, couldn't put it together.

"No. No. Not like that." He gripped the edge of the counter tightly. "I—it was my fault he was killed. When we broke them out and I took Alan and two other guys, I figured he was my death warrant. His physical condition wasn't good. He'd had pneumonia the winter before, and his chest hadn't really recovered. He had a cough, and he was thin, under-nourished. Couldn't speak a word of German and had an absolutely atrocious French accent."

A watery little chuckle escaped. "He was terrible at languages; he thought everyone should speak English."

Stephen smiled faintly. "Yeah. And he had that limp way of talking that some upper-crust Englishmen have, like they've never done anything tougher than knock a croquet ball around a lawn. I thought he would be useless, a hindrance. But through it all—the snow and the mud and the hiding, walking until I thought our feet would fall off, sleeping in barns and out in the open, starving all the time—he never complained. And he never stopped. One of the other men died. The other one gave up and went back to surrender. But Alan kept plugging along, bad cough and all. I realized he was tough as an old boot and braver than I was. He wanted so desperately to come home to you. I was almost jealous of him for the love he had with you."

He paused. Tears sparkled on the ends of Jessica's eyelashes, but she sat quietly, her hands folded in her lap, looking at him, waiting for his explanation. Stephen let out a heavy breath. "*I* was the one who blew it. I honestly hadn't expected to come back from that assignment. It had been so damned tough. But all of a sudden there we were at our rendezvous point. We'd made it. We spent the night in a hayloft of a farm owned by a Belgian couple, and the next day we went down to the boats. I saw my contact waiting, his fishing boat ready to go. It was dusk. I knew we'd made it; I was flooded with relief. And I said, 'Son-of-a-bitch, we're home free.'"

His face twisted. "In English!" He slammed one fist down on the counter. "I was the big expert, the one who was supposed to save him, the one who knew exactly what to do. And I made the simplest, stupidest mistake you could make. The kind of mistake the rawest trainee would get canned for. This old lady standing there gasped and began to babble. Suddenly there were a bunch of people around, gabbing and gesturing. Two soldiers up the street noticed the commotion and started toward us. Alan and I broke and ran. I was hoping we could make it to the fishing boat. But Alan got hit. It was my fault. I killed him. Every time I look at you, every time I want to kiss you or hold you, I think about it. How your husband is dead because of me. And I feel like I'm betraying him all over again—taking the woman he loved so much."

Silence lay like shattered glass around them. Jessica's throat was clogged with tears, and she wasn't sure for who she wanted to cry. "Oh, Stephen…"

He turned away from her huge, pain-filled eyes.

"Is that what you've been doing the past few months, torturing yourself over that? You think you failed Alan and me and headquarters, too?"

"I did."

Jessica went to him. "You made one mistake. One simple little mistake because you were tired and overjoyed to think you were going to make it home. Anyone could have done that. You aren't God, you know."

"Alan's dead because of me. Don't you understand? He could have been here with you now if it weren't for me."

"If it weren't for you, he would still be in that stalag where you found him! How many times did you speak French or German because Alan couldn't? How many times did your expertise get both of you away from patrols or guide you across Germany? Alan would have been caught and shipped back in a day if you hadn't been with him. And when he was shot that day, it was you who pulled him into the boat at the risk of your own neck."

"That's what I'm supposed to do."

"That doesn't make it any less important. Any less courageous."

"I'm responsible for his death!"

"You were also responsible for his freedom. Look—you didn't have the power of life and death over Alan. He knew what his chances were, and he took them. I know Alan; he would have risked anything to be free. I know he must have been going insane in prison. Alan couldn't stand being penned up; that's why he loved flying so—that ability to soar free and unrestrained by even physical limitations. I'm sure he was desperate to get out of there. He chose to run and fight instead of staying cooped up. He chose to risk death. His choice is not your burden."

"But I made the mistake…"

"So what? That proves you were human! It was a costly error, but that doesn't make you evil. It doesn't make me hate you. You've been grinding yourself into the dust over this, and you know what it's accomplished?"

"What?"

"You've lost your confidence in your abilities so that you're scared to go out in the field again. The war has lost a damned fine agent. And you've kept us from having love and happiness."

Stephen stared at her, unable to speak. He was shaken and confused; her reaction had been nothing like what he had expected. For the first time since Alan's death he felt tendrils of hope creeping through him. "How can you—after what I just told you—"

"I still love you," Jessica said simply. "I loved Alan, and I'm horribly sorry he's dead. But that doesn't mean I blame you. Or that I don't love you anymore. It's you who are keeping us apart." Jessica's hands clenched with the tension of pleading with him. "Stephen, please don't waste your life regretting something that can't be changed. What happened is in the past; you can't change it, no matter how much you rake yourself over the coals. Don't continue to punish yourself. To punish us. Give us a chance for the future."

Tears shimmered in her eyes. Stephen had never seen her look so lovely. His insides were ripping apart. He turned and walked away. Then, slowly, he turned back. And opened his arms.

Jessica went running into them.

They made love in the girlish room where Jessica slept, their mouths slow and hungry on each other. Stephen undressed her slowly, savoring the sight of her body. His hands drifted over Jessica, his roughened fingertips drawing from her every sensation of pleasure she had ever known, and more. He kissed her deeply, lingeringly, as though to learn all of her in this first tasting. He was gentle until he became too greedy to be gentle any longer, and his hands and mouth consumed her.

Jessica loved it all, the soft touches and the demanding ones, the slow fires he built carefully and the swift, raging ones that flashed into being under his expert mouth. She panted and twisted and tore at his clothes, as eager to see and taste and touch his body as he was for hers. His tongue was agile, wet, and fiery, and it found all her secret places, even ones Jessica hadn't known existed. Everywhere he touched he brought her to new, trembling heights, so that she shuddered and moaned, even sinking her teeth into his shoulder. Afterward he would touch the mark she made and joke that she wasn't the lady he thought, his eyes dark and dreamy with the memory. But now the pain-pleasure of her sharp teeth hurled him deep into the dark realm of passion, and he came into her with a hard, wild force.

She took him with equal fervor, skimming her hands down his back and muscular buttocks, pulling him closer, deeper. He moved, and she answered. "I love you," He whispered, driving into her, and she moved beneath him, too aching and hungry to even answer. But he felt her love in the arching of her hips and in the breathy, involuntary noises she made as he moved within her. He felt the sweet ripple of ecstasy take her, heat flooding her skin. And he could hold back no more, no longer stem the hot tide of rapture. Stephen shivered and cried out, and for a single instant they were joined in a swirling, timeless realm of joy.

*****

Philippe returned to his apartment shortly after lunch to find Alyssa dressed and waiting for him. Philippe barely glanced at Alyssa as he came into the bedroom, but as he walked past her, he silently dropped three pills in her lap. Alyssa glanced down, astonished. They were the three capsules that she had stuck in the drawer and which had since disappeared. He obviously had found them, but why was he giving them back to her?

Hastily she broke a few threads in the hem of her dress and stuffed the three pills into it. Philippe pulled a small suitcase from the wardrobe closet and packed a few pieces of clothes for both of them. He turned back to Alyssa. "Ready?"

She nodded. He was as cold and distant as a stranger. It seemed impossible that only a few hours before he had made love to her with such fervor.

Alyssa rose, and Philippe led her from the room, his hand firmly under her arm. They went down to the street where Philippe's chauffeur waited for them beside the long, sleek limousine. Walther started the engine, and the car pulled away from the curb and drove slowly through Paris. Alyssa didn't look at Philippe; she wondered if he, like her, was recalling their journey out of Paris together two years earlier. The trip took longer than it had that summer, for they had to stop at German army checkpoints three times and present their papers. They were always waved through with a minimum of fuss; but often there was more than one car waiting in front of them, and those were scrutinized carefully.

It was late afternoon when they entered the village close to Philippe's estate. Alyssa glanced over at Philippe and found him watching her. For a brief, unguarded moment, his eyes were dark with sorrow. Involuntarily, she moved toward him.

"Philippe?"

He took her hand and pulled her the rest of the way across the seat. He squeezed her hand. "We are almost there. Are you tired?"

She shook her head, still puzzled by what she had read in his eyes. His other hand came up and gently cupped her chin. "Good, for I have a certain amount of activity in mind." He bent and kissed her lips, not with hunger as he had earlier today, but lingeringly and with softness, as it to capture each nuance of her taste.

He lifted his head, and for a moment their eyes locked. His were unreadable, but Alyssa was afraid he could read all too clearly the love and despair written in hers. She turned her head and moved a safer distance from him. Philippe watched her without comment.

The dusk deepened, and Walther turned on the headlamps. He rounded a curve. A barricade of tree limbs blocked the road.

The driver slammed on his brakes, and the car came to a skidding halt. "*Maquis!*" Philippe exclaimed.

The chauffeur straightened dazedly, blood starting from a gash on his forehead where it had hit the steering wheel. Clumsily he reached inside his jacket just as a rifle came through his window and jammed into his chest. The man carrying the rifle reached inside and removed Walther's Luger from its holster, pocketing the gun.

The doors on both sides of the limousine were thrown open, and a man reached in and jerked Alyssa out of the car. "Traitor! Informer!" he hissed, and Alyssa stared at him in astonishment. "You're coming with us. We'll show you what happens to informers."

"No!" Alyssa protested, stunned, as the man dragged her away from the car. "No!" She turned her head in panic to where Philippe stood on the opposite side of the car, two men beside him.

"Let her go!" Philippe shouted, starting after them, but one of the men swung his rifle, cracking the butt against the side of Philippe's head. He crumpled into the dirt, blood welling from his head.

"Philippe!" Alyssa screamed, struggling to escape her captor. But the man swung his gun over his shoulder and wrapped both arms around her, pinning her arms down and holding her still.

The man who had hit Philippe stood over him. He turned his gun around so that the barrel pointed at Philippe, and Alyssa realized in horror that he meant to shoot him. Hysterically she screamed and struggled. "Such concern for your lover," said the man holding her. "You better save your concern for yourself, whore."

The man who stood over Philippe swung his gun up, his lip curling with contempt. "He's not worth killing. Let him live to see what happens to the woman."

Alyssa sagged in relief. The man turned to Alyssa. He was a wiry man with dark hair and a flamboyantly thick black mustache. His face was hard as a rock. "You were one of us and betrayed us, and that makes you worse than this filth. You will die a slow, painful death, as our men die in Nazi prisons. You will be an example to discourage others who might decide to save their own necks by informing on their comrades."

Alyssa's mouth was dry as cotton and her skin suddenly cold in the warm summer air. Philippe was hurt, perhaps even dead, and her own people were going to kill her for something she hadn't done!

"Let's go." The man started off, and the other men followed, dragging Alyssa with them. She began to kick and scream and scratch wildly, fighting for her life.

The man who held her muttered an oath and neatly clipped her on the chin. Her head snapped back, and she sank into a fathomless blackness.

Chapter 22

Louis Bousquet took a final assessing look at himself in the mirror. He had cut and dyed his hair earlier this afternoon and combed it to the side in the style that Midnight used. Next, he had pasted a thin mustache across his upper lip. He had practiced until he had Midnight's walk down pat. Then he had gone to the Gestapo headquarters, where he'd been very relieved to find out that they didn't plan to beat him to make him look bruised and bloody, as he'd half feared.

Instead, one of Schlieker's underlings dressed him in an actual prisoner's stained clothes, which stank so of sweat and old blood that it had made him gag. Afterward, the man stained his hands and feet with animal blood and matted it in his hair, dripping a realistic trail of blood down his face. Again Bousquet had had to swallow his revulsion at the smell and fix his mind firmly on the money Schlieker would pay him if he played the role—and the punishment Schlieker would inflict if he did not.

Stage makeup provided the bruises in shades of blue, purple, and black, and a pasty mixture thickened his eyelids so that they looked swollen. The same mixture, colored red, made a gory wound near his eye. When Schlieker's man, who Bousquet presumed must once have been a makeup artist, was through with him, Bousquet looked nothing like himself and fairly similar to Midnight after a beating—as long as one didn't look closely enough to see that the marks were all fake.

Schlieker was pleased with the result and reassured his informer again that Dragon would not be able to see him well. Two guards took Bousquet up to the fourth floor, where important prisoners were kept. The closer he came to the thick wooden doors with the heavy metal locks, the sicker he felt. He thought of the door shutting and locking on him, of Schlieker never getting him out, and he had to fight to control his panic.

The guards unlocked one of the grim doors and threw him inside. Bousquet stumbled and fell into the cell. Behind him the door slammed shut. He rose to his feet slowly. The single window high up in the wall had been boarded shut, and only a small barred grate in the ceiling, opening onto the roof, allowed in any fresh air. The atmosphere was fetid with the smells of excrement, blood, and the sweat of fear. Bousquet fought his rebellious stomach as he looked around the room.

There was one cot in the small cell, and in the dim light Bousquet could see only that someone, or something, lay on it. He waited for his eyes to adjust to the dark and moved closer. Immediately he regretted it. The man who lay there was a bloody mess, completely unrecognizable. He could see now why Schlieker had said the man would hardly be able to see him. One eye was swollen shut, and the other was a mere slit. His stomach heaved and Bousquet whirled and rushed to the corner to retch violently.

Sometime later, trembling slightly and carefully not looking directly at the man on the cot, he crept closer. Was the man looking at him? Was he awake? Was he even alive?

"Dragon?" he asked tentatively, remembering to keep his voice low and hoarse, as if he'd screamed his throat raw, for he couldn't imitate Midnight's voice. He had forgotten to walk like Midnight in his distress, but he though Dragon was past noticing it.

There was a long silence, than a weak whisper came back to him. "Do I know you?"

"God, it is you, then?"

"Yes. Who are you?"

"Midnight. One of Allegro's men."

Dragon jerked and made a feeble attempt to sit up. "Allegro? Is he here?"

"No. He got away. They burst in on us, and he managed to run out the back door."

"Thank God.

Bousquet waited. He didn't want to make the other man suspicious by broaching the subject too soon, even though he was anxious to get out of there. Cautiously he squatted down on the floor; he hated to think what kind of vermin might be there.

Dragon's mind was hazy, aware of little but the sensations of pain throughout his body. He was reaching the end, he knew. He had the blessed pill safely in his mouth. Soon he would have to use it; he couldn't hold out much longer. He wouldn't have waited this long if it hadn't been for his worry about Philippe.

He was the only person in Paris who knew the identity of le Duc. What would happen to Michaude if he died? How could he get his messages out of France? To whom could he go even to ask Mother for another contact? There must be someone to help Philippe. Someone who knew Philippe was not a collaborator but a true hero of France. A man of strength and courage.

The resistance had wanted to make an example of Philippe time and again, and many times Dragon had calmed them without giving away the true reason. What if an assassin got to Philippe at last, and he died with the world thinking he was a collaborator? Dragon couldn't let that happen.

Over the past two days of ceaseless pain, Dragon almost lost his mind. There were now only two clear thoughts in his head: he must not tell the Germans who le Duc was, and he must reveal the man's true name to someone safe.

Now, like a miracle, one of his cousin's men was in his cell. Had his mind been clearer, he would have questioned the fortuitous event. But at this moment he was only grateful, a man released. If he could get word to Allegro—that was more than he could have hoped for. He was sure he could trust Allegro. It was difficult to speak, but he ignored the pain, "Can you—get word to Allegro?"

Bousquet hid his excitement and raised his head, trying to look puzzled. "If I am sent back to prison, yes. There is a network of criminals there that communicate with the outside all the time. I could get word to him. But why?"

Tears leaked from Dragon's eyes. The agony had been worth it. He had been given the chance to help the man he admired, to do one last thing for his beloved France. "Come closer. I have a message for Allegro. It's very important."

Bousquet swallowed the bile that rose in his throat and crept closer. "What?"

"Tell Allegro that I was le Duc's contact. He must find a way to get in touch with him. He must be his new liaison. Tell him the real name of le Duc is Philippe Michaude."

"Michaude!" Bousquet repeated in astonishment. "But he is a…"

Dragon gave a ghastly imitation of a smile. "Yes. So he pretends."

"My God!"

"Will you tell him?"

"Yes. Yes, I swear."

"Good. Bless you." Dragon moved the pill over with his tongue, and his remaining teeth came down upon it. It burst, spilling powder into his mouth. He swallowed, his mouth still twisted into a smile, and died.

Bousquet didn't notice what had happened to the other man. He was too astounded by what he had just learned. The spy who had baffled the Germans was Philippe Michaude! The most infamous collaborator in Paris. A friend of Schlieker himself. A small smile touched Bousquet's lips as he thought of Schlieker's face when he told him the Duke's identity. How it would puncture that proud bastard's vanity to know that he had been duped. That he knew the spy personally and had probably even given him information!

Bousquet wished he could leave right now. He wanted to run to Schlieker with his information, but he waited. Schlieker wouldn't know how long it would take him to get the information. He wouldn't send for him for several hours—perhaps even all night. The thought chilled his blood.

He glanced over at Dragon. His arm dangled off the bed. His face was frozen, contorted in an awful grin. Dragon was dead. Oh, God! He was stuck in a cell with a dead man. Bousquet shivered and huddled within his arms. The room seemed suddenly very cold.

*****

When Alyssa regained consciousness, she was lying on the ground, trees branching thickly above her head. She was no longer bound. Slowly she sat up, and her head swam. She held herself very still until everything righted itself, then looked around her. She was in the midst of trees. Some distance away men were grouped around a low fire. She turned her head the other direction and jumped. The mustachioed man sat not two feet away, watching her.

Strangely, he smiled. "Hello, I'm Scorpion. Abominable way to meet. Are you all right? Philippe will murder me if you so much as get a bruise."

"Philippe!" His name was the only thing that made sense to her of what the man had said, and in her confused state, she tried to rise to her feet. "Oh, my God, he was hurt!"

The other man shook his head and laid a restraining hand on her arm. "Don't worry about him. Just a tap on the head in the place most likely to create a little bleeding. He'll be all right, I promise you. He always had a hard head."

Alyssa's head was aching and foggy. "You hit him! And kicked him!"

"He didn't warn you at all, did he?"

"What are you talking about?"

He sighed. "Typical of Philippe. It would make you behave much more realistically if you had no idea we were going to stop the car." He laid a hand on his heart theatrically. "I swear to you, he's fine. That was just a charade we played for the German chauffeur. So he'll report to his masters that you were seized by the resistance and are probably dead by now. We hope that will keep Philippe in the clear while you escape to England."

She continued to stare, and he grinned. "We pulled our punches, of course. You can't think I'd really hurt le Duc, can you?"

"What!" Her jaw dropped, and she put a hand up to her head as if to anchor it firmly in place. "The Duke!"

A look of guilt flitted across the man's face, and he muttered a curse. "You didn't know, did you? He didn't tell you a thing!"

"No! What are you talking about? Are you saying that Philippe is...the Duke?"

"Now I've really done it. He *will* have my head. But I never dreamed—Georges called you his 'duchess,' and I presumed that—well, that you knew. I should have known better."

"He's the spy? But he's a—"

Scorpion smiled. "A collaborator. Of course—what better way to get information from the Germans?"

Alyssa gaped at him for a moment. The world spun around her. Philippe was the Duke! She burst into a grin, dazzling the man before her. Suddenly her heart was alive and singing with joy. Philippe wasn't helping the enemy at all! He wasn't dishonorable or cowardly. Just the opposite—he was risking his life playing a most desperate, dangerous game with the enemy. He had endured the contempt of the woman he loved and of the people he was working to save. She had reviled him; resistance fighters had tried to assassinate him. And he had kept silent, all the while chancing his life by stealing secrets from the Nazis. Why, if he were found out—"

Alyssa shot to her feet. "Oh, my God!"

"What?" He was instantly alert.

"He's in danger! Philippe's in terrible danger. And to think I knew all this time! If only I'd known who he was, I could have warned him. Scorpion, please." She reached out a hand to him, her face pleading. "You have to take me to him. I must see Philippe."

"What? Are you insane? He'd murder me if I brought you back to him. You're supposed to leave for England tonight."

"But I know who the traitor is. And the Gestapo has Dragon."

"Dragon? What traitor?"

"Dragon is connected to the Duke. I sent a message for him, and it said it was from the Duke. A man named Unicorn saw the message. He realized who Dragon was and he betrayed us. The next day Dragon and I were arrested when we met at the Brasserie Lipp."

"And you are sure it was this man who turned you in?"

"Only two other people besides Dragon and me knew where and when we were meeting. One of them was Allegro, whom Dragon told me was his cousin. He said he'd trust him with his life. The other man was Unicorn, who had been in the same group I was it but had escaped with me when about half the network was blown. He has to be the informer. I think he must have betrayed the first group, too."

Scorpion's face hardened to stone, and his eyes were like bright black marbles. "He will be taken care of. I promise you. I have contacts in Paris, and I will let them know. You must tell me everything you can about this man."

"But what about Philippe? I have to tell him that Dragon was captured."

"Yes, yes, I'll go to him immediately. He's at his château, resting after Georges came along and 'rescued' him and his Nazi guard. I will call Paris from there."

"And you'll take me with you?" Alyssa gripped his arm anxiously. Her eyes were huge and swimming with tears. "Please, I beg of you. I must see him. I didn't know what he was doing. I said terrible things to him. I can't leave him with that between us. I have to talk to him, apologize. I have to tell him how much I love him."

Scorpion hesitated, then nodded. "Yes, all right. Now tell me about Unicorn."

*****

Schlieker had the guards bring down Bousquet shortly after supper. He couldn't wait any longer to find out if he had learned anything. Surely after two hours the man would at least know if it was likely that he would get any information.

The guard opened the door, and Bousquet entered, bringing with him the awful stench of the cell. Schlieker's nostrils tightened, and he brought out a handkerchief to shield his nose from the worst of it. He looked into Bousquet's face and immediately forgot about the smell. Bousquet's eyes glittered; he was bursting with excitement.

"Did you find it out?" Schlieker dropped the handkerchief on his desk and rose.

Bousquet had never seen Schlieker display such interest or emotion. He luxuriated in the moment, stretching it out as long as he dared. "Yes, I did. He asked me to give the name to Allegro, so that he could become the Duke's new contact."

"And? Damn it, man, who is the Duke?"

"Philippe Michaude."

All the color in Schlieker's face seeped out. Bousquet carefully kept his expression blank, despite the spurt of delight it gave him to see the officer so stunned. "Michaude?" Schlieker asked in a voice not quite his own. "Are you sure?"

It seemed impossible to Schlieker. Could he have been such a poor judge of character? Philippe Michaude was one of the few men he liked. The man was sophisticated and intelligent; Schlieker had enjoyed conversing with him. He wasn't like the other French flunkies, always groveling, soft and spineless. There had been something hard and confident in him, something strong.

But, of course, he would be strong if he were playing such a dangerous game. He wouldn't be like the others. No wonder he had seemed almost an equal. In a way he was—the enemy, but a man of courage and daring and brains. A man fighting for his country.

Albrecht Schlieker could understand that. He could even admire Michaude for it. And he hated him to the depths of his soul.

Michaude had fooled him. Humiliated him. He had taken secrets not only from German army officers, but from Schlieker himself! All the time that he was so anxiously hunting the Duke, he'd been right at his side. Michaude must have been laughing with glee at Schlieker's blindness. Red rage filled Schlieker, and he slammed his fist down on the desk. "I'll kill him!"

Bousquet wisely kept still. Schlieker struck the desk again and again. The whites shone all around his eyes, and his pupils were pinpoints of black. Bousquet wouldn't have been surprised if he started foaming at the mouth.

But Schlieker quickly regained control of himself. He clenched his fists and forced himself to sit down. His eyes flickered to Bousquet. "You may leave," he said in a voice like ground glass, and Bousquet didn't stay to inquire about his reward.

Schlieker watched him leave, hardly seeing him, his mind on Philippe. He thought about the information Michaude had given him this morning. No doubt the great majority of it was false and the rest of it unimportant. The girl would probably mysteriously escape while they were at Michaude's country house. Michaude must have known that providing him with false information and letting a prisoner escape would increase his risk of discovery. Why had he done it? The woman must mean something very special to him indeed.

If Philippe lusted after her that much, Schlieker didn't imagine Philippe would forgo the pleasure of her body just yet. She would doubtless remain at the château for a day or two before her "escape." If he acted quickly, he could get both Philippe and the woman, and with her in his hands, he would be able to get any answer he wanted from Michaude. He would make him beg.

A frosty smile touched Schlieker's lips, and he picked up his telephone. When Dieter Gersbach answered at the other end, Schlieker said crisply, "I've decided to give you what you requested. Drive down to Philippe Michaude's estate immediately and bring both him and the girl back to me." He paused, listening to the man on the other end, then said, "Yes, you shall have the girl. Just as soon as I am through with the two of them."

*****

Alyssa described everything she could remember about Unicorn, including the false name he had used on the identity papers he secured for them. She knew nothing about his job or his true identity, but she pointed out that if there were any members of Allegro's or Oak's cells still alive and free, they would be able to recognize him.

It seemed a pitifully small amount of information to catch the traitor, but Scorpion smiled and told her not to look so downcast. "We will find him. Now it's time for us to go."

He said a few words to the men around the fire and returned to her. He no longer carried the rifle, but now he slid a German Luger into his belt at the back beneath his light jacket. He settled his soft cap on his head at a jaunty angle, grinned, and motioned for Alyssa to follow him.

He struck off briskly through the trees, but Alyssa had no trouble keeping up. If anything, she was so impatient to see Philippe that Scorpion's pace seemed too slow. They walked along narrow paths through fields and trees, crossing fences and once jumping from stone to stone over a small stream. Finally they emerged from a stand of trees, and Alyssa saw that they were behind Philippe's house. Scorpion left her in the shelter of trees and walked through the garden into the house. Alyssa sat waiting for what seemed like ages, clenching and unclenching her fists and watching the upper stories of the house.

"Alyssa."

She whirled. Georges, Philippe's valet, stood a few feet from her. He had come from the side of the house, around the formal garden, and had moved so softly she had had no inkling of his approach.

"Georges!" She let out a sigh of relief.

"Sorry if I startled you. Scorpion said you wanted to see Philippe."

"Yes. Very much."

He smiled. "Good. Scorpion is using the telephone. I will take you to Philippe."

She followed him as he circled the garden to the side entrance, set into one of the ornamental round towers.

"I've never been in this way before," Alyssa commented.

"It isn't often used." He ushered her inside the door and stood in a dimly lit stairwell. "The servants here are good Frenchmen, no Nazi spies, but the less anyone knows, the better."

Georges led her up a flight of stairs into a wing of the house she had never entered before. It, too, was dark, but Georges knew his way, and he led her down the hall. When they rounded the corner, they were in the main section of the second floor, an area with which Alyssa was familiar. The hallway was deserted. The door to Philippe's bedroom stood open, and a small light burned within, casting a dim yellow square of light into the hall.

Alyssa looked at Georges, and he smiled before walking away in his silent manner and disappearing down the main staircase. Alyssa's heart pounded inside her chest as she crossed the hall to Philippe's door.

Philippe sat across the room, gazing out the window into the night. A cut-glass decanter and a half-empty glass of whisky sat on the small table beside him. He turned his head to stub out a cigarette, and Alyssa saw the darkening bruise on the side of his forehead. Her heart contracted with love and anguish.

How hard it must have been for him! Hated by the woman he loved, despised by the very people he was trying to save, pretending to like people he hated, he had constantly walked the razor's edge of danger for the past two years. It was no wonder he had seemed hardened and careworn. It must have been awful for him to be friendly to the Germans, to see the things they did and even have to act as if he approved. Alyssa remembered how much she had hated her role in Washington, when she had had to pretend to like the enemy. There had been times when she had been hard pressed to continue—and she hadn't had to face the scorn and hatred of her own people, as Philippe had. Nor had she had to live under that constant pressure for two years.

She stepped inside. "Don't you know you shouldn't drink after a head injury?"

Philippe whirled, leaping to his feet. "Alyssa! What in the name of God are you doing here?"

Alyssa closed the door and turned back to him. It occurred to her that her hair and clothes must be a mess, and she wished she had on a little makeup. She wanted suddenly, desperately, to be pretty for him. "I came because I love you."

"Alyssa." The word was barely more than a breath, and he crossed the room to her in a few long steps. He had been drinking and thinking of Alyssa all evening, and now her appearance seemed like a vision. A vision with leaves in her hair. Philippe smiled and plucked a curl of green leaf from her tousled mane.

"I must be a mess," Alyssa said quickly, her voice breathless.

"You are beautiful," he corrected. He dropped the leaf and cupped her face with his hands. His thumbs gently caressed her cheeks and chin and outlined her lips. When he touched her mouth, she kissed his skin. Philippe's blood began to thunder within his veins.

"I love you," he told her hoarsely, and his mouth came down to meet hers. The kiss was tender and seeking. There was none of the harsh, eager desperation that had been between them this morning. Their physical thirst had been slaked. Now it was love that touched, tasted, lingered.

His fingers trailed lightly down her back and smoothed over her buttocks, then slid back up her sides and brushed the edges of her breasts. Tongues teased and glided, wet and silken and pleasure giving.

Their loving turned bright and fiery, but it was still infinitely slow. Philippe undressed her, his eyes as hot as his fingers upon her skin, and Alyssa undressed him. They came together, skin against skin, his arms hard around her. He pulled her into him, and her breasts pushed against the hard cage of his ribs. They kissed, their mouths straining against each other, seeking every bit of sweetness. Alyssa dug her fingers into his hair, urging him even closer. Her fingernails skimmed down his neck and across the bunched muscles of his shoulders. Philippe shuddered. His arms were so tight around Alyssa that she thought she might break in two, but she didn't care. She wanted him even closer. She wanted him inside her.

Philippe swung her up into his arms and carried her to the bed, nuzzling at her neck and earlobe as he walked. He put her down on the bed and sat down beside her, gazing down at her body. Slowly he ran his hands down her, exploring her soft flesh. His mouth was full, his face heavy and flushed with desire. His eyes ate her up.

Alyssa stretched, loving his gaze, loving his hands. They had been separated so long. She wished their lovemaking could go on forever. Her own hands went to his hard thighs and the smooth wall of his abdomen. He sucked in his breath at her touch, and his fingers tightened on her.

Stretching out beside her on the bed, kissing her as his hand caressed her breasts. Philippe moved downward, sliding his lips over the tender skin of her throat to her breast. He kissed the soft, quivering flesh, and his tongue circled her nipple, turning it into a hot, tight bud. He moved to the other nipple, tracing and teasing until Alyssa trembled and arched upward, seeking the full pleasure of his mouth. His lips closed around her nipple, rubbing it gently, and at last his mouth pulled at her breast. She was flooded with warmth, liquid with the exquisite pleasure.

Alyssa moaned his name, and his fingers slipped between her legs, so that the pleasure arced from her in two places, meeting in sizzling excitement in her abdomen. She could not keep still. She moved her hands restlessly over Philippe's shoulders and back and slid them through his hair. His hair was damp around the edges, and she could see the faint sheen of moisture on his bare shoulders.

Philippe moved to her other breast, loving it too. His breath was ragged. He was frantic to have her now, pounding with need, but equally determined to miss none of the pleasure, none of the love. He kissed her everywhere with lingering, arousing kisses that made Alyssa writhe with desire.

He moved between her legs, and she took his hard maleness joyfully, pushing up to meet his thrust. He groaned out loud, his fingers digging into the sheets beside her. His face was contorted, his eyes closed, his sight turned inward to some deep, magical place. He moved, gloved by her tightness, aware of nothing but the shimmering reality of her love, and then he was plunging faster, rushing past sanity to the blissful point beyond. They crashed into a sparkling, white-hot world, melded together for a moment. For an eternity.

"My love," Philippe whispered. "My love."

Chapter 23

Philippe rolled onto his back, wrapping his arms around Alyssa and pulling her with him. She nestled contentedly against his shoulder. She didn't know if she had ever seen his face look this relaxed, this open and peaceful. Alyssa smiled; she couldn't stop touching him—light little brushes of her fingertips, as if to reassure herself that she was there and he was real.

He sighed and said with more resignation than anger, "You know who I am?"

Alyssa nodded. "Yes. Scorpion let it slip. He thought I knew."

Philippe smoothed his hand along the line of her waist and hips. "You are so very lovely. I've ached for you a long, long time."

"Why didn't you tell me?" Alyssa rose on her elbow to look into his face. "Why did you let me believe you were a traitor?"

His hand brushed her cheek. "I had no choice. No one could know."

"I would never have told anyone! Never! You must know that."

"Yes, but the more people who know, the more dangerous it is. The only others are my contact in Paris and Scorpion."

"And Georges."

"Yes. You see how many that is already, and those are out of sheer necessity. When you left France, I was afraid that once you were in the United States, you might tell a friend what I was really doing, thinking it safe to reveal it there. Or you might defend me if you heard someone condemn me as a collaborator. Most of all, I knew you would want to stay if you knew the truth, and I couldn't risk that."

"You could have told me since then. You saw me playing a double game in Washington; you must have known I could keep my mouth shut. Or when you got me out of prison. Why didn't you tell me then?"

"I wanted to. God, how I wanted to! I couldn't bear the disgust in your eyes whenever you looked at me. I knew you hated me for being cold and cruel. I had to do it; it was part of the act for Gersbach and Schlieker." His voice dropped, hoarse, barely above a whisper. "I couldn't endanger everything for the sake of my own selfish desires. You had to despise me; I couldn't risk your knowing the truth. You might have looked at me with love. You wouldn't have seemed scared. It would have tipped them off."

"Who? Frau Heuser? Walther?"

"Yes. They were Schlieker's spies—" He managed a faint smile. "Given to me, of course, under the guise of great kindness."

Alyssa ached for him. "How hard it must have been for you. No privacy. Living with spies in your own house, having to keep up the front all the time."

"The worst was pretending to be friends with the bastards. Fawning, flattering, smiling, all the while hating their guts. I began to feel stained by their dirt. Filthy myself."

"I know." Alyssa's hand caressed his cheek. "I felt that way in Washington. But at least I could go home afterwards and be myself. My countrymen didn't look on me as a traitor or try to assassinate me. I didn't lose everyone I loved—and at least I had Blakely to talk to."

"Who?"

Alyssa saw the little flare of jealousy in his eyes, and she chuckled. How nice it was to have something so ordinary between them. "My contact when I was in D.C. Nothing to worry about; he was hardly even a friend." She paused and her expression turned serious. "You believed me, didn't you, when I told you in Washington that I hadn't slept with Paul?"

"Yes, I believed you. I knew you better than that. I was just crazy with jealousy. I'm sorry for the things I said to you."

She shook her head. "It doesn't matter."

"Of course it matters. Everything to do with you matters." Lazily his fingers tangled in her tumbled hair. "Your love is the most precious thing on earth to me. It's just that the world got in our way. Sometimes I think I hate the Nazis most of all for that." He sighed. "We must get up. You have to return to Scorpion; the sooner you get out the better."

Alyssa sat up abruptly, her face registering horror. "Oh, God, how could I have forgotten! When I saw you, everything left my head." She slipped out of bed and began pulling on her clothes as she talked. "Come on. You need to get dressed. We're both leaving."

"What? What are you talking about?"

"I know who the traitor is in the Rock network."

"Who? How did you find out?"

"His name is Unicorn. I told Scorpion, and he promised that they'll find him. But the important thing is—my group wasn't the only one he betrayed to the Nazis. Dragon was arrested with me."

"Dragon!" Philippe jumped out of bed. "Are you sure?"

"Yes. He had given me a message to transmit from the Duke—from you, though I didn't know it at the time. When I met Dragon to give him the reply from Mother, we were arrested. Only Unicorn and Dragon's cousin knew about our meeting."

Philippe closed his eyes. "Poor Charles." He sat down on the bed and ran his hands through his hair. All the years had come back to his face.

"I know. But the important thing now is for you to get away. At any moment he could reveal your identity to the Gestapo."

Philippe shook his head. "No. Not Charles. He will never tell, no matter what. He's a tough old soldier."

"Philippe!" Fear and frustration ran through Alyssa. "You can't know that for certain. Anyone could be made to talk. Anyone. It's too big a risk to take."

"No. It's a slight risk. But reasonable. Charles has one of your L-pills; he will take it if he has to."

Frantically Alyssa tried to think of something to say to convince him. "It's not cowardly to run. There's nothing to be gained by staying here for certain death. You could do things for France in England now, important things. You'd be far more helpful than you would be dead."

"If I thought the Gestapo knew who I was, of course I would go. But with Charles, I don't think the risk outweighs the—"

"All right, then," Alyssa broke in, "I'll stay here with you. You'll need someone to transmit your messages."

The horrified expression on his face clearly told his answer. "No! Don't be absurd! It's too dangerous."

"If it's not too much risk for you, then why is it too much for me?"

He glared at her and started to speak, but he stopped, his attention caught by a noise outside. Raising his hand to her to be silent, he padded over to the window and looked out. "*Nom de Dieu!* It's Gersbach."

"They've found out. You have to go."

Philippe dressed quickly, his brow knitted in a frown. "It's too soon for Walther to have reached Paris to tell Schlieker of the attack. You must be right."

The door flew open, and Georges rushed in. "Monsieur! Gersbach is outside, and there are six men with him."

"Get Alyssa out of the house. Where's Scorpion?"

"He returned to camp to set up your departure."

"Take Alyssa to him. I will go down and talk to Gersbach."

"No!" Alyssa exclaimed. "You have to come with me!"

"Don't argue! There isn't time." Downstairs they heard the loud thud of the heavy metal knocker against the door, again and again.

"I'm not going without you!"

"You have to. If we both run, Gersbach will immediately institute a search, and we'll both be caught. But if he's looking for me, he probably won't even bother to search for you. If he does, at least I will have delayed him long enough for you to get away."

"What do I care about getting away if you're here?" Alyssa cried.

"If you are caught, do you know what would happen? They would torture you in front of me. How long do you think it would take before I told them everything I know to keep them from hurting you? My love for you would make me vulnerable. The only way you can help me is to go with Georges. I must know that you are safe."

Tears clogged Alyssa's throat. There was something in Philippe's face that she had never seen there before, a touch of fear. She knew that her presence had put it there. He was right. She made him vulnerable. "All right," she said. "I'll go." She stiffened her spine and, with a single backward glance at Philippe, she followed Georges from the room.

They ran along the deserted hall which they had used earlier and down the stairs to the ground floor. Georges reached for the door, but Alyssa stopped him. "No! Isn't there someplace you could hide me in the house where they couldn't find me?"

"Probably in the wine cellar, but—"

"I know what Philippe said. But if Gersbach doesn't know I'm here, we might be able to rescue Philippe. I'm not going to just run away if I can save Philippe's life."

A smile touched Georges's lips. "Yes, mademoiselle. This way."

They walked along the hall to the kitchen. Alyssa saw Philippe come down the huge main staircase and start toward the front door as Georges whisked her into the kitchen. It was late enough that all the servants were in bed, so that the kitchen was deserted. There was no one to see them cross the huge room and open a door in the far wall. Georges turned on the light switch and motioned for Alyssa to precede him down the steep stairs. Georges pulled a lantern and some matches from a cabinet and followed her.

"This is the basement, mostly storage," he told her, lighting the heavy lantern and switching off the stairway light bulb. "Better that they not see a light down here if they happen to walk through the kitchens. Follow me." He led her past boxes, crates, and bins of food to an even narrower set of circular stairs. He preceded her, and Alyssa was glad; she didn't relish descending the stone stairway into the unknown.

When they reached the floor below, the glow of Georges's lantern revealed a room filled with racks of bottles. He took her to the back of the room, where a low doorway opened into a small cubicle. He handed her the lantern. "There is a blanket there. I've hidden a refugee or two down here." There was also a candlestick with a thick candle in it, and Alyssa lit it gratefully "I'll pull a couple of casks in front of the doorway to conceal it. I'll come back as soon as I find out anything."

Alyssa nodded. She handed him the lantern back, and he crawled out of the room. He shoved two barrels in front of the low door, cutting off most of the light from his lantern.

When even the edges of light from around the casks were gone, she knew that Georges had left the basement. Alyssa glanced at her candle's low glow and hoped fervently that it wouldn't go out. She settled down to wait.

*****

Philippe pasted a smile on his lips as he strode forward to greet Gersbach. The Gestapo agent stood in the middle of the entryway, hands belligerently on hips, glaring at the tongue-tied servant before him. Five armed guards filled the foyer behind him. "Dieter! What a pleasant surprise."

"There you are!' Gersbach's fearsome gaze swung to Philippe, and the servant eagerly scurried out of the room.

"I'm sorry," Philippe went on calmly. "If I'd known you were coming, I would have had a room prepared. I shall send a maid to look after it right now. And for your men." He sent a questioning glance toward the crowd behind Gersbach.

"Where is the girl?"

Philippe assumed a puzzled look. "But surely Walther told you—no, no, I suppose he can't have reached Paris yet. You don't know. The girl is gone."

Gersbach looked singularly unsurprised. The dancing nerves in Philippe's stomach increased.

"The *maquis* took her," Philippe continued. "They stopped my car and pulled her from it. Gave me this bump on the head." He gestured toward the dark bruise on his face and sighed. "They're going to execute her for giving me information. Poor girl. She was so lovely, too."

"I'm sure she still is," Gersbach replied with heavy sarcasm. He turned and snapped an order to the men behind him. "Search the house for her. Everywhere. Don't miss a spot. Except Braun. You stay here."

The men trotted off, guns in hand, to search for Alyssa. Philippe smiled sardonically and crossed his arms. "What's the matter? Don't you trust me?"

The remaining guard stepped to the side of Gersbach, his rifle pointed at Philippe. Gersbach smiled evilly. "No, as a matter of fact, I don't. Let's go into a more comfortable room where we can sit and talk—Monsieur le Duc."

Philippe managed a smile of disbelief. "Is this a joke of some kind?"

"I am not fond of jokes, Michaude." Casually Gersbach raised his hand and struck Philippe backhandedly across one cheek. Philippe staggered backward. He tasted blood. Fervently he hoped that Alyssa had gotten well away. Gersbach motioned forward. "Now, shall we go?"

Philippe turned and led them into the drawing room.

*****

Alyssa could hear nothing in her cubbyhole. It seemed as if hours had passed. She rested her head on her pulled-up knees and tried to think how she could help Philippe.

There was a noise outside. Alyssa's head flew up, every sense alert. The sound came again. Boot heels on the stone. Someone was coming down the steps! Hurriedly she blew out her candle. They mustn't spy the light around the edges of the casks. She waited.

There was a light in the cellar outside her room and the sounds of someone walking. A man spoke in German, and she heard a whistle of surprise. Another man laughed and replied. They must be admiring the cache of wine bottles. The steps came closer, and Alyssa shrank as far back into the corner of her room as she could. She wished she'd thought to grab some sort of weapon.

The steps halted outside the small doorway. They talked again, but Alyssa's German was too poor to understand what was said. One of them kicked casually at one of the casks, and it wobbled. Alyssa stopped breathing.

After a moment, the footsteps retreated, and the light was gone. Alyssa was left in utter darkness. A shudder of relief ran through her. Sweat was trickling down her sides; she hadn't noticed it before. She unbent her cramped muscles and moved forward, her hands slowly sweeping the floor until she encountered the candle, then the box of matches beside it. By feel she pulled out a match and lit it, touching it to the candle. Light sprang up in her cell again, and she released a shaky sigh. She had feared she would be doomed to complete darkness until Georges came back.

Again she waited. After some time there were noises on the stairs again, and she jumped to blow out the candle. A man walked very quickly, close to running.

"Alyssa! It is I!" Georges hissed in a stage whisper. Alyssa relaxed and crept to the doorway. Georges rolled the casks aside and helped her out. His heavy, square face, normally so stolid, was pale and frightened.

"You were right. Gersbach knows who Philippe is. He plans to take him back to Paris to be questioned."

Alyssa couldn't say anything. She was more scared than she could ever remember, even when the Gestapo had come for her. She knew how Philippe must have felt when he saw her escorted from Gestapo headquarters.

Georges stared back at her, his face mirroring her fear. "What shall we do?" he asked.

Alyssa swallowed. Georges was a good man and a brave one, but it was obvious he was used only to taking orders. She must decide what course of action they should follow.

She shook off the freezing fear. It wasn't as if this were a surprise. She had spent most of her time in this cubbyhole trying to think of a way to rescue Phillippe. "Go get Scorpion. Tell him what's happened. They can set up a blockade for Gersbach's car, as they did with mine, except for real this time."

Georges shook his head. "There isn't enough time. Gersbach plans to leave immediately. It would take me twenty minutes to reach Scorpion, and another hour for them to set up the roadblock. It's impossible."

"What are Gersbach's men doing?"

"They're in the kitchen eating at the moment. As soon as they've finished, they will leave for Paris."

"They're eating? All of them?"

"Gersbach has a tray in the drawing room, and there are three soldiers eating in the kitchen. When they are through, I assume they'll change places with the two guarding Philippe. There's one outside watching the car."

Alyssa fumbled with her skirt, ripping at the hem. Three pills tumbled out. "Put these in their food. This one makes a person ill for a few hours. This is what we call a 'Mickey' in the

U.S. Knocks one out. And this is pure poison. Are they drinking out of the same bottle?"

He smiled. "I will bring up a bottle of wine for them from the cellar—already treated."

"Good. Be sure to break this pill; it won't dissolve. Can you do that?"

"Yes, of course." Georges was steadfast and confident as long as someone told him what to do. "And I will take a tray of food and wine to the one guarding the car."

"Can you get me a handgun?"

"Yes. More than one."

"A small one. Like a derringer." Alyssa demonstrated the size, and Georges nodded. "Take care of the men eating first, then come back here with the gun."

She followed Georges through the wine cellar to the bottom of the circular stone steps leading up to the basement. She waited for interminable minutes before he opened the door above and trotted back down the stairs. "They're sick as dogs. I dumped the men in the pantry and locked it and collected their weapons. I've armed the servants." He reached in his pocket and extended a small, snub-nosed revolver to her. "Here's the gun you wanted. What do we do now?"

Alyssa took the gun and slipped her hands into the pockets of her dress. With the full-skirted dress and both hands in her pockets, the larger lump of the gun was hardly visible.

"I want you to go to Gersbach and offer to bring me to him for a payment. Then come back and get me."

"Yes, mademoiselle."

Hearing Georges's footfalls, Alyssa hurried up the stone steps into the basement to meet him. "Did he believe you?"

"I think so. Philippe nearly took my head off when I made my offer to Gersbach. He knows I wouldn't betray you, but he's sure we're up to something that could endanger you, and he was furious." Georges grinned. "I think his reaction convinced Gersbach I was telling the truth."

"Good." Quickly Alyssa sketched out her plan, what little there was of it, and they sat down to wait for enough time to elapse for Georges to have brought her back from a hiding place in the woods. After twenty minutes, Alyssa stood up. "All right, let's go."

Chapter 24

They emerged from the second set of stairs into the kitchen and paused to listen for a moment before continuing into the hall. The house was abnormally quiet. Their steps on the wooden floors reverberated in Alyssa's ears. Her fingers clenched around the revolver in her pocket. The blood was racing through her veins, and she felt amazingly clearheaded, aware of every tiny detail. Her stomach was cold as ice, and her heart was pounding so hard, it felt as if it might shoot straight out of her chest. She didn't feel frightened, only determined and pumped full of adrenaline.

Georges walked a little behind and to one side of Alyssa as they approached the formal drawing room, and he held a large pistol pointed at the back of her head. A Gestapo agent stood guard outside the door to the drawing room, arms crossed over his chest. He glanced at Alyssa and Georges and motioned for them to go inside. Georges pushed open the door, and Alyssa walked into the room.

A guard stood near the marble fireplace, a Luger in his hands. Gersbach was several feet away. In front of him Philippe was seated in a straight-back chair, his hands pulled back and tied behind the chair, stretching his arms painfully. One of his eyes was reddened and swelling, and there was another red, swelling area beside his mouth. His lip was split. Rage and nausea added to the tumult in Alyssa's stomach, and she looked at Gersbach with loathing.

Fire shot from Philippe's eyes. "Damn it, Alyssa!"

"Well, well, well." Gersbach grinned and walked toward her, running his eyes down her in a vulgar assessment. "Even prettier than before." He stopped in front of her and ran a hand over her breasts. Alyssa was so intent on what she was doing that his touch hardly registered. She stared back at him without a trace of fear on her face, knowing that would annoy him more than anything.

It did. He frowned and snapped at Georges to leave.

"What about my reward?" Georges asked, not budging.

Gersbach smiled. "Your friendship with the Gestapo is your reward. Your neck is your reward." He gestured. "Get out."

Reluctantly Georges left. Alyssa knew he would linger in the hallway as long as he could, but the Gestapo guard would soon chase him off. Things had to move quickly. She continued to stare coolly at Gersbach. "I give myself up in return for Philippe's life."

Gersbach laughed at the ridiculous statement. She had known he would, but she wanted to present a fighting front to Gersbach, for that would arouse him the fastest. "So you are offering me a deal?" he asked. "I would say you aren't in much position to offer me anything. I can take whatever I want." Gersbach glanced over at Philippe, whose eyes flamed with hatred. "Schlieker said I wasn't to interrogate you, Michaude; he wants you all for himself. Special hatred, you see, because you made him look like a fool. So I have restrained myself with you. But Schlieker didn't say a word about not touching the woman."

"Goddamn you, Gersbach," Philippe said in a grating voice. "You hurt her, and I'll kill you."

"You will kill me?" Gersbach was highly amused. "So you don't like me touching your whore, eh?" He squeezed Alyssa's breast, and she tried not to wince.

The German was close enough to her, but Alyssa waited, hoping he would send the guard outside. If he didn't, she would simply have to go ahead and play her hand. She cast a sideways glance at the guard. At least he was getting very interested in the action and was holding his rifle loosely.

"This should be quite entertaining," Gersbach said, taking Alyssa's arm and dragging her over to stand directly in front of Philippe. Philippe was deathly white, his eyes blazing green. He had been cursing Gersbach vividly, but now he fell silent. His jaw was set, his body taut and straining forward against his bound arms. "It would be interesting to take her in front of you, Michaude," Gersbach continued slimily. "Something I haven't done before." He slid his hand over Alyssa's backside and she hoped fervently that he didn't get too near her pocket with the gun in it. Luckily he was more concerned with upsetting Philippe than anything else. He described in disgusting detail what he would do to her and Philippe lunged forward. The chair he was tied to toppled over, crashing with him to the floor.

Gersbach laughed. "Braun, turn our turtle here right side up again. He can't see as well that way."

The guard laid down his gun and heaved Philippe's chair upright. Alyssa knew this was her chance. Her grip tightened in her pocket. Gersbach pulled her closer, his fleshy lips coming down to her face.

Alyssa raised the gun, still inside her skirt pocket, and jammed it hard into Gersbach's groin.

Gersbach froze, grunting in pained dismay. Alyssa smiled. "Yes, it's a gun."

Braun, who had just finished setting up Philippe's chair, whirled at her words. His mouth fell open, and his eyes went across the room to his automatic rifle. "No!" Alyssa jabbed her weapon deeper into Gersbach's flesh. "Tell your boy not to try anything, or you'll be missing a vital piece of your anatomy."

Sweat broke out across Gersbach's forehead, and he spoke to the guard. The guard nodded and stood with his arms dangling loosely, making no move toward the gun.

"Tell him to untie Philippe."

"No!"

"Yes, unless you'd like me to squeeze the trigger."

"If you shoot me, the guards will shoot you."

"All the other guards have been taken care of, and I could probably shoot both you and Braun here before he reaches his gun. Even if I didn't make it, you'd be dead anyway—and rather painfully, too. Tell him to untie Philippe."

He barked out an order to the guard, and Braun began to untie the knots that bound Philippe. Braun was nervous and fumbling, and it took him several minutes to unfasten the bonds. Sweat poured down Gersbach's face. Philippe tugged sharply against the rope, and his arms were free. He was up in an instant and used his ropes to bind Braun's hands and feet, finishing by gagging the man with his handkerchief. He crossed the room to pick up Braun's gun and leveled it at Gersbach's spine. "All right, step back."

Gersbach did. Alyssa lowered her arm; it began to tremble. She felt as though she might start shaking and not stop until she lay in pieces on the floor.

"Tie him up, my love. Take the cord from the inner curtains."

Alyssa obeyed Philippe, going to the curtains and jerking down the thin white cord. Slipping her own gun back into her pocket, she returned to Gersbach, reaching out to bind his hands. But with a swiftness that surprised her, he grabbed her hands and jerked her toward him, twisting to place Alyssa between Philippe and himself.

But he couldn't move fast enough. Philippe fired and the bullet blasted through Gersbach's chest. Alyssa dived to the floor as Philippe fired, Gersbach's blood splashing over her. Philippe whirled around, dropping to his knee, to train his gun on the door. There was the sound of three quick shots in the hall. The door flew back, and the German guard fell into the room. Georges stepped over the body, a Luger in his hands, ready to fire. For a moment all three stared at each other, frozen.

Georges relaxed. "Thank God." He bent to feel the neck of the guard he'd shot. "He's dead. What about that one?" He motioned to Gersbach.

Philippe shrugged, and Georges cast a glance at the guard Philippe had bound and gagged, who was staring at them in wide-eyed fear. "He seems secure enough."

"Where are the others?" Philippe asked, his gaze still fixed on the door.

"Incapacitated. I'll have all of them taken down to the cellars. Him, too." Georges jerked a thumb at the bound guard. "We'll figure out what to do with them later." The bound guard, looking, if possible, even more terrified, began to babble, the words muffled by his gag. Georges ignored him, going over to take Gersbach's pulse. "Gersbach's dead, too."

Philippe looked at Georges, who was now helping Alyssa up, and scowled at him. "I ought to beat you senseless—except you're obviously already in that state! Do you realize how crazy that was? What could have happened to Alyssa?"

"Do you realize what could have happened to you?" Alyssa retorted crossly.

Philippe took her in his arms and held on to her as if for dear life. "I've never been so scared in my life as when you stepped into this room."

Alyssa hugged him back fiercely. "Then you know how I felt when Georges told me Gersbach was taking you back to Paris."

He rubbed his cheek over her hair. "Please, don't ever do that to me again."

Georges had been busy confiscating the German's weapons, and now, arms full, he turned to Philippe and Alyssa. "I'd suggest that we get out of here. You'll need all the time you can get to escape."

"Right." Reluctantly Philippe released Alyssa, but kept an arm around her shoulders as they walked out the door. "Now, tell me. How did you two 'incapacitate' four Gestapo guards—without any noise?"

Alyssa laughed and began her story.

The final Gestapo agent lay on the grass beside the Germans' cars. Georges siphoned gas from one car into a can and stuck it into the trunk of the other car, which they took to leave the estate. Georges drove about ten minutes, taking increasingly poorer roads, then stopped the car.

"Where are we?" Alyssa asked.

"As close as we can get by car to the Scorpion's camp," Philippe replied. "We'll have to walk from here."

They climbed a fence and trudged through the trees until at last they saw the glimmer of a campfire. Seconds later a voice demanded their names, and they were spotlighted in the beam of a flashlight. "All right." A man stepped out from behind a tree. "Go straight on."

Scorpion rose from the ground when he saw them approaching. "What took you so long?"

Briefly Philippe explained what had happened, and Scorpion's eyebrows rose. He thought for a moment, then said, "It doesn't matter. Our plan will still work. Mother instructed us to send you to Laval when I told them you were probably blown. They're sending in a plane tomorrow night to pick you up."

"I'll take the German car and drive in the opposite direction," Georges offered. "If I abandon it in the south tomorrow, it will look as though you're escaping to Spain."

"But, Georges, aren't you coming with us?" Alyssa protested.

He shook his head. "What would I do in England? I'll stay here, join Scorpion or one of the other groups. I'm not important enough for the Gestapo to hunt for me."

They argued over it for a while, but in the end they did as Georges suggested. Camp was broken up, and the men scattered, taking the confiscated German weapons and ammunition with them. Georges dressed in a uniform he had taken from one of the Germans and stuffed the man's papers into his pocket, then, Luger beside him, drove off in the staff car.

Scorpion walked with Philippe and Alyssa to the nearby village. He disappeared inside his house to whisper good-bye to his wife, then returned, and the three of them rode northward in Scorpion's old, battered truck.

As they rattled along the back roads, avoiding German checkpoints, Alyssa glanced over at Philippe. His face was less careworn now, and there was a brightness to his eyes that hadn't been there earlier. He seemed excited, almost happy. Philippe felt her gaze and turned his head. He smiled and leaned over to kiss her. Alyssa realized that he must feel free now. The matter had been taken out of his hands; it was no longer possible for him to spy on the Germans. He had been released from the role of collaborator which his stern sense of duty had impelled him to play. Even though they were in danger, at least now he could fight it openly. Alyssa was sure that he would face it eagerly.

She snuggled up against him and closed her eyes, drifting into sleep. She was awakened sometime later by the truck's jouncing over rough ground. She opened her eyes and straightened to look around her. They were off the road behind a group of trees. Scorpion stopped the truck.

"We'll go the rest of the way on foot," he told them, and they swung out of the truck after him.

They walked along the road for a few yards, then turned onto a smaller dirt road. Before long they came upon a small gray stone farmhouse. Scorpion led them to a wood-sided flatbed truck beside the barn and instructed them to get inside. He disappeared in the direction of the house and came back a few minute later with a middle-aged farmer. The farmer handed them shoes and clothes more appropriate to a farm couple than their own conspicuously elegant attire. Philippe and Alyssa changed clothes inside the barn, and when they returned they found that Scorpion and the other man had laid a thick layer of straw on the truck bed.

"You can sleep here for a couple of hours," Scorpion told them as the farmer walked back to his house. "Early in the morning he will hide you in a load of vegetables and take you to Laval." Scorpion paused and thrust out his hand to Philippe. "Good-bye, sir. I—it's been an honor to work with you." He flashed a smile at Alyssa. "Mademoiselle."

Alyssa gave him her hand and he shook it as well. "Good luck."

"Thank you."

Scorpion vanished down the dark dirt road, and Philippe helped Alyssa into the truck. The straw made a passable bed, and they snuggled up together on it, gazing up at the remote black sky, sprinkled with bright pinpoints of stars. Gently, leisurely, they made love again, the summer night cool against their heated skin, their bodies open to the vast night. They touched and explored and rediscovered the delights they had known together so long ago, moving without urgency, seeking the sweetness of each moment as much as the end itself, and exploding at last into a hot, dark fury of love.

Afterward, they cuddled and talked, too much in love, too happy to be with each other to waste the time in sleep. They talked of the golden Paris spring when they had met and loved and of the years between, the things they had done and seen.

"Why did you start this?" Alyssa asked him.

"What? My masquerade?"

"Yes."

"It was suggested to me by a mutual friend of ours."

Alyssa's brow wrinkled. "A mutual friend? Who?"

"Pliny."

"Ian Hedley?" Alyssa's voice rose in amazement. "You know Claire's uncle?"

"I've known him for several years. We met through a friend of mine." He sighed. "Actually, it was Charles—the man you knew as Dragon—who introduced us. We saw how things were going. Charles knew the army and how foolish their reliance on the Maginot Line was. The army refused to listen to any of the younger men who pointed out how vulnerable we were, like de Gaulle."

"The man who's heading the Free French in England now?"

He nodded. "Yes. He was regarded as a renegade and a hothead. Anyway, it was obvious that if it came to war, as we thought it would, the Germans would overrun France without much trouble. As events turned out, the invasion was accomplished even more easily than we had feared. If France were occupied by the Germans, a spy among them would be invaluable. I was the logical choice. I had no family who might be hurt. I traveled to Germany on business and could build friendships there. And I had a business that would be of value to the Germans."

"So you laid the groundwork to become a collaborator."

"Yes. It had been decided long before I met you. Then you came along and made me regret bitterly what I had pledged myself to do." He shrugged. "But I had no choice. I had to do it.'

"How awful for you! And I was so harsh and unforgiving."

"I could hardly expect anything else from you. I knew your principles. You wouldn't have been the woman I loved if you had been able to live with a collaborator. I returned to Paris after you left and dropped by to see my German friends who were now there. It was easy to make more friends in the army, and I was able to get a good bit of information from them. But I soon realized that I wasn't doing as well as I could. So I contacted an old friend of mine, Geneviève. You remember the woman you saw me with in Paris?"

"I certainly do."

He chuckled. "There was nothing between us. She was a friend of mine from long ago. I knew she was a successful prostitute—and patriotic as well. I set her up with a house and a complement of young girls, and she's obtained more facts than I ever could have hoped to."

"You mean you set up a brothel to spy on the Nazis?"

"Most of the girls have no idea what Geneviève is doing. But she is very adept at getting information, both from the officers she knows and from the girls who work for her." He paused. When he spoke again his voice was low and dark. "Can you accept that—what I was, what I did?"

"Oh, Philippe!" Alyssa rose up on her elbow to look down into his face. Her eyes glittered with tears. "Of course I can. I'm hardly one to cast stones; a lot of the things I did in Washington weren't exactly pure and sweet. Whatever you did, you did for your country. For what you believe in—and what I believe in. I love you, and I'm very, very proud of you."

She bent to kiss him, and his arms went around her tightly. She felt the salty warmth of his tears on her cheek.

*****

The sun had just begun to rise when Louis Bousquet emerged from his apartment and glanced cautiously around him. Schlieker had called last night and told him to report to Gestapo headquarters this morning. When Bousquet started to protest, Schlieker cut him short. "There's no need for secrecy now. You are of no use here any longer. I realized it after you left—Cleopatra is sure to figure out who betrayed her to us, and she was given to Michaude. That means that what's left of the Rock network will soon be looking for you. You'll have to start operating in a different region."

Bousquet's heart had jumped into his throat at Schlieker's words, and he cursed the man's casual attitude, as if the only concern was whether Unicorn could be used again in Paris—it was his life at stake here! He knew how the resistance rewarded traitors.

"You'd better come in tomorrow morning, and we'll give you a new identity and a ticket to—oh, Marseilles, I think."

Bousquet strode off briskly toward the Métro. Schlieker—that bastard! You'd think he could have sent a car and guard to pick him up last night and escort him to headquarters instead of making him wait out the curfew alone in his apartment. But, no! He wasn't important enough. Just a lowly French informer, not one of the super race. He should probably feel lucky that Schlieker had even thought to call him.

Bousquet rode the Metro through Paris and exited near Avenue Foch. Almost there. He walked quickly. He could see the building a block ahead now, and his pace increased. His eyes were trained on his destination, relief already beginning to flow through him, and so he missed the man standing partially hidden behind a tree on the side street.

But the man knew him well. His name was Devigny. Bousquet knew him better as Allegro.

When he'd heard that his cousin had been taken by the Gestapo, Allegro knew who was responsible... the same man who'd sent the police to Allegro's own house. Allegro was fortunate enough to be at the market when the Gestapo came; his wife had not been so lucky. Neither had the other members of his cell.

No one knew where Unicorn really lived, so Gestapo headquarters and the Left Bank cafes he had frequented seemed the most likely places to find him. Allegro had taken up his post at the headquarters before dawn this morning. It didn't matter that it was a dangerous place for a wanted man to loiter. He had no family. His cell was destroyed. Sooner or later the Gestapo would find him. There was nothing left for him but a thirst for revenge.

And God had just delivered his enemy to him. Allegro smiled and reached beneath his coat for the knife. Finding Unicorn had been quick. He'd make sure the traitor's death was slow.

Bousquet heard the steps behind him, and a thrill of fear ran through him. Where had they come from? He'd seen no one on the street a moment before. He glanced ahead. Half a block to go. His steps quickened. Would the guards hear him if he yelled? Would they bother to come to his rescue? He wanted to turn around, but didn't dare. Maybe he was imagining things. The man walking behind him might just be going to work early.

A hand grabbed his arm, and a sharp point penetrated his clothing, pricking his back. "Don't speak. Turn around and walk back the way you came."

Bousquet hesitated, and the knife pierced his skin. He jumped, stifling a cry of pain. "Who are you?" He changed directions, as ordered. The man stayed glued to his back.

There was a low, humorless chuckle. "Look and see."

Bousquet turned and looked at his captor, and he knew that he was staring into the face of death.

Chapter 25

Close to dawn, the farmer reappeared and had Alyssa and Philippe lie down against the side of the truck directly behind the cab. He set a sort of wooden cage over them, which stretched from their heads past their feet and was built of solid wood planks spaced two or three inches apart. Alyssa and Philippe looked at each other in puzzlement. They understood the reason for the cage later when the farmer and his wife began to pile cabbages on top of and around them. Without the cage the vegetables would have weighed heavily on them. As it was, they were encased in a dark, hot, smelly cocoon.

The farmer climbed into the cab and drove off. They drove for a long time. It was difficult to retain any sense of time in their dark, claustrophobic cell. The truck bounced over ruts and holes, and the load shifted and settled around them. The roar of the engines and the noise of the road made any sort of communication impossible, so they simply held each other and tried to sleep through the jarring ride.

Every once in a while they came to a halt; and on occasion when they were stopped, Alyssa felt a blow against the side of the truck. They could hear voices, but no words were distinguishable. Each time, the truck started up again.

Finally the truck stopped, and the engine was turned off. They assumed they had reached their destination and expected to leave immediately, but instead they waited. Sweat trickled down Alyssa's sides. It was extremely hot in here, and the smell was loathsome. Panic tickled at the edges of her brain—what if something had happened to the farmer? How would they ever get out?

They heard the sound of unloading, and soon light and air grew increasingly plentiful. The area at their feet was cleared, and Philippe and Alyssa slid gratefully out of their cage. They hopped down from the truck, smoothing out their clothes and shaking numbed limbs. The farmer instructed them to walk to a café down the street, where they were to wait for their next contact. He would be carrying a copy of an Alexandre Dumas novel, and when he left the café, they were to follow him.

Alyssa and Philippe set off down the street, thankful to be away from the truck. "Do you think they'll let us sit down at the café?" Alyssa asked, giggling, "Smelling the way we do?"

Philippe smiled. "You are beautiful, even smelling like cabbage soup. Here, put your scarf around your head. You look too lovely for a farmer's wife."

They found the café the farmer spoke of and sat down at a table at the edge of the sidewalk to eat and wait. After a while, Alyssa began to grow nervous. But then a man with a copy of *The Man in the Iron Mask* tucked under his arm strolled up and sat down at the table nearest them. Alyssa swallowed her excitement, and they waited for the man to drink his cup of coffee. The man paid for his coffee and walked out of the café. Alyssa and Philippe followed him. He walked a couple of blocks and turned the corner, Philippe and Alyssa on his heels, and ran into a line of people. At the front of the line stood two German soldiers, checking identification papers.

They had no papers. When Alyssa was arrested, hers had been taken and never returned. Philippe had left his behind; they would be more dangerous than helpful now that he was wanted by the Gestapo. But anyone without papers was automatically subject to arrest.

As soon as they rounded the corner behind their contact and saw the soldiers, Alyssa and Philippe did an abrupt about-face and started back the way they had come. One of the soldiers saw the sudden movement and shouted at them to stop. They did not, an immediate admission of guilt. The soldiers pushed through the crowd after them. Philippe took Alyssa's hand, and they ran.

Something whizzed past Alyssa's head, and a split second later she heard the sound of a shot. The Germans were firing at them. Philippe jerked her to the right down a side street. They ran, unfamiliar with the city, not knowing where they were going, turning again and again in an attempt to lose their pursuers.

It took a moment to realize that there were no longer footsteps behind them. Philippe slowed and glanced back. There was no soldier in sight. Alyssa sagged against the building, catching her breath, but Philippe pulled her upright, and they began to walk at a brisk but normal pace. They emerged from the side street onto a more traveled thoroughfare just as an open gray car with a black swastika on the side turned onto the street a block away from them. It was moving slowly, the soldiers in it looking carefully all around them.

Philippe uttered a short, bitter expletive, and they ducked back into the side street. They couldn't run. If the soldiers looked down the side street as they passed, they would be sure to be alerted by the sight of a running couple. A couple walking might escape their attention. Alyssa's back crawled; it was almost impossible to resist the temptation to turn around and look. Philippe's fingers gripped hers reassuringly.

Then she heard the awful screech of brakes and the clanging of gears changing, and a car roared up the street. Alyssa and Philippe took off running. There were shouts in German to stop. The vehicle passed them and swung crosswise in front of them, blocking their path. They stumbled, trying to stop and turn back, but the soldiers were out of the car before they could take two steps. A soldier grabbed Alyssa's arm and flung her against the wall, striking her head painfully and knocking the breath from her. Next to her she could see the same thing happening to Philippe. Rough hands ran over her body, and there was a low exclamation of triumph when the soldier pulled the snub-nosed revolver from her pocket. As she had been warned in training school, their guns indicted them.

They were finished.

*****

They were separated in jail, and Alyssa didn't see Philippe again until the next evening. When she was asked a few preliminary questions about her identity and address, she gave the name Marie Benoit and a street number in Marseilles. She was locked up in a cell, and several hours passed before she was taken out again and brought into a small, windowless room with a single chair. Her stomach roiled in fear. She no longer even had her L-pill. Whatever happened to her, she would simply have to endure.

An army officer with short brown hair and a young-looking face came in to question her. He asked her hundreds of things about herself and her life, and Alyssa used the biography she had made up for her character before she left England, so that she was able to answer most of the questions quickly and naturally, without tangling herself up. He watched her, frowning, then suddenly snapped out in English, "Why are you lying to me?"

Alyssa managed a blank stare. "What? I don't speak German."

"It wasn't German. It was English."

"I'm sorry. I don't speak English," she replied.

He sighed, crossing his arms, and leaned back against the wall. "You are a beautiful woman," he told her, and she glimpsed something like regret in his eyes. She wondered if it was real or an act. "But you are making it very difficult for me not to turn you over to the Gestapo."

She said nothing, and his mouth twitched in irritation. There was a knock at the door, and another officer stuck his head in. "Herr Demmler, I have received a message from Paris, sir. A man and woman are wanted by Albrecht Schlieker of the Gestapo." He cast a glance over at Alyssa. "Their descriptions fit the man and woman arrested today."

Demmler took the sheet and skimmed it. "Cleopatra, eh?" he murmured. "A fitting name." He sighed. The Gestapo official wanted to be notified immediately if either was arrested, with clear instructions specifying that neither was to be questioned or harmed. Demmler thought of the woman prisoner's silky hair and dark blue eyes, the shapely legs. And he thought of what she would look like when the Gestapo was finished with her; he had heard stories of their methods.

He crumpled up the paper. "Take her back to her cell. I will call Paris."

Alyssa's heart sank as the other man took her arm and led her from the cell. Demmler returned to his office and sat down to work on the papers on his desk. It was two hours later before he placed the call to Paris, well after seven, and Schlieker had already left the office, as Demmler had hoped. He left a message that he had taken prisoners answering the descriptions of Michaude and Cleopatra. It wasn't much, he knew, but at least it would buy the woman one more night. He didn't know that Schlieker had left orders that he be contacted immediately when any news arrived regarding Philippe Michaude, no matter what the time. Less than an hour later Schlieker and his driver were on their way to Laval.

*****

Jessica closed the snap of her suitcase and set it on the floor. She glanced at her watch. She and Stephen would have to leave in thirty minutes in order to catch their train back to London. She carried the bag outside and met Stephen coming out of his door down the hall. They smiled at each other, slow, secret smiles, and Jessica's heart swelled with love.

Downstairs the telephone rang, and Jessica's mother answered it. Moments later she appeared at the bottom of the stairs. "Stephen? There's a man on the telephone asking for you."

Stephen's brows shot up and he exchanged a look with Jessica. "I'll be right down."

He trotted down the stairs and took the receiver. Jessica followed more slowly and sat down on the bottom step, watching him. Stephen's end of the conversation was largely grunts. Once he glanced up at Jessica, then quickly away. At last he said, "Yes, I'll be there. I'm catching the next train out."

He hung up the phone and turned to Jessica. "Let's walk for a minute."

Concerned, Jessica followed Stephen out the front door. "What's happened?

"That was a man named Pliny. He says he knows you."

"Yes. Very well. What's the matter? What's going on?"

"Pliny said that a resistance group in France contacted them. Your friend was taken in by the Gestapo."

There was a roaring in Jessica's ears, and suddenly Stephen seemed very far away. Stephen grabbed her and helped her to the ground. "Here, put your head down. I'm sorry. I said it too bluntly."

Jessica lowered her head, and the momentary faintness receded. She shook her head. "How else could you say it?" Huge tears formed in her eyes. "Oh, God, poor Lyssa."

"She was freed by someone whom Pliny called vital to the organization. The Duke. They were supposed to leave France tonight, but they were taken up again. Both of them are now in a German jail in Laval, but as far as we know, the Gestapo doesn't have them yet. We're mounting a rescue operation."

"Thank God!" Jessica's eyes shone, and she looked up at him. "But why did Pliny call—" She stopped suddenly as the implications became clear to her. "Oh, no. No! You aren't going in to rescue them, are you?"

"I have to. I'm the only one qualified who's close enough to leave this evening. I may be rusty after this long, but I can still do it."

Jessica leaped to her feet. "No! It's too dangerous. You don't go on missions now! You're a liaison…"

"Which any idiot can do. You know why they put me in that job; you told me so yourself. Because I was too lacking in confidence to go out in the field again. I was hiding from the botch I'd made with Alan, terrified I would make another mistake." He smiled tenderly, and his hands came up to cup her face. "But you've changed all that. You made me believe in myself again. Until yesterday, I wasn't a whole man. I lost something vital in Belgium." He kissed her softly on the lips. "You gave it back to me."

"Not to have you kill yourself!" Jessica protested frantically. Her lips were bloodless, her face starkly white beneath the blazing hair. "Please...I can't bear to lose you, too!"

"Don't worry. You won't." His thumb traced her lips. "I have to go. I would have gone on another mission if this hadn't come up. I had already planned to request active duty as soon as I got back to work tomorrow."

Jessica knew he was right. Stephen had been released from the guilt of Alan's death. He had forgiven himself for the failure and turned his face forward again. His doing so had allowed him to love her, but she knew that the same release would just as surely send him back to his work. He was too good at it, too brave, not to return to duty.

Jessica closed her eyes, tears seeping past her lids. She wrapped her arms around him tightly. "Please come back. Please, please come back." She couldn't bear it if she lost him. She had loved Alan dearly, but she knew that the sorrow she had felt for him would be as nothing compared to what she would feel if she lost Stephen. He had become her world, her life. "I love you so much."

"And I love you." He kissed her fiercely, his lips pressing into hers. He pulled back at last and gazed down at her. "Will you marry me when I get back?"

"Yes, oh, yes!" She cried, tears coursing down her cheeks, and held on to him all the more tightly.

He smiled. "Then I'll be back. You can count on it."

*****

Having heard Demmler's conversation with his subordinate, Alyssa wasn't surprised when a guard released her from her cell several hours later, informing her that she was about to be transferred to Paris. She followed him down the long hall to the interrogation room where she had been questioned before. Philippe sat alone in the room, his hands manacled in front of him, as hers were.

He jumped up at her entrance. "Alyssa!" He came to her, taking her face between his cuffed hands. "Are you all right? Did they hurt you?"

"No," she whispered.

For a long moment they gazed at each other. There was no need for words. They knew they might not see each other again, or if they did, it could be under the most horrible of circumstances. Philippe's eyes were full of love and regret, speaking in an instant all the tangled emotions that lay in his heart. He kissed her softly and laid his cheek against hers. "I'm sorry, my love.'

"Don't be. I'm glad for every moment."

He kissed her again and stepped back, his gaze still locked on hers. Alyssa knew what he was thinking—that if there was any way, he would suffer the agony of torture for her.

"Thank you," she whispered.

She sat down on the single chair in the room, and Philippe stood beside her, his hand resting on her shoulder, giving her strength and comfort. As long as he was there, Alyssa thought, she could face anything. She looked up at him. "I have no regrets," she said, "except for the times I refused your love."

He smiled and trailed a wistful finger down her cheek.

The door jerked open, and Philippe straightened. Albrecht Schlieker stood framed in the doorway. His face was cold, but the pale blue eyes were bright and alive, gleaming with hatred. "So," he began, his voice clipped, "Monsieur Michaude." He gave him a parody of a smile. "Fooled us very cleverly, didn't you?"

Philippe said nothing, merely continued to gaze expressionlessly at him.

"It is not often I make such a mistake in my judgment of men," Schlieker continued. The frozen fire in his eyes promised that Philippe would pay for that mistake. "I am here to take you back to Paris. It will be more convenient to question you there. I imagine the interrogation will take a good deal of time." He smiled again, a real smile this time, and it chilled Alyssa's blood. "You are one prisoner I shall take great pleasure in breaking, Philippe. I only hope you don't give in easily."

Again Philippe made no response, and it seemed to irritate the other man. He jerked his head in an impatient gesture for them to leave. "Let's go."

Schlieker strode out of the small jail building, Alyssa and Philippe following him, two guards with guns behind them. Schlieker's armed driver snapped to attention and opened the front door for him. The guards shoved Alyssa and Philippe into the rear seat and one of the guards sat beside them. A moment later, the long black car zoomed off.

*****

Stephen Marek crouched in a ditch by the bridge, watching the road. A bicycle appeared, its rider pedaling furiously, and Stephen stood up. The cyclist stopped and jumped from his bicycle, panting. Stephen knew he had come from the small house only minutes down the road, where two members of the local resistance waited. "Bluebird just phoned. Le Duc and Cleopatra have left the jail with a Gestapo officer in a black car."

"Good." Stephen had hoped fervently that the car would take them back tonight instead of waiting for the morning. A daytime rescue was far more dangerous, especially since the rescue plane would only fly at night, forcing them to hide out all day, waiting for it.

The messenger hopped back on his bicycle and rode across the bridge toward his home. Stephen crawled partway down the bank of the stream and checked the charges high under the two posts supporting the small bridge on this side. Moving quickly and efficiently, he attached the wires to the explosives and scrambled back up the bank. The estimate was that it would take a car thirty minutes to reach the bridge from the jail, which didn't leave him a lot of time. He ran through the ditch, the wire spinning out behind him from the spool in his hands.

He reached the trees, where three men waited for him. He snipped the wires and attached them to the detonator. And they waited.

"I hear an engine."

The man closest to Stephen raised his binoculars and sighted down the road. "A big black car. Mercedes. This is it."

Stephen fixed his eyes on the hood of the car. Closer, closer. The explosion had to come at exactly the right moment. Not close enough to hurt the occupants of the car, but close enough to shake them up and make the driver jam on the brakes. He drew a last steadying breath and shoved down the plunger.

The near end of the bridge exploded, sending wood and stone flying. The car skidded, brakes squealing, and fishtailed to a stop. Stephen and his men were already out of the trees and running toward the car.

Inside the car Alyssa, Philippe, and the guard were flung to the floor. Alyssa heard Schlieker bite out a curse as he bounced off the dashboard. The driver pulled out his gun and began to fire out the window toward the men running at them. The guard had hit his head when he fell, and struggled groggily to rise. Philippe reached down, grabbing the guard and pulling him up. Schlieker ripped his gun from its holster and whirled to aim at Philippe, but Philippe twisted, jerking the guard in front of him, and Schlieker's bullet struck the guard.

Alyssa grabbed Schlieker's gun arm, and his second shot went wild. Philippe shoved aside the guard's body and lunged at

Schlieker, struggling to pry the gun from his hand. Silently, desperately, they struggled for possession of the weapon. "Run!" Philippe roared to Alyssa. "Run, damn it!"

Bullets thudded into the front doors, but they were obviously armored, for the shots had little effect. Alyssa threw open her door and tumbled out onto the road in a crouch, intending to open the front door and attack Schlieker from behind. But she was thrust aside by a hard arm, and a rifle barked beside her. Suddenly Schlieker's head was bathed in red, shattered glass falling around him.

The German slumped forward, and Philippe jerked the gun from his limp hand. The driver continued to fire out his window at their attackers, who were now stretched out in the grass as they fired back. Philippe brought the gun down hard on the back of the driver's neck, and he collapsed against the door.

The man beside Alyssa shouted at his men to cease firing. Philippe crawled out of the car, and Alyssa threw her manacled hands around his neck, clinging to him. He kissed her hair and eyes and mouth, murmuring, "My darling, my darling, are you all right?" He ran anxious hands down her.

"Yes, yes, I'm fine. What about you?"

"A scratch." He glanced down at one arm, and Alyssa saw that blood stained his shirt. Clumsily she ripped away the sleeve. "It's nothing," Philippe assured her. "I was grazed by one of the bullets from outside, that's all."

But Alyssa had to clean away the blood with the remnant of his sleeve and see for herself before she believed him. The man who had shot Schlieker reached into the car and pulled out a set of keys from Schlieker's pocket. Quickly he unfastened their manacles, and for the first time Alyssa looked straight at him. She gaped.

"I know you!"

"Uh-huh." The man grinned.

Her mind was whirling, full of jumbled fragments, and it took her a moment to place him. "You're Jessica's friend."

Jessica had written her about Stephen when Alyssa was training in Hampshire, and she had met him briefly one day at Jessica's house when she returned to London.

"That's me." He stuck out his hand to shake Philippe's. "Stephen Marek. Pleased to meet you."

"Philippe Michaude." Philippe grinned. "We owe you a great deal of thanks."

"No time for it now. We have to get this show on the road. There's a plane waiting for us, if the pilot hasn't lost his nerve. The longer it sits, the more danger it's in. And if I lose a Lysander to the Germans, I might as well not go back with you."

The other three men had come up to the car, quiet men in rough, dark clothing. They helped Philippe and Stephen pull the driver and Schlieker from the car and into the ditch. Then one of the men hopped in the front to drive, and Stephen got in with him, his gun across his lap. Alyssa and Philippe climbed in the back. The other two men melted into the dark trees. The driver wheeled the car around, and they zoomed back down the road in the direction from which they had come. In a few miles they turned off onto a side road and bumped along it at a slower pace.

Philippe wrapped his arms around Alyssa and held her close. It was difficult to absorb the sudden change in their circumstances, the fact that Schlieker was dead and they were racing for a plane that would take them to safety in England. He kissed the top of Alyssa's head. She could feel the thudding beat of his heart beneath her. This was real. They were nearly out of danger.

"Is there time now for our thanks?" Philippe asked Stephen lightly.

Stephen swiveled around in the front seat to grin at them. "No need. I had to get you two home. Jessica agreed to marry me, and she needs a bridesmaid."

"You and Jessica are getting married!" Alyssa gasped. "But how marvelous!"

Philippe chuckled. "Congratulations." He squeezed Alyssa a little tighter. "Perhaps we should make it a double ceremony."

The car slowed down and stopped. "We have to hoof it from here." Stephen shook the driver's hand, and they got out of the car. The driver stepped on the gas and roared off down the road. "He'll dump the car somewhere else so they won't find their landing strip," Stephen explained. "Come on, it's this way."

He disappeared into the trees beside the road, and Alyssa and Philippe followed. A few minutes' walk brought them out of the trees into a long, flat meadow. The dark, squat shape of a Lysander loomed on the field. Alyssa's heart leaped into her throat. They walked faster, then broke into a run.

The pilot, pacing nervously beside the plane, saw them and scrambled into the cockpit. He fired up the engines as soon as they climbed into the plane. On both sides, men ran along flicking on the rows of lanterns that served as their primitive runway lights. The three passengers settled in, Alyssa cuddled in Philippe's arms, as the plane lumbered through the meadow, gaining speed at what seemed an alarmingly slow pace. Then, abruptly, amazingly, the plane lifted, and they were off the ground, climbing upward into the dark night sky to safety. To freedom. To love.

Epilogue

Alyssa breathed in the heavy scent of the pale pink rosebuds. Philippe had sent her a vaseful. She smiled, thinking of him. No doubt he was already seated in the audience, waiting for her to appear onstage. Her father would be sitting beside him. With the war over and Roosevelt dead, Grant's duties had greatly diminished, and he finally retired. Now he spent several months out of the year in Paris.

On Philippe's other side would be Jessica and Stephen. They were married soon after Stephen returned from his rescue mission, and Alyssa and Philippe followed suit only a few weeks later. Over the years the two couples remained close friends.

After their return to England, Stephen and Philippe worked together in the organization and were even involved in the same mission once or twice. Somehow they both managed to come through the war alive, though Stephen broke a leg in a parachute drop in Yugoslavia in 1943, and it had been poorly set, leaving him with a slight limp. Philippe was with him on that expedition, and it sealed their friendship, though Alyssa and Jessica were never able to find out exactly what happened there.

Alyssa glanced through the pile of telegrams on the table beside the flowers. There was one from each of her grandmothers, of course, and her mother. Ky and Claire sent their best wishes; they were unable to come because Ky had finally been allowed inside Poland to search for relatives who might have survived the war. There were wires from a number of Philippe's business acquaintances and the friends they had made since they returned to France after the Liberation. Even Ian

Hedley, still snowed under with secretive work—though at least his offices had been taken out of the damp basement of Evington Court—sent words of encouragement.

Alyssa pulled out one telegram to read again. It was from Lora and Kingsley Gerard, encouraging her to "break a leg" and promising another joint assault on the Parisian fashion houses before the year was out. Alyssa smiled. How terribly long ago that seemed. Six years.

Tonight would be her first stage performance since then. Her first ever in France. It seemed odd to be back in the theater after so long—not just in terms of years but in what she had done. Her work in Washington, in France, then at Evington Court with Jessica. She left Evington Court three years ago, pregnant with Philippe's child, and became a full-time mother to little Charles. It was hard to leave Charles for several hours each day when she began rehearsing, but she knew he was in the care of not only his efficient French nursemaid but also Georges, who loved Charles as if he were his own grandson. It was strange to return to the stage after so long, but it was dear and familiar, too, like coming home. The theater, no matter where, was always a family place.

For Alyssa and Philippe it was all part of picking up the pieces again, adjusting to life after the years of devastating war. They had returned to France soon after the Allied troops freed Paris, and for the nearly two years since, there was a long, hard process of rebuilding—a business, a country, a life. Like finding all the pieces of a shattered glass and painstakingly gluing them back together, what they achieved was not quite the original but a newly conceived mosaic. It hadn't been easy, but slowly everything was coming together for all of them.

Jessica, who had always been a homebody, had become a citizen of the world when Stephen returned to his career as a foreign correspondent. They were living in Berlin now, but there was no telling when he would be assigned elsewhere. Strangely enough, Jessica enjoy the life, despite having to pack up two children under three and a nanny in order to follow him. She was in a way still a homebody, but her home now was wherever Stephen was.

Alyssa checked her makeup in the mirror again. Her stomach was a knot of nerves. She had never performed Molière, and she had never performed in French either—unless you counted the part she had played here in Paris four years ago. The part of a lifetime.

The war days were over now—the fear, the wreckage of lives, the demands of duty. But there was still one thing that had lived then and lived now, the single lodestar, the bright and shining essence of her life: her love for Philippe, and his for her. That love was true and never-changing, and she knew that it would carry her always, even past this life.

There was a knock upon the door. It was time for her to go to the wings and await her entrance cue. She looked at the picture of Philippe on her dressing table, the snapshot of him holding their son tucked into the corner of the frame. She smiled and opened the door and walked forward.

Candace Camp is the NY Times best-selling author of over 70 novels, including the popular *Mad Moreland* series, *The Rainbow Season*, and *A Momentary Marriage*. Her books have been published in twenty-three countries and 17 languages. She wrote her first novel while in law school and happily gave up her work as an attorney to pursue her lifelong dream of writing books. Born in Amarillo, Texas, she now lives in Austin, Texas with her husband, Pete Hopcus. Her daughter is young adult author Anastasia Hopcus.

For a complete list of her books, go to candace-camp.com. You can also visit her at **facebook.com/candacecampauthor/ or @campcandace on Twitter.**